SoulQuest

Book 1 of

The EGYPTIANS! Trilogy

by

Jay Palmer

ISBN-10: 1-7324989-0-3
ISBN-13: 978-1-7324989-0-7

Books by Jay Palmer

The VIKINGS! Trilogy:
- DeathQuest
- The Mourning Trail
- Quest for Valhalla

The EGYPTIANS! Trilogy:
- SoulQuest
- Song of the Sphinx
- Quest for Osiris

Jeremy Wrecker, Pirate of Land and Sea

The Magic of Play

The Seneschal

Viking Son

Viking Daughter

Dracula – Deathless Desire

The Grotesquerie Games

Cover Artist: Jay Palmer

Website: JayPalmerBooks.com

ACKNOWLEDGMENTS

Thanks to those researchers and authors who provide the rich source material to indulge enquiring minds!

Bibliography (and recommended reading!):

- "The Ancient Egyptian Books of the Afterlife", by Erik Hornung, translated by David Lorton
- "Dictionary of Ancient Egypt", by Ian Shaw and Paul Nicholson
- "Book of the Dead", by E.A. Wallis Budge
- "Egyptian Magic", by E.A. Wallis Budge
- "Bulfinch's Mythology", by Thomas Bulfinch
- "Dictionary of Occultism", by Lewis Spence
- Marvel Comics, by Stan Lee

Special thanks to Edith Hamilton, author of "Mythology", for introducing me to the intricacies of my favorite subject!

To a lovely lady, a wonderful proofreader,
and a dear friend, Kelly Bowen.

(From The VIKINGS! Trilogy, which ended eight years before …)

Pretending to be an ambassador from the king of Norway, Eric Bjornson, an aging Norse warrior, arrived at Castle Bristlen intending to rob it, and bought his entrance with a golden heirloom stolen from his vengeful best friend, King Svenson Two-Sword. Knowing that he was being pursued, Eric deceived the baron of Castle Bristlen, and then robbed his treasury and fled out the castle's postern gate … just as King Svenson Two-Sword arrived at the main gate … leading seven thousand Viking warriors … to reclaim his stolen heirloom.

Behind Eric, and the four Saxons that fled with him when the Norse army arrived, Castle Bristlen was sieged and burned. As intended, the long siege delayed King Svenson, which allowed Eric to flee on horseback into a nearby forest, carrying with him the plundered wealth of the castle's treasury.

Chased across England by King Svenson Two-Sword, Eric and his companions, Karl, Rafe, Roselyn, and Eloise, plowed a Blood Trail, leading Svenson's army on a merry chase deep into Northumbria. In their wake, the savage Norse warriors left a line of ruined and plundered towns, and in retaliation, the Saxons raised an army to destroy the Norse invaders … and the companions found themselves hunted by two armies.

After the war, while mourning their losses, the companions were forced to flee … as half of them bore death sentences decreed by the Eorl of Northumbria. Forced to backtrack their own regretful path of destruction, where they witnessed the suffering that they'd caused, the companions were waylaid by a terrible curse, which repeatedly delayed their escape.

Finally they embarked on a quest that led them through a 'crack in the world', bridging Midgard with the legendary realms of Yggdrasil, the home of the Norse Gods. Joined by Athelwynne the Seer, a small, arrogant, and dangerously-powerful Druid priest, and Seren, an elderly prostitute with uncanny street-smarts, the companions faced the myriad mythological horrors of Yggdrasil. Accompanying Eric through each dangerous realm, young Karl found himself torn between the tall, beautiful Countess Roselyn and the fiery, passionate Baroness Eloise, both of whom fell in love with Karl's handsome, muscular looks and honest, courageous nature.

Not all of them made it home. Eric had never hoped to return to England, Athelwynne became the chief servant of the Lady of the Druids, and Roselyn had to choose between death and remaining in Valhalla. With no other choice, Roselyn surrendered Karl to Eloise, allowing her lover to marry her best friend, but with the commitment that, upon his death, Karl would return to her.

Back in England, by marrying Baroness Eloise, Karl became a wealthy baron. Rafe and he were knighted, and soon afterwards Lord Sir Rafe and Seren also wed. Eloise bore Karl three beautiful children, and their lives together were mostly happy.

Yet not all celebrated as eight years slowly passed. Sleeping alone in Valhalla every night, Roselyn grew tired of waiting for Karl to die …and her patience reached its end.

All that she needed was one excuse to seek him …

Chapter 1

The Search Begins

REGINLEIF

"Valkyrie never die!" Reginleif screamed, and she rose to charge up onto the blood-drenched knoll, her sword tight in her fist.

"Get down!" Geirahöd shouted, and her strong right hand grabbed Reginleif's ankle and yanked her back; both clanged and crashed onto the muddy, gore-soaked dirt, and they slid down the short slope into the tiny ravine on their newly repaired armor, the plates of which were already scratched and dented, their mail rings clogged with muck.

Reginleif glared at Geirahöd as death screams and the stench of war filled the air. The fighting was especially fierce today; the Black Bear clan had them surrounded.

"There are seven of us … and six hundred of them!" Reginleif snarled.

Grim faces stared back at her; Geirahöd, Hrist, Mist, Skeggjöld, Skögul, and Hildr's expressions matched

Reginleif's undaunted determination. Reginleif frowned: *she hated dying.*

"If Róta were here, then we'd be charging already," Reginleif complained.

"We charge when I say!" Skeggjöld shouted angrily. "They know we're here; Mist, blind them."

Slender, lithe Mist slipped up the steep slope like a vapor. Despite the bright blue sky above them, Mist always walked surrounded by a thin aura of fog that suddenly, as Mist raised one hand, expanded, rose over the edge of the ravine, and poured toward their foes. Furious cries burst amid deafening shouts; their enemy had lost to this tactic before.

"On three," Skeggjöld said. "One, two, …"

"Footsteps!" Hildr shouted.

A dozen warriors of the Black Bear clan burst over the edge of the hill, jumping into the ravine, wielding wide-bladed pikes, bows, and arrows. The Valkyrie rose instinctually, shields high and swords slashing. Arrows pincushioned the dirt behind them, barely avoided by dexterous feminine dodges. Slashes, stabs, and decapitations followed; bear-cloaked bodies fell pierced, muscular limbs sliced, and necks severed. Bows and pikes rained, dropped from hands unclenching, as the bloodbath sprayed everyone.

Their attack lasted only seconds. In the end, six gore-dripping Valkyrie stood, looking down upon their fallen foes.

"Norn's doom!" Hrist cursed; Mist was laying on the ground, clutching the shaft of a black-fletched arrow sticking out of her throat, writhing in the death-agony.

"Is she …?" Skeggjöld asked.

"Lost," Skögul declared with a glance. "Reginleif, spare her."

"I don't need the practice . . .!" Reginleif argued.

"You're still the new girl," Skögul grinned nastily, ". . . Roselyn."

Reginleif glared at Skögul; she didn't like being called by her human name; *she wasn't Roselyn anymore.* With a snarl, Reginleif straddled Mist, inverted her sword, and dropped to her knees. Mist's eyes widened with the shock of pain, and then her eyes glazed over. Thick mists covered her entirely, shone pure white, and then faded away, leaving only her corpse. Reginleif pulled out her bloody sword; later that night, in Elvidner, the grand feast hall of the einherjar, Mist would have to pour her an ale.

Skögul chuckled.

"Valkyrie never die!" Skeggjöld snarled. "Valkyrie avenge!"

As one, they charged up the hill. Reginleif wished that Randgríðr was there; she had the biggest shield. The Black Bear clan weren't slouches, but Reginleif was a Valkyrie. Although the youngest of her sisters, she rose fearlessly; the ground trembled beneath Hrist, and Skeggjöld's axe could chop through any shield or helm. Skögul and Hildr drove into their foes with unequalled fury, and Geirahöd's spears were thrown with such force that they pierced whole shieldwalls. Reginleif charged in behind them and fell upon her foes with matchless ferocity; arrows rained upon her shield and ricocheted off her silver and gold-decorated armor and helm, but she kept attacking.

The Black Bear clan charged forward, eager for the glory of slaying the Valkyries, even if it cost them every man that they had. Cries echoed across the battlefield.

Suddenly an explosion of rolling thunder deafened them all, shaking the ground like Thor's dwarven hammer crashing upon the land, a deep *'Boom!'* resounding across

Valhalla. Lightning flashed … and incinerated every man that it touched. The blue sky above them darkened to blood red, and the white clouds blackened like Niflhiem.

"Valkyrie!" cried Odin's grim, resonating voice, louder than all of the sounds of battle. "*Come, my shield-maids! Odin requires you!*"

All fighting instantly stopped. Angry complaints filled the air, but six warriors, the only women among millions of fierce combatants, proudly walked through the heart of their enemies, ignoring furious glares. The King of the Gods, the Master of Battles, wouldn't have called upon his chosen amid the frenzy of a sunny day's war without urgent need. The einherjar moved aside to let the women pass; they were the hand-picked warriors of Odin, and none defied his will.

Approaching as if summoned, great winged horses flew over the battlefield to greet them, and the Valkyrie mounted with practiced ease. Smiling, Reginleif mounted her stallion along with her shield-sisters; *she wouldn't die today!*

Hooves raced and mighty wings beat the air; the Valkyrie rose and soared over the wide fields of Valhalla, watched by tens of thousands of sweaty einherjar. Soon, the golden Gates of Valhalla quietly slipped beneath them as they winged toward Asgard, the fabled City of the Gods.

Asgard, the stronghold of the Aesir, shone in the sunlight like a tall mosaic of gleaming gems. Vast halls and palaces glowed with the vibrancy of the Norse gods, and gems twinkled in the sunlight as brightly as stars at night. Green courtyards and gardens of colorful flowers peeked between polished walls of dark granite and gleaming marble. From the sky, Asgard was a jewel of beauty and elegance.

Six magnificent winged horses flew over the formidable, giant-built wall and landed on the wide red flagstones before the largest building. The Valkyrie dismounted; ten minutes after the blood sky and black clouds had reverted to blue and white, six beautifully armored, blood splattered women warriors marched through the renowned doors of Válaskjálf into the gold-roofed Hall of Odin.

Upon his mighty throne, the Alfather sat waiting. His heavy beard covered his mail-armored chest, and on each of his thick, aged shoulders sat a sly, watchful raven. A worn leather eyepatch hung strapped across his rugged face. His shield-maids approached without ceremony, their footsteps echoing through the vast hall. The other gods of Asgard watched the Valkyrie cross the throne room in silence; only Thor, Loki, and Baulder dared to meet their eyes. Resentment filled the chamber; the Norse gods were doomed to die, and their only hope of winning Ragnarrock would come from the swords of the einherjar; those countless puny humans chosen by the Valkyrie.

As the women approached, their weapons rose in salute, but Odin stopped them with a gesture.

"Where are your sisters?" Odin demanded.

"Mist lies dead in Valhalla, my lord," Hildr said. "Prudr, Göll, Herfjötur, Hlökk, Randgríðr, and Róta are fetching new einherjars."

Odin nodded slowly, then frowned.

"Reginleif, come forward," Odin said.

Reginleif startled; she hadn't spoken to Odin for eight years, not since the day that he'd brought her back to life. Yet she was a Valkyrie; she stepped forward and bowed.

"Reginleif, the Seer is missing," Odin said. "He left Niflhiem eight days ago to meet with me, and he never arrived. Know you where he is?"

"The Seer …?" Reginleif asked. "No, my lord; I haven't seen him for months."

"He must be found," Odin said with unquestioned finality.

"Your will commands," Reginleif said, and she bowed again.

With curt salutes, the Valkyrie walked back toward the massive doors trimmed with gold. The Norse gods watched them depart with grim respect; *the fate of their universe traveled with these few women.* Yet Reginleif walked with clenched teeth and every muscle tensed.

What could have happened to Athelwynne …?

"Seer?" Skögul scowled. "Isn't he that short, skinny …?"

"You know who he is!" Reginleif snapped.

"No time for jokes," Skeggjöld said. "Odin has commanded; we must obey."

"Few could delay a sorcerer as powerful as the Seer," Hildr said.

"We can't search everywhere," Geirahöd said. "Someone should head for Niflhiem and learn what happened."

"I'll go," Reginleif said. "Hel will tell me anything, and I won't rest until I know that he's safe."

"I'll join you," Skeggjöld said. "Geirahöd, come with us. The rest of you; begin the search."

"Where?" Skögul asked.

"Odin wants him found," Skeggjöld shrugged. "Find him."

"The Seer's greatest enemy is Loki," Hrist said. "I'll take Mist and talk to him."

"Mist is dead," Hildr said, "and Loki will always lie."

"We'll ambush him tonight, after Mist arises, when Loki leaves Válaskjálf," Hrist said. "Mist helped the Seer defeat Loki; he's sure to lie to her, and it's easier to deduce the truth when you know that a liar is lying."

"I'll join you," Hildr said. "Loki mocked the Valkyrie, and I never forget an insult."

"Approach Loki cautiously," Skeggjöld said. "The Norns were surely commanding our actions that day; we mustn't become their pawns again."

"Loki shall answer us … or he'll smart for his silence," Skögul said.

"We're decided," Skeggjöld said. "Farewell, sisters … until Odin's will is realized."

In thoughtful silence, Reginleif watched her sisters slip back into Válaskjálf. She liked Skögul the most, although she'd never admit it. Skögul was the shortest of her shield-sisters, and she kept her brown hair equally short, but she was also the most fun, and the most reckless Valkyrie, always boasting, regardless of truth, with a mouth so eager to spew insults that she practically spat venom. Hrist was Skögul's best friend, the giant of the Valkyrie, a head taller than Reginleif, and Hrist's bulk matched her height, as if her body struggled to find new places to add muscle. Only a few men excelled Hrist in size, or could vie with her in wrestling, and when she stomped, the ground trembled. Hildr, whose hair vied with roses for being the reddest, was their surest killer; Hildr could walk across grass without leaving a bent blade, and dispatched her foes so quietly that they often died before they realized that they'd been slain.

"We must go," Skeggjöld said.

"Supplies first," Geirahöd said.

Turning their backs upon their sisters, Skeggjöld, Reginleif, and Geirahöd flew back to Valhalla, winging their mounts to the rear doors of Elvidner, the great hall of feasting, where kitchen helpers loaded their mounts with packs kept ready for long journeys; smoked meats, hard breads, and skins of mead and ale, along with bedding rolls, torches, ropes, and large bags of oats for their horses. Then they flew off, for hours flying across the wide skies over green fields, forests, rolling hills, and deep valleys. Heading for a distant, far corner of Asgard, their mounts winged them to an unkempt road that ran through the trackless wastes behind Alfhiem, out to the very border of Yggdrasil. There, ages before, on a great limb, Odin had once hung himself in a deadly noose. He died, his own spear stabbed through him, but so strong was the King of the Gods that Odin fought his way back from death, stealing with him the fabled Nine Secrets of the Dead; Odin prized wisdom above all things, and would risk everything to know all. Reginleif eyed the famous limb, trying to hide her concern, but like Odin, she'd give all she possessed to know what had happened to the Seer.

With wide, circling glides, they descended their horses to land before the ominous mouth of a dark cave, into which ran their worn, rutted path. Reginleif and Geirahöd paused and stared at the bleak aperture, rank and overgrown with twisted, hanging vines. Skeggjöld never hesitated; Skeggjöld was fearless, a natural leader, and a natural beauty, with the thickest blonde hair that Reginleif had ever seen, a slender, muscled frame, and smooth, taut, unscarred skin. She cantered right through the opening, into deep shadow, without slowing down or a backward glance.

Reginleif and Geirahöd glanced at each other; they couldn't allow Skeggjöld to appear braver than they, although they drew out torches and pulled off their covers before they followed Skeggjöld. Like those of Nidavellir, the halls of the dwarves, these torches instantly burst aflame, illuminating the entrance to the long tunnel. Reginleif knew this legendary, cursed aperture; they rode upon the main passage to the Norse underworld, and at its end lay Niflhiem.

Geirahöd wasn't as muscular as Hrist, but she was almost as tall, and she wore a long harness down her back that held ten spears, which would refill itself whenever it emptied. Geirahöd was a redhead with golden highlights, such that she sparkled in the sunlight. She was also trim and muscled, but not as slender as Skeggjöld; Geirahöd was the best spear-thrower in Yggdrasil, and not even Odin vied against her skill. Few shields could deflect her spears, and her muscular right arm threw so hard that many einherjars were usually impaled on each cast; when a path needed to be plowed, Geirahöd was always the first to be called upon. Yet Geirahöd was also quiet, wise, and usually soft spoken; she didn't brag unless encouraged by Skögul.

Reginleif had ridden this dark tunnel once each year; during the week before the anniversary of her rebirth, when Odin had made her a Valkyrie. Reginleif rode to visit Hel, her closest friend in Yggdrasil. Hel was the Goddess of Death, eons old. From the waist up, Hel was divinely beautiful, such that all mortal women envied her. But Hel was Loki's daughter: from the waist down, Hel was a rotting corpse. In her realm, the subterranean Land of the Dead, Hel leeched, from her mindless subjects, the fresh blood that she had to bathe in to keep her dead legs supple. Everyone in Yggdrasil hated Hel, and many thought her friendship with a Valkyrie was obscene, but Hel and Reginleif were more than friends; the Nine Secrets of the Dead were the only mysteries that Hel refused to surrender, and Reginleif supported Hel's resolution to keep those hidden. In every other aspect, they were confidants, the only one whom either would entrust with their deepest, darkest thoughts.

The road to Hel's domain was dark, and deadly to any who traveled it lightly. Terrors older than time filled the Norse underworld, and when Reginleif traveled alone, she practiced every skill of caution and concealment taught to her by Hildr. Some new threat always haunted the lightless tunnels beneath Asgard, and surprise was the surest path to death on any battlefield. But this time, Reginleif wasn't alone; Skeggjöld and Geirahöd rode with her, and in their company, Reginleif rode confidently.

The tunnel was rocky, rough, and in some places opened into large caverns, never the two alike. They often halted, guessing which route would be wisest. The gloom seemed ever threatening, despite their bright torches, and shadows constantly wavered, mimicking movement upon the uneven stone walls. In many places, footprints in the dirt, or arrows chiseled into stone walls, marked their path, but many signs had been scratched out, or marked as misleading. In some of the bigger caverns, large growths blocked their way, strange trees and thorny bushes planted to create obstacles; one Valkyrie always watched behind them while the others cleared their path. In dangerous places, their passage grew narrow, such that the Valkyrie had to dismount and lead their magical steeds afoot, often squeezing them through doorways not designed for winged horses. There they watched most … and kept their weapons ready.

Countless evils dwelt down here, ever hungry, hoping to lure the unwary into deadly traps.

Two days and nights they traveled by the light of their torches, and they glimpsed few other sets of eyes. A contingent of dark elves welcomed them at the entrance to their realm, but Reginleif was the only Valkyrie allowed to enter Svartalfhiem; her friendship with Ruthedhel made her a guest. No other Valkyrie would be admitted through their forbidding gates, and dark elves were fighters as fierce as the einherjar.

A few cowardly dwarves fled from them on sight; Reginleif wouldn't enter Nidavellir, certain that she'd murder Radsvid, if she ever crossed paths with the greedy, lecherous dwarf who'd fouled Seren and betrayed them. The rest of the eyes that spied upon the three sisters stared silently from shadowy alcoves, and those eyes looked increasingly fearful; none dared attack three watchful Valkyrie. The sisters rode unaccosted, and the few foolish animals brave enough to hunt them were butchered and roasted.

All the while, Reginleif thought about Athelwynne. In Castle Bristlen, they'd briefly become lovers, but that was long ago; Reginleif tried to think of her days as Countess Roselyn as a previous life, totally separate from the life of the Valkyrie Reginleif, yet she knew better. Reginleif still held a deep fondness for the Seer, and he was more than mildly attractive; Göll had once claimed him as her lover, but Reginleif doubted her wild tale; the Seer had a different immortal paramour.

For the Seer to go missing was absurd. The Seer worshipped the Lady of the Druids, a goddess who existed in another universe, but who had many dealings with the gods of Asgard. The Seer was Her ambassador, sometimes in Yggdrasil, but mostly in Her universe, which the Seer described as a vast land of the most beautiful gardens anywhere, and dark, forbidding forests which only fools entered. By will of Odin and the Lady, the Seer could traverse between their universes at will, and he bore incredible power, such that the Seer was almost a god himself. Few deities could delay him, yet the Seer and Reginleif shared a powerful enemy: Loki. Reginleif felt certain that, if anything had harmed the Seer, Loki was to blame.

In a remote corner of a large wooded cavern, the Valkyries found a small cave, slew the trolls inhabiting it, and settled down for their last night before arriving at Niflhiem. They had only a little mead left; they'd conserved their mead by drinking all of their ale first.

Skeggjöld rekindled the troll's dying fire while Reginleif scavenged for more wood, and Geirahöd cared for their horses, giving them the last of their water and plenty of oats. They threw dice for guard duty; Reginleif lost: she'd take the midwatch, between the watches of the others. Skeggjöld and Reginleif untied and spread their thick bed rolls while Geirahöd stared at the flames and kept one hand upon a spear.

When Geirahöd awoke Reginleif, the two exchanged places. The hours wore on, and Reginleif struggled to stay awake, often coaxing their sleepy horses to flap their powerful wings to expel the excess smoke in their cave. Eager to awaken Skeggjöld and return to sleep, she kept poking their small fire just for something to do. Twice she thought that she'd heard something, but it was only an echo of a distant rock falling, or a creak of the thin woods outside their cave, but Reginleif grew suspicious. Leaves outside their cave occasionally seemed to move, as if blown by a gentle wind, but there was no wind in these deep caverns. Finally Reginleif uncapped a torch and moved closer to their cave's mouth, only to be surprised by what she saw.

"Danger!" Reginleif hissed softly.

Instantly Skeggjöld and Geirahöd awoke. Weapons raised, both glanced in all directions, and then focused on Reginleif.

"What …?" Skeggjöld whispered.

"The leaves outside … are coming in," Reginleif whispered back.

"Leaves …?" Skeggjöld scowled. "You woke us for …"

"There were no leaves against the mouth of the cave," Reginleif whispered. "Now the entrance is choked with them."

"Perhaps a tree fell," Geirahöd whispered.

"During your watch?" Reginleif asked. "I would've heard a tree fall."

Geirahöd inched closer, sliding up behind Reginleif.

"Either the forest has grown much larger in a few hours … or it has shifted to block our exit," Geirahöd whispered.

"Either way, we're trapped," Reginleif said.

"Trapped by leaves?" Skeggjöld scowled.

"We don't know what we're up against," Geirahöd said.

Geirahöd placed a hand on Reginleif and raised one of her spears. Reginleif froze to help steady her aim, and braced; Geirahöd cast hard enough to impale a stone wall. Yet her spear crashed through the growth, tore through the foremost leaves with ease, and vanished into them. No impact sounded, no thud into a tree truck or scream of a hidden enemy.

"Just bushes!" Skeggjöld laughed.

"That cavern isn't infinite," Reginleif said. "Geirahöd's spear didn't thunk into a tree or the far wall; what stopped it?"

Nervous glances exchanged.

"I won't rest until we're far from ... whatever this is," Geirahöd said.

"I'll test it," Skeggjöld said.

Reginleif hated magic; better an invasion of giants than a mysterious enemy wielding powers unknown. Skeggjöld drew her sword and inched forward, ready for anything. Reginleif and Geirahöd stayed only a few feet behind her, ready to help; *better to die than to sacrifice a shield-sister ... unless by her death ultimate victory could be achieved.*

As Róta had taught her, Reginleif surveyed the setting; the mouth of their cave was roughly six feet tall and four feet wide, barely big enough for their horses to enter. The leaves pressing into its entrance were dark green, heart shaped, and identical to any bush that they might walk past without noticing. According to Róta, the key to wrecking the plan of any enemy was understanding their plan, but how could a bush have a plan?

Skeggjöld held out her gleaming sword, slid it closer, and touched a leaf. Instantly little vines sprouted and wrapped around the tip of her blade, pulling hard at it. Yet Skeggjöld was a Valkyrie; she ripped back her keen blade, slicing off several wriggling tendrils, which clung to her blade as she retreated. The severed tendrils spouted new, tiny shoots, miniature tendrils, like wiggly green hairs, each trying to reach around her sword and increase their hold upon it. Skeggjöld shook her blade to try and flick them off, and finally banged its flat against the stone floor, forcibly dislodging the wriggling growths; Geirahöd stamped on them as they tried to take root. Each tendril took several stomps before it finally stopped moving.

"A formidable trap," Skeggjöld said.

"Is it just a cannibal plant … or did someone enchant it to trap us?" Reginleif asked.

"We've no way to tell," Geirahöd said. "Regardless, we can't let it keep growing; it'll consume us once our supplies run out."

"Resources …?" Skeggjöld asked.

"Our weapons, horses, saddles, bridles, the torches, a little mead, bread …," Geirahöd said.

"Fire," Reginleif continued. "A limited supply of wood, a few rocks, some rope, bedding, our armor, our hair …"

"Let's try fire," Skeggjöld said.

Reginleif laid her sturdy shield beside the fire, and with her sword, she scraped some flaming wood and coals onto its edge. Carrying it carefully, she approached the cave's mouth and cast the flames upon the greenery; the leaves were unaffected, but the tiny tendrils upon them recoiled violently.

"It doesn't like fire," Geirahöd said.

"If we had a bigger fire, maybe we could burn our way out," Skeggjöld said.

"The smoke in here is pretty thick already," Reginleif said. "Fire consumes air, which we need to breathe."

"How strong are those tendrils?" Geirahöd asked.

"Too strong to break through," Skeggjöld said. "Prudr might make it, but it almost kept my sword."

"There's a key to every puzzle," Reginleif said. "Our wits are our best weapon."

"Let's put the rest of the fire against it," Geirahöd suggested.

Slowly they slid their fire, careful to keep from extinguishing it, and transferred it to the mouth of their cave. They added half of their reserve of firewood; the smoke grew thicker, but the flames only shriveled a few leaves, making their tendrils writhe. Overtop the flames, new leaves grew.

"They're growing closer," Reginleif said.

"Suggestions …?" Skeggjöld asked.

"Build the fire as much as we dare, and then try to fight our way out," Geirahöd said.

"We can't abandon our horses," Skeggjöld said. "They can barely squeeze out, and if those tendrils wrap into their feathers …"

"Magic," Reginleif said.

"What …?" Skeggjöld asked.

"The only way to fight magic is with more magic," Reginleif said.

"We have no magic," Skeggjöld said.

"Yes, we do," Reginleif said. "We have Geirahöd's spear case."

"What're you suggesting?" Geirahöd asked.

"We have an endless supply of spears," Reginleif said. "The spearheads are metal … and the hafts are wood."

"We can burn the hafts," Geirahöd said.

"We can do better than that," Reginleif said.

An hour later, they lifted a large section of wall, four feet wide, formed entirely of seven foot spears, crossbraced by spearhafts, and tied with all of the rope that they had. Every spearhead was carefully aligned to form one great serrated blade. Then they threw all of their spare wood onto the fire, and amid thick smoke, they used their swords and shields to hurriedly pile many red hot coals onto the spears' wooden hafts. While their horses stood saddled and ready, they braced, with Skeggjöld and Reginleif on the sides, and Geirahöd on the end; *this would be her mightiest cast.*

As one, they ran at the greenery. With Skeggjöld and Reginleif helping, Geirahöd cast her flaming wall of spears forward, striking low and crashing through the foliage. Green leaves were ripped apart, stalks severed, and tendrils writhed away from the scattered coals that fell upon them in its wake; a four foot wide path appeared as if a large scythe had mown their exit, and paved it with red glowing coals. Skeggjöld kicked the remains of their fire through the cave door, scattering more burning wood over their escape.

The Valkyrie grabbed their reins and, kicking the flaming sticks before them, they hurried through the momentary gap, leading their faithful mounts, before the tiny vines could regrow. The thickest growths had congregated before the mouth of their cave, and soon as they pushed past them, Skeggjöld and Reginleif slashed with their swords at all remaining creepers, and as fast as they could, they mounted, and their horses leaped into the air, flying over the remaining carnivorous plants, winging across the wide cavern. Geirahöd came last, jabbing with another spear at several clinging tendrils clutching at her boots, wrapped around her spurs. They glided to land near the mouth of a tunnel leading out of the tall cavern, but they didn't proceed until every tendril was scraped off and stomped to death.

"Well, that was unpleasant," Geirahöd said.

"We'll be safe inside Niflhiem soon," Reginleif said. "Yet this is an ill omen; whatever was powerful enough to overcome the Seer may have other threats to hurl at us."

"I won't feel safe anywhere near Niflhiem," Skeggjöld said. "I go because Odin commands us, but Hel is a sworn enemy of the Valkyrie; her countless minions shall battle against us in Ragnarrock."

"Led by Loki, not by Hel," Reginleif reminded her. "Hel's my friend."

"I'll speak no evil of your friend," Geirahöd said to Reginleif. "But Hel's no friend of mine. They say that she's beloved by the Seer, but also that he betrayed her. She's Loki's daughter, and the Seer was last reported in her realm; until she's proven innocent, Hel's my chief suspect."

Reginleif glared at her shield-sisters, but they stared back undaunted. Together they mounted, raised their torches, and rode off into darkness.

Chapter 2

The Baron of Castle Bristlen

KARL

"Father!"

Little Roselyn and Eric ran to embrace Karl, and he bent down and opened his arms to snatch them up. Both were lifted in great hugs as tiny little Athelwynne started to cry. Baron Sir Karl du Harmonn carried his two eldest children toward his youngest, who was sitting on Seren's lap and refusing to eat mushed porridge.

Castle Bristlen was a wonderful home. In the great hall, jugglers tossed flaming sticks and bright polished knives, minstrels played lutes and sang merry songs, and everyone seemed happy despite the hard times. A guard was posted at every door, each handpicked and devotedly loyal; few men didn't like and admire Baron Sir Karl du Harmonn.

But someone hated Karl; two attempts on his life had been narrowly foiled, and so serious were these threats that one assassin, whom they'd caught red handed, slew himself before they could discover who'd sent him … or why. Karl suspected that Roselyn's father, Eorl Sir Guldwin, was behind the attacks; he'd never forgiven Karl for usurping the barony which he'd hoped to usurp. His claim of avenging his youngest daughter, Roselyn, who'd been lost under very mysterious circumstances, was just an excuse; he'd prostituted his own daughter for political profits, and beaten her whenever she'd defied him. Yet Karl had no proof of Eorl Sir Guldwin's involvement, nor any idea of what could be done even if he had proof.

Karl held his children lovingly, but the frown on his face couldn't be hidden.

"What wrong?" Seren asked.

Karl glanced suspiciously about the noisy great hall.

"Not here," he whispered.

Foisting all three children onto a pair of wet nurses, Karl and Seren walked behind the throne through a door hidden by a tapestry, down a narrow sconce-lit hallway, and into the baron and baroness' bedroom.

Eloise wasn't there … again.

"Hiding in her tower …?" Karl groused, looking around.

"Assume so," Seren said.

"What's she doing up there?"

"Eloise tell nobody," Seren said. "That tower trouble you?"

"Yes … no … I don't know," Karl said. "du Harmonn is broke, and we can't survive much longer. There's so much going on, I don't know which way to turn …"

"Eloise love you," Seren said.

"I can't trust her," Karl said. "She vanishes for months, and then donates more than we can afford to a bunch of Druids; Bishop Duncan threatened to excommunicate me …!"

"Trust Eloise," Seren said.

"Eloise won't trust me!" Karl fumed. "Why won't she tell me what she's doing … or where she's going?"

"Seren talk to Eloise …?"

"Rafe already tried; you could hear them shouting all the way to Demril."

"Some things women only speak to women."

"Try, then; I can't bear this much longer."

"What else bother?"

"Everything," Karl replied. "The king wants more taxes than we can collect. He also wants more Water of Life, like we can just go and get some. He wants us to support his invasion of France, but he didn't even invade the last time, he just took our tribute and kept it. Eorl Sir Guldwin is raising troops again; I suspect that the king's command for him to stay out of du Harmonn isn't important now that all of the Water of Life's been drunk. In fact, the king's request for troops may be part of a conspiracy, to deplete our reserves while Guldwin invades; the king was never happy about making a farmer Baron du Harmonn."

"Prepare for war?" Seren asked.

"Preparations are expensive," Karl said. "At the very least, we must feed those we conscript, and we can't hope to raise as big an army as Eorl Sir Guldwin will have."

"What Eric do?"

Karl smiled; ever since they'd returned from their insane adventures beyond the 'crack in the world', that had been their motivation: *What would Eric Bjornson have done?* Everything reminded him of Eric; Karl had first seen his bedroom when Eric had forced him here at the point of a sword. Karl had first touched his bed when he and Eric had awoken Eloise's father in it … and then knocked him unconscious. Karl had first held his beloved sword when he'd helped Eric rob the treasury, and he'd first lit a fire in his bedroom fireplace when they'd returned to Castle Bristlen, with Seren and the Seer, following Eric's ghost. Now Eric was an einherjar in Valhalla, living near Roselyn, who was now Reginleif the Valkyrie, yet that had been eight years ago; Karl wondered if she even remembered him.

Roselyn was Karl's true love, yet she'd had to remain in the immortal lands of Yggdrasil, while Karl returned to England and married Eloise. Several times, in the heat of battle, Karl had wondered if Roselyn were watching him from a magical flying horse, but she'd never appeared, and as the long years passed, Karl wondered if he'd ever see her again.

At first, their return to England had been delightful. Eloise was a fiercely passionate lover, and Karl would always love her deeply, and he was blinded by carnal pleasures and dazzled by his elevation to Lord of Castle Bristlen and ruler of the Barony du Harmonn.

Eloise had tried to make Karl happy. They were wedded as soon as they'd returned to Castle Bristlen, and Eloise had borne him three wonderful children, but Karl's unquestioned love for Roselyn had always stood between them, a splinter in an otherwise perfect union; it was the greatest sadness in Eloise's life.

Seren hugged Karl, and held him protectively in her thin, aged arms. Seren was Karl's most trusted confidant; when they'd first met, Seren had been an elderly prostitute in the seediest tavern in Madrone. Now Lady Seren was minor nobility … and the loyal wife of Lord Sir Rafe, Karl's best friend, the horsemaster of Castle Bristlen. Seren had accompanied Karl on the most incredible adventure of his life, but age had finally taken its toll; Seren was now frail and delicate, no longer able to slay giants or deflate the Goddess of Death. She spent her days caring for Karl and Eloise's children, and they looked upon her as a mother during Eloise's unexplained absences. Karl trusted her implicitly; Seren's wisdom made her invaluable.

Karl accepted her embrace warmly; there was no other way that Seren could aid him, but during troubled times, hugs were immensely helpful. She had no wealth to pay the king's taxes, and no troops to offer, but Seren never failed to give whatever she had. Her devotion was inspiring and steadied Karl whenever he started to sway, when his hate of politics soured his love of being baron.

The crash of a distant door flying open was almost immediately followed by rapidly pounding knuckles on his door. Karl opened his door to find two eager, familiar faces staring back at him.

"Message from the king!" Nate and Philip shouted simultaneously, as if racing to say it first.

"Get in here," Karl scowled at both of them.

The young men entered, breathless from running, and both bowed to Lady Seren while Karl unsealed their scroll and read it. Nate and Philip Tiller were Karl's first squires, the sons of a wealthy farmer who lived in the valley, on the far side of Wolven Forest, and who was Karl's staunchest supporter. Farmer Tiller had helped them twice during their adventures with Eric. He always rode to the castle when important news reached his ears, and he was a leader of the peasants, and spoke for many. Nate and Philip had only been boys when Karl had first met them, but now they were young men, strong and sword-trained. As brothers, they competed at everything; their current rivalry was over whose beard would be the fullest when it finally came in; neither could yet call their youthful scruff a beard.

"Damn!" Karl cursed. "His Royal Self-Importance has again refused to change the name of du Harmonn; Eloise won't be happy about that. And he's ordered another conscript: a hundred men; he knows we don't have them!"

"We didn't even get to see him," Phil said.

"We only talked to some minister!" Nate exclaimed.

"He's mad," Karl said.

"King not mad; all he do is to his purpose," Seren said. "No point getting upset: you not meant to fulfill obligation; if you suddenly have extra hundred soldiers, then the king be really upset."

"Listen to this," Karl scanned the letter. "*'Mindful of your failure to pay the taxes you currently owe, I make this request doubtful of your competency and with an eye toward your replacement.'*"

"King goading you," Seren said. "You done more to restore strength and prosperity in these lands than anyone since Eloise's stepfather arrive at Castle Bristlen, and you sent him two hundred excellent soldiers in last four years; remind him of that."

"So what should I do?" Karl asked. "I can't send money or troops I don't have."

"Send king diapers," Seren said. "Tell him you working day and night to fill diapers with sons."

Nate and Phil looked shocked, but Karl broke out laughing. Suddenly he and Seren were hugging again, and Nate and Phil both joined in the merriment, although worry marred their expressions. When he and Seren broke apart, Karl put his hands on his squires' shoulders.

"Boys, I'm sorry about your horses," Karl said. "That's terrible luck, having both of your horses go lame on the way back here."

"What …?" Nate asked.

"Our horses are fine …," Phil said.

"No, your horses went lame … and you had to walk home," Karl insisted. "So … by my reckoning … you won't be able to deliver the king's message to me for another three days; by then I'll have a proper reply for the king."

"As you command," Nate bowed while Phil chuckled.

"Make yourselves scarce, boys," Karl said. "I'll call for you when you finally arrive at the castle."

With wide grins, both boys bowed and departed. Seren stayed, and stared at Karl appraisingly.

"You need rest," Seren ordered him.

"I can't sleep," Karl said. "I just lay awake and worry. And I can't leave the castle, not after two assassination attempts."

"Brooding no help," Seren said. "Do swordpractice … or take walk."

Karl escorted Seren back to the main hall, where she sat upon his throne and took little Athelwynne back into her lap. Karl fetched his sword, then went looking for his squires, but he'd told them to vanish, and both were good at being elsewhere. Karl wandered around the courtyard, the stable, the kitchen, and even checked the two gate towers, but no one had seen either Nate or Phil.

Karl was just about to give up, walking along the tallest battlement behind the castle keep, when he heard running footsteps. Ever vigilant, Karl turned just in time to see a stranger rush at him, swinging a long, heavy knife. Karl wasn't armored; he dodged aside, and the blade sliced a thin gash into his skin just below his elbow. It missed a vital target, but Karl fell, off-balanced, and the stranger collided into him and pinned him against the stone battlement.

The two men grappled on the brink, leaning over the battlement, overlooking the top edge of the great cliff of Othar. Karl seized the wrist holding the thick, sharp knife, his other hand wrestling to pull his attacker's hand from his throat. The attacker twisted his blade and added several small slices to Karl's forearm, but only scratches; none were serious wounds. Knees kicked, and muscles strained, but neither could get the upper hand, and they were too close for effective punching. Karl had his longsword scabbarded on his belt, but he couldn't reach it, and the moment that he took to draw it might give his opponent the chance to shove him over the edge.

Inch by inch, the assassin pushed Karl, who was clinging to a stone battlement with one leg, farther over the edge. Karl resisted, but he'd stumbled at a bad angle, his thighs resting on rough stones, his weight mostly over the precipice. He tried to cry out, but the hand around his throat strangled his shout. His attacker was strong, fierce, and desperate; Karl glanced straight down over two hundred feet to the distant village of Demril far below; if he couldn't win, then he, or both of them, would arrive in Demril in the next few seconds.

Karl felt himself being pushed another inch over, and knew that he couldn't stop it; his balance teetered. *What would Eric Bjornson do?* Desperate, Karl released the grip on the hand clenching his throat; instantly it tightened, cutting off his breath, but Karl reached down; his opponent wasn't wearing armor, either. Karl reached between the stranger's thighs and seized his soft balls and squeezed, and his attacker's grip faltered. Karl lifted him by his most-delicate organs and flipped him overtop himself, hurling him out over the void. Their combined weight proved too much, and pulled the both of them over the edge, but Karl was closer; Karl seized the stone battlement in a deathgrip and clung for dear life. Crying out in terror, his opponent dropped his knife and tried to cling to Karl's legs, but as they both kicked and struggled, his grip on Karl's boots proved insufficient; vainly scrabbling his soft shoes against the rough stones for a foothold, the assassin's hands slipped … and he plummeted with a trailing wail the quick way down the white cliffs of Othar.

Frightened shouts echoed in Karl's ears as frantic hands seized and pulled him up, back onto the battlement. Gasping for breath, Karl fell into his shouting guard's grasp, sweat pouring down his face: three assassination attempts; *he'd sealed the castle days ago … and an assassin had still gotten in.* Voices of his familiar, trusted guards yammered, but Karl couldn't hear any of them; his ears were pounding with the pulses of his own heartbeats. Without him, Eloise would lose control of du Harmonn, and then the king could sell their barony to Eorl Sir Guldwin; *that was why he was being hunted.*

Hours later, as Seren was holding Karl still and making him drink many ales, a young page ran into the castle keep.

"Your Excellency, permission to open the castle gate …?" the boy asked.

"No one goes in or out," Karl said absently, staring at the aged rafters while a servant pressed a wet cloth to his cuts and bruises.

"But … your Excellency … it's Lord Sir Rafe!"

Karl reached the gates just as the guards raised the mighty portcullis enough for Rafe and his company of guards and squires to ride into the courtyard.

"It's started," Rafe said without dismounting or commenting on Karl's unexpectedly scuffed appearance. "Eorl Sir Guldwin is marching his troops up the King's Road toward Grusshire; he'll be here in five days … four, if he pushes his men."

"How many …?" Karl asked.

"Over two thousand footmen," Rafe said. "At least five hundred knights, and an equal number of archers."

"That's ten times more than we have," Karl said.

"Send a fast messenger to the king …," Rafe said.

"The king knows all about it," Karl said. "We're on our own."

Rafe and Karl stared at each other, and all of their guards, squires, workers, women, and even the little children, fell silent.

"What would Eric do?" Rafe asked.

Karl glanced about at his anxious people. They depended on him to protect them, to keep their laws honest, and dispense true justice. All of them remembered the rule of Baron Vandeslidge du Harmonn; suffering plagued their lands after Eloise's mother was forced to marry that French bastard, and they all knew that Eorl Sir Guldwin, angry at being denied ownership of the barony for the last eight years, would be even worse.

"Prepare for war," Karl said.

Not one mouth cheered.

Preparing Castle Bristlen to withstand a siege required intense labor. Messengers were sent to every corner of du Harmonn; all crops and livestock were to be sent to Castle Bristlen, taken away and hidden, killed, burned, or cast into the sea. All women and children, especially those in the invader's path, were to flee and hide, preferably as far away as possible. Every weapon and available man, capable of fighting, was summoned to defend the barony, and cartloads of every resource that could be gathered and hoarded, even fresh water, was driven to Castle Bristlen. Rationing began that day.

Construction began on the battlements; the great portcullis was permanently sealed and braced from the inside, murder holes were inspected and cleared, and wooden palisades and shelters were built around the two gate-facing towers and along the battlements not facing the cliff.

A hundred men arrived the next day to help prepare the castle for assault, and a hundred more were expected. Training began for those who needed it, which included all of the local farmers and tradesmen, which composed the bulk of their army. Rafe oversaw their training, since Karl couldn't be spared; after three assassination attempts, Karl's squires wouldn't let him out of the castle keep unless he was completely surrounded. Despite Karl being the baron, Rafe's orders that he be protected day and night seemed paramount. Yet it wasn't enough.

"Eight years ago, King Svenson Two-Sword's host arrived in dragonships with no knights, no battering rams, no siege towers, and only a few archers," Rafe scowled. "They overran Castle Bristlen, and killed every person in it, within hours."

"Eorl Sir Guldwin will have all of those things, plus strict organization and a defended supply route," Karl said. "He won't act foolishly; he'll overwhelm us … or siege us, and wait for our supplies to run out."

"That bastard won't put any more scars on my back," Rafe promised.

"We can't buy him off; he wants everything that we have," Karl said.

"If can't win, should flee," Seren said. "Take everybody."

"You should've left by now," Karl said to her.

"Seren no leave without husband," Seren said, and Rafe scowled again.

"If we tried to take everyone, then we'd fail," Rafe said. "We can't take people's homes and farms; where could our people go where they won't starve?"

"Eorl Sir Guldwin doesn't just want our barony; he wants to make examples of us," Karl said. "We've publically humiliated him for eight years; he'll never stop hunting us."

"What Eric do?" Seren asked.

"We must do the one thing that Eric would never do," Rafe said.

"What's that?" Karl asked.

"We must pray," Rafe said.

Rafe bowed his head, made the sign of the cross, and began to speak the familiar liturgy. Everyone bowed their heads and joined him.

Chapter 3

Return to Niflhiem

REGINLEIF

"Garm!" Reginleif shouted.

Skeggjöld and Geirahöd reined in short, but Reginleif dismounted and hurried forward. The massive walls of Niflhiem towered above them, and before the ancient iron gates stood a fearsome terror of old, entirely blocking the wide wooden bridge over the icy river Gjoll.

Bigger than the largest horse, Garm towered over them, a giant gray wolf of threatening aspect. The rumble of its growl shook the ground, its huge teeth bared, and its deep, red eyes focused on Reginleif. Her shield-sisters paled; Skeggjöld drew her sword and Geirahöd raised a spear to cast, but Reginleif dashed forward to embrace the neck of the fearsome giant wolf, who wagged his tail and licked her with his giant slimy tongue.

"He's safe," Reginleif called to her companions. "Garm's my friend, Hel's pet."

With grave concerns, Skeggjöld and Geirahöd rode closer, dragging Reginleif's winged mount. Garm glanced up at them and growled, but Reginleif pulled his head back down and scratched between his eyes.

Suddenly the closed iron doors rumbled with the grindings of a hundred avalanches, and the towering gates creaked open. Looking inside, Reginleif gasped.

Never before had Reginleif seen the infinite hosts of Niflhiem arrayed for war. The only armor that she'd ever seen in Niflhiem had been on herself and her companions, on the day that they'd entered Niflhiem to save Eric's soul. Now she saw a hundred thousand armed and armored dead men and women, crowded together, filling the vast plain of Niflhiem as far as the eye could see. Each holding weapons in both hands, the dead stared back at them, fierce and threatening, blocking their path; *all of the Valkyrie could never defeat such a force!*

"Hel!" Reginleif shouted over the horde of warriors. *"Hel! I've come!"*

Unexpectedly, despite being tightly pressed together, a hundred thousand dead warriors noisily bowed as best they could.

"Enter," a hundred thousand mouths said in unison.

Struggling to make room, the dead separated, leaving a narrow gap between them. Reginleif exhaled heavily, then took her mount's reins and led it across the bridge over Gjoll, and her sisters followed her. Garm ignored Skeggjöld and Geirahöd; he snarled at their winged horses, but made no move to attack. Skeggjöld and Geirahöd never hesitated; *they couldn't let Reginleif appear braver than they.*

Their path to the Hall of Eljudnir was long, with gruesome dead warriors pressed close on each side. Unlike the brave einherjar of Valhalla, these lost souls still bore the wounds and likenesses that they'd suffered upon their deathbeds, and many appeared to have rotted, or been unwashed for centuries. Ghastly eyes followed the Valkyrie from the visors of countless helmets. Reginleif had never asked Hel if she had any armories, as she apparently did; doubtless she hosted several thousand blacksmiths who'd been pounding metal for an eon.

They approached an enormous hall built around four great towers, and atop each tower glowed a blazing bonfire. Crackling flames reflected their bright red light off the moist cavern's ceiling and the massive hanging stalactites towering over them, illuminating all of Niflhiem. The hall itself was brightly lit, but of such dark ruin and dilapidation that it was difficult to see how it remained standing. Two great doors marked the only entrance to its hall; the Valkyrie led their horses to its massive doors, which opened as they approached.

Reginleif handed her reins to an armored deadman, then walked fearlessly inside Eljudnir. Skeggjöld and Geirahöd gritted their teeth and followed her.

"Hel . . . ?" Reginleif called.

Unlike the stony wastes of Niflhiem, Eljudnir, Hel's hall, was brightly furnished, with glints of silver and gold sparkling from all over, reflecting the burning torches set in sconces on every wall. Dust and cobwebs thickly buried its corners, and in the center of the room rested a great firepit with a huge, roaring bonfire that poured black smoke through a wide hole in the ceiling. Several large wardrobes, elaborately carved, rested in one corner beside a many-pillared bed shrouded with black lace curtains.

From behind the black lace curtains floated soft, agonized sobs.

"Hel!" Reginleif cried, and she ran forward.

Beside the bed stood two old people, and man and a woman: Ganglot and Ganglati, Hel's servants, who moved so slowly that it was hard to see any motion. Behind Glimmering Misfortune, Hel's sparkly black lace curtains, Hel lay weeping upon her bed.

Reginleif shoved aside the thin curtains, and upon seeing her, the Goddess of Death threw herself into Reginleif's arms, sobbing upon her armored shoulder.

"Hel, what is it?" Reginleif demanded.

"A-Athelwynne …!" Hel's voice sounded crushed by misery. *"Athelwynne …!"*

"Where is he?" Reginleif shook the Goddess of Death. "Where's Athelwynne?"

"I don't know!" Hel sobbed. "He walked out of here, across the bridge over Gjoll, and then …!"

"Then what …?"

"I don't know!" Hel practically screamed. "Never, never in thousands of years has this happened …!"

"What happened?"

"I … I can't remember!"

"What …?"

"I passed out … and when I did, all of my subjects swooned. Ganglot and Ganglati alone didn't pass out, but from inside my hall, they never saw a thing! A whole day passed before they could awaken me, and when they did, Athelwynne was gone!"

"You've no clue …?"

"I've lived eons in this hall, and I remember every day as clearly as you recall yesterday," Hel said. "All but this … one day … the worst day ever … it's gone!"

"We're here," Reginleif said. "We'll find Athelwynne."

"We …?" Hel startled, and then she looked past Reginleif, shocked to see that she wasn't alone.

Skeggjöld and Geirahöd stared back, frowning.

"Valkyrie …?" Hel gasped. "You bring … *Valkyrie … into my domain …?"*

"I'm a Valkyrie," Reginleif said, "and I'd drag Odin himself here, if I thought that it'd find Athelwynne."

Hel ceased crying; she seemed to transform in less than a second. Suddenly she became aloof and imperious, glaring formidably at her guests despite the tears dripping down her cheeks. Gracefully Hel extricated herself from Reginleif's arms and rose from her bed with all the poise, majesty, and dignity of an immortal. Hel stood, gorgeous beyond description, dazzling, more perfect in form and figure than any mortal woman could ever hope to be, and more; Hel was Loki's daughter, a half-goddess, radiant with divine loveliness, and darker, more mysterious than forgotten legends and myths of terror. Taller than Reginleif, Hel wore a tight gown of darkest black, which matched her long, raven hair, and contrasted with her pale, perfect skin. Despite the presence of three beautiful Valkyries, Hel excelled them all; her smooth oval face and trim figure defied mortal description, and her large breasts protruded against her black dress, round, firm, and hovering as if weightless.

"Welcome to Eljudnir," Hel said coldly.

"We seek the Seer, not welcome," Skeggjöld said harshly.

Hel's brows furrowed, as if she were considering crushing both of these impudent Valkyrie, but Reginleif looked at her imploringly.

"For Athelwynne's sake …," Reginleif whispered.

Hel frowned.

"Every service that the dead may render is yours … *until Athelwynne is found,"* Hel said meaningfully.

Skeggjöld nodded, and Geirahöd slightly inclined her head. They understood her meaning; once the Seer was found, all hatreds would remanifest.

"Perhaps we should ascertain the order of events …?" Reginleif asked. "Where did you last see Athelwynne?"

"On the bridge over Gjoll, right before my gates," Hel said. "I always walk him to the gates, for a last … good-bye … and from there, he vanishes. He thinks that my godly eyes can't see him when he's cloaked in illusion, and I allow him that. After he hides himself, he walks away quickly; no troll, dark elf, or any other can sense him when he walks unseen, and the Seer walks very quickly. He gave himself four days to reach Asgard; he had an appointment with Odin; that was eleven days ago.

"I don't remember him vanishing. The Seer walked out onto the bridge … and that's the last thing I recall. The gates of my land were wide open … and all of my subjects swooned; anyone could've entered. When I awoke, I was lying on the ground just outside my gate, Ganglot and Ganglati beside me. I could've been attacked, but I wasn't. Athelwynne was gone, and it wasn't until I returned here that I learned that a whole day had passed … and I have no memory of it."

"Why was the Seer here?" Skeggjöld asked.

Hel's black eyes suddenly narrowed and her tone became icy.

"The purposes of my visitors are no business of the Valkyrie …," Hel said.

"Odin commands … and you will comply!" Skeggjöld ordered.

"No one commands Hel!"

"Enough!" Reginleif said. "I know why Athelwynne was here, and it's no one's business but his and Hel's."

Skeggjöld started to argue, but Geirahöd stepped between them.

"Goddess of Death, forgive me or not; anything which might have a bearing on the Seer's disappearance is a clue …," Geirahöd said.

Hel paused and took a deep breath before replying.

"I will tell Reginleif all that I know," Hel said imperiously. "You two … are dismissed."

"No one dismisses the Valkyrie!" Skeggjöld snarled.

"Odin commands you to find Athelwynne," Hel said. "You need information which only I know. I will only divulge that information to Reginleif, and only when we are alone. By command of Odin, you must leave us."

Their war of glares threatened to equal Ragnarrock.

"Valkyrie fear you not, Queen of Niflheim," Skeggjöld said. "On the Last Day, we'll ride beside Odin, and lead the einherjar against those you've armed and armored; great news we'll spread of your preparedness for war. As warriors, even in death, no Valkyrie shall come to your cursed lands; Niflhiem and Valhalla shall perish at the same time, along with us … and you."

"Then you'll die as you've always lived … as servants," Hel said. "Speak softly before your betters; I serve none but myself."

"You …!" Skeggjöld started, but Geirahöd interrupted her.

"Await me outside, if you're my shield-sister," Geirahöd said to Skeggjöld.

After murderous glares, in a barely-restrained rage, Skeggjöld stormed out of Eljudnir, stomping her feet like Hildr, save that Hel's hall didn't shake from her stomps. After she'd exited, Hel's doors closed of their own accord.

"For now, we seek the same goal," Geirahöd said softly to Hel. "Someday we'll be enemies, but that must wait. I came here doubting you, but I've seen your tears

… and I believe them to be real. Only love forces such tears from a woman; I no longer suspect that you abducted or killed the Seer. But Odin's commands can't be dismissed; if the Seer isn't found, then I'll return, and all your dead hosts shan't stay my punishments for mocking the Valkyrie."

Geirahöd nodded, not deeply enough to be considered a bow, but as a show of respect to an honorable enemy, and then she turned and walked toward the tall doors, which opened before she reached them.

"I … am despised," Hel said softly as her doors closed again. "Like countless others, those two have never met me … and they loathe me."

"I've tried to make them understand," Reginleif said.

"Of all in Yggdrasil, only I understand my father," Hel said. "Loki's madness, and the coming of Ragnarrock, were predicted by the Norns when he was a child, even before I was born. In all the eons since, even before the lands of Midgard were peopled, Loki's reputation preceded him; when his madness comes, it will be the predictions of the Norns that caused it, rather than any event they foretold. The Norns made similar predictions of me, and everyone hates me; will their hate be the cause of my madness?"

"I'll never hate you," Reginleif promised.

"We must find Athelwynne," Hel said. "I … *need him.*"

Hel's face tightened, as if she couldn't decide whether she was going to smile or burst into tears. Slowly she reached down and plucked at her long black skirt, and finally she lifted it high. Reginleif glanced down and almost screamed: Hel's dead legs, exposed to her thighs, were sickly green, but whole and unrotted.

"What happened …?" Reginleif gasped. "*How …?*"

"Athelwynne," Hel managed a troubled smile. "The Lady of the Druids is a great healer; although it costs him most of his strength, Athelwynne can heal me, and his magic takes weeks to wear off."

"Athelwynne healed your dead legs …?"

"Only temporarily," Hel smiled mischievously. "Just long enough to …!"

"Oh, blessed be!" Reginleif cried, and the two women fell into the tightest of embraces. "I'm so happy for you!"

"Now we share another thing … literally," Hel whispered into her ear.

Reginleif's hug never faltered, but she recalled the drunken night when she'd lain with the Seer; she had no desire to repeat that lovemaking.

"Athelwynne is yours," Reginleif whispered back. "I'll have no one but Karl."

"You mustn't tell the other Valkyrie …"

"Sleipnir couldn't drag it out of me."

They embraced long, too glad for words. *Hel, the Goddess of Death, had her first lover!* Reginleif couldn't be happier. Yet that made her mission even more important.

"You know that only Loki could've stayed Athelwynne …," Reginleif said.

"Even if we could prove that, what could we do?" Hel asked. "My father is always my greatest fear, but I can't believe that Athelwynne is dead; if his body were found, then Odin's wrath would be more than Loki could withstand."

"Have you no clues?" Reginleif asked.

"I've perused the minds of thousands of my subjects, seeking any hint," Hel said. "Only Father knows me well enough to cause my incapacitation, and is powerful enough to challenge Athelwynne, and sneaky enough to get away with it. But we have no proof."

"Athelwynne will be our proof," Reginleif said. "We'll find him; I promise. We have no choice; the Valkyrie can't rest until Odin's command is fulfilled."

Hel opened a bottle of wine, and then fetched a silver bowl of delicious golden apples while Reginleif poured two goblets to the brim.

"Will you keep your … *unseemly friends* … waiting?" Hel asked.

"They could've chosen to act civilly," Reginleif said. "My shield-sisters remind me of the knights of England: personified arrogance."

"They're queens in Valhalla, and some have known no other realm," Hel said. "They answer to no master but Odin, and his manners are contemptible."

"If I ever behave so, cast me out of Niflhiem," Reginleif said.

"If you were ever that rude, then I'd assume that you were playacting for a good reason, even if I didn't know what it was," Hel said. "It's not in your nature to be purposefully rude, but you're not the same woman whom I first met; Roselyn kept far better company than Reginleif."

Reginleif frowned; from any other person, man or woman, she'd consider those words an insult worth fighting over, but didn't that attitude prove Hel's argument? Reginleif wasn't just far stronger these days, she was more determined and confident, quicker to judge, and like any Valkyrie, she killed at will. *Was she doomed to become as haughty as her shield-sisters?*

"Thank you," Reginleif said. "I need you to keep me grounded."

"I pray that you always feel so," Hel said.

"Am … am I really changed that much? Do … do you think … that Karl … will still want me?"

"Karl will always love you," Hel smiled. "Karl has already proven that his love for you is the strongest that exists."

"How can you know that?" Reginleif asked.

"He chose you …" Hel smiled, "… over me."

Chapter 4

Eloise's Private Tower

ELOISE

"What're you doing up there?" Karl bellowed from the foot of the stairs.

Eloise froze abruptly, and stared down at her husband; around him stood a crowd of men, most of whom she didn't know well, with expressions horrified by Karl's caustic outburst. Eloise paused, and her handmaiden gasped softly; they were descending the stairs after a trying ordeal, their hair askew, garments crumpled, and faces weary. Eloise had been too tired to check to see if the hallway was empty before she descended into full view.

However, Eloise was born to be a baroness; she lifted her chin, assumed a pious air, and in silence descended the stairs. After stepping onto the flagstones, she calmly and demurely bowed before her husband, and then met his eyes without saying a word.

"I asked you a question!" Karl shouted.

Little Edith Tiller, now ten years old and Eloise's personal handmaid, blanched at Karl's vehemence, but she stayed behind her mistress and said nothing.

"I'll speak in our chambers," Eloise said, and she made to depart.

"You will …!" Karl shouted, but Rafe's voice cut him off.

"Baron Sir Karl!" Rafe shouted. "You're needed in the courtyard!"

Enraged, Karl turned to see Rafe and Seren standing before the door to the castle kitchen. At first, Eloise thought that Karl was going to shout at Rafe, his best friend, but then Seren intervened.

"I escort Eloise," Seren offered, and she let go of Rafe's arm and approached Eloise.

Eloise wanted to run away from Seren even more than she wanted to avoid Karl; their last conversation hadn't ended well. Yet Seren bowed deeply to Eloise, her gray-white hair now so long that it piled upon the floor as she bent over, but then Seren calmly waited, as if she'd stand contented until the world ended, patient and demure, until Eloise decided to move. Eloise envied her control, but to refuse Seren would expose her to more of Karl's shouting, and Eloise didn't think she had the strength to endure that.

Despite her exhaustion, Eloise walked, with every ounce of regal bearing, toward her bedroom, leaving Rafe to deal with Karl. She entered her bedroom with Edith and Seren in tow.

"Seren, I'm sorry to ask this, but I'm tired …," Eloise said.

"Then Seren watch over as you sleep," Seren said.

"You don't need to …," Eloise began.

"You pale," Seren said. "Perhaps company of another woman comfort you."

"I'll call you when I awaken."

"No need call: Seren be here."

Eloise sighed; this was getting nowhere. She was exhausted, and the strength to fight with Seren wouldn't return until after she'd slept. She'd prefer to send her away; Seren knew her too well, and Eloise had secrets that she couldn't reveal.

"Seren, if I could tell you, then I would."

"You can."

"If you knew, if anybody knew, then they'd be in grave danger."

"Eloise never seen Seren afraid."

"What about Nidhogg ...?" Eloise asked.

"No dragon in Bristlen," Seren said.

"Please; I need sleep ..."

"Sleep."

"I can't risk the ones I love ...!"

"Guldwin coming."

"I know."

"How Eloise know...?" Seren demanded. *"Eloise locked in tower when Rafe bring news!"*

Eloise gritted her teeth; *she shouldn't have said that.* Eorl Sir Guldwin's coming was known to her weeks before anyone else knew of it, but if she'd told anyone, then they'd demand to know how she knew it. She was too tired to argue with Seren; *she couldn't win.*

"Sleep beside me," Eloise said reluctantly, hoping to delay the conversation.

Minutes later, each in a sleeping gown, Eloise, Seren, and Edith crawled into the huge bed and pulled the covers up to their chins. Eloise tried to think about ways to sneak out while Seren was asleep, but moments after her head touched her pillow, blissful relief overwhelmed her.

Hours later, Eloise was dimly aware that her door opened suddenly, and one set of heavy footsteps entered, paused, and then departed, closing the door behind them. Eloise felt certain that it was Karl, that he'd seen the women sleeping and went elsewhere. Eloise felt ashamed for all of her secrecy, but she had no choice; *she was so close that she could almost taste it.* Yet mostly, she was just glad that she'd shown no outward sign of awakening; the last thing that she needed was another argument with Karl.

The first light of dawn shined through their open window, offering the rare promise of another hot day. Eloise liked the heat, but she knew that it wouldn't last; she had to be finished before it rained again. Slowly, cautiously, Eloise lifted one hand and rested it on Edith's shoulder; Edith opened her eyes and stared knowingly at her mistress. Signaling for silence, Eloise pointed; Edith nodded and slipped out of bed. Eloise crept to the edge to follow her.

Suddenly Eloise felt an unexpected tug; around her other wrist was a thin loop of long human hair, tied to her like a shackle; Seren stopped snoring and opened her eyes at once.

"Did you do this?" Eloise demanded, holding up her bound wrist.

"Must have happened while sleep," Seren said, but not one girl believed it.

As they dressed, again in silence, Eloise knew that she had to go back.

"Seren, I know that you …"

"Seren no leave."

Eloise stared at Seren; she loved her too much to offend her, but also too much to endanger her; *what she was doing could get them all killed.*

"I need to eat," Eloise said.

"We go eat," Seren said.

Less than an hour later, after a silent and very uncomfortable breakfast, Eloise emerged from the privy to find Seren standing placidly before her.

"I need a bottle of wine," Eloise said. "Would you …?"

"No leave you," Seren said.

"Seren, you've always trusted me …"

"No."

"As baroness, I order you to …!"

"No."

"I have work to do …!"

"Seren help."

"You can't."

"Then Seren watch."

"No one can enter my tower!"

"Seren no leave your side."

"I'll call my guards."

"I call Karl."

Eloise fumed, then steeled herself, as if reaching a serious conclusion.

"Very well," Eloise said. "But we can't talk here; let's go to your bedroom."

"Lead, I follow," Seren said.

Frowning, Eloise led the way. Rafe and Seren had the room next to hers and Karl's; Eloise's old room was now a nursery for her children. They entered the familiar bedroom and Eloise sat upon Seren's bed.

"Sit beside me," Eloise said.

Seren complied, and Eloise gritted her teeth; *she didn't want to do this, but Seren gave her no choice.*

If it worked at all …

Eloise closed her eyes and focused her inner thoughts. Her unwillingness to deceive someone that she loved troubled her, but she pushed her private feelings away; *she had to concentrate.* She had to use all of the training that she'd received, all of the knowledge that she'd learned. She stretched out an arm to keep Seren safe; *Seren would never know what hit her.*

When Eloise's mind was prepared, the sensations began to flow within her. She felt a wonderful openness to all of the worlds around her, a harmony that she felt nowhere else but upon the Magic Isle. Silently, Eloise chanted with her mind and her heart.

Blessed Lady, Hear my plea,
Your will and power grant to me,
Soft and gentle, restful and deep,
Grant now thy blessed sleep.

The sway of subtleties wafted Eloise in a dreamlike fog, and then she felt a hand pull her back; Edith was holding her, carefully keeping her from falling off the bed. Eloise opened her eyes; the bedroom appeared as if magically molding itself out of the fabric of another reality, and Eloise felt inexplicably tired. Beside her, Seren lay unconscious on her bed … as if she'd swooned.

Instantly Eloise regretted what she'd done, but she had no choice; Rafe was the most Christian man that Eloise knew, and Seren was his wife; Eloise wouldn't be the cause of another schism between them, like the one that Radsvid had caused. The barony du Harmonn was being threatened, and Eloise couldn't allow her barony to fall.

After arranging Seren into a comfortable position and covering her with a quilt, Eloise had Edith check the hall to make sure that it was empty, and together they slipped out and hurried toward Eloise's tower. Practicing Druidism was grounds for excommunication, and Eloise couldn't let it be known that an English baroness was learning forbidden magics. They unlocked her door, entered her tower, locked the door behind them, and then ascended her stairs to the one room in Castle Bristlen that no one else was allowed to enter.

Eloise's tower was small, barely eight feet in diameter, but crammed so full that, except for the narrow windows and one gap opposite the door, its curved walls were covered in shelves. Upon the floor was a pentagram inside a circle, all painted in dried lamb's blood. Painted on the wall, in the gap, was a tall, flowering tree, whose branches rose high and entwined on the ceiling. Foremost in her tower, before the trunk of the painted tree, was a white marble statue of the Lady of the Druids, which Eloise had commissioned; after seeing the Goddess Herself before the Well of Mimir, Eloise knew that its likeness was true. Around Her statue was arranged Eloise's most prized possessions; seven books written in the small, artistic handwriting of Athelwynne the Seer, and at the feet of the Lady lay her slate altar, holding her tools of magic, including the Blessed Moonstone which had illuminated their path all the way to Niflhiem, home of Hel, the Norse Goddess of Death. Her shelves held countless books, scrolls, and clay jars of ingredients; raven feathers, snake fangs, and of course, herbs and roots of every variety. Yet her greatest trophy was sitting upon the white marble shoulder of the statue of the Lady: Talita, a tiny, winged fairy.

"You're tired," Talita scolded, her high-pitched voice like that of a singing bird. "You're supposed to be rested."

"Forgive me," Eloise said, and she explained how she'd been forced to put Seren into an enchanted sleep.

"On any other day, I'd congratulate you," Talita said. "Perhaps we should wait until tomorrow."

"We can't," Eloise said. "Eorl Sir Guldwin will reach Grusshire tomorrow, and then he'll be too close to turn back. I must do it today."

"This will be the most demanding spell that you've ever attempted," Talita warned. "If you fail, it will kill you."

"Eorl Sir Guldwin will kill all of us, if I fail," Eloise said. "I made this decision long ago: Eorl Sir Guldwin dies today."

Talita rose on her colorful monarch butterfly wings, amber and black, and flew to hover before Eloise; from her auburn hair to her tiny feet, she was no more than a finger's height, less than half the size of Glororil or Silvana, and yet Talita was Eloise's teacher, sharing fairy wisdom that even the Seer's Master didn't know.

"To toy with death risks all life," Talita said.

"My dearest friend, if you wish to depart, I won't blame you," Eloise said.

Talita stared at Eloise as if estimating her strength.

"If I say stop …!" Talita warned.

"I'll do as you ask," Eloise promised.

"There's a point," Talita said, "after which we can't stop. Once Death is summoned, someone must die."

Eloise nodded.

"Let's begin," Talita said.

Eloise turned to Edith.

"Edith, Talita is right," Eloise said. "This will be dangerous. If you want to leave …"

"I stand with you, mistress," Edith said softly.

Eloise looked down at her beloved Edith; Edith was her only confidant, the only one who knew all of Eloise's secrets. Edith had even been allowed to accompany Eloise to the Magic Isle, where they'd both learned from her Master, who'd once taught Athelwynne the Seer. Edith had also gone with Eloise to visit the fairy well, although Titania didn't grace her with a second appearance, and from which they'd summoned Talita, the learned fairy who'd become her second teacher. Edith had a beautiful face with huge brown eyes, but they might as well have been the aged eyes of Seren; Edith was wise beyond her years, and deeper than her outward appearance of youthful innocence. Sarah Tiller would never forgive Eloise if anything ever happened to her only daughter, but looking into Edith's calm, focused eyes, Eloise had no fear for Edith.

"Let's begin," Eloise said.

Edith lifted the pitcher and poured fresh, clean rainwater into her silver basin, then dropped in a dozen rose petals, three sprigs of blooming violets, and powdery, crushed juniper. Then she lifted a small gray stone, breathed upon it, and dropped the stone into the water. Lastly, Edith lit a tall white candle and held it over the bowl.

"Blessed Mother, Lady White,
Holy is all within your sight."

Edith plunged the lit candle into the water and stirred three times in slow, round movements.

Eloise stood patiently as Edith removed Eloise's garments, carefully folding each and setting them onto the only empty shelf. Eloise closed her eyes and emptied her mind; to begin any complex spell, she had to be clean inside and out. Cold water splashed upon her naked skin, and Eloise's mind rebelled against its chill, but she forced her discomfort away; she had to stay focused. Eloise knew that Edith was cupping the water in her tiny hands, so the bathing took longer than Eloise liked; on the Magic Isle, a dozen bathers cleaned the spellcaster at the beginning of each ritual, and while Eloise liked their rapidity, she much preferred the longer and more private ritual of Edith alone washing her. Yet these thoughts weren't part of the ritual; Eloise shivered when the first handful splashed onto her hair and trickled down her bare shoulders, but she tried to ignore her discomfort and concentrated only upon the purity of the Lady as Edith's young voice chanted again.

"Blessed Mother, Lady White,
Holy is all within your sight."

When she'd been washed completely, a dry towel visited every inch of her; Eloise moved only enough to allow its touch, as she had to be completely dry. Then oily fingers marked her centers of vitality, her sacred places, and afterwards she heard Edith washing her young hands. Then the robe came: *the black robe.* Eloise had six robes, each that she'd spun and woven herself, as soft as silk, and of a specific color. The white robe was for pure connection to the Lady, the most powerful experience that a Druid could have, for it bound their heart with Her immortal perfection. Gold was for knowledge, blue for emotions, green for growth, and her red robe was for desire. Never before had Eloise worn her black robe: *the robe to summon Death.*

"Blessed Mother, Lady White,
Holy is all within your sight."

Edith stripped and washed next, but she wasn't anointed; nothing that Edith did was to draw attention to her. Edith dressed in a soft robe of gray and tied its sash tightly around her. Then she took the long white candle, which had been extinguished in the bathing water, and reignited it upon the eternal candle; they were done with the cleansing and ready for the illumination.

Eloise spread her arms and raised her eyes to the twisting patterns of white branches and green leaves that she'd painted upon her ceiling, and she took up the chant.

"Blessed Mother, Lady White,
Holy is all within your sight.
Upon Your glory I now call.
Unto Your will I submit my all."

Eloise paused to breathe, and then continued her chant. It was long and complex, and she couldn't blink … or hurry her chant so that she could blink. Her eyes began to sting; Eloise knew that this was the initial suffering, the first step to prove that she was worthy of the Lady's attention. Her eyes were burning and tearing before she finished, and her prayer was answered; through her blurry sight, the swirling, random patterns of leaves on the ceiling above her seemed to writhe, to form themselves into countless eyes staring back at her.

When her chant concluded, Eloise closed her burning eyes, feeling a flood of tears drip down her cheeks, and waited until the burning faded. Then Eloise again glanced skyward, but she saw no eyes; she hadn't expected them to stay. The eyes of the Lady had graced her, but this was just the second stage.

Lights stung her eyes; while Eloise had chanted, Edith had lit all of the many candles, in the correct order, and she was just finishing lighting the last of the nine black candles that encircled them upon the floor just outside of their circle. Then Edith lifted up the tiny cage and held it patiently.

"Blessed Mother, Lady Blue,
All my feelings I give to You.
Blessed Mother, Lady Green,
I give to You my future unseen.
Blessed Mother, Lady Red,
Receive all lovers upon my bed,
Blessed Mother, Lady Gold,
Yours I am until all is old."

Eloise knelt and reached out to the feet of her statue of the Lady and lifted her square slate altar, upon which lay all of her tools of magic. She set it inside of her circle. Each item she took and lifted up to the statue, as if presenting each for inspection and approval. When done, Talita suddenly flew down from her perch; she landed on Edith's head, and the large young eyes lifted, trying to see her.

"You can stop now without penalty," Talita said. "If you continue, you'll pay a price."

"You're disturbing my concentration," Eloise said.

"I'm your teacher; listen to what I say."

"I hear and trust, but I'm decided."

"Look at the bird," Talita said. "Be the bird."

Inside the tiny cage in Edith's hands was a brown and rust colored sparrow, flitting nervously about in its cramped wire enclosure. Some aspects of magic disgusted Eloise, but she'd learned how disgusting magic could be from Athelwynne, who'd practiced his arts upon the Wolfqueen more than once. Eloise focused on the bird, closing her mind to all else. She imagined being tiny, trapped, and scared; the bird had every reason to be afraid. It didn't know what was happening, how it had gotten trapped here, and its puny awareness never thought to ask why. Eloise delved into herself, became the bird, and held out her hand.

Edith opened the cage; Eloise reached inside, seized, and drew forth the trembling prisoner, its soft wings almost a caress, its tiny shape so weak that she could crush it in one hand. Eloise lifted the frightened bird to her cheek and brushed it against her, feeling its soft feathers upon her cheek, a mere whisper against her skin, relishing it, wishing that she could comfort it and set it free. Then Eloise carefully set it down, upon its back, and pressed her palm over it, feeling the rapid hammering of its tiny heart. She didn't like doing this, but the ritual required it; *she was playing with death.* Slowly Eloise lifted her athame in her other hand, determined to make it as quick and painless as she could.

"Blessed Mother, Lady White,
Accept now this sacrifice.
Take its spirit into Your own.
As one eternal, never alone."

The sharp silver blade scraped against the flagstones as she cut quickly and completely; instantly Eloise used the feathered body as a paintbrush and marked with death the whole circle around her, on top of the dried lamb's blood: a fresh circle of protection to strengthen the old.

Edith held open the cage, and Eloise deposited the sad remains into it. Edith picked up the head and reverently placed it beside its body; later she'd bury it with more prayers to the Lady … if they lived.

"Blessed Mother, Lady White,
Accept Thee now my life.
Whether I win or be won,
Let now Thine own will be done."

Their circle was set. Eloise glanced at Edith and Talita; none of them could leave the circle now.

The cup stared up at them; it was a plain, simple chalice, originally made of hardened clay by some unknown potter, but it had been ornamented with silver bands and masterfully decorated with the faces of twelve bearded men. Eloise didn't know whose faces they were, but they looked grim; the cup was a gift from her Master, and she'd learned to trust him. Into the cup, Eloise slowly placed the ingredients that Talita had so carefully measured; if the ingredients weren't measured properly, then Eloise would die.

Eloise lifted her silver athame, bloodied by the sparrow, and stared at it, admiring its artistic beauty, yet repulsed by the cruel evidence of its sharp blade. For what she was about to do, she had to prove that she was worthy; *magic is not for the squeamish.* Eloise bared her arm and held it up before her, seeing the faint scars of her prior spellcastings. With her athame, Eloise had to pay in blood; she set its sharp silver edge against her white flesh, took a deep breath, and slashed in a sudden jerk. The pain was always more than she could bear, but Eloise couldn't cry out, couldn't risk someone breaking open her tower door to find out why she'd screamed.

Unexpectedly, Eloise felt a soft hand grab her arm, and when she opened her eyes, Edith was holding the cup under her cut, dripping her red essence onto the deadly ingredients, filling the chalice with her blood.

"Do not gasp," Talita said. "Breathe slowly. Control your mind."

Eloise knew how to breathe properly; she just wasn't as good at resisting pain as her fellow novitiates, but after this ritual, Eloise would no longer be a novitiate. Any spell of this magnitude was the final test; if Eloise succeeded, then she'd be a full Druid priestess. If Eloise failed, then she'd be a corpse.

Slowly the cup filled. This was her last chance to quit, but Eloise steeled herself, took the cup from Edith's hands, and raised it high.

"Blessed Mother, Lady White,
The final door is in my sight.
Let now this dread door open
And all beyond to me send.
In life or death, my soul to Thee.
As Thou do will, so mote it be."

Eloise dipped the tip of her athame into the chalice, stirred nine times, watching the deadly herbs swirl, and then she drank. The taste made her want to gag, but Eloise choked it down.

There was no going back now.

"Control!" Talita shouted. "Face your fear!"

Edith took the empty cup from Eloise's shaking hands. The poisons worked fast; Eloise felt unwell, then sick, and finally waves of agony exploded from her stomach. Eloise struggled; *she had to stay aware!* The pain was staggering, she felt feverish, and suddenly she vomited all over the floor. Yet it was too late; Eloise had studied this spell since her first day on the Magic Isle; *she knew what this would cost her.*

Sweat beaded upon her face, and a burning slowly arose within her gut. Eloise clutched her stomach and doubled over, gritting her teeth to keep from crying out. She was dying; that was the prime requirement of her spell. She forced her eyes back open every time that the pain squeezed them shut, and she kept staring at her statue of the Lady; *surely She wouldn't let her die.*

Minutes passed, each more agonizing than the last. Swirling colors filled her sight, darkness closing in; Eloise was dying.

Had she already failed?

Was she doomed?

Slowly she glanced about her tower, but every vision flashed in rapid succession, distorted and confused: Talita was ten feet tall, sitting upon the shoulder of Edith, who was no bigger than her hand. Her shelves were empty, then full of magical treasures, and then empty again. The sunlight entering through her window was formed of golden spears aimed straight at her; Eloise was blinded, but she had to see. The statue of the Lady moved, raised a skeletal face, and grinned the morbid smile and deathly teeth of a glaring, empty skull.

Wracked with agonies both physical and mental, Eloise struggled; Death had come, and she had to face him. She was within her circle, and Edith would hold her, keep her from falling outside of it, but neither Edith nor Talita could defy his strength; if Death claimed her, then she'd be his.

Death hovered hungrily, angrily; Death didn't like being defied. *Death could not be denied.* Death didn't take orders; Eloise had summoned him … and Death wanted her.

Eloise fumbled, her trembling hands crawling across the flagstones; upon her slate altar was a scroll. Despite her pain, Eloise lifted the scroll and opened it to face Death; upon the rolled parchment Eloise had drawn a realistic picture of Eorl Sir Guldwin. Eloise tried to control her breathing, tried to restrain her gasps, and focus on his image; she wished that she'd gotten a lock of his hair or a garment that he'd worn. Instead, she pictured Sir Guldwin in her mind, imagined where he was right now, and remembered his voice, his arrogance, and his overwhelming greed and callousness. Eloise hated Eorl Sir Guldwin with every ounce of her being; she had to focus her pain into pure hate.

Eloise understood the power of magic. Casting such a spell might kill novices, or drive them insane, or trick them into attempting to murder their target physically, falsely believing themselves capable, despite innumerable proofs to the contrary. However, Eloise wouldn't give in to Death or madness; Eloise concentrated with all her will upon Eorl Sir Guldwin.

Death screamed in outrage. Empty eye sockets burned with fury, clenched jaws opened, and gray, rotting teeth gnashed; *Death didn't want Eorl Sir Guldwin.* It wasn't Guldwin's time; he wasn't Death's errand. Eloise was dying; *Death had come for her.*

The pain was too much. Eloise didn't want to die, but she'd drunk her own blood mixed with poison; *this was her doing, the death that she deserved.* She was failing; once unconscious, her circle would collapse, and then she, Edith, and Talita would all succumb to the ultimate inevitable. She didn't want to die, and would spare her companions, if she could, but her last ounce of strength was fading; she was helpless before the eternal appetite of Death. Her pain was growing, her sickness overwhelming; *she wasn't going to make it.*

A brief thought flitted through her; Eloise hoped that Death would take her quickly. She couldn't endure long suffering, or the tormented mental burden; she'd challenged Death to a battle of wills, and realized too late that she couldn't win. Her Master had told her that this spell was folly, that hate couldn't hold back Death, but she'd ignored him; Eloise was the second-best student that he'd ever had … mostly because she'd read and reread the secret grimoires of Athelwynne, the most powerful seer ever trained upon the Magic Isle.

Eloise struggled to remain conscious even as the blackness stole over her. She vomited again; bile splashed upon her altar, painting her tools, but she didn't care. She pushed her drawing of Eorl Sir Guldwin at Death, praying that he'd heed her, but he only leered and seemed to grow bigger, as if swallowing her whole fading circle.

Eloise felt herself slipping and redoubled her effort; she had to keep concentrating on Eorl Sir Guldwin, to force Death to take him. Eorl Sir Guldwin was an evil man, who'd paid to have his virgin daughter raped, and then he'd beaten her, and had Eloise and Seren bound helpless inside a tent while he'd had Rafe and Karl lashed …

Karl … tears burst forth; *Karl would never know what happened to her.*

"No tears!" Talita shouted. "Tears open a doorway for Death …!"

But Eloise couldn't stop crying. Eloise loved Karl more than she could say, and had cast this spell to save him, and her barony … but mostly him. She couldn't imagine living without him, especially since that would mean Roselyn would claim Karl, and Eloise couldn't enter Valhalla; she'd never be a warrior. Karl … the only man that she'd ever loved; *how appropriate that her last thoughts were of him.*

Yet suddenly, inexplicably, Eloise felt stronger. Death hesitated and drew back. Despite the agony burning through her, Eloise took a deep breath and focused; but not on Eorl Sir Guldwin; Eloise focused on Karl.

Death recoiled. Karl was the greatest love of her life, and only love defeated fear. Eloise lifted her face and stared into the endless eyes of Death, using her love for Karl as a shield, and her drawn picture as her sword. A newfound resolution filled her, and she shoved the scroll showing Eorl Sir Guldwin at Death's skeletal face; *she wouldn't give in.*

Death vanished. The choking, smothering air was suddenly wholesome and fragrant again. Her tower was cleansed.

"It's done!" Talita shouted happily. "He's gone!"

Nauseated, Eloise fell over and passed out.

Chapter 5

The Well of Urd

REGINLEIF

"The Valkyrie have failed!" Hrist bellowed angrily.

"We haven't failed," Róta said. "We're still trying."

Standing beside tall, massively-muscled Hrist, amid towering trees and thick greenery, Róta looked small. Róta resembled Mist, a wisp of a woman, but where Mist was white and flowing, Róta was dark and forbidding, her feral features edged with sharp angles, shifty black eyes, and she was sly and devious. Many considered Róta an equal to Loki's cunning.

"We've searched everywhere," Mist said. "Where else should we look?"

"I'll aid Herfjötur," Randgríðr said. "She can't escort every einherjar alone."

"I'll join you," Geirahöd said. "I tire of pointless searching."

"Go," Skeggjöld said. "We'll continue."

While Randgríðr and Geirahöd mounted and flew off, Prudr snarled, her deep voice strong and defiant.

"We should ambush Loki again," Prudr said. "*I'll make him talk!*"

Prudr was the one Valkyrie that the Norse Gods feared; Prudr had the most sculpted physique, was massively muscled, able to lift weights and snap chains that no other could manage, and no einherjar could outwrestle her. Her long, thick hair flowed down her back, brown as polished rowan, and her face rivaled the chiseled beauty of Greek statues. Prudr was the most direct of all her sisters, and she prided herself on being fearless … moreso than any other Valkyrie.

"Can you stop Loki from vanishing?" Skögul demanded. "We caught and bound him, but the instant that he got his bearings, he exploded in a blast of green flames; the cursed one singed my best fur vest!"

"Then we inflict so much pain that he can't get his bearings," Prudr said.

"Without his bearings, how will he answer our questions?" Skeggjöld asked. "If he's screaming in pain, how will you tell his truths from his lies? Starting another war with Loki won't help. We need a foolproof plan."

"Heid could make him talk," Reginleif said.

All of the Valkyrie gasped and stared at her.

"I never said that we should seek her," Reginleif said quickly. "But, for enough gold, Heid will do anything, and I'd see Odin's command accomplished."

"Heid could make the Valkyrie into mindless slaves," Skeggjöld said. "I'll not approach her."

"I'd rather bargain with Mimir," Róta said. "Better death than enslavement."

"We've no choice," Mist said slowly, and the fog encasing her grew dark and still. "We must look into Urðarbrunnr, the Well of Urd."

"The well of madness …?" Prudr exclaimed.

"The well of lies," Göll said. "I'll not go there."

"I'll go," Róta said. "I'm the least-easily fooled."

"You're our loremaster, not our wisest," Skeggjöld said.

"No, that would be Geirahöd," Róta said.

"We'd best not all go," Skeggjöld said.

"Yet we dare not approach too few," Hlökk said. "Urd's deceptions deny safeguards."

"I'll take Róta, Prudr, Mist, and Hlökk," Skeggjöld said.

"I'll go," Reginleif said.

"You're not ready …," Skeggjöld started.

"I watched the Seer die in the Well of Mimir," Reginleif argued. "I've fished for Hel in the Well of Hergelmir."

"Urd is the most dangerous well in Yggdrasil," Skeggjöld said.

"The Twelve gather there every day …," Reginleif argued.

"Odin commands that they gather there," Skeggjöld said. "The Well of Urd reflects the thoughts of the Norns, and no danger will Odin not face to gain wisdom. Yet most gods fear that well; it's frequently their chief cause of trouble."

"I would go," Reginleif said.

"Very well," Skeggjöld said, "but beware; Urðarbrunnr offers only torment … and the touch of its waters brings eternal madness."

"Reconsider, Reginleif," Hlökk said. "I predict grave danger, should you challenge the Well of Urd."

Reginleif hesitated; Hlökk was the Valkyrie gifted with second sight; her eyes weren't as keen as Heimdal's, yet she saw things no other did, and felt sensations too mild for her shield-sisters. Hlökk often made predictions that her sisters doubted; not all came true, but most did, and many considered her a half-seeress. She looked the most like Reginleif; Hlökk had hair of shining gold, and a very strong chin, but her eyes changed color frequently, matching her mood and her visions, even if no other could see them. Physically, they were little different; she and Reginleif could wear the same armor, since Hlökk was thinner but with hard, bulging muscles. Reginleif paled; she didn't doubt her words, but she couldn't show cowardice.

"Valkyrie fear nothing," Reginleif said.

All the sisters nodded.

"Let's go," Skeggjöld said.

The Well of Urd lay in a far corner of Asgard, surrounded by green hills and deep woods, but the winged horses of the Valkyrie reached there quickly and with little effort. The well was much smaller than Reginleif had expected, barely as wide as she was tall; a third of the size of the Well of Mimir, and only a puddle compared to the mammoth Well of Hergelmir, where all the rivers of Yggdrasil were born. They arrived in the middle of the day; the sun was high, yet no reflection of its brilliance shined upon the water, nor did its surface darken from the shadows of those leaning over it. None saw their reflection in its water; the Well of Urd was dark, like a shaded pond in a midnight swamp, and the ripples of the wind across its surface only showed as a black movement overtop a black stillness.

Surrounding Urðarbrunnr was a single thick circle of stone the like of which Reginleif had never seen, a dark purple marble, etched with runes and magical symbols. Róta knelt and examined the markings closely, tracing them with her thin fingers, and slowly whispering to herself in a tongue that none of the others knew. Outside the ring of purple stone grew tall grasses that were heavily trampled, such that most lay flat; the Norse Gods rested upon these hills, the Twelve who assembled each day: Odin, Thor, Baulder, Heimdall, Loki, Hod, Vidar, Tyr, Bragi, Vali, Ull, and Forseti. With them sat Njord, Frigg, Freyja, Gefion, Eir, Vili, Ve, Lofn, Sif, Saga, Aegir, Freyr, Idun, and others of great wisdom, each fearing, yet hoping for wisdom from the Well of Urd.

Suddenly Róta cried out and fell back, shaking, trembling upon the grass.

"What did you see?" Skeggjöld asked.

"My death," Róta said slowly, forcibly regaining control of herself. "Don't fear; I've seen it before."

"How … how do you …?" Reginleif asked.

"That's my concern," Róta said. "It's not wise to seek your own future, and less wise to share that vision; I've wrecked countless plans, but my own death stymies me; I fear that it shall come to pass."

"Your doom is not our quest," Skeggjöld said. "Perhaps you should let another look."

"Be my guest," Róta scowled, and she gestured toward the well.

Skeggjöld stiffened, then cautiously approached the water. She stepped carefully upon the ring of purple marble and leaned over. Long moments passed.

"I see nothing," Skeggjöld said.

"Patience," Róta said. "It will come."

Minutes ticked by, each longer than the last. Finally Skeggjöld gasped and her eyes opened wide; with the swiftness of a warrior, she drew her sword and raised it to strike.

"Don't disturb the water!" Róta shouted.

Skeggjöld hesitated, her teeth gritted in anger, her tense swordarm shaking, barely holding back her swing.

"Sister, if that black water splashes upon you, then your mind is lost forever," Hlökk warned. "If you strike its surface, then you'll be drenched, and the Valkyrie can't tolerate a madwoman; we'll have to kill you outside of Valhalla, and let your soul crawl to Niflhiem, where you'll bow before Hel … unable to resist her commands."

"We'll all be dishonored, and from you Hel shall gain the Fighting Secrets of the Valkyrie," Prudr said. "Her dead will fight against us with our own skills."

Mist raised her lithe hand; from her foggy aura flowed the white mist that eternally shrouded her. It swept over the grass and stone circle, and covered the black waters of Urðarbrunnr; whatever Skeggjöld saw, Mist hid it from her eyes. Prudr stepped forward and seized her from behind, her fingers locked beneath Skeggjöld's breasts, and she lifted her and carried her back.

"What did you see?" Hlökk asked.

"Lies," Skeggjöld snarled. "Shameful … disgraceful …!"

"Deceptions flow deep in Urðarbrunnr," Róta said. "The Norns prize madness. They want you to attack its waters."

"Tell us what you saw," Mist said.

"Never," Skeggjöld said. "You'd cease to respect me …"

"No Valkyrie would judge you by a lie," Hlökk said.

"I've looked into those waters before," Mist said. "I know what they show, but Reginleif doesn't; we must prepare our sister."

"You look and tell," Skeggjöld scowled.

"I will," Mist said. "But you looked first; it's your turn to speak."

Skeggjöld scowled, then closed her eyes, turned her head away, and spoke through gritted teeth.

"This cursed well showed Heimdal winding his great horn; Ragnarrock had begun, and Loki was leading infinite forces of evil, backed by the legions of Hel, against the walls of Asgard. The Valkyrie proudly rose to face the final threat … except me: this … evil thing … showed me … fleeing … in terror …"

"Skeggjöld bows to no terror!" Hlökk shouted.

"It's a base lie," Mist said.

"Blasphemy," Reginleif said. "No one would believe it."

"Why?" Róta asked.

All of the Valkyrie looked shocked.

"How dare you …?" Prudr shouted.

"Skeggjöld would never show cowardice, not even if all the offspring of Loki had her bound like Fenris," Róta said. "What I meant was: *why did the well show her this particular vision?"*

All of the Valkyrie paused, taken aback by the question.

"How should we know …?" Prudr asked.

"Plans," Róta said. "All things act for a reason. It wanted Skeggjöld to attack it; if Skeggjöld had splashed the water of insanity upon herself, then Skeggjöld would become a tool of Urd, rather than a threat to her."

"Then … you speak … a compliment?" Mist asked. "You say that Urd fears Skeggjöld …?"

"The Norns fear nothing," Róta said. "Even Mjollnir is no threat to them. However, the Norns have cruel desires; if the Norns plot against Skeggjöld, then they must see her as a threat to their plans."

"What are the Norn's plans?" Reginleif asked.

"Not even Odin knows the hopes of that evil trio," Róta said. "Yet Odin has suspicions, derived from clues like this; I'll report this evidence to him. But let this be our warning; the Norns despise the Valkyrie, and we'll each be tested."

Mist insisted on going next. Reginleif stepped closer to watch, but Mist glanced at her, frowned, and then spread out her fog, encircling the foretelling pool, and hid its black waters from all but her. Reginleif went back and sat beside her sisters, upon the grass.

Long minutes passed, nearly half an hour, and then Mist screamed in outrage. Her fog became a violent white whirlwind, and suddenly expanded, engulfing all of them in a blinding hurricane. Caught off balance, Reginleif stumbled, blown over, but Prudr's hand clenched around her arm and held her, keeping her from being blown away. All the other Valkyrie threw themselves flat upon the ground, seizing thick tufts of grass, their cries lost in the roar of wild wind; only Prudr stood, her immense strength resisting the gale.

As quickly as it had come, the fierce wind dissipated. The mists lowered, and became a thick fog that covered the ground. Yet it was an icy fog, chill, bluish, and Mist appeared, standing alone by the Well of Urd. Slowly she turned her head, then walked she directly towards the Valkyrie, past Skeggjöld and Róta, to face Hlökk.

"Prince Olaf of Sweden is mine!" Mist screamed at Hlökk, her voice deep and threatening, her brows furrowed with accusation. *"You know I claimed him!"*

Hlökk said nothing, just stared at her shield-sister; *all of the Valkyrie knew this!*

"Did you lie a'bed with Olaf?" Mist seethed.

All looked shocked, and before anyone could say anything, blood-red mists exploded about them, Mist leapt forward, and she and Hlökk rolled on the grass, punching with the fists of hardened warriors.

Skeggjöld and Prudr jumped into the fray and pulled the two apart.

"I never …!" Hlökk shouted.

"I saw you …!!!" Mist screamed.

"The well lies!" Skeggjöld shouted.

"I saw you exchange looks …! I saw you touch him …!"

"Calm yourself!" Róta shouted. "Urðarbrunnr doesn't always lie; sometimes it shows visions of the past; truths deceive better than lies, if revealed partially … or out of context. You've failed, Mist; the Well of Urd defeated you!"

Mist gave Hlökk the blackest of stares, such that all of her fog turned black.

"I never touched Olaf!" Hlökk insisted.

"That's not true," Skeggjöld said. "You helped me turn him over once, to see if he was dead."

"That doesn't count," Hlökk said.

"Showing that from specific angles, the Well of Urd could make it look like it counted," Róta said. "You can't trust anything that the well shows you. We've all looked at Olaf as you lead him to your chambers; none would dare to challenge you."

"If we can't trust it, then why are we here?" Prudr demanded.

"Urd knows why we're here, and we must endure her taunts," Róta said. "Eventually, she'll show us what we need to know …"

"Why?" Skeggjöld asked. "Why would Urd show us where the Seer is?"

"Because," Róta smiled, "that's how she'll kill us."

"The Well of Urd … will show us … where the Seer is …," Hlökk said slowly, in the voice that they all knew marked a prediction.

"How do you know?" Prudr demanded.

"I simply know," Hlökk said.

"You have the sight," Skeggjöld to Hlökk, and she shook her head. "We'll stay until you're right."

"Mist, we have millions of warriors to choose from," Hlökk said. "I wouldn't take yours."

Mist glared blackly, and inhaled deeply before speaking.

"If I've falsely accused, then I'm sorry," Mist said.

"Enough of this," Prudr said. "I'll look."

Without hesitation, Prudr stomped toward the well.

"Do not splash the water!" Róta reminded her.

For almost an hour, Prudr impatiently glared at the black water, and when Prudr swore that she could look no longer, Skeggjöld ordered her to keep watching for a vision. Róta suggested that Urd knew that waiting would infuriate Prudr, and probably hoped to make her angry before showing her anything. Prudr loudly complained, but she kept watching. Mist and Hlökk remained silent, but they cast occasional glares at each other; both looked ruffled from their fight, stray broken grasses sticking out of the tangles in their mussed hair.

Suddenly Prudr gasped. Reginleif stared amazed; normally Prudr could double her muscle-girth just by flexing arms, but Prudr seemed to shrink; her shoulders slumped, her head drooped, and her spirit crumpled. She seemed about to topple into the well.

"Stop her!" Róta shouted, and she dashed forward.

Never hesitant, the Valkyrie ran; they seized Prudr and flung her back, away from the well. Reginleif glimpsed a brief view of the water before the vision faded: *a landscape of eternal death.*

Prudr toppled onto her back, tears moistening her closed eyes. She never sobbed or whimpered, but when she opened her eyes, despair filled her gaze.

"Death … everywhere …," Prudr whispered. "The Valkyrie, the gods, giants, horrors of old, and all the einherjar …!"

"Another lie," Mist said.

"Perhaps not," Skeggjöld said. "Urd could have given Prudr a glimpse of the aftermath of Ragnarrock."

"Impossible," Reginleif said. "Ragnarrock will end, as I understand it, when Black Surt envelopes all nine worlds with fire; in the aftermath of Ragnarrock, everything would be burned."

"Another lie," Hlökk said.

"Let's pray that we never know," Róta said.

"All were dead …," Prudr said softly. "My strength … couldn't help …"

"Enough of this," Hlökk said. "I'm next."

Hlökk stormed up to the Well of Urd and looked into it.

"Show me the Seer!" Hlökk commanded, and when no image appeared, Hlökk added: "Toy not with me, Urðarbrunnr!"

Two hours passed, and the other Valkyrie sat and waited, yet Hlökk never moved, never glanced away from the water.

"I see you!" Hlökk said suddenly.

Abruptly, the still black waters of the Well of Urd began to bubble and froth. The Valkyrie jumped up, but Hlökk held out her hands, knotted fingers stabbing over the vile vapors that suddenly arose, and she glared into the boiling well.

"I see through your lies!" Hlökk seethed. *"You can't defeat me! Show me what we seek! Show me the Seer!"*

Suddenly a thousand dark images burst upwards into the air around them, turning the bright day to blackest night. Urðarbrunnr blasted forth a sickly, rancid green brilliance, blinding all but Hlökk, who stared undaunted into its bright glare. The other Valkyrie cried out, and some closed their eyes, but Reginleif strained to peek, shielding her eyes from the worst of the glare. She dared not approach the well; the visions flying about her were too many, too confusing, and moving too fast. Lost amid the swirling images, Reginleif might fall into the well … and end every thought in her mind.

Images of everything blew about the gusty air and swept around them in never-ceasing torrents. Wars raged, babies slept, and hungry beasts hunted; endless landscapes and oceanic horizons stretched around them, deserts, mountains, and forests without end. Billions of humans were born screaming … and billions died with the same sounds. Men collapsed from weariness, women from exhaustion, and everywhere swelled despair and suffering. Scenes of all places and times opened before their eyes.

"No!" Hlökk shouted. *"Too much …! Urd! Stop …!"*

Suddenly the air was clear; bright daylight streamed upon them, birds sang in the distance, and the tall grasses smelled sweetly. Reginleif glanced at the well; the sickly green light and countless images were gone, and Hlökk lay sprawled upon the ground, unmoving, unconscious. Róta was holding her hand.

"She lives," Róta said. "She challenged Urd … and fought a war of seeresses. It was brave, but foolish."

They carried Hlökk away from the stone ring and set her to rest upon the grass. No one spoke, but then

Reginleif slowly turned, walked to the well, and peered into its infinite dark waters.

"Urd, show me what you will," Reginleif said gently. "Please."

Apparently Urd was appeased, for her vision came at once: Eloise was screaming, sweat pouring down her face, and then she almost fainted. Karl's reflection came into view, holding a newborn infant in his arms: *a boy, their son.* Smiling, Seren took the infant from his hands, and Karl leaned over and tenderly kissed Eloise's sweat-wet forehead.

Reginleif bit her lip; *this was Karl's son!* Eloise and Karl had children … a family. *This was why he hadn't died …!*

Karl and Eloise were sitting upon the baronial thrones of du Harmonn; two small children, a boy and a girl, sat in Karl's lap, and Eloise was nursing their six month old baby at her breast. Smiles beamed from all of them.

A deep heaviness fell upon Reginleif's heart; she'd sent Karl, her true love, back to England to marry Eloise … not considering what that meant: *she'd sent her only love into the arms of another woman! She'd given him away!* Eloise was no longer a child; she was a beautiful, strong woman, such that any man would desire. While Reginleif was fighting and dying in savage Valhalla, or drinking herself into oblivion each night, only to stumble to her chambers alone, Karl was enjoying the life that she'd always wanted, full of love, family, and friendship … *without her.*

Rafe appeared, and he gave both Karl and Eloise large goblets of wine; they were still together, the closest of friends, while Reginleif sat frowning in Elvidnir, surrounded by millions of laughing warriors … yet always alone.

An old man and woman entered Castle Bristlen and bowed before them … and never were smiles brighter. Reginleif recognized Farmer Tiller and his wife Sarah, the smartest farmer and the best cook in du Harmonn, and as Eloise's young handmaiden ran to embrace them, Reginleif realized that this grown child must be Edith, the two year old that she'd played with at the Tiller's farm; *had it really been so long ago?* The young girl looked about ten, which added correctly; whole lives were being lived on Earth while she flitted about Yggdrasil, flying over battles and fetching the best warriors, attending to her duties, each day exactly the same. As Karl, Rafe, Eloise, and Seren warmly greeted their guests, two strange young men joined them, both with scruffy, thin beards; *could that be Nate and Philip Tiller, boys no longer?*

Reginleif had dreamed of having a daughter like Edith, a little darling of her own, back on Earth*; no, that was Roselyn's dream.* No longer was she a mortal woman to fantasize of marriage and growing old in peaceful harmony; Roselyn had surrendered that dream when she'd accepted Odin's offer and become Reginleif. She was a warrior now, her sword-skills already legend; even Eric Bjornson and Svenson Two-Sword regularly fell beneath her blade.

However, seeing Karl enjoy the life that she'd given up, and watching Eloise bask in the delights that she'd never have, Reginleif felt pangs of regret that impaled more deeply than Geirahöd's spears.

The reflections on the black waters darkened. At first, Reginleif couldn't recognize them; then the scene coalesced in her eyes: moonlight pouring in from the window illuminated Karl and Eloise deeply entwined, fervently kissing, lost in lustful ecstasy. Their naked bodies enmeshed, hands grasping, backs arching,

Reginleif could almost hear their gasping breaths, the groans and grunts that only lovers know, sounds that Reginleif hadn't heard in eight long years. Roselyn had once stumbled upon Karl and Eloise in these positions, back in the Silver Swan Inn, and then she'd been so relieved that she'd thrown back her head and laughed.

Tears dripped from her eyes; *she could bear this no longer!*

Yet another vision came, still and silent. Karl was sweating while sleeping, ghastly pale and sallow, and his face was covered in crusty red sores. He was lying in bed; Seren pressed a wet cloth to his spotted forehead while Eloise frantically shook his arm, gripping his hand as if she'd never let go. Rafe stood behind them, reading aloud from a bible; never had Roselyn seen Rafe look so sad. Slowly Karl's breathing depleted … failed … and died. Eloise and Seren burst into sobs, and Rafe closed his bible and bowed his head.

Fingernails gouging rents out of her temples, Reginleif was unaware that she'd screamed until she heard it burst out of her, and then hands grabbed and pulled her back, yet Reginleif resisted; she couldn't turn away, couldn't stop watching: *better to fall into the pool of madness than live with nothing!*

She bounced hard onto thick tufts as Valkyrie hands yanked her backwards. Grips upon her arms that could only be Prudr seized and held her, and several voices called her name. She didn't care; she was Roselyn, not Reginleif, and the one man that she loved, the man for whom she'd become a Valkyrie, was dead … and he'd died a'bed of a sickness; *no Valkyrie could come for him.* She'd lost Karl forever. His spirit could go anywhere; to Christ in Heaven, to the Lady of the Druids, or to Hel in Niflhiem … no, they'd all seen the living death that Hel's subjects endured. No one would willingly spend eternity in Niflhiem; no matter what faith Karl truly embraced, he'd never come to Yggdrasil.

Roselyn had lost her one true love!

"Lies …!" Róta shouted.

But it had been too real …!

"Valkyrie!" Skeggjöld shouted, but Reginleif turned away from her.

"Hold her down," Hlökk said. "She's too new; we shouldn't have brought her."

"Gently," Mist said. "Reginleif, we're here … your shield-sisters …"

Slowly Reginleif realized where she was … and what had happened. Yet she couldn't force the images from her mind, any of them …

Stern, strong, feminine faces; Reginleif saw them as never before. Above her stood true Valkyrie, warriors centuries old; she'd never really be one of them. Her friends were gone, her love was gone: *Roselyn had nothing.*

"She's not going anywhere," Prudr said firmly.

Minutes later, they released Reginleif, and sat together upon the grass, huddled tightly. Almost an hour passed before Reginleif could stand without falling; her whole universe had tilted off-balance. She didn't know if any of the visions that she'd seen were true or false, but never had she felt so miserable; Urðarbrunnr had wholly defeated her.

"Let's finish this," Reginleif said.

As one, the Valkyrie stood and walked to encircle the Well of Urd.

"Hail, Urd, Giantess of Jontunhiem," Róta said. "We've faced your will and still live; if you would do your worst, then show us what we came to see."

A vision of thick white mists appeared upon the black waters of Urðarbrunnr, slowly churning. All of the Valkyrie stared, but only Mist gasped.

"What is it?" Skeggjöld asked.

"I … I don't know," Mist said. "I've seen every type of fog and wisp of cloud; I've never seen anything like this."

"What's wrong with it?" Hlökk asked.

"What's right with it?" Mist replied. "It's cold, so much that it should crystalize into snow, yet it swirls as if heated by all the fires of Muspell. No mists should act like this …!"

"This vision tells us nothing," Róta said to the well. "Urd, show us the Seer … or where we must go to learn of him."

The strange, twisting mists vanished, and the black water became as still as ice. Another vision appeared upon the shifting surface, a large symbol drawn upon faded yellow-gray sands; a single runic eye, with a long, thick brow over it, and what looked like a shadow of a nose, with a long, curling line extending from between the eye and the shadow, ending in a spiral.

"Is that the eye of Odin?" Skeggjöld asked.

"I've never seen this symbol," Róta said. "Recall it well, sisters; this may be important."

The unknown symbol of the eye vanished, and again the black water became as still as ice. Slowly an image rose out of it; three horrible, shadowy giant women surrounding a cauldron of churning bile. One worked a large spinning wheel thick with new thread, and another weaved on a huge loom, and the last held a golden pair of deadly scissors.

"We can't …!" Prudr gasped.

"We've no choice," Hlökk said.

The image faded, leaving only black waters surrounded by stunned Valkyrie.

"It's decided," Róta said. "We must face … *them.*"

Skeggjöld bowed and shook her head at the same time. Reginleif understood: *they had to face the Norns.*

Chapter 6

Death and Secrets

RAFE

"Eorl Sir Guldwin is dead," the bristling guard said.

Lord Sir Rafe's eyes opened wide from atop his horse, taking in the guards and the familiar foothills beyond the steep ridge of Grusshire.

"Dead ...?" Rafe asked. *"How ...? When ...?"*

"The devil alone knows," the other guard said. "He screamed suddenly, not four days ago, and his eyes blazed as if he were staring into the face of Satan himself. He clutched his chest ... and fell off his horse ... and he was dead before he hit the dirt."

"Eorl Sir Guldwin ... dead," Rafe mused, and then he bowed his head. "Forgive me; we were mortal enemies, but I can't learn of the death of any Christian soul... not even that of a foe ... without speaking a prayer for him."

Rafe dismounted, took out a small silver and brass crucifix, and knelt upon the dirt road. Both guards seemed to approve this behavior; they made the sign of the cross and bowed their heads.

"Requiem aeternam dona eis, Domine, et lux perpetua luceat eis," Rafe said. "Blessed Lord and Almighty God, Father of all, receive into Your care this fallen soul, and grant him Your eternal mercy …"

At the end of his long prayer, Rafe again made the sign of the cross, and then he rose and faced the guards.

"I have a scroll from Baron Sir Karl du Harmonn to Eorl Sir Guldwin," Rafe said. "Is there someone else to whom I should deliver it?"

"Sir Aledard Guldwin is the eldest son of Eorl Sir Guldwin, and he's assumed command of the army," one guard said.

"May I see Sir Aledard?" Rafe asked.

"I'll send a runner to inform him of your coming."

Sir Aledard was a tall man, thin and impressively muscled, with a Norman-cut beard, like his father wore, but a younger and more handsome face. He wore no armor, but rather a white tunic, as was proper for a son mourning his father, but he also wore a thick and heavily-ornamented crown; he was leaving no question as to who ruled his father's lands.

Wearing his fanciest armor, Rafe bowed deeply before him, holding only his scroll.

"Greetings in this troubled time to Eorl Sir Aledard, son of …," Rafe began.

"Eorl of Northumbria," Sir Aledard interrupted.

Rafe hesitated; Eorl Sir Guldwin ruled half of Northumbria, but the other half consisted of nine independent baronies, including du Harmonn. Yet Rafe was alone in a vast enemy camp …

"Greetings to Sir Aledard, Eorl of Northumbria," Rafe said reluctantly. "I come from …"

"Upon your knees!" Sir Aledard ordered.

Rafe swallowed hard.

"I'm an official messenger …"

"You're a lowly stablemaster who blackmailed the king into confirming an undeserved knighthood … *knighted by a woman …!*" Sir Aledard scowled. "Where's my sister?"

Rafe had always known that his chances of escaping this audience alive were slim; he'd known this when he'd determined to undertake this mission, yet he wouldn't die groveling.

"Roselyn chose to remain behind," Rafe said, "rather than let your father continue to prostitute her."

All of the soldiers within the sound of Rafe's voice snarled.

"I'll kill you for that insult …," Sir Aledard said.

"You may want to delay my execution," Rafe replied curtly. "I'm not done insulting you."

More snarls and hisses arose from the many knights watching and listening; all would've liked to kill Rafe, and an army of thousands backed them …

"My father's lashes scar your back …," Sir Aledard sneered. "Perhaps I should add to them."

"If you're that witless, then you probably can't read this scroll," Rafe said, and he threw the sealed scroll onto the ground between them. "If you're worth that crown, then what message have you for Baron Sir Karl du Harmonn?"

"I don't bandy words with farmers' sons," Sir Aledard said. "The Barony du Harmonn will be mine in five days."

"Five . . . ?" Rafe laughed. "King Svenson Two-Sword marched his men here in only three days, and he took Bristlen in less than an hour. Is Sir Aledard less than a viking king?"

Sir Aledard glared daggers.

"Castle Bristlen will fall in three days," Sir Aledard promised.

Rafe bit his teeth to keep from smiling; *he'd goaded Sir Aledard into rash foolishness!* If Aledard pushed his men that hard, then his troops would arrive at Castle Bristlen exhausted, and if they were rushed into battle, then they'd be easier to kill. Their weariness would slay more men than any sword that Rafe could wield, now that he'd grown too old to fight; since he'd returned from Yggdrasil, Rafe's life had been delightfully soft, and he'd given his old bones more rest than he should've. Now his mission was accomplished; all that he had to do was escape from a huge enemy camp where every soldier wanted him dead.

"When I first saw you, how tall and handsome you are, I thought that I may have made a mistake saving Eloise from having to marry you," Rafe said.

"Eloise should have been my wife eight years ago!" Sir Aledard said. "du Harmonn was slaughtered by the viking barbarians, and my father stopped them . . .!"

"Your father never understood what that war was about," Rafe said. "Eric Bjornson was the only thing that Svenson Two-Sword wanted, and he would've traded anything to have him."

"Nobody cares what heathen vikings want!" Sir Aledard said.

"The two thousand Saxons that died that day cared," Rafe said. "As will the knights and soldiers of your army that will die before the walls of Castle Bristlen, of which there will be not a few. I brought you an offer of peace, of annual tribute, to spare those lives, but if all that you care for is death …"

"Baron Sir Karl will swear fealty to me?" Sir Aledard asked.

"Yes, if you will spare du Harmonn," Rafe said. "That way you'd gain du Harmonn … and leave your army intact, undiminished, and ready to invade other baronies."

Rafe had done it; he'd committed treason. The scroll was a lie; Rafe had written it himself and forged Karl's name upon it, and ridden out to risk this gambit: either Sir Aledard would attack too soon, with unready troops, or Sir Aledard would attack too late, after he learned that the offer of fealty was false. Karl would've had time to gather more men and truly fortify Castle Bristlen, while Sir Aledard depleted his army fighting other barons. Either way, Rafe would succeed; the only question now was: *how much longer Rafe would live?*

"I'll have to confer with my officers," Sir Aledard said.

Rafe stood uncomfortably alone, hopelessly encircled by guards of Sir Aledard … and this time, the Seer wouldn't be coming to his rescue. He placed his hand upon the large brass cross riveted across his breastplate; just in case, he'd best spend his last few moments in prayer. However, thoughts of Seren kept invading his silent prayers; *if what he did today would spare her life, then Rafe would be content, even if he died.* Yet Rafe doubted if his tactic would work; *the clearest message that Sir Aledard could send to Karl was Rafe's severed head.*

Finally Sir Aledard and his knights and councilors returned.

"Here's my only offer," Sir Aledard said. "I'll be at Castle Bristlen in three days: if the gates of Castle Bristlen are open wide, and every weapon in the barony is laid upon the grass outside of its walls, and I'm presented with the head of Baron Karl du Harmonn, and the hand of Baroness Eloise du Harmonn in marriage, then I'll spare the Barony du Harmonn. Otherwise, everyone inside Castle Bristlen will be slain, down to the lowest thrall, and every peasant in the barony will swear to me or die."

Rafe hesitated; he hadn't expected this. *Karl's head?* Rafe would rather cut off his own. He considered asking about Karl and Eloise's children, whether or not Sir Aledard would let them live, but it didn't matter; *he never meant to relay any message.*

"I'll report your message exactly as you've said," Rafe said, and he bowed deeply, and then walked away.

Farmer Tiller smiled as Rafe rode into his open wooden gateway; their greetings were always glad. Rafe glanced around the farm, rustic no longer; ten grown men and their wives worked Farmer Tiller's fields, and where once they'd lain choked with weeds, wheat and vegetables now grew as far as Rafe could see. The Tiller's house had been recently repainted, and countless chickens squawked and clucked from a huge fenced pen. Farmer Tiller rose on his cane, for he had difficulty walking; he was slightly older than Rafe, and he'd spent his life doing backbreaking farm chores; now he mostly supervised, but he was still the wealthiest peasant in du Harmonn.

"Eorl Sir Guldwin is dead," Rafe said, "but you still need to clear out."

"Why?" Farmer Tiller asked. "If Eorl Sir Guldwin has died …?"

"Sir Aledard, his son, is continuing his plans," Rafe said. "Their army should be here in a day and a half."

"What will Castle Bristlen do?"

"We've no choice but to fight," Rafe said. "Sir Aledard has proclaimed himself the Eorl of Northumbria, and he'll stop at nothing to own all of it."

"That's a tall order; the king may not like it," Farmer Tiller said. "Every king is different; this one seems to want his barons to be constantly fighting; he sends other men's troops to the weakest baronies, and when the fighting escalates, then both sides lose … while the king remains strong."

"No one is coming to help du Harmonn," Rafe said. "Karl believes that the king and Eorl Sir Guldwin were secretly colluding …"

"Possible, but those two would never bargain honestly; chances are that each is just awaiting the opportunity to betray the other," Farmer Tiller said.

"Either way, both have chosen Karl and Eloise to be their sacrificial lambs," Rafe said. "I've just left Sir Aledard and have to hurry to Castle Bristlen."

"You can't stay for supper?"

"No, and neither can you," Rafe said. "Clear out, and tell all of your neighbors; despite what he says, I suspect that Sir Aledard intends to kill everyone in du Harmonn."

"Once Sarah and my animals are safe, then I'll help defend Castle Bristlen," Farmer Tiller said.

"Send your men to the castle after you ride away," Rafe said. "If Sir Aledard succeeds, then Sarah will need you."

"Do think his victory is likely?"

"He's another Svenson Two-Sword," Rafe said. "Like then, we're vastly outnumbered. Once that siege began, everyone trapped in Castle Bristlen died. Only, this time, we can't flee into Wolven Forest."

Farmer Tiller smiled at Rafe's reference, but his deep-set eyes showed no trace of innocence; *he knew what Rafe meant.*

Castle Bristlen could be heard before it was seen; hammers pounded, axes chopped, and men could be heard shouting before Rafe rode out of the trees and into view of the only home that he'd ever known. The stone crenellations of the twenty foot walls were capped with newly-built wooden palisades, some with long spikes sticking out of them, and men were still constructing them. The two towers flanking the gate were especially protected, as they'd bear the brunt of the attack. The tallest tower, Eloise's tower, alone was unchanged; it abutted the formidable cliffs of Othar, from where no army could attack.

"Sir Rafe has returned!" the men shouted. "Sir Rafe approaches!"

Rafe had to canter to the backside of the castle to enter the postern gate, for the main gates had been braced; only a crew of workmen, or a powerful battering ram, would ever reopen those gates. He rode inside to cheers, but the looks on the men were worried; if Rafe had good news, then he'd be shouting it. Several questions were asked of him, but he ignored them.

"I must report to Baron Karl first," Rafe said in his deepest voice.

As Rafe dismounted in the courtyard, Karl stormed out to meet him. Six guards, Nate and Phil Tiller the most prominent, came with Karl, raising large shields as if expecting arrows to suddenly fly at them.

"Where have you been?" Karl demanded. *"You leave here without a word to anyone …!"*

"To visit our enemy," Rafe said boldly, and every eyebrow rose.

"You went to see Eorl Sir Guldwin …?" Karl asked.

"Eorl Sir Guldwin is dead," Rafe said. "He died several days ago; that's why his army stopped. But they're still coming; Guldwin's son, Sir Aledard, is leading them, and he won't stop until all of Northumbria is his, starting with du Harmonn."

Every listener strained to grasp the totality of this, but it slowly sank through every skull.

"Dead …?" Karl asked with a bitter sneer that he couldn't hide. *"You're sure …?"*

"Everyone in his army knows it," Rafe said. "Many saw it happen; he just …"

Unexpectedly, Karl turned away from Rafe and stormed back inside the castle keep. His guards ran to catch up with him, and Rafe hesitated only a second, then followed. Karl marched fast, with stomping feet, so much that Rafe had to run as best he could to catch up. Karl headed straight for Eloise's tower.

"Wait here," Karl ordered his guards at the foot of her stairs, yet Rafe pushed past them and climbed up the winding steps in Karl's wake.

The thick door to Eloise's tower was closed; Karl's fist hammered upon it.

"Eloise!" Karl shouted. *"Now! Come out … or I'm coming in!"*

"Karl, the whole castle needn't hear this," Rafe suggested, but Karl only pounded louder.

"Eloise, open this door … or I'm fetching an axe!"

Impatiently Karl waited, glancing from the stout door to Rafe, and then back again. Finally they heard soft footsteps.

"Karl, you vowed upon your immortal soul …,"
Eloise's voice came through the wood.

"Never have I regretted a vow so much!" Karl said irritatedly. "But I won't enter; open the door!"

Several braces scraped, two locks clicked, and the door to Eloise's tower creaked open. Eloise was dressed in blue and white; she looked as pretty as a flower, but exceedingly pale, and her eyes were red and weary.

Karl stared at her, but he said nothing for a long time; Karl was no longer the boy who'd mindlessly marched back and forth guarding the battlements of Castle Bristlen.

"Eloise, Eorl Sir Guldwin should've been here yesterday," Karl said slowly, as if fighting for control. "I … I don't think … that he's coming here … ever."

Eloise couldn't help it; a grin widened her lips; too late she tried to cover it.

"You know that he's dead!" Karl shouted. "*How …?*"

"Quiet!" Rafe hissed, and he grabbed Karl's arm and shook it.

Karl relented, but he continued to glare at Eloise.

"How could I know …?" Eloise began.

"Swear it," Karl said.

"What …?"

"Swear it upon every deity that you know," Karl insisted. "Upon God, Jesus, the Lady, Odin, Hel, … all of them!"

"Karl …"

"Swear!"

Eloise looked at Rafe exasperatedly, but she couldn't speak.

"Don't lie to me," Karl said. "Three days ago, I asked aloud *'when would Sir Guldwin get here?'* ... and despite being sick, you smiled. How did you know that he'd died?"

"It took me two days to ride back," Rafe whispered. "Eorl Sir Guldwin perished in his saddle five days ago."

"How did you know ...?" Karl demanded.

"I ... I ...," Eloise stammered.

"Karl, let me speak to Eloise," Rafe said.

"No! I ...!" Karl started.

"Please," Rafe interrupted him. "If you're my brother, closer than friend, then let me talk to Eloise ... alone."

Karl glared at both of them, snarled a guttural, angry growl, and then he pushed past Rafe and stormed back down the stairs. Rafe and Eloise watched him, and didn't speak again until he was gone, taking his guards with him.

"He's a good man," Rafe said.

"... A good husband," Eloise said sadly.

"How much longer do you think he'll tolerate this?" Rafe asked. "You're poisoning your marriage."

"There are worse things," Eloise said dejectedly.

"Guldwin's son, Sir Aledard, is marching here with thousands of men," Rafe said. "We can't hope to defeat him. He wants the barony ... and nothing can stop him."

"His ... *son ...?"* Eloise asked, looking surprised.

"The one whom you were supposed to marry," Rafe said. "He said that he'd spare everyone, but only if we kill Karl ... and you marry him."

"Karl will not die!" Eloise said firmly.

"How can you prevent it?" Rafe said.

Eloise didn't reply.

"Eloise, are you doing ... what I think you're doing?"

Eloise opened her eyes and looked up; once Rafe trusted those eyes, but no longer. Now Eloise was shrouded with mystery.

"Angels don't make repeated visits, so you wouldn't need to be closeted in your tower every day," Rafe said, trying to restrain the contempt in his voice. "Is … will … *are you dallying with the Seer?"*

"Athelwynne …?" Eloise looked honestly shocked. "Rafe, how could you think …? You were there: the last time that we saw the Seer … before the Gates of Valhalla!"

"I was the first person this side of Grusshire who knew of Eorl Sir Guldwin's death," Rafe said. "How did you know? Is Roselyn visiting you?"

"We watched Roselyn fly off together, standing beside the king," Eloise said.

"Then how …?"

"Rafe, please don't ask …"

"How …?"

"I …!"

Suddenly a large, colorful butterfly flew down from inside Eloise's tower. Rafe gasped; between the fluttering monarch wings floated a tiny girl, her skin like glowing cream, with auburn hair and large eyes. She was wearing a tiny green dress that couldn't have slipped over Rafe's smallest finger.

"A … *fairy …?"* Rafe gasped.

The fairy landed upon Eloise's head and smiled at Rafe while Eloise frowned and closed her eyes.

"Rafe, meet … Talita," Eloise said softly, looking very ashamed. "Talita is my …"

"… *Friend!"* Talita beamed.

"This is your big secret?" Rafe demanded. "You've been up here … all these years … playing with a fairy?"

Eloise bowed her head. Rafe clenched his teeth, knotted his muscles, and squeezed his hands into fists.

Not again!

"Why …?" Rafe demanded, shouting for the first time. "I thought that we put all of this … *pagan nonsense* … behind us! What are you trying to do … bring it all back?"

"If I could bring Athelwynne here, then I would," Eloise said. "He'd crush their army …!"

"Didn't you listen to the Lady's words?" Rafe shouted. "The old gods are dying, driven out by Christ; why would you befriend this relic …?"

"I'm the baroness of all the people du Harmonn, Catholic and Druid," Eloise said.

"It's your duty to lead your people to God's church, not to pagan forests!" Rafe said.

"I … *ummm* …, please don't tell Karl," Eloise said. "I know that I can't be seen talking to a fairy; that's why I hide …"

"No more!" Rafe said. "I'll have no more of this in Castle Bristlen!"

Rafe glared at Eloise, careful not to bend his fury upon the fragile fairy.

"Talita, my respects to Titania, but I must ask you to leave," Rafe said. "There's a chapel of Christ upon these grounds, and I can't allow its sanctity to be defiled."

Talita frowned.

"Blessings upon you, friend Rafe," Talita said. "Eloise has told me all about you; you know more truths about religion than most people guess, but you're blind to the fullness of all, to the universe wherein all universes exist. I'll leave here and not return, if that pleases you, but mistake not my politeness for truth; you do great wrong here."

Talita rose upon her monarch wings and performed a graceful midair bow to each of them.

"Farewell, Sir Rafe, and all my blessings go with you," Talita said. "Farewell, my sweet Eloise; I'll always be your friend. If you want me, you know where you can find me. I'll say farewell to Edith before I leave."

Talita rose on her wings, fluttered up the stairs toward Eloise's tower, and vanished around the curve of the stairs.

Eloise turned her angriest glare upon Rafe.

"You shouldn't have done that!" Eloise said coldly.

"Me …?" Rafe asked. "You sit in the Lord's chapel … and then hide up here with one of Titania's …"

"Talita's my friend …!" Eloise seethed, and she turned to face away from Rafe. "I'm … not sure if I can forgive this."

"Then you should be more attentive to your prayers," Rafe said. "All forgiveness comes from God."

Fury in her eyes, Eloise stepped backwards, slammed her door in Rafe's face, and the sound of her locking it seemed unusually loud. Rafe stared at the closed door, and then descended the stairs alone. He'd done the right thing, but … *what would he tell Karl?*

Chapter 7

Vanahiem

REGINLEIF

After long debate, the Valkyrie separated; most refused to approach the Norns.

"It's a fool's errand," Mist said. "I've seen the Norns; they aid no one."

"The Norns are our ultimate enemy," Prudr agreed.

"By command of Odin, we must go," Róta said. "I'll lead us, and I'll take Geirahöd, Skögul, Göll, Herfjötur, and Randgríðr."

"I won't visit the Norns," Geirahöd said defiantly.

"I'll take her place," Reginleif said.

"We don't need a novice Valkyrie taking stupid risks," Skögul sneered.

Reginleif stepped forward angrily, tired of being insulted, but Skögul's attempt to leave her behind failed before the argument began.

"She swore the same oath to Odin that you did," Róta snapped at Skögul. "Come, let's go."

The company trooped out of Elvidner into heavy rain drenching Valhalla, hearing the distant crashes of steel and the screams as several million warriors waded through the droning splashes of bucketfalls upon the wet, muddy fields. Before they reached their saddles, they were already soaked, but no complaints were uttered. With contempt for the bad weather, their winged horses flapped their powerful wings and galloped to catch the wet winds, and then rose toward the dark, stormy clouds.

Reginleif gritted her teeth against the rain; Valkyrie armor didn't protect against water or cold, and both seeped through mail and articulations. She loved to fly, but no one knew what weather those fighting in Ragnarrock would face, so Valhalla suffered every extreme, including baking heat which scorched the ground, and frozen snows so thick that armies had to tunnel to reach each other. Tiny rivulets of water streamed and pooled inside her armor; she'd be glad get away from Valhalla today.

Quickly their mounts carried them into better weather; Asgard gleamed bright and shining beneath the sun. Below them stretched the wide fields around the city of the gods, the best lands in Yggdrasil when riding for pleasure. Distant Alfhiem looked to be simply a tall forest, deep and mysterious, but Reginleif knew that countless fairies dwelt in the shelter of those trees, and entrance to their realm was forbidden. Yet no threat equaled their destination; they flew far past Asgard and Alfhiem, mile after mile, into dark and empty hills.

Vanahiem appeared as a collection of sharp-edged shadows amid endless rubble. Nestled between four huge brown mountains, under clouds even darker than those that capped Valhalla, Vanahiem was a crumbling, broken city, deserted and forbidding. Ruins of a once unbreachable wall now lay in broken sections upon dead, thorny brambles that seemed to have overgrown everything, and each building looked likely to collapse at any second. The tall, sharp spires of Vanahiem rose like rusty spikes into the unforgiving sky; once, these stone walls and shale roofs had gleamed like Asgard, but time and nature had consumed its beauty with eons of neglect. Vanahiem was now only a monument to the majesty it had once boasted, a legacy of gods and goddesses that had once lived as immortals, but died fighting giants … and each other.

Róta led their descent, down onto a courtyard of worn, cracked flagstones, which was once a mosaic of a person's face, but now too stained and shattered to tell if the figure were a man or a woman. They landed with ease, but none wanted to dismount; the grimy courtyard looked unsavory.

"We'll have to send our horses away while we search," Róta said.

"Can't we bring them?" Göll asked.

"No," Róta said. "The Norns would eat them."

Reluctantly, they bid their horses to fly away; hooves bounced tiny stones as their mounts galloped to gather speed, and a large section of slate roof broke off, slid down its steep roof, and crashed loudly onto the courtyard, shattering into a cloud of gray dust as tiny fragments flew high and then rained upon the company. Their mounts winged up toward the clouds; *they'd return when called.*

"I hope that we don't need to get out of here in a hurry," Skögul scowled, watching their horses fly away.

"Speed wouldn't avail us," Róta said. "Not even the gods can escape the Norns."

"Which way?" Herfjötur asked.

"The Norns don't like their location known," Róta said. "After they're found, they always move, so that they must be found again."

"Then how do we know that they're here?" Herfjötur asked.

"Hlökk said that we'd find them here," Róta said. "Besides, the last three times that they were found, and the searchers escaped, they were somewhere in Vanahiem."

"Escaped . . .?" Skögul asked.

"Winged horses aren't the only food the Norns eat," Róta said.

Reginleif glanced about at her sisters' expressions; none of them would ever show fear, but the apprehension on their faces couldn't have been greater. Róta led them down a narrow roadway, where a flowering bush had to be pushed aside by Randgríðr, who used only her great shield; they were careful not to touch the delicate flowers, whose beauty looked out of place amid the jagged ruins.

Randgríðr was the stoutest of the Valkyrie, solid as a rock, and ever-vigilant; of all the Valkyrie, Randgríðr was most like Heimdal, the watchman of the Norse gods. She had a rugged face, with ancient scars that were mostly faded, and she wore a corselet of thick steel rings, an easy target for arrows, but Randgríðr bore a great steel-rimmed shield that was made of many thin layers pressed together, and only she knew the secret of all of them. Legends said that her shield was made of a thumbnail of Ymir, the hide of a black dragon, wood from the core of Yggdrasil, the flattened bones of a troll, the skin of the first man that she'd ever killed, and a cloth woven from the threads that formed the noose upon which Odin had hung himself. All of this was conjecture; no one knew, but nothing in Yggdrasil, not even Geirahöd's spears or Mjollnir, had ever penetrated her shield, and she wielded it as if it were part of her body. Randgríðr was also the best drinker in Elvidner; only Thor and Loki could defeat her, and ale vanished into her at a rate that would drown most warriors. Yet her often jovial expression was deadly sober as she held back the flowery bush to let her sisters pass.

Following her sister's example, Reginleif peered into many windows and entryways whose doors were mostly absent. Like Asgard, most of Vanahiem's buildings were huge, capable of housing giants, and included wide halls; the floors of the largest halls lay buried under their collapsed roofs. All of the stonework was heavily carved with runes, spirals, knotted designs, or the artistically twisted shapes of animals; Vanahiem had been a palace of intense creativity, especially around the many open archways that never seemed to have had doors, yet everything was windworn, eroded, and in some places the carvings were faded beyond recognition. Deep holes existed in the decorations, as if gems or metallic castings had once been displayed there, but Vanahiem had been abandoned for eons, its treasures scavenged countless times. Statues remained, scattered about, most partially crumbled, or walls with ancient faces chiseled into stone, and each seemed to stare at the trepidatious Valkyries. Not even Skögul risked a sarcastic remark; the sisters traveled as quietly as they could, ever watchful for any threat. Every building loomed ominously, and every road and courtyard seemed empty … save for tall weeds and occasional trees pushing through the broken masonry.

Suddenly Göll exhaled between her teeth and held up a hand; the company froze. Softly, in the distance, the wee voice of a small child echoed. They listened; it sounded like an infantile song, sung in a voice so youthful that it lightened their hearts. As silently as Hildr, the Valkyrie followed the gentle music, which grew louder as they approached.

They entered a dilapidated courtyard and saw the child; three children were far above them, playing on the rooftop of a tall building; one was singing, skipping along its edge in rhythm with her song. Her words were of a strange language, but even the most guttural sounds seem sweet and innocent in the laughing voice of a child. To Reginleif, the singer looked like a girl of five or six, wearing a white dress, with yellow flowers in her hair.

Suddenly the little girl slipped on a stone, tilted over the edge, and screamed as she fell. With the trained reflexes of a Valkyrie, Reginleif dashed forward, dropping her sword and holding out both arms to catch the falling child. Yet she never made it; Róta jumped her from behind, seized her legs, and both tumbled to the ground two feet shy of catching the innocent girl. Then an explosion blasted the courtyard at the base of the building: where the little girl had struck the flagstones, a huge boulder, an ancient statue whose original shape could no longer be determined, crashed to the ground in a thunderclap of dust and flying shards; if Reginleif had reached that spot, then she'd have been crushed.

"Trust nothing!" Róta whispered, releasing Reginleif's legs and climbing to her feet.

"How did you know …?" Reginleif asked.

"What would innocent children be doing here?" Róta asked. "Be careful; those that dwell here don't welcome our presence."

"Who dwells here?" Reginleif asked.

"The dead," Herfjötur answered.

"And the Norns," Randgríðr said.

The sisters continued their trek, even more apprehensive. Vanahiem was a vast city, and they walked for an hour seeing nothing else, only empty ruins, when suddenly, with a staggered *tap-tapping*, an old, raggedy woman walked around a corner. Bent and withered, the crone limped upon her rickety cane, a bare, gnarly branch striped of leaves. Many thick knitted shawls lay layered over her shoulders, hanging to her cloth wrapped feet. She glanced up at the sisters, her eyes widening as if surprised, but her wrinkled sneer showed only disgust. Frowning at them, she slowly limped down the empty street.

“Do we follow her?” Herfjötur asked in a whisper.

[illegible] think we're meant to,” Róta said. “That doesn't [illegible]hat we should.”

[illegible]Vhere else are we to go?” Skögul said. “Better a [illegible]an searching empty ruins.”

[illegible]o one argued, so they followed the old woman, [illegible]getting close, but walking so slowly that they [illegible] grew bored. Finally, the old woman led them into [illegible] building built of some reddish stone, and they cautiously followed. The building seemed to have been a palace or a temple: a shrine to a goddess; a strong, smooth skinned face stared from several mosaics, and upon a great dais was an ornate throne of blue granite, now thickly layered in dust and dead leaves that had blown in through open windows.

The old woman *tapped* on her cane toward a shadowy corner, and then through a dark doorway into a lightless room. The sisters followed warily; *they'd brought no torches.*

Göll cried out, and all of them froze; Reginleif felt a hand grab her leg, but she recognized the grip of her sister.

"Pull her back!" Herfjötur shouted, and the sisters backed out of the dark room, back to the light, dragging Göll with them.

"It was a well," Göll said, breathing hard. "I almost fell into it; I dropped backwards when I realized there was nothing beneath my foot."

"Another trap," Skögul scowled.

"Should we go on?" Herfjötur asked.

"We've no choice," Róta said. "We won't find the Norns stumbling about, no matter how long we search. The ghosts of the gods that lived here are taunting us, trying to lure us to join them. If we're careful, and don't die, then eventually they'll lead us to the one peril that we can't defeat."

"Keep risking death … until we're led to certain death?" Reginleif asked.

"That's what we're here for, isn't it?" Skögul sneered.

"They only have one lure: the location of the Seer," Göll said. "Eventually they'll have to use it."

"We were fools not to bring torches," Róta said.

"I can make a lantern," Herfjötur said. "Let's go back outside."

After a brief search, Herfjötur located an ancient window with some thick shards of dirty glass still in it; Herfjötur took out her empty drinking horn, half filled it with crumbled stone chips, and then shattered the remaining window, sweeping all of the broken glass fragments into her horn, until it was fully topped with broken glass.

"The trick to capturing anything is to make the right container," Herfjötur said, and she held her horn up into the sunlight. Reginleif watched fascinated: the name Herfjötur translated as 'Host-Fetter'; she was the bondage-master. Whenever the Valkyrie wanted someone captured or bound, or to reveal secrets against their will, no warrior proved better than Herfjötur. Herfjötur was tall and muscular, but she didn't look like any other Valkyrie; Herfjötur was dark, her skin tanned so deeply that she was golden-brown, and her hair was as black as Hel's. Few could bear the challenge of Herfjötur's gaze, and no one argued with her twice; once the Valkyrie had to restrain her from dragging the corpse of a warrior who'd argued with her outside of Valhalla so that his fatal injuries wouldn't be undone at sunset. Her sense of humor was dark and perverse, and her armor consisted of thick leather straps tightly buckled all over her, some with steel rings or plates riveted to them. No one trapped within her bonds enjoyed themselves. In the late evenings, when some of the Valkyrie wandered through the legions of warriors to choose a mate for the night, Herfjötur was the one Valkyrie that most of the men hoped wouldn't choose them.

Herfjötur held her horn high, pointed it at the sun, and whispered a long chant of guttural, arcane words. Finally she clapped her other hand overtop the mouth of her drinking horn and smiled wickedly.

"It's done," Herfjötur said. "I've captured the sunlight."

Herfjötur led them back into the building that they'd entered, only as soon as darkness veiled them, Herfjötur uncovered her horn, and from its mouth beamed soft yellow light, shining up from her horn, making a glowing circle upon the ceiling. It wasn't brilliant; Herfjötur's lamp shone dully, as if blurred by its dirty glass, but its glow thinned the shadows.

The well that Göll had almost fallen into was small, only three feet around, in the center of a room which appeared to have existed just to house it; upon the floor lay the powdery remains of a wooden barrier that had once encircled the well. The room was otherwise empty, save for bracken strewn in the corners. They peered into the well; even the glow of Herfjötur's horn couldn't illuminate its bottom. Only one other door awaited; the old woman, if she was real, must've gone through it … or silently thrown herself into the well.

This closed door was rotten, but not crumbled. While they held their swords ready, Róta pushed against the door, but its hinges were long rusted; her hand pushed right through the rotten wood. Disgusted, she gently swiped her sword against the door and the once-sturdy wood fell apart like spiderwebs, barely tangible; they let Herfjötur hold her horn out to illuminate the next room, and then they entered.

The next room was only slightly larger than the last. A brass mirror hung upon one wall, but so ancient and tarnished that any hope of a reflection was lost. A broken stone slab and a pile of rotted powder beneath it appeared to be the remains of a table, but nothing else showed. This room had three other open doorways, but no doors remained on any of them. Two doorways led to empty rooms, and the third to a long hallway; they proceeded down the hallway.

Suddenly a different woman stepped out of a doorway right in front of them. She showed neither fear nor surprise; she was middle-aged, with a jagged scar upon one cheek, and she glared at the foremost of them.

"*Where are my grandchildren?*" she demanded. "*Why did you kill them?*"

After a stunned moment, Skögul shook her head.

"You're not real," Skögul said, and she turned to the others. "Ignore her."

"How could you do this … to me?" the woman shouted angrily. "*Answer me!*"

"My mother's dead," Skögul said to the woman. "You're not her."

The other Valkyrie exchanged startled looks.

"I gave you everything that I had; I gave you life …!"

"Eating again?" asked a deep male voice, and they turned to see an old, worn man in farmer's clothes standing behind them.

"Father …!" Randgríðr exclaimed.

"I work myself to death in the fields, and you eat more than the rest of us put together …!"

"No, I …!" Randgríðr started.

"Don't acknowledge him!" Róta said. "None of these people are who they appear to …"

"Am I a false image?" a familiar voice rumbled, and the tall, mighty shape of Odin came striding out of a room to stand beside Skögul's mother, glaring at them with his one eye. "I ordered you to find the Seer, a simple request, and here you are wandering around Vanahiem …!"

Bristling, Odin faced his Valkyrie, his ravens flapping their wings as they clung to his mailed shoulders. The Alfather looked furious.

"You're not our liege!" Göll shouted. *"Begone, false likeness!"*

Odin didn't vanish. Reginleif would've sworn that it was the real Alfather; even the aura around him radiated tangible strength.

"We mustn't listen," Róta said.

"Roselyn …?"

Reginleif spun around, astounded by the voice.

"Karl!" Reginleif shouted as her eyes flew open, and she started to dash toward him, but Skögul seized her.

"It's not him!" Skögul said. "*It can't be …!*"

"Sister, don't be fooled," Randgríðr said. "My father isn't here, Odin isn't here, and Skögul's mother isn't here …"

Reginleif's eyes moistened; *the Well of Urd showed her that Karl was dead!* But … *was anything connected with the Norns to be trusted?* It was Karl, standing meekly, looking sad; her desire to rush to him surged, but she knew that it couldn't be him. She glanced around the hallway, which was blocked on both sides, the Valkyrie stood trapped between their liege, their kin, and her lover.

"No one mocks the Valkyrie!" Reginleif shouted. "*I'll see what's true!*"

Facing Karl, Reginleif swept out her sword, but Göll waved her back.

"Touch not what you don't understand," Göll said warningly. "I'll deal with these deceptions."

"No," Róta said. "If you shout, then you'll collapse this whole palace upon us."

Róta stepped forward and continued walking; she passed right through the images of Odin and Skögul's mother, and they could hear her footfalls continuing down the hall.

"Come back, I order you!" Odin shouted at her, but Róta ignored him.

Skögul went next, and before she walked through her mother, she slashed with her sword, but her legendary blade passed through her mother without affect, and then Skögul was gone, passed through the images of god and mother. With a last, longing glance back at Karl, who frowned sadly at her, Reginleif followed, walking through Odin and Skögul's mother with no more fear than stepping through the shade of Yggdrasil. It couldn't be Karl; he wouldn't let her walk away.

"Sisters, wait!" Skeggjöld's voice shouted. *"The Seer has been found!"*

They all stopped; standing behind them, amid the illusions, was their leader, Skeggjöld, who hadn't come with them, holding a burning torch.

"Come back to Valhalla, sisters," Skeggjöld said. "We have the Seer. We've no need to seek the Norns."

The company exchanged glances, then turned their back upon the illusion of Skeggjöld.

"Odin orders us to return!" Skeggjöld shouted behind them. "Where're you going? Heed me!"

As they walked away, suddenly Skögul hissed softly, and they all raised their weapons, ready for anything.

"What is it?" Herfjötur whispered.

"Róta," Skögul whispered. "She was right in front of us ..."

Herfjötur tilted her horn, beaming the trapped sunlight ahead of them; the long hallway was empty.

"Róta ...?" Göll called softly.

"Forward," Randgríðr whispered, "slowly."

Leaving the crowd of illusions behind them, they inched down the hallway, swords raised, and passed several open doorways to empty rooms. The hallway turned a corner, and there they saw the last person that Reginleif expected to meet.

"Ruthedhel ...!" Reginleif shouted.

In the light of Herfjötur's horn stood a dark elf, warily watching them. He was shorter than any Valkyrie, so much that he'd have to look up to admire Skögul's breasts, and he was thin, almost skeletal. His skin was stark white, as if he'd never endured sunlight. He had thin, pointed ears, like a fairy, but he was wearing a suit of articulated metal plates, blackened and polished like new.

Each of his hands held a thin sword, and he stood, blocking their passageway, as still as stone.

"Roselyn," Ruthedhel bowed slightly.

"Another illusion …!" Skögul said.

"I don't think so," Reginleif said.

Ruthedhel glared at them.

"Normally no dark elf would raise a sword against a Valkyrie," Ruthedhel said, "but I'm commanded to kill you all."

"We've been friends for eight years …!" Reginleif argued.

"This isn't your friend," Göll said.

"Whatever it is, I'll kill it," Skögul said.

Skögul eased forward like oil flowing across a level floor, with a balance and poise that her shape belied, her sword raised and inverted; a classic stance when facing a skilled opponent if you had a shield, but a foolish stance without one. Yet none of the company was concerned; as the combatants closed within range, Skögul righted her blade, holding it between herself and her foe; she'd only been testing him, to ascertain his reaction. Then she froze; dark elves were legendary fighters, and Skögul and Ruthedhel were observing each other; even the tiniest twitches could warn of an impending attack, and reveal the angle that a sudden slash or thrust might come from, giving the defender the advantage … and advantages in combat defined the victor and the vanquished.

Reginleif held her breath; she knew that it wasn't Ruthedhel, but she wouldn't enjoy watching him die. Of course, the real Ruthedhel was a renowned champion; even a Valkyrie couldn't guarantee victory.

Steel clashed, a gambit of slashes, but nothing came close to drawing blood; the combatants were still testing each other, identifying their opponent's styles. Reginleif had hoped that Ruthedhel was an illusion, that Skögul's blade would pass through intangible nothingness, but she'd suspected not; the first illusion, the children upon the roof, had failed to kill them, and then the old woman had almost dropped Göll into a well, and then their kin and Odin; *each threat was increasingly more dangerous.*

Skögul and Ruthedhel exchanged a blinding flurry of swordplay, the clangs of their combat echoing distressingly through the hallways; *any hope of secrecy was lost.* Yet neither made an inroad through the other's defense; not one drop of blood spilled. Only expert swordfighters could equal a dark elf or a Valkyrie; this was a duel of masters.

Reginleif watched intently; *this was the one area where she had the most to learn.* Most Valkyries had sworn their allegiance to Odin eons ago. Several were only a few centuries old, gathered when the Viking Age had first started, while the others came from ages past memory.

Reginleif had become a Valkyrie only eight years ago, and despite learning from the best, she was still the rank novice. Learning to evaluate an opponent in a glance was an art that took even the best warriors decades to learn, and learning how to anticipate your opponent's attacks, without falling victim to feints and counterfeits, was an eternal process that could only be learned through experience. Knowing the Fighting Secrets of the Valkyrie helped; without them, she'd only be Roselyn, the worst fighter in Valhalla. Yet, when fighting deadly foes, knowledge wasn't as efficient as skill and experience.

Ruthedhel swung two swords, while Skögul only had one. Ruthedhel's blades were thin; they moved at blinding speed, were hard to anticipate, and could stab and slash without warning. Skögul's blade was long and thick, but she wielded it as a dancer, moving her body as much as her sword, and when her heavier blade met Ruthedhel's, his were knocked aside. Yet suddenly Skögul cried out and fell back, clutching one arm; one of Ruthedhel's blades was dripping blood.

"Something's amiss!" Skögul shouted. "I watched his blades; they didn't touch me!"

"Together!" Randgríðr shouted.

Reginleif jumped forward with her sisters, attacking simultaneously. Ruthedhel managed to block most of them; the one blade that he missed was Göll's. Ruthedhel cried out, but not in the voice of a dark elf; the sisters gaped, horrified: the false image of Ruthedhel faded, and where the dark elf had stood, Róta appeared. Alone, with only one sword, Róta had defended herself against the weapons of Reginleif, Skögul, Herfjötur, and Randgríðr, but the bloody sword of Göll lay stabbed through her chest.

"Róta!" Reginleif cried.

Róta collapsed; *every Valkyrie could ascertain the dying at a glance.* Göll pulled out her blade; Róta's blood streamed onto the ground as she lay coughing.

"Dis ... disgraceful," Róta croaked. *"A Valkyrie ... felled by dark elves ..."*

Róta stopped breathing and moved no more.

"It wasn't your fault," Skögul said to Göll. "We were cloaked like she was ... made to look like dark elves."

"We should've guessed," Göll said.

"We must take her back to Valhalla," Randgríðr said.

"What of our mission?" Herfjötur asked.

"Some must go on," Skögul said. "Róta was our leader, but we can't let it be voiced that the Valkyrie feared to face the Norns without her."

"The path towards wisdom isn't cowardice," Reginleif said. "Róta knows more about the Norns than the rest of us combined."

"I'll continue," Skögul said, glancing at her bloody arm. "Alone, if need be; I must avenge this wound."

"Not even Odin can avenge himself upon a Norn," Göll said. "If you seek anything but wisdom from the Norns, then you seek death."

"I ask no company," Skögul said.

"You have my company, shield-sister, like it or not," Göll said. "They made me kill my sister."

"Then I must stay," Randgríðr said. "You'll need my shield."

"Reginleif, you carry Róta home," Skögul said.

Reginleif glared at Skögul, her anger welling.

"Reginleif, we've fought enough amongst ourselves," Herfjötur said.

"I'm not a novice to be dismissed!" Reginleif snarled.

"You're novice enough to argue over nonsense," Herfjötur said nastily. "If you try to fight, I'll bind you. Would you stay or go?"

"I must face the Norns," Reginleif said defiantly. "One illusion tells me that my mortal lover is dead, and another shows him living; I must know the truth."

"Then I'll carry Róta, bind her to her horse, and fly her back to Valhalla," Herfjötur said, and she took out of her horn one tiny glowing fragment of broken glass, and then handed her glowing horn to Reginleif. "Take this, that you may continue with my light. I'll fly home, and insure that Róta arises with the sunset."

With her sister's help, Herfjötur shouldered Róta's limp body and turned back, holding aloft her tiny fragment of shining glass to light her way. Reginleif watched her go regretfully; she should be the one to carry

Róta back, as she was the youngest, but Reginleif resented that all of her shield-sisters were such better fighters than she; she wanted to learn everything about Yggdrasil, to someday rival Róta's knowledge. In time, even Skögul might come to respect her. Yet her chief concern was Karl; the Well of Urd had broken her heart, and now their illusions showed him alive; even her hopes for the Seer couldn't equal her prayer that Karl could still be hers.

Without him, why was she here?

Their footprints tracking Róta's blood across the stone floor, the four Valkyrie continued down the hallway, which ended only a hundred feet beyond where Herfjötur had left them. There stood three doors, one of which opened into a large chamber whose ceiling had collapsed, and they could see cracks of daylight peeking through the ceiling of the room above it. Behind the next door lay a small, empty room, and the last chamber held a large, long stairway leading down. Beside the stairway was a tall, naked male troll, smiling at them … and pointing their way downwards.

"This is bad," Göll said. "The illusions are helping us."

"Without Róta, we're probably not considered a threat," Randgríðr said.

"We'll teach them not to mock the Valkyrie," Skögul said.

"If we accomplish Odin's will, then our duty's to return to him, not to fight the Norns," Reginleif reminded them.

Skögul scowled, but Göll and Randgríðr agreed. Together they approached the naked troll, who roguishly grinned at them, and then they descended the stairs.

Chapter 8

The Norns

REGIINLEIF

At each turn through the winding labyrinth, some illusion appeared to point them in the right direction. A dead woman from Niflhiem directed them, then a mockery of Loki, a huge, muscular giant, the Lady of the Druids, and the head of Mimir, who silently laughed at them and gestured with his eyes. The shield-sisters walked carefully, determined not to be ambushed or deceived, and never losing sight of each other; *they didn't want to risk another Róta.* Twice they avoided more traps; a large chamber where thorny vines reached for them like hungry tentacles; Skögul cleaved them a path. Another room, with a crumbling ceiling, collapsed upon them; Randgríðr protected them all beneath her shield.

Finally, a stench that equaled the black healing mists of the Wolfqueen assailed them, and strange noises reached their ears: a loud bubbling and a repeated creaking, which tensed the muscles of Reginleif's spine and clenched her teeth. Skögul led the way, Göll and

Randgríðr close behind her, and they emerged into a filthy chamber, layered with black molds and mosses, larger and brighter than any room they'd yet seen.

Three monstrous giantesses loomed over them, horrible faces topped with long, thin, matted gray hair, each almost brushing the ceiling. These weren't giants like Utgard-Loki, smooth, clean, and sophisticated; they reminded Reginleif of Skaldi, the twisted, malformed giant that had almost killed them atop the Druid hilltop outside of Madrone. The massive sisters looked lopsided, their dark countenances horrendous distortions of normalcy, with greenish-black hues that closely resembled Hel's usually-rotting legs. Rags barely covered the worst of them, and threadbare rents exhibited grotesque flesh. Their movements flowed eerily, their curved arms bending like the legs of spiders, horribly slow and at odd angles, yet deftly controlled.

The closest Norn was sitting on a sawn section of log easily ten feet in diameter, her foot working the pedal of a giant spinning wheel, which gave off a loud *creak!* with each rotation; she was huge, with rolls of fat dripping off her, and arms like the torsos of flabby horses. Her bloated face bore the deepest frown that any of the companions had ever seen, and she looked down at the Valkyrie hungrily. This was Urd, Mistress of the Well, the diabolical Spinner who draws forth the thread of each life, mortal and immortal. From Urd comes all nightmares … all fears of the unknown.

Against the back wall stood a great loom of the earliest and crudest style, an ancient wooden framework upon which was wound a thick bolt of cloth, the fabric of time, whose ends were stretched out, unfinished; hoary, long clawed fingers of the giantess deftly wove and intertwined the living threads which Urd fed her. This giantess stood tallest of all, her back the least hunched, and her expression as she stared down upon the Valkyrie beamed pure loathing. This was Skuld, the Weaver, who enmeshes all into her tapestry of life, and chooses the path which every living thing must travel. From Skuld comes all suffering and the pains of reality.

Near them, but not between them, stood the last Norn sister, the most dreadful and menacing. Her twisted spine bent her skeletal-thin frame, and where her ghastly skin showed, it lay taut over bones so evident that she could've been a prisoner of Niflhiem that had starved to death. Her expression was wicked delight, and no skull ever grinned as loathsome. She was Verdandi the Slayer, who severs each thread at the end of life, and dooms all to die, mortal and immortal. As the Valkyrie watched, she lifted her ancient shears, which looked to be of rusted iron decorated with gold, and whose fell presence struck each Valkyrie like a fist. She displayed her ghastly shears as if exhibiting a prized trophy … or a warning of what was to come …, and then she turned her weapon toward the weaving hands of Skuld, and a tiny *snip!* whispered through the chamber, followed by hideous evil cackles and wheezes as the terrible sisters laughed, an ear-clawing torment which tortured the Valkyrie, who cringed sickeningly; *their ghastly laughter would haunt Reginleif's nightmares forever.*

Between the horrible sisters raged a fire that lit their soot-blackened, moldy chamber, a huge blaze whose flames licked their cursed legs unheeded, and climbed up the sides of a vast black cauldron. None of the Valkyrie could see what boiled and bubbled within that monstrous pot, but vile, reeking fumes rose from it, and Reginleif was glad that its height hid her view of its innards.

In silence, the Valkyrie stared up at the three awful giantesses, the legendary Norns who defied even the wills of all gods. Reginleif struggled to hide her trembling; perhaps Róta knew how to deal with these three weird sisters, but all that Reginleif could think of was how desperately she wanted to run away.

Yet she didn't; Roselyn would have fled in terror, or perhaps fainted, but Reginleif the Valkyrie couldn't show cowardice. However, for the first time, she was glad that she was the youngest of the Valkyrie, that she wouldn't be expected to approach the Norns first.

Skögul looked scared for the first time that Reginleif had ever seen, but Skögul hesitantly stepped forward; *no Valkyrie could submit to fear.* Göll cringed close to the edge of Randgríðr's great shield. Reginleif tried to scold herself to boost her courage; she'd seen many of the worst creatures in Yggdrasil, even Nidhogg, the Devourer of the Dead, the great stone dragon who tunneled beneath the roots of Niflheim, and Mjollnir, the mighty hammer of Thor, but nothing equaled the fell radiance of the Norn witches.

"Come to see the sisters three,
Prowl the tasty Valkyrie!"

Reginleif startled; the voices of the Norns, if voices they were, screeched high and squeaky, almost sing-song, echoing like clanging bells in an empty cathedral. Yet she wasn't sure if any of them had spoken; their mouths moved as if they were chewing their own tongues, like a cow upon its cud, and she couldn't discern if one or all three had spoken; their eerie voices defied description, and its source was unfathomable.

"They failed to find the one they seek,
In waters black and tunnels deep,
Unto three sisters bring their fears,

To die upon Verdandi's shears."

Skögul drew cautiously back, and Randgríðr raised her shield to protect all four of them; Reginleif slipped into the shadow of her invulnerable shield.

"Bitches of Odin, women slaves,
Fetching those whom Skuld saves,
From those doomed to Loki's power,
Whence Heimdal calls the final hour."

"Enough of your taunts, unless you'd feel ours!" Skögul shouted back.

Abysmal laughter filled the air, deafening the Valkyrie, such that they plugged their ears as best they could without dropping their clutched weapons, although none could hope to use them with any success. Their vulgar peals of dreadful mirth echoed throughout all of Vanahiem, and the Valkyrie cowered.

"Urd!" Reginleif cried, despite the pain in her ears, which she struggled to plug while holding the horn of Herfjötur, whose light still glowed. "Urd, please tell us what we must know!"

The weird sisters laughed louder, dropping Skögul and Göll to their knees in agony. Randgríðr remained standing only because her huge shield made kneeling difficult, but she bowed beneath it, her hands pressed to her ears. Reginleif similarly tried to protect her ears, but she seemed to be less affected; at the Well of Urd, her politeness had spared her the waiting that the others suffered. Perhaps she was being spared the brunt of their laughter's stabs.

"Great sisters, I pray you, heed me!" Reginleif shouted. "Speak, and we'll listen!"

Slowly the evil laughter died away.

"Blind they sought Urðarbrunnr,
Their funerals in the black water,

With eyes unseeing what they see,
Pathetic, puny Valkyrie!"

"Urðarbrunnr, yes," Reginleif said, placing a hand on Skögul as she started to rise to the insult. "We seek to understand your visions: where is Athelwynne the Seer?"

"Lost, lost, his battle won,
In distant lands rides no sun,
Forgotten, disremembered, never to return,
His fate one must die to learn."

"We seek not his fate," Reginleif said. "Where is he? Where was the fog that Urðarbrunnr showed us, and what was the symbol of the eye?"

"Death, demise, murders foul,
Between lovers darkness prowls,
Across rivers, cold sands,
Blind he walks in hopeless lands."

Reginleif glanced at her sisters confused, but Göll nodded to her, and Randgríðr gestured for her to keep going. Even as she cringed, Skögul looked disgusted and angry.

"Where, oh great ones?" Reginleif asked.

"Colder than cold, 'ere Odin hung,
A land ancient when Yggdrasil young,
Imprisoned where a second crack dwells,
The terror of frozen Mistyhel."

Reginleif had no idea what that meant, but Skögul, Göll, and Randgríðr suddenly startled, as if more stunned by these words than by the sister's ghastly laughter. They looked up, eyes wide, and Göll's mouth fell open, her lips making the motions that would've repeated *'Mistyhel'* had she uttered a sound. Reginleif didn't know what *'Mistyhel'* meant, but she guessed that the riddle of the strange fog, that had baffled Mist, had been answered.

"The eye, blessed ones," Reginleif continued. "What was the symbol of the eye?"

The Norns laughed again, louder than ever, and their howls pierced every eardrum. Long the laughter continued, but when it ceased, the voices changed, as if coming from different directions.

"Eye of a God dead in the sand,
Willingly slain by his own hand."

A voice responded, but from behind them.

"Speak not of Gods forever lost,
These Valkyrie must pay the cost."

A different voice came from their left.

"In darkness forever, eternal strife,
Only a life can buy a life."

The Valkyrie stared at each other; the Norns seemed to be arguing, ignoring them. Finally their original voices chorused:

"The time comes for endless grief,
The mortal lover of Reginleif,
The cold eye of immortal strife,
Speaks the mother of his wife."

The laughter bellowed, such that all of them, Reginleif, Skögul, Göll, and Randgríðr, collapsed to the stone floor, unable to bear the deafening chortles that stabbed at their souls, the humor of the witches' malevolence, the spinner of life, the weaver of fate, and the chooser of death. Then the last echoes of their laughter slowly died, and with their laughter died the light of their flames. When the Valkyrie finally, with tears of anguish wringing from their eyes, lifted their heads and looked about, the vast chamber was dark and empty: *the Norn witches were gone.*

Reginleif, Skögul, Göll, and Randgríðr stared in every direction, into every shadow not penetrated by the failing light of the shards of glass in which Herfjötur had trapped the radiance of the sun, which lay fallen and spilled upon the floor. Save for them, the huge room was vacant; the fire, the vast cauldron, the great spinning wheel, the ancient loom, and the terrible scissors had all vanished with the evil trio. Only molds, mosses, slime, and stink remained.

Weapons instantly rose, held ready by pure instinct, but the Valkyrie stood alone.

"How dare you let them mock the Valkyrie?!?" Skögul shouted at Reginleif, finally breaking the silence.

Göll rolled her eyes as Randgríðr shook her head.

"I achieved the will of Odin," Reginleif seethed, glaring at Skögul. "You would've succeeded in getting us killed."

"You disgraced us!" Skögul screamed.

"Some battles are best won without swords," Reginleif said.

"I pray Ragnarrock isn't one of those," Randgríðr said. "It's done; we know where the Seer is."

"But what of the other clue?" Göll asked. "What is the symbol of the eye?"

"The mother … of the wife … of Reginleif's love?" Randgríðr asked.

"Eloise," Reginleif said bitterly.

"The girl that you told to marry your lover?" Skögul sneered.

"My loves are no concern of yours!" Reginleif snapped at Skögul.

"Mistyhel …," Göll said. "What a horrible doom!"

"What's Mistyhel?" Reginleif asked.

"No one knows," Randgríðr said. "Mistyhel is a cave, or a tunnel; no one knows … because none who have ever entered it returned."

"Mistyhel lies in the farthest corner of Niflhiem," Göll said. "Many thousands have tried to learn its secret, but none succeeded."

"Niflhiem?" Reginleif asked. "Perhaps Hel would know …"

"Then we must force its secret from Hel," Skögul said flatly. "Mistyhel is the font of all the cold and mist in Niflhiem. If the Seer entered Mistyhel, then he's lost forever."

"He might not have entered of his own will," Göll said.

"How one enters Mistyhel changes nothing," Randgríðr said. "The Norn witches may be trying to trick us into entering Mistyhel. We must seek the meaning of the symbol of the eye."

"Then we must go to Midgard … to England," Reginleif said.

"If we go where the Norns direct, then we may be walking into a trap," Skögul said.

"Let's gather our sisters," Göll said. "The Valkyrie shall ride together."

Reginleif gathered the spilled glass of Herfjötur, whose light was starting to dim, and followed as Skögul, Göll, and Randgríðr led the way back to the surface. She had no idea why they were seeking Eloise's mother, but the words of the Norns were indisputable.

Half of her felt delighted; she was going home, with all of her sisters to support her, and there she'd see Karl, and learn the truth of his condition. Yet she'd also have to face Eloise, whom she loved, but whom she resented so strongly that it tore her heart in two every night while she lay alone, unable to sleep, as Eloise lay cuddling with the man whom Reginleif loved, and who was living the dream that Roselyn had fantasized of. However, she was no longer Roselyn; *despite their deep friendship, when faced with her romantic rival, what would Reginleif the Valkyrie do?*

Chapter 9

The Siege of Castle Bristlen

SEREN

The plodding of countless weary footsteps, the *clip-clop* of a thousand hooves, the *creaks* of strained wagon-wheels, and the *clanks* and *clangs* of men marching in armor filled every ear around Castle Bristlen. Seren stood upon the battlements beside Karl and Rafe, watching the hosts of Sir Aledard march up the hill, out of the woods, and towards the castle. The anxious days of waiting couldn't equal the tension that they all felt; *the day of battle had come.*

Rafe had reluctantly reported their conditions of surrender, but none had considered them worth listening to, and Seren doubted if their enemy had ever expected them to be heeded.

Flags on tall poles had appeared first, followed by horsemen brightly-arrayed. They preceded a pair of drummers, who walked pounding their skins in unison to the clomps of thousands of boots. Knights in the finest armor followed them, riding in pairs; they spread out as they emerged from the narrow forest trail onto the wide field leading up to Castle Bristlen. More knights emerged behind the first, over a hundred, and then the nobles appeared, riding around the flag bearers to the fore, to gaze upon their objective.

Over twenty nobles silently stared while more knights rode onto the field, and slowly their lines moved forward as even more poured from the woods. Finally, the parade of armed horsemen, riding from the woods, changed to marching archers, easily five hundred strong, slowly filling in behind the knights, and lastly, almost an hour after the flag-bearers had first appeared, the footsoldiers marched to join them. The vast army spread out before them, in all its majesty, a fearsome force arrayed to face the relatively few trapped inside the barricaded walls of Castle Bristlen.

Seren didn't have to be a warrior to sense the dismay of the defenders. The upcoming battle seemed hopeless; their twenty foot stone walls, raised to twenty six by wooden palisades, were slitted to allow their archers to shoot from behind cover. However, Seren wasn't sure if they had enough arrows to equal the thousands arrayed against them, which looked even more dangerous than Rafe had reported. The army of Sir Guldwin, led by his ambitious son, wasn't as big as the force that had fought and defeated King Svenson Two-Sword, but it was at least ten times the numbers of the guards, farmers, and old sailors inside Castle Bristlen.

Lady Seren shook her head; she was an honored and respected woman, part of the minor nobility of England, who lived inside a castle, which was a far cry from the filthy brothel where she'd been born and had grown up prostituting herself for coins. For most of her life, Seren's body had lain open to any man, but since she'd returned from her insane adventures, her life had been wonderful beyond her wildest dreams. Now, she suspected, her life was about to end, but she wouldn't choose to be anywhere else; she'd rather die beside Rafe than live anywhere without him.

She glanced at Rafe and met his eyes; he was angry at her for staying, but they'd argued over that decision until both their throats were raw; there was no point in arguing anymore.

"Just a little closer …," Karl said, frowning. *"Come on, you louts; take the bait!"*

Trumpets blared from the army, and a troop of six men rode forward. Karl cursed.

"What wrong?" Seren asked.

"They want to parley," Rafe said. "We'd hoped that they wouldn't, that they'd rush their troops forward as soon as they arrived."

"We could fire upon their ambassadors," Karl said.

"You'll lose the respect of your soldiers, if you do," Rafe said.

"They'll drag out the parley for hours … just to rest their men," Karl said.

"Don't let them," Rafe said. "End the parley quickly."

"How?" Karl asked.

"Do what Eric Bjornson would do," Rafe said.

The six riders took their time, ambling their horses slowly, their white flag leading them. They rode close to the barred gate, and Karl raised a hand in salute. The company were all old men, save for one young page, who carried their flag of truce and looked very anxious. Three were knights, resplendent in their polished armor, with bright red cloaks and gold chains around their necks, and their helmets bore high plumes. One elderly man wore a rich ermine robe, and the last man was a priest.

"Hear the words of Eorl Sir Aledard, son of Eorl Sir Guldwin, the rightful heir, and ruler of Northumbria," the elderly man in the ermine robe spoke, his aged voice reaching every ear upon the walls. "In mighty arms we come to avenge the foul rape and murder of Countess Roselyn Guldwin, and to end the tyranny of the usurper and false-knight, plow-born Baron Sir Karl du Harmonn. All who fight against us shall be justly slain, yet mercy shall be bestowed upon those who aid us. If you would avoid your most assured destruction, then noble Eorl Sir Aledard shall hear your pleas for clemency. Yet you, false Baron Karl, must come before him alone, unarmed, and beg from your knees before all of your watching company. Beg for mercy from Eorl Sir Aledard, or he, with the support of all the hosts of Heaven, shall descend upon your fortress with no more effort than stomping upon an anthill, and everyone within these walls shall die before sunset. Thus speaks Sir Aledard, rightful Eorl of Northumbria."

The elderly man fell silent, and all eyes turned to Karl. Karl stepped up onto the palisade so their whole army could clearly see him.

"Thus speaks Eorl Sir Aledard," Karl said, "… and this do I hear: *yap, yap;* the shrill barks of a small, weak puppy … to be kicked aside with ease."

Many gasped at this insult, and a few laughed.

"Dare you come before me?" Karl demanded, raising his voice in anger. "The hosts of Heaven are preparing deep pits in Hell for you, and for all of your host, as your criminal trespass into these sovereign lands do most assuredly earn. Not one man in your army truly believes that Roselyn is dead, nor that she was ever abused by anyone but her besotted father, Eorl Sir Guldwin the Unworthy and Most-Vile. God's curse shall fall heavily upon any man who attacks an enemy knowing that his cause is unjust, and trusting lies only because their overreaching son of a cur pays them to be false! Begone … or die, faithless scum!"

Rafe and Seren smiled; *Eric would be proud!*

The expressions upon the parley company were comically horrific, mouths open and eyes wide, as if disbelieving their ears. The page boy looked as if he'd faint.

"Hear now the words of Baron Sir Karl du Harmonn," Karl shouted threateningly. "Send to me the ass of Northumbria, Sir Aledard, naked and crawling upon his hands and knees, with the thorny stems of a hundred roses sticking out of his stinking butt, and return to your homes in shame and disgrace, or the Heavens themselves will open, and God's fist shall descend upon you."

Cheers rose from the castle walls, and many men raised and shook their weapons. Those who came to parley glanced at each other, and then they began to turn their horses around, all but the priest.

"Tell Sir Aledard that we have a large pigpen full of slop, in case he wants to lie in the only bed fit for him!" Karl continued to shout at them. "Tell him that every man in Castle Bristlen thirsts for his blood upon their sword. Your army doesn't look fit to wear armor, let alone fight in it. Your knights are all the sons of whores and bastards …!"

Karl's stream of insults failed as he saw the eyes of the priest staring at him. The rest of their company was riding back, but the priest sat alone, hearing Karl's insults and the cheers of the men behind the parapets.

"Great evil you have done this day," the priest said aloud after Karl waved for his men to be silent. "As your death is certain, the best that you could've done is to spare the lives of those sworn to you, whose loyalty must mean nothing. Because of your vanity, many shall die today … instead of just one."

"Hide in the woods until the day is decided," Karl said to the priest. "We spare none who ride against Castle Bristlen."

"Before the sun sets, you'll need me," the priest said, "… to perform your last rites."

The priest turned his horse around and started to ride away.

"Insult priest!" Seren whispered urgently to Karl.

"Seren …!" Rafe scolded.

"Do," Seren said. "Last words before battle important!"

Karl considered, then raised his voice.

"More shall die outside of Castle Bristlen than inside it! Pray that your deaths don't exceed your numbers!"

More cheers came from the shielded walls, but none of the parley party turned back to look at Karl. Karl spat at their whole army, and then he climbed down behind the palisade.

"Well said," Rafe grinned.

"Words don't win wars," Karl said, and he turned to his guards. "Men du Harmonn; pass this news: we've provoked them into attacking us right away, while they're still tired from marching. Give them no chance to rest; kill as fast as you can, and see that none of them gain the wall! Remember our plan; stick to it, and we'll rule the day!"

Some cheered while others repeated Karl's words, but Seren shook her head; Sir Aledard undoubtedly had plans of his own, and he had many more men to enact his campaign.

"This is it," Rafe said, and he grabbed Karl's shoulders and stared into his eyes. "I'm on the left, you're on the right, and we both watch the gate."

"Victory or Valhalla," Karl said to Rafe.

"Victory or Heaven," Rafe said to Karl.

Both men embraced, and then Rafe turned to Seren.

"Seren, you must go now," Rafe said.

"Seren go," she said. "Need hug."

Rafe and Seren embraced, and Seren couldn't help but fret that she might never hold him again. Yet she was no young lass; Seren held her composure, kissed Rafe, and then she kissed Karl.

"This from Eloise," Seren said.

"I haven't even seen her today … or last night," Karl said. "Now I don't have time …"

Trumpets sang from the enemy forces. With a frown, Karl turned away, and Seren started to walk toward the stairs, knowing that Rafe wouldn't go to the left wall until she'd departed, as she'd promised. She descended to the courtyard, and from there she watched Rafe cross through the towers to the far wall, where he'd command their defenses. Only then did she allow her eyes to leak.

Loud shouts rose from the enemy, and then the charge began. The wide field between the castle and the woods became filled with rushing men. Even as innumerable battlecries reached her ears, Seren knew what would happen: hidden amid the tall grasses, within fifty feet of the wall, were many short, sharpened stakes, driven into the ground, their points upwards. Karl wanted Sir Aledard's men to reach those stakes, to impale their feet upon those points, to trip over them, leaving them easy prey for the archers, or better yet, to fall upon them and be stabbed to death. Even as she reached the doors to the castle, Seren heard the first screams of pain from the enemy. They'd come slower now; the castle archers would have time to practice their art.

"Archers!" Karl shouted.

The air was filled with hisses and twangs as the archers released. More screams sounded; Seren prayed that those screams would come only from outside the castle.

"Keep the ladders back!" Karl shouted. *"Ready the furniture!"*

Seren stopped at the castle door and looked back. Many men held long, forked poles; they'd push back any ladders that Sir Aledard's troops laid against the wall, hoping to climb. If the enemy gained a foothold upon the walls, then all would be lost. The insides of the ramparts were lined with furniture; large chests, wardrobes, heavy benches, and many wooden boxes filled with rocks; when the enemy pressed thickly against the walls, then they'd throw these heavy objects down upon them. Eric had given Karl the idea in Grusshire; Seren didn't care about the rocks, and she thought that using beautiful furniture as weapons was a waste, but Rafe and Karl had planned their defense carefully; the furniture was a weapon that they could use twice.

"Arrows!" many men shouted.

"Shields!" Rafe's voice rang out.

A rain of arrows came into view, making the sky gray, and Seren hurried inside the castle keep and closed the door. Several light thuds echoed from the other side, and many *plinks!* as arrows bounced off the stone walls near her. There was nothing left that she could do; *again, her fate was out of her hands.*

"Lady Seren!" cried a youthful voice.

Little Edith came running into the great hall, making several servants jump aside to avoid being plowed into by the child, who was running as fast as she could. She ran to Seren, grabbed her arm, and pulled.

"Hurry!" Edith urged, tears flowing down her cheeks.

"What matter?" Seren asked.

"Eloise ...!" Edith cried. *"She's going to kill herself!"*

Aged Seren couldn't run anymore, but she hurried along as best she could. All of the guards were upon the walls, and she couldn't bother Karl or Rafe; she alone could deal with this. Although Edith looked frantic, she never let go of Seren's hand, helping her to balance as she hurried too fast for her aged legs, and she led her straight to Eloise's tower. Like Karl and Rafe, Seren had sworn never to enter that tower, but the door was open, Edith dragging her, and Seren was too practical to worry; the Virgin Mary, the Lady of the Druids, and the Goddess Freyja would all forgive her for breaking her vow when someone that she loved was in danger of dying. For the last eight years, Seren had wanted to climb those steps so badly that she'd have gone even if the Great Ladies forbade it. Seren's feet met the first stair and she climbed as fast as she could, and for the first time in eight years, she entered the forbidden door, which had never been left open and unlocked.

The expression on Eloise's face as she looked down from the top of the stair was pure horror.

"No!" Eloise screamed. *"Seren, stop! You promised ...! Edith, how could you ...?"*

Seren climbed the stairs without hesitating. Eloise came halfway down, blocking her path. On the wooden steps, the three women met and glared at each other.

"Talita said that you must wait three months …!" Edith shouted at Eloise.

"I have no choice!" Eloise argued.

"Talita …?" Seren asked.

"You swore …!" Eloise shouted at Seren. *"You made an oath …!"*

"No more," Seren said. "Now I go up."

"No!" Eloise shouted.

"I go," Seren said firmly, "or Eloise push me down."

"Seren, please …!"

"Seren easy to stop," Seren said, and she reached into her cleavage and drew out a small dagger, which she held out to Eloise. "If would stop, Eloise kill Seren."

Horrified, Eloise stared at the little knife.

"Please, Mistress," Edith pleaded. *"There's no point in hiding anymore …!"*

"There are worse things than death," Eloise replied to Edith.

"Seren faced death before," Seren said.

A moment passed, and Eloise didn't take the knife. Seren pushed past her, and Eloise slumped up the stairs behind her.

Seren's eyes widened as she reached the top of the stairs. Instantly she recognized the image of the Lady of the Druids, whose white marble statue gleamed in the sunlight. All around the room were books, scrolls, and the tools of magic; the blackened circle of blood painted upon the floor revealed everything. Seren hesitated, then entered the circle, bent down, and picked up the moonstone.

"You like Seer now?" Seren demanded, holding the moonstone out as evidence.

"I wish I were," Eloise sighed. "I'm a Druid priestess, but just barely; I'll never be as powerful as

Athelwynne. Please, Seren; you have to leave. I'm trying to fight Sir Aledard's army …"

"Edith say you suicide," Seren said.

"It's a great risk …," Eloise said.

"Talita said …," Edith began.

"I know what Talita said!" Eloise shouted. *"If I'm going to die anyway…!"*

"Eloise no die," Seren said firmly. "Trust Karl."

"Karl has less than three hundred men!" Eloise shouted. "How's he going to defeat three thousand knights and archers …?"

Seren glanced down at Edith.

"Can Eloise defeat army?" Seren asked Edith.

"I forbid …!" Eloise shouted at Edith.

"If false, Eloise not forbid," Seren said.

Seren stepped to the window and looked out, across the wide roof of the castle keep. The courtyard was hidden from her, but she could see everything upon the castle walls. No enemy soldiers had topped the wall, but they were trying; archers were shooting as fast as they could, and men with long, forked poles were frantically busy, and those with swords or pikes were hurling huge pieces of furniture up and over the wooden palisades protecting them from arrows; thousands of men were shouting … or screaming in agony. Many were dying on the grassy fields outside the castle walls, but occasionally an arrow would fly through the defenses and strike a defender. As Seren watched, an archer stumbled back, clutching a feathered shaft sticking out of his head, and he fell off the parapet; no one rushed to his aid.

"That's one," Eloise said, staring past Seren at the battle. "How long before they all fall?"

The battle raged on. Trumpets sang, more men screamed, and occasionally someone upon the wall fell dead; the wounded kept fighting. Then came the largest roar of all; the enemy was charging the wall en masse; *their whole army was coming.*

"Oils!" Karl shouted.

"Oils!" Rafe echoed.

Each man that could grabbed a large earthenware jug, covered bowl, or wooden bucket; these were filled with a few rags floating in animal fat and grease. Fires were set to each, and then these were dropped over the palisades, to ignite as they splashed upon their foes pressed against the base of the walls, climbing upon the smashed furniture and the corpses of their fellows. Screams echoed from all around, so horrible that Seren winced; men were burning, trapped by their fellows, and as planned, the oil that didn't land upon enemy soldiers splashed onto the broken fragments of wooden chests, wardrobes, and benches that they'd already thrown down; a circle of fire erupted around the base of Castle Bristlen.

"Retreat!" many shouted before the trumpets sang.

As Karl and Rafe had planned, Sir Aledard's soldiers fled back, unable to reach the castle walls through the smoking flames. Screams and moans of helpless agony came from the dying, but few could help them.

"Save the arrows!" Karl shouted. "Let the burning burn!"

Seren grimaced; Karl had not only become a powerful thinker, but cold-hearted, not the indecisive child that she'd first met. He was doing what needed to be done, no matter how horrible, much like Athelwynne had when he'd tried to restrain the Wolfqueen.

"Can Eloise summon Seer?" Seren asked.

"I've been trying day and night for the last three days," Eloise said. "I've tried before, but every attempt failed almost instantly; maybe he's in Odin's realm."

"Can Eloise summon Lady?" Seren asked.

"The Druids serve the Lady," Eloise said. "I've prayed to Her, but I can't make Her appear."

An arrow suddenly flew towards them out of nowhere, but less than a foot from Seren, it bounced off thin air.

"This tower is protected," Eloise said. "One of my few spells that worked."

"Why not protect castle?" Seren asked.

"How could you explain that to Christian soldiers?" Eloise asked. "If I'd done that, then no one would be defending the castle. Please, Seren, go back downstairs; let me do what I must."

"What can Eloise do?" Seren asked, looking out at the retreated army.

"I can try to kill Sir Aledard," Eloise said.

Seren glanced at Eloise.

"You kill Guldwin?" Seren asked.

"Yes," Eloise admitted.

"Kill Guldwin, no stop army," Seren said. "Kill Aledard, will army stop?"

"Probably not," Eloise said, "but at least, when we lose, I won't have to marry Karl's murderer."

"It takes three months to get the poisons out of your body," Edith said. "If you summon Death again …"

"No summon death," Seren said. "Fires last at least an hour; then we see."

The women stared out the window, moving aside to let little Edith move in front. The men were busy; flaming arrows which had stuck into the wooden palisade had to be extinguished, arrow-quivers had to be restocked, more heavy rocks were carried up to the parapets and towers, to be dropped upon the enemy, and finally, the dead were carted away and the badly wounded were attended. Water was drunk from barrels placed at strategic locations; most of the servants and women had been sent away from Castle Bristlen days before, so few servants remained. Each of the three women wanted to do something to help, but all that they could do was stare at the smoke rising from outside the walls; *when those fires died, so would more men.*

Finally, the battle began with another charge, heralded by trumpets, but this charge was different.

"*Focus on the ram!*" Rafe bellowed. "*Kill the carriers!*"

Amid the tumult, a terrible thunderclap resounded, and the massive gate shook.

"*Rocks and archers!*" Karl shouted. "*Shoot when their shields tilt!*"

After a few moments, the thunderclap repeated; *they were ramming the gate!*

"*Invaders!*" Rafe shouted.

Enemy soldiers had topped the palisade on the left, and swords rang and spears jabbed. Rafe ran into the thick of it, and others rushed to help him; three enemy soldiers jumped off the parapet down into the courtyard, and a dozen men rushed to engage them. The soldiers on the parapets fought madly, and finally their ladder was cast back and the last of the invaders were slain. Their enemies down in the courtyard must've also been slain, but Seren, Eloise, and Edith couldn't see the bloody dirt. Ten defenders had obviously died upon the battlement, and twice that many soldiers of Sir Aledard's forces, but the defenders could least afford the loss. Rafe's face was covered with blood, but from her distance, Seren couldn't tell whose blood it was.

The hammering of the battering ram ceased, but all too soon it thundered again. Karl was shouting. Innumerable war cries rose, and a frenzy seemed to have seized every heart. Screams of men dying echoed unrelenting.

Suddenly the thick gates of Castle Bristlen smashed apart, cracked and broken, but sufficient to block passage. Moments later, the battering ram struck again, and the rough, yellow wood of a newly felled tree trunk became visible through the gaps that appeared in the gates as boards shattered and fell away. A few moments later, the battering ram punched through, and the gate burst open; a passageway five feet wide appeared where before not even a mouse could squeeze.

Sir Aledard's men poured through the gap. Karl and Rafe both shouted something, but their words couldn't be heard over the chaos.

The trap was unleashed; a huge wall of loose stones, that had been built over the inside of the gate, was pushed over the brink, on the inside of the gate, and men screamed as the falling rocks crushed them. The men of Castle Bristlen ran or jumped down to dispatch the survivors, but then trumpets rang again, and a hail of flaming arrows flew through the open gate; several men fell screaming, stabbed and burning.

"They're drawing back!" one guard shouted. "They're massing for a charge!"

"Raise the flag of parley!" Karl shouted, and when the guard hesitated, "Raise it!"

A white flag was lifted and waved upon the battlement. Almost instantly, trumpets rang.

"Let's go," Seren said.

"I'll not marry Sir Aledard," Eloise said. "I'll kill myself first."

As Seren and Edith started down the stairs, Eloise grabbed a silver chased chalice and a bottle of wine, which she poured into the chalice.

"There's poison in that cup," Edith whispered.

"Me know," Seren said.

The women emerged to find Karl and Rafe whispering in the middle of the courtyard, surrounded by grim-faced warriors, including Nate and Phil, both of whom had blood trickling from rips in their tunics. Rafe had a long, shallow cut that stretched diagonally across his face.

"What are you doing here …?" Karl demanded when he saw them.

"We stand beside our husbands … always," Eloise said.

"We can't defend walls and a broken gate," Karl said. "We've lost."

"The only hope that we have is to spare our men," Rafe said.

"We with you," Seren said.

"And us!" Nate said.

"To the death!" Phil agreed.

"No," Karl said to his squires. "We started this … and you need to protect your sister. Go home to your mother; *that's an order, boys."*

"Clear the gates," Rafe ordered.

No words needed to be said. Reluctantly the warriors of Castle Bristlen moved to the gates and began to pull away the bodies, large rocks, and broken boards. Karl, Rafe, Eloise, and Seren stared; *the end of their lives had come.*

When a path was cleared, the quartet walked forward, skirting only the still-flaming arrows and dead bodies. They passed under the broken remains of the once mighty portcullis, and then walked outside the gate. Cheers rose from the enemy; *the siege was ended; their battle won.*

A company of six riders came forward; the same that had come to parley at dawn, to demand their surrender and offer conditions. The three knights glared, but they were smiling. The elderly man in the ermine robe looked delighted. The priest looked disgusted, and the page boy beamed a triumphant smile.

"It's over," the old man said.

"We are defenseless," Karl said. "We ask only for clemency for our soldiers and our women."

"For our soldiers and women inside the castle," Eloise said emphatically. "We four are those who defied Eorl Sir Guldwin and all of his family; we'll share the same fate, one and all."

"No," the old man said. "Clemency will be granted only if Baroness Eloise agrees to wed Eorl Sir Aledard."

"Very well," Karl said.

"Never," Eloise said at exactly the same moment.

"Let's just kill them all," one of the knights said.

"The death of Baron Sir Karl du Harmonn is inevitable," the old man said. "Baroness Eloise, this is your last chance to spare your life and the lives of your soldiers; *choose now."*

"I will not live without my husband," Eloise said.

"Those will be the last words you'll ever speak," the old man said. "We go to report your foolishness."

The parley company rode away, all but the priest.

"When you stand before God, the pains of all who've died this day will be shackled to your soul," the priest said nastily to Karl, and then he rode after the others.

"Let's pray," Rafe said, and he knelt in the road, right where he was.

Taking hands, they all knelt down … to pray before they died. Behind them, all of the men of Castle Bristlen, on the wall or in the courtyard, knelt to pray. Beside her brothers, little Edith was the last to kneel, and she burst into tears.

Chapter 10

The Unexpected Reunion

RAFE

Sadistic murmurs of Sir Aledard's men filled the air, whispers heard even from a distance. Weapons were raised, sharp edges fingered, and grim slaughter anticipated. Rafe glanced up from his prayers just long enough to notice: *they were gathering for a final, dramatic charge.* At great cost, the three hundred defenders of Castle Bristlen had managed to slay almost eight hundred enemy soldiers, but over two thousand remained … *and they wanted revenge.* Tonight, the souls of every man in Castle Bristlen, and the souls of Eloise, Seren, and Edith, would stand before the judgement of St. Peter at the Gates of Heaven. Rafe bowed his head and continued to pray.

Trumpets sang. The roar of a thousand angry cries rose above all other noises, and then hoofbeats hammered, along with the deafening thunder of countless booted feet running across the grass. Rafe didn't stand;

for his soul's sake, best that death came while he was deep in prayer.

Karl alone stood; he drew his sword and raised it threateningly, but he was hopelessly outnumbered.

Suddenly a scream filled the air, inhuman, with ample intensity to burst every eardrum. Many stopped and plugged their ears, while others fell, overcome by the deadly volume of the single high-pitched scream. With it, the deafening roar of angry shouts became cries of dismay; Rafe glanced at their foes, all stopped in their tracks, less than twenty paces away, looking up, northward, high into the sky. Rafe followed their line of sight, and there he saw the last thing that he'd expected to ever see again.

Thirteen great horses rode across the sky, flapping wings like monstrous eagles, and each bore the form of a beautiful woman warrior. Eloise looked up and gave a cheer …

The Valkyrie had come!

Like a troop of avenging angels, thirteen Valkyrie swooped down from the clouds, swords raised and voices lifted in challenge. They flew swiftly; some landed in the narrow space between the companions and the horrified army, many of whom had fallen to their knees, started to run away, or simply fainted. Other Valkyrie flew low over their enemy and dropped from their saddles; wherever any Valkyrie touched the ground, any enemies within sword-reach died instantly. Screams of terror filled their hosts, yet some stood amazed and, seeing only beautiful women in armor, they advanced; *those fools didn't live long.*

One Valkyrie screamed at those closest to her, so loudly that a fierce wind seemed to blow her foeman backwards. Another Valkyrie hurled spears so forcefully that a whole line of men were impaled on each cast, and she threw so fast that none could rush her. A huge armored woman cried out and stomped the ground so hard that the entire mountain shook beneath her boots, and foe and friend alike struggled to keep from being tossed off their feet. One robust woman, with a huge shield, rammed into her foes and sent a whole squad of men flying backwards as if they'd been punched by Utgard-Loki. The others held their shields high and attacked with sword or axe, and one woman, the strangest of the lot, a frail woman surrounded by a white mist, sent forth a thick cloud of vapor which seemed to suffocate a hundred men at once.

The battle against the Valkyrie lasted only a few minutes. Most of the footmen ran off or threw themselves down and begged for mercy, most knights were thrown by their rearing horses, who seemed terrified of their winged cousins, and some men were so frightened that they ran headlong over the edge of the great cliff of Othar and plummeted down to Demril village. Those who dared approach any Valkyrie died, and in the end, every man alive fell onto his knees, save for those in the very back, who stood in stunned disbelief as their unstoppable army was decimated by thirteen angry women.

One Valkyrie approached the companions, who remained beside the dropped battering ram, surrounded by many dead soldiers, before the broken gates of Castle Bristlen.

"*Roselyn!*" Seren shouted joyously.

"Reginleif," the Valkyrie corrected her sternly. "Come. Follow." Then she turned to face her quailing foes. "*Make a path!*"

Hundreds of men jumped back to clear her way. Reginleif led, and closely behind her followed her shield-sisters; those who'd dropped into the midst of the enemy joined them as they walked, and behind them followed Karl, Eloise, Rafe, and Seren. The wide eyes of the vanquished stared dumbfounded as they passed, and most bowed to them, made the sign of the cross, or covered their faces, afraid of being cursed.

Reginleif led the procession to the very back of the army, where its commanders stood aghast, disbelieving what they'd just seen. Reginleif ignored them all save for one: *Sir Aledard.* Reginleif walked right up to him and punched him in his shocked face, and so mighty was her blow that he flew six feet backwards and fell down.

"Brother, why are you here?" Reginleif demanded. *"This castle and my friends are protected by divine providence; such am I, your sister, who hasn't forgotten the torments of our childhood …!"*

Reginleif strode forward as her brother tried to stand, seized him, and shoved him to his knees. Then she kneed him hard in his chest, backhanded his face, and drew her glittering sword and held its point against his throat.

"Speak, brother, or die and be damned!" Reginleif shouted. *"What are you doing here?"*

"A-avenging … y-your death," Sir Aledard stammered.

Cruel, mocking laughter spewed from Valkyrie lips, but not one man dared speak.

"Fool!" Reginleif cursed. "All of the puny armies of England can't threaten the shield-sisters! This land is sacred, and any army that invades it, ever again, shall be slaughtered to the last man. Where's our father?"

"D-d-dead …!"

"Too bad," Reginleif sneered. "I'd hoped to settle that score myself. Now get up! March these fool soldiers back to our lands … and let every man here now witness:

if any of you dare return, you'll each suffer a fate worse than mortal death!"

Reginleif kicked him again, and he collapsed before her.

"Roselyn . . .!" he said as she started to walk away.

Faster than a cornered snake, Reginleif struck with her sword; almost instantly, her brother's face bore the same diagonal wound that marred Rafe's face.

"Never call me that again!" Reginleif shouted. "My name is Reginleif, Valkyrie, Queen of Valhalla, Battle-Maid of Odin the Terrible, God of Gods. Speak that mortal name again and die!"

Reginleif stood, tall and defiant, and not one man moved for fear of her.

"Gentlemen, if I may?" Karl asked, looking around and addressing all of their army. "If you'd take my advice: *run! Now! Leave your weapons and horses! Run! And never return!"*

Sir Aledard was the only man who didn't move instantly, dropping whatever they had, even to the smallest knife, and some pulled off helms and dropped them as they hurried toward the mouth of the trail from where they'd emerged only a few hours ago. A thousand soldiers followed them, while others fled into the trees toward Wolven Forest, or down the steep trail toward Demril; whatever road offered the quickest hope of escape, without having to approach the warrior maidens who'd descended upon them like Hell from the Heavens.

Rafe stepped up beside Reginleif and addressed Sir Aledard, who still knelt unmoving upon the dirt.

"When last that we met, you spoke in a most unchristian manner," Rafe said seriously. "Now we'll both wear a memory of this day unto the end of our lives. Let this be a warning to all who follow in the footsteps of their fathers … and not in the footsteps of our lord, Jesus Christ, Savior and King. Go forth and be a man that the angels will praise, merciful and just, or I'll send your very alive sister to talk to you again."

Sir Aledard opened his mouth to speak, but Karl waved him silent.

"Can you really say anything to make today better?" Karl asked. "Your sister's immortal, almost a goddess, and she's angry; *do you really want to antagonize her?*"

Sir Aledard glared at Reginleif, glanced once at all of her shield-sisters, and then he drew his sword, stabbed it into the ground, and walked away, following his soldiers as they fled down the path. Rafe smiled as he watched him go; *no army would ever follow him again … especially not into du Harmonn.*

Within ten minutes, every enemy soldier was out of sight, vanished into the trees.

Rafe didn't wait; he embraced Reginleif with a wide smile upon his bleeding face. She allowed his hug, but didn't reciprocate; Rafe noticed that she seemed stiff and unresponsive, as if softness no longer existed in her.

"We need to talk privately," Reginleif whispered.

Rafe nodded, and then Seren pushed past him and hugged Reginleif. Rafe watched them embrace, then noticed the worried look on Eloise's face; Reginleif had promised to come for Karl. *Was it Karl's time to die?*

"Most beautiful Reginleif," Karl said, and he sank to his knees and reached up to take her hand, which he drew to his lips and kissed.

"Beloved Karl, when I saw you about to die, I was tempted to allow it," Reginleif said. "It was good of you to raise your sword as you faced death … or I might've been angered. But we're on a mission for Odin, and we come seeking wisdom. By the will of the Norns, we are commanded to find … Eloise's mother."

Eloise's mouth fell open; her expression of terror intensified as all eyes fell upon her.

"W-what …?" Eloise asked.

"Comfort before discussion," Rafe spoke up.

"Yes," Karl said as he rose. "Most worthy Valkyrie, greatest of warriors, the thanks and hospitality of all du Harmonn is yours."

"Valkyrie have no use for mortal gratitude," Skögul said. "But we will judge the merit of your beer."

Karl smiled and faced the distant walls and ruined gate of Castle Bristlen, which had a large section of palisade burning.

"Men du Harmonn, open every keg of beer and ale that we have!" Karl shouted as loudly as he could. *"The Valkyrie thirst!"*

Karl took Reginleif by the hand, and then took Eloise's in his other hand, and escorted both of them toward the castle. The Valkyrie marched behind them, ignoring the vast number of slain bodies. Rafe held Seren back until they'd all passed, and then they trailed the procession. Rafe was greatly torn; he was delighted to be alive, which was undoubtedly a miracle, yet he was also disgusted that the might of the Valkyrie had saved them.

If they had to be saved, why couldn't it have been by the power of Christ?

First, Eloise was playing hostess to a fairy, and now Reginleif had brought all of her shield-sisters to Castle Bristlen.

Were their lives again to become enmeshed in pagan troubles?

The surviving soldiers of Castle Bristlen stared amazed as the Valkyrie entered through the remains of their sturdy gate. Everyone had heard the wild stories of

Karl and Eloise's great adventure, but few believed them; tales of fighting giants with illusions, and being chased by the Goddess of Death through another world, were too fantastical to be accepted, yet the Valkyrie marched fearlessly, casually, over the fallen, after decimating several hundred hardened warriors, including many tough knights and squires, in only a few minutes. Behind them, their winged horses, no less unbelievable than these amazing armored maidens, grazed upon the tall grass heedless of the bleeding corpses.

"Have no fear!" Karl shouted to his men as he led the procession across the courtyard. "If the Valkyrie wanted us dead, then you wouldn't be hearing my voice."

His pronouncement didn't seem to comfort the men. Rafe frowned; the men may be frightened for now, yet their shock would soon wear off. *It'd take him years of preaching to undo the men's belief in pagan deities and return them to the True Faith.* The sudden appearance of the Valkyrie had saved their lives, but would it cost these men their souls?

"Take buckets of water out to their horses," Rafe ordered disgustedly. "Do not try to ride them!"

As they entered the castle keep, they found two barrels of beer already being carried in, several soldiers struggling to carry each, while Nate and Phil stood nearby, each carrying a tray piled with empty tankards. With difficulty, the men wrestled the heavy kegs onto the tables, and one man tapped the first, and then both squires began filling the tankards.

By the time that Karl reached them, Nate was holding out a tankard to him and Reginleif. Reginleif took one, but Karl gestured behind him to the next Valkyrie, refusing to take a drink before their guests. The

Valkyrie didn't wait upon ceremony; as soon as any tankard was grasped, it was raised to thirsting lips.

One of the largest Valkyrie, Randgríðr, scorned her tankard, and went to stand before the untapped keg, pointed one finger at its tightly wedged cork, and suddenly, with ease, she pushed it all the way down inside the wooden barrel. Then, with no more effort than lifting a cordial, Randgríðr seized its wooden sides and lifted the whole keg to her mouth. She held it aloft, and as every man watched in stark amazement and disbelief, she drank long and deeply.

"Fetch more kegs," Karl said to the six men who'd struggled to carry the kegs in, and they hurried off, their faces pale.

Nate and Phil filled and refilled every tankard, hurrying to swap full beers with those emptied by the Valkyrie, some of whom tossed them back with amazing speed. Repeatedly Karl thanked them as Rafe had his men rearrange the tables, and bring out all of the food that had been cooked and left for them, which was pathetically little, and of common fare. Soon the Valkyrie were seated at the high table, and before them was a single table where Karl, Eloise, Rafe, and Seren sat, and all of the men of Castle Bristlen stood behind them, Edith beside her brothers.

"We thank you for this show of hospitality," Skeggjöld said as she sat centermost on Karl's throne. "Although it is a sad reflection of the tables of Elvidnir, we recognize that it's all that you have, and we thank you for your generosity. Yet we didn't journey across Bifrost to fight your war or save your lives; we come seeking the answer to one question: *Baroness Eloise, where is your mother?*"

"I … I don't know," Eloise said. "I assumed that she was killed, since she never sent me a message. She was stolen from Castle Bristlen when I was a child."

"We must find her," Skeggjöld said. "Have you any clue …?"

"I wish that I had," Eloise said. "I'd give anything to know what happened to her."

Every Valkyrie frowned, and Skögul scowled.

"All that killing … just for the fun of it," Skögul sneered.

An uncomfortable silence filled the hall; their lives had just been saved, and the one gift that their rescuers wanted … they didn't have.

"I … I have a clue," Rafe said slowly, and he stood and faced the Valkyrie.

"Speak, Giant-Bane," Reginleif said.

"I … I know who took Baroness Elaina, Eloise's mother," Rafe said.

"You know …?!?" Eloise gasped, but Rafe bowed his head.

"I know nothing," Rafe said quickly. "I suspect, but I have no justifications for my speculations, and I feared that they'd cause more harm than good."

"Tell us your suspicions," Skeggjöld commanded.

"It was long ago, on the day that our adventures started," Rafe said. "We'd fled from this castle, and had just made it to Karl's …, I mean, the Baron's Hunting Lodge in Wolven Forest. Karl, Eloise, and … Reginleif … took our treasure bag and went inside to light the fire, and I had an argument with Eric. We didn't know each other then, and I didn't like traveling with a viking. He admitted that he was the reason why Svenson Two-Sword had razed Castle Bristlen, and that … that he'd been there when the vikings stole Baroness Elaina."

"Eric Bjornson …?" Hrist asked Reginleif. "That einherjar who brings you your first ale each night?"

"Eric must know," Karl said. "He was Svenson Two-Sword's best friend."

"Eric knew … *all this time …?"* Eloise seethed.

"I assumed that something bad had happened to her, something that you needn't know," Rafe said to Eloise.

"All this searching," Herfjötur grimaced, "and the answer that we seek drinks with us in our hall each night."

"At least we know where to find him," Geirahöd said.

"Why?" Karl asked. "Why do the Valkyrie seek Eloise's mother?"

"She possesses wisdom that we must have," Skeggjöld said.

"Athelwynne has vanished … and failed to appear for a meeting," Reginleif said. "Odin commanded us to find him, and the Norns said that Eloise's mother could identify our last clue."

"How could my mother …?" Eloise began.

"The Norns often deceive, but they're never wrong," Mist said. "Our only other hope is to enter a cave where even gods fear to tred."

"We must return to Valhalla," Skeggjöld said.

"Where we can get better beer," Skögul added.

"Again, we thank you for your courtesies," Skeggjöld said, and she rose from Karl's throne. "Come, sisters."

"Wait!" Eloise jumped to her feet. "You can't … I must know what happened to my mother. Please, take me with you."

"That's not allowed," Skeggjöld said.

"Eric might not tell you willingly," Eloise said. "I'll get it out of him … even if I have to cut off his arm again."

The Valkyrie looked reluctant.

"They do carry the favor of Odin," Hrist said.

"Who will vouch for their conduct?" Skeggjöld asked.

"I will," Reginleif said. "Although Eloise is not a Valkyrie, she was a sister to Roselyn."

Skeggjöld shook her head, but acquiesced.

"Only the four who bear Odin's favor may come," Skeggjöld said.

"No!" Eloise said. "I mean … maybe just I should come."

"I come," Seren said, and she put great emphasis on her words. "Want see Eric … and protect Eloise."

"I don't need …," Eloise began, but Seren raised one eyebrow as a warning, and Eloise fell silent.

"None of us should go," Rafe said. "If we want to communicate with the lands after death, then we should do so in church, not in Yggdrasil!"

Karl eyed each of his companions carefully, and then stared at Reginleif.

"We'll all go," Karl said firmly. "Eloise must know if her mother lives, and Seren must chaperone her, since only she seems to be able to do it. I want to see Eric; all of these years we've been asking what he'd do in a hundred situations; I'd like to ask him directly. Rafe, we'll need you there to protect our souls; no baron or baroness of England could keep their coronets if they were believed to be consorting with pagan deities. The Barony du Harmonn should be safe while we're gone; once Sir Aledard's men spread the tale of how his own sister and a dozen women defeated his army, no enemy will dare enter our lands again."

"Then, let's go," Skeggjöld said.

"No!" Eloise said. "I mean, I need to get some things …"

"We'll wait until you return, if you're quick," Skeggjöld said.

Eloise got up and hurried from the hall. Rafe sat wondering, and finally he rose and went after her.

Eloise was nowhere to be seen, but Rafe knew where she was going; he headed toward her tower. As he reached the base of her steps, he saw the door to her tower wide open, and knew that he'd judged correctly. He stood waiting, and finally heard footsteps coming down.

Eloise appeared carrying a small leather satchel. She stopped and almost stumbled when she saw Rafe.

"What's in the bag?" Rafe asked.

"Nothing," Eloise said. "Just some …"

"Show me," Rafe said.

Eloise turned and locked the door to her tower behind her.

"Rafe, we don't have time …," Eloise said.

"Roselyn won't leave without us," Rafe said.

"Without Karl, you mean," Eloise said.

"Is that why you invited fairies into our castle?" Rafe asked. "Because of Roselyn and Karl?"

"He's my husband," Eloise said.

"You knew his intentions when you married him," Rafe said. "You knew what Roselyn intended, and you had no objection then."

"I won't give him up," Eloise said.

"If I thought that your plans were to inter Karl's soul into the bounty of Heaven, then I'd help you … and you know that," Rafe said. "The solution is simple: Karl must not die with a sword."

"I won't kill my husband," Eloise said.

"I wouldn't allow it," Rafe said. "Nor will I allow you to abscond to the afterlife of the Druids with Karl's soul … or your own."

"I don't care where I go," Eloise said, "as long as it's with Karl."

"That's blasphemy," Rafe said.

"Christ is not the only god," Eloise said.

"Not yet," Rafe said. "But the winter of the pagans is coming; they may not survive."

"Show me a way to get Karl to choose Christ over Odin, and I'll follow wherever you lead," Eloise said.

"First you must choose Christ over the Lady," Rafe said.

"I'll choose Christ … if Karl does," Eloise said.

"Love of another can't supersede your love for Christ," Rafe said. "Show me what's in the satchel."

"No," Eloise said.

Rafe and Eloise exchanged glares.

"No good will come of this journey," Rafe warned. "You can't seek Christ in the lands of the Norse gods."

Chapter 11

The Hall of Elvidnir

ERIC

In Valhalla, the day's battle raged on. The sun was near setting, but neither side had triumphed. Eric fought under the red and purple snake, the symbol of Svenson Two-Sword's great, great grandfather, Olard Longbeard, who led a company of only four hundred men. Many thought that Olard was a fool, as they were wiped out so frequently, since four hundred was too small a company to hope to conquer much, yet Eric understood; Olard didn't want victory. Too many victories made one overconfident, self-assured, and conceited. Olard wanted to always be at risk, to always be fighting as hard as he could.

His company was scorned as imprudent because so many others were ten times bigger, but Olard's warriors had proven themselves many times; when some fool boasted that their company was stronger, Olard challenged their leader to an equal fight, four hundred against four hundred; Olard Longbeard's company had never lost to equal numbers.

Eric and Svenson peeked over the boulder; they were in the high mountains today, atop a long range of snow-capped peaks. Below them waited the vast army of AnTyr, an ancient Germanic tribe that had died out on Midgard, but numbered almost three thousand einherjar … with a well-earned reputation for cruelty. Only two trails offered hope of ascension to the chilly heights, and the remnants of Olard's forces had defended both since noon. They'd retreated to this defensible position, but sunset was two hours away, and the AnTyrians would consider the day wasted if they didn't slay every man who opposed them before the feasting began.

Several dozen arrows flew at their heads, and Eric and Svenson ducked to avoid losing their eyes. Several old soldiers cursed at them for peeking, for drawing enemy fire; their opponents were unlikely to run out of arrows.

"There's plenty of rocks," Svenson said. "We should start an avalanche."

"That would kill us," snarled a youthful face belonging to a cousin who had been fighting in Valhalla for centuries. "If we lose these boulders, we'll expose ourselves."

"They outnumber us eight to one," Eric said. "Do you really expect to win?"

"I always expect to win," the cousin said.

Eric mused in silence; every einherjar debated the best philosophy for fighting Ragnarrock with hope of victory. Some felt that killing as many enemies as possible was paramount, no matter how many lives it cost, to leave the surviving gods free to resist Black Surt. Others insisted that the gods might need their help against Black Surt, so their best option was to stay alive as long as possible, to kill only where victory was assured. It was generally agreed that Black Surt wouldn't come from Muspell until the end of Ragnarrock, but how long would the Great Final Battle last; weeks, months, or years? Would its outcome be decided before Black Surt came? These questions had been argued for centuries, and no vehemence or explanations had ever convinced anyone of anything.

"They're coming," said an old graybeard, resting beneath his shield with a bloody axe in his hand.

There was only room for about twenty defenders at the gap nearest Eric and Svenson. Eric had only arrived in Valhalla eight years ago, and despite his unique and highly-celebrated entrance, most of his fellows still considered him a novice. The cousin with the youthful face was an archer who'd practiced his art every day, in every terrain, and under every type of weather, for three centuries; he could shoot both eyes out of a diving falcon as it swooped past him. Eric and Svenson had both become far greater swordsmen than they'd been on Midgard, but in training sessions against Olard's heavy spiked maul, even the two of them working together didn't have a chance. Fighting was the ultimate art in Valhalla, and victory was the only measure of any warrior.

Slowly Eric and Svenson inched forward toward the narrow, frosty ledge where the trail below arose to their ridge. Each enemy charge killed off several of Olard's men, even if a dozen of their own men fell, and the dead had to be cleared before another charge could be attempted. The rough stones scraped, and the uncomfortable positions that they had to maintain to keep from being exposed strained Eric's aged joints; he wished that he'd come to Valhalla younger.

Suddenly gleeful cheers rose above the clangs and crashes of battle.

"They've broken through behind us!" the cousin yelled. "*To arms! Valkyrie!*"

Enemy soldiers came running up the slope on both sides; falling on top of Svenson's kinsmen and burying them in grappling matches, while more enemies ran overtop them, pouring up the slope. Eric and Svenson rose, shields first, and arrows thudded into their shields before they'd climbed to their feet. Both slashed their swords as the same instant; Eric killed his opponent, but Svenson's foe blocked his blade. Svenson punched with his borrowed shield, lifted the man high into the air, and threw him over the brink. But his shield had been protecting him; Svenson staggered back from the cliff with ten arrows stabbed deep within him.

Eric charged his second foeman. The second man jumped back, and Eric stumbled forward; suddenly he was facing five men, three of whom had long spears, and his shield was trapped at his side, protecting him from the arrows which had claimed Svenson.

Eric threw himself down onto his back, laid his shield atop him, and kicked as hard as he could. His feet met a small, icy boulder, weighing little more than he did; he kicked the boulder off the edge, and it rumbled and rolled down the mountainside. Smaller, but still formidable rocks fell with it, causing showers of snow, and many screams came from their path; Eric knew that he couldn't win this fight, and the rolling boulders could kill or wound dozens of enemy warriors.

Spears pierced Eric's flesh, and he cried out as agony washed over and consumed him. Eric hated to die, but lingering deaths were even worse, especially if you were mortally wounded right after dawn and had to suffer all day; *better a clean death.* If possible, a fellow soldier would end your pain, but when your entire company was defeated, often there was no one left who'd aid you. Killing yourself was frowned upon even in Valhalla, if you were alive, then you might yet distract some enemy with a shout, and help a fellow soldier. Yet Eric had no hope; he could barely move his limbs, and his enemies trod over him with sadistic smiles as they rushed to kill off the last of Olard's men.

"Eric ...?" came Svenson's weak, feeble voice.

"I thought ... you were dead," Eric moaned.

"Can you move?"

"No."

"Try."

"You kill me, and then ... I'll return the favor."

Both men tried to laugh, and then both men began coughing up blood.

"I hate this part," Svenson finally managed to say.

"There's one good thing ...," Eric said.

"What?"

"Your loud-mouthed cousin was beheaded."

Both men laughed ... and coughed up more blood.

A long, agonizing hour later, Svenson Two-Sword died. Eric cursed his eternal friend, secretly wishing that he'd been the one to die. The low sun beamed upon him, and the cold, high mountain air swept across his face, but he couldn't move; the enemy's blades had done him to death, just not quickly enough. The AnTyrians had long since departed, having overwhelmed and defeated Olard's company, but they'd only laughed at Eric and Svenson as they'd lain, mortally wounded, unable to move; AnTyr never showed mercy. Eric stared into the darkening sky, impotently suffering.

The sun finally set, and a tinkling chime filled the air. From the sky came a great rainbow, a reflection of Bifrost, which descended upon the whole of Valhalla like a blessed cloak from the gods. Multi-hued colors swept over the mountains, and swathed the ancient battlefield in lights of every shade. Eric felt his pains vanish at once, and he became almost spectral, a spirit such as he'd been when walking across the vast ocean toward the 'crack in the world', the secret doorway to Yggdrasil. Slowly he sat up, and saw dead Svenson Two-Sword open his eyes. As Svenson rose to his feet, the ten deadly arrows shot into him fell right through his ethereal form and clattered onto the trail atop the mountain.

The severed head of the youthful cousin vanished, then reappeared upon the stump of his ghostly neck. Other dead men shuffled, slowly standing.

"Here it comes," Svenson said.

The world changed. Where once there'd stood towering mountains, now millions of men stood upon countless gentle rolling hills. Valhalla was as wide as it needed to be, ever expanding as more einherjar were ferried to Yggdrasil by the Valkyrie, and yet its borders never seemed to change. Many newcomers wondered about this, but the old timers simply accepted it as part of the magic of Odin's battlefield.

Standing amid a crowd of friends and enemies, Eric and Svenson waited, and finally the rainbow colors vanished, and they became solid again. Daylight could still be seen in the distance, but the first stars were already visible, and soon it would be blessed night. In the failing light, each man scavenged for weapons, especially those most-treasured, engraved with their runes or symbols, and then every man began walking east. There, near the Gates of Valhalla, stood Elvidner, the Hall of Odin, where the Valkyrie hosted exuberant feasts each night. All of the einherjar headed there, after locating the weapons that they'd need come the dawn.

Every evening, the walk to Elvidner was the same, some already smiling, eager to boast about their feats of the day to a tableful of drunken listeners, but it was usually a silent walk, some hurrying to get the best seats nearest the table of the Valkyrie, others walking slowly, not wanting to get stuck in the crowd pressing to enter Elvidner's wide doors.

Suddenly something unexpected happened. Without warning, over the battlefield swept one name, shouted from a thousand lips, and repeated, echoing across Valhalla.

"Eric Bjornson!"

Eric and Svenson stopped suddenly, not knowing what it meant; in the eight years since they'd come to Valhalla, the evening walk to Elvidner was always quiet, a time to recover after a hard day's fighting and prepare for a night of drunken revelry. Never had so many voices been raised during this walk, chanting a single name, and never had that name been Eric's.

"Here!" cried the undecapitated cousin, pointing. "Here is Eric Bjornson!"

The cousin's cry was relayed back, and hundreds pointed. Slowly the sound of rushing wings grew, and all thirteen Valkyrie flew low over the heads of the einherjar. Men rushed to get out of their way and clear a space as the great horses beat their powerful wings, blasting the faces of the einherjar with mighty gusts. The flying steeds landed and settled onto the grass, and all of the nearby einherjar dropped to one knee or bowed deeply, as did Svenson and Eric. Foremost of the Valkyrie was Reginleif, whom Eric had once known as Roselyn, the daughter of Eorl Sir Guldwin, who'd been one of the renowned companions who'd brought his dead arm from Midgard to the Gates of Valhalla. Eric brought her a brimming cup of ale at the beginning of each feast, in remembrance that he'd be groveling in Niflhiem if not for her courage and sacrifice.

"Eric!" shouted a familiar voice.

Over one shoulder of Reginleif, Eric saw a face that he treasured above all others; *riding behind Reginleif, sharing her horse, was his dear old friend.*

"Karl!" Eric shouted, and he rose in surprise.

"Eric Bjornson, tonight you will join our guests at the Table of the Valkyrie," Reginleif said.

"As you command, my Queen Reginleif," Eric dropped to one knee and bowed as best he could.

Karl dismounted and ran to embrace his old friend. As they hugged, Eric glanced behind Karl; Rafe had also dismounted, as had Seren, and they were rushing to greet him. Eloise had also dismounted, but she was standing beside Skeggjöld, looking unusually grave.

Eric hugged his old friends, and then Svenson insisted on shaking each of their hands, introducing himself, and insisting that Eric had described each of them many times. Eric broke free and hurried forward to hug Eloise, but her hug was perfunctory; *something was wrong, but Eric suspected from her expression that it had best wait until they were alone.*

"Conclude your greetings, but don't discuss the reason why mortals stand in Valhalla," Skeggjöld commanded. "We'll await you at the High Table; be prompt."

"Yes, Queen Skeggjöld," Eric bowed deeply.

The steeds of the Valkyrie reared, flapped powerful wings, and leaped into the air. The Valkyrie flew away, back toward Elvidner.

On the walk to Elvidner, Eric asked many questions about their lives since he'd last seen them, and Karl related all that had happened since he'd become Baron du Harmonn, about the wars that he'd fought in, about the amazement of his family to learn that he'd become royalty, the refusal of the king to remove the name du Harmonn and restore the barony's true name, and of the collusion between the king and Eorl Sir Guldwin to seize control of the barony. Eric was delighted to learn that Eorl Sir Guldwin was dead, and laughed uproariously at their descriptions of Reginleif confronting her brother, Sir Aledard, and the Valkyrie sending his whole army fleeing back home with their tails between their legs.

The walk back to Elvidner wasn't short; Rafe required a spear to use as a staff, which one of the einherjar, walking close to overhear their tales, was glad to offer. Seren simply couldn't make it, and two of Eric's muscular cousins held a new shield flat so that she could sit upon it, and they carried her the rest of the way.

The main doorways to Elvidner were usually packed, such that men often pushed to get through, but the einherjar held back, allowing a path for those brought or summoned by the Valkyrie. Eric led them to the taps; a hundred barrels of beer were stacked against one wall, and Eric lifted a gold drinking cup, untied it from his belt, and filled it with the best ale. Ceremoniously he carried it before him all the way across the vast hall, and up the wide steps to the High Table, where the Valkyrie were already sitting, with Reginleif on one end, and servants were carrying chairs forward for Eric and the companions.

To both sides of the hall were many doors, all opening to other halls, identical to theirs; Eric passed these by, but noticed how the companions stared through them.

"Prepare yourselves," Eric said. "The view from the High Table can be … unsettling."

As they reached the top of the stairs, Eric bowed deeply to the Valkyrie, and then approached Reginleif, presenting her with the golden cup. Reginleif accepted the drink, and nodded to the chairs beside her.

"Karl will sit beside me, and Eric will sit beside him," Reginleif said.

Eloise choked softly, but Eric pretended not to notice.

As Eric had expected, the companions stared amazed; the view from the High Table was vast, as if they were staring into countless huge halls, thousands of different rooms, each filled with thousands of warriors.

"This is the magic of Elvidner," Eric said. "There's always room for everyone, in some version of the Great Hall, and those who know their ways may traverse between the countless halls, but the Valkyrie can be seen from each of them, and they preside over all."

"How do you get used to looking at them?" Karl asked, amazed, staring into the kaleidoscope of images.

"It takes a while," Reginleif said.

"Einherjar, be seated … and be silent!" Skeggjöld shouted, and men hurried to take seats at the foremost tables and fell utterly silent and still. Skeggjöld waited several moments for them all to find places, then turned her head to look at Eric. "Eric Bjornson, the will of Odin commands the Valkyrie, and long we've sought to fulfill his desires. All that we've learned has led us to one question: *where can we find the mother of your mortal companion, Baroness Eloise du Harmonn?"*

Eric paled, and then he seemed to steady himself and rose to stand before speaking. He glanced worriedly at Eloise, and bowed his head shamefully.

"My Queen Skeggjöld, and all of my other queens, this secret I did promise to take with me to my grave, but every einherjar is long past such trivialities, and never would Eric Bjornson deny the will of the Valkyrie.

"On Midgard, many years ago, I and King Svenson Two-Sword led a fierce army against Castle Bristlen in England. Wergild we agreed to accept, but only if the beautiful Baroness Elaina, whose virtues were so renown that tales of her had reached us in Norway, would deliver it to us. Baroness Elaina had been recently force-wedded to a French knight, and she was glad to demonstrate his weakness before all of their people. She alone pushed a wheelbarrow full of treasure out of the gate of Castle Bristlen, and we were delighted to receive it. She asked if we'd speak privately with her, and then she begged us to siege the castle and kill her husband, promising any honor that was hers to give, if only Svenson would agree to leave her in charge of the barony, and leave her daughter and her peasants unharmed.

"Yet we didn't travel alone. Skafti, Svenson's most powerful wise-one, a necromancer of dread reputation, traveled with us, and upon seeing Baroness Elaina, he performed fantastic feats of illusion … and made an ominous prediction: *if Baroness Elaina ever saw her daughter's face again, if she even went back inside Castle Bristlen, where her daughter would see her, then her daughter would know only sadness for the rest of her life.*

Baroness Elaina argued, and we restrained her just long enough to convince her that Skafti had never made a prediction that didn't come true. Baroness Elaina couldn't bear to be parted from her daughter, but neither could she doom her daughter to eternal unhappiness; in the end, Baroness Elaina chose to depart with us, and she never saw her daughter again."

"You never told me …?!?" Eloise shrieked, and she leapt from her chair and attacked Eric, teeth gritted, snarling, and baring her tiny fingernails as if they were the claws of the Wolfqueen. Many einherjar laughed, but Eric stood and took it, letting her strike him as hard as she wanted, until Karl and Rafe pried Eloise off him.

"I was obeying your mother's wishes," Eric said to Eloise. "I, too, didn't want to be the cause of your unhappiness."

"Where's my mother?!?" Eloise demanded.

Eric shook his head and said nothing. Eloise renewed her struggles, but Karl and Rafe held her back.

"The will of Odin can't be thwarted for fear of a mortal's happiness," Skeggjöld said. "Eric Bjornson, by command of the Valkyrie, reveal this secret."

"Many miles north of the innermost tip of Olso Bay is a large lake," Eric said reluctantly. "Upon a small island in the lake stands a single tower made of gray stones, so light that it vanishes in fog and at twilight. When last I stood in Norway, before I killed Prince Thorland, Baroness Elaina lived in that tower."

"We leave at once …," Skeggjöld said.

"Tomorrow!" Skögul insisted. "We've been riding for weeks; a night of rest will help us think more clearly, and Odin ordered us to find the Seer, not to bring him back; we ride for wisdom, not to battle."

The Valkyrie looked at each other uncertainly, and several looked doubtful.

"We're neglecting our other duties," Geirahöd said. "Our involvement in the siege of Castle Bristlen was fun, but there are einherjar to be chosen, and there's no war at this tower; we need not all go."

"Very well," Skeggjöld said. "Reginleif must come, and I'll go; we need two more to ferry the mortals …"

"I'll go," Skögul said.

"I'll join you," Róta said.

"We leave at dawn," Skeggjöld said.

"Excellent," Skögul grinned. "At least we'll all get a pleasant sleep, *won't we, Reginleif …?"*

Reginleif said nothing, but she glared daggers at Skögul, who smiled back. Several of the other Valkyrie seemed to be hiding mischievous grins, and Prudr burst out laughing. At this, several einherjar joined in the laughter.

"Be silent!" Reginleif shouted at a thousand halls, and their laughter died instantly.

Eric sat back down, and Karl and Rafe forced Eloise to return to her chair, where Seren patted her comfortingly.

"See mother soon," Seren whispered to Eloise.

Eloise stared at Eric as if she'd consume him.

Eric stared at his plate, but he wasn't hungry. As the serving wenches arrived, the beer-maids of Valhalla, carrying huge platters of roasted pork and braised beef, steaks, cooked fowl, and huge fish, the clatter of the hall rose, but still no einherjar spoke; Reginleif may be the youngest Valkyrie, but she was a Queen of Valhalla, and her commands were no less paramount than those of Herfjötur or Hlökk, the eldest Valkyrie.

Eric drank his beer in silence, but he couldn't enjoy its taste; to his knowledge, the only time that Skafti had ever been wrong was the time that he'd linked his spirit with Skaldi, a brutish, illusion-casting giant from Jotunhiem, to bring him to Midgard. Then, the Seer's illusions had triumphed, and with all of them helping, they'd defeated Skaldi, although it had almost killed them; when Skaldi the giant had died, Skafti the wizard had also perished*; Svenson had watched him die … and he still shuddered whenever he recalled it.*

Eric risked a glance at Eloise; she'd helped give him everything that he had, praise that even the oldest einherjar couldn't claim, and personal attention from Odin. The thought of condemning her to eternal sadness troubled him. He'd spared her this knowledge for eight years, but he couldn't defy the Valkyrie; many of the einherjar considered them to be goddesses, and as far as Eric was concerned, the difference between the Valkyrie and the gods of Asgard wasn't enough for him to draw a distinction.

Yet his knowledge of Baroness Elaina didn't end with her location; Eric knew things about her mother that Eloise must never know. If possible, he had to convince Eloise to return to England, to stay inside Castle Bristlen, and never seek the truth about her mother.

The feast was subdued, and Eric had lived and died in Valhalla long enough to notice the tension. He tried not to look at the miasma of halls before them, ever shifting; he came to the High Table before each feast to bring Reginleif her first ale, so he saw this sight every night, but he usually sat at those lower tables near Svenson and his father, and from there, the High Table of the Valkyrie looked fixed and unmoving. Reginleif had commanded silence, so no one was speaking, boasting of their victories that day, or laughing, or flirting with the beer-maids, but they did that every night; tonight every eye watched the High Table.

"Skeggjöld," Skögul broke the silence, "perhaps we who travel with you tomorrow should get a good night's sleep."

All of the Valkyrie glared at Skögul, as if she'd said something terrible.

"Valkyrie sleep when they choose," Skeggjöld said.

"And with whom they choose," Skögul agreed.

Eric startled; he knew why Skögul was speaking so: Reginleif had been sleeping alone for eight years, and everyone in Valhalla knew that she'd been awaiting Karl, her mortal lover, to join her as an einherjar. Yet now Karl sat in Elvidner, still mortal, and on Eric's other side sat Eloise, Karl's wife; *where would Karl spend his night?*

Eric wondered what Karl had been thinking all of these years; Eric had shown him how to earn an honorable death: *make them want to kill you!* Nevertheless, Karl hadn't put his life in certain peril; he'd stayed with Eloise, growing older and wiser, making his eternal love wait. For the first time, Eric worried for Karl; Roselyn may have been patient and restrained, but Reginleif was a Valkyrie, proud and strong. Eric had watched her slowly change over the years; *she wasn't Roselyn anymore.*

Slowly, Eric pushed back his chair, rose to his feet, and bowed.

"Queen Skeggjöld …," Eric said. "If I may speak …"

"Weren't you ordered to be silent?" Skögul shouted. "Dare you defy the Queens of Valhalla?"

Eric looked horrified, but he quickly regained his composure, bowed silently to Skögul, and returned to his seat. He would've preferred to have escorted Eloise out of Elvidner for a private talk, but that was impossible now.

"Eric Bjornson," Reginleif said softly. "Escort our guests from the hall."

Eric glanced at Reginleif; she'd understood what he'd tried to do. Perhaps later, they'd have the chance to speak privately, but now wasn't the time. Eric bowed to her, then pushed back his chair and rose, and the companions followed his example.

"Baron Karl, you will remain," Reginleif said adamantly.

Karl hesitated, then sat back down; Eric suspected that Karl hadn't guessed why he was being kept at the table, but Eloise burst into tears. Eric hurriedly wrapped his arms around her, and as a million warriors watched, he led Eloise from the hall, with Rafe escorting Seren behind him.

Outside, many warriors were gathered, lounging in the grass with tall beers and whispered conversations. Eric led Eloise, Rafe, and Seren into their midst, and gave his fellows a pleading glance; warriors of countless centuries needed no words to communicate. Within two minutes, the crowd of warriors had slid back into the great hall, leaving them alone.

"He … He's my husband!" Eloise sobbed.

"Reginleif has no choice," Eric said. "She's not a countess anymore; she's an immortal queen, a Valkyrie, and she can't allow another woman to take from her side the man that she's sworn to make her own. Her reputation would be damaged for all eternity."

"I agree with Eloise," Rafe said. "Their marriage was sanctified by God; damn the reputations of these pagan …"

"Speak no ill of the Valkyrie!" Eric interjected quickly, silencing Rafe. "You stand in their lands, not before the Gates of Heaven. The vengeance of the einherjar, however misplaced you believe it, is swift and terrible."

"If I must die for my faith, then I will," Rafe said.

"What's death in Valhalla?" Eric scoffed. "I could kill you now, or you could kill me; each evening, Odin's rainbow graces these lands, and we'd both rise to continue our argument as if nothing had happened. Yet there are torments the einherjar know, deaths beyond death, which I wouldn't wish upon my worst enemy; you mustn't anger the armies that dwell here."

"Karl didn't have to . . . !" Eloise sobbed.

"Yes, he did," Eric said. "If Karl had refused Reginleif, then he would've shamed her for all eternity, and she'd have to kill him. Then she could raise him as an einherjar, or send him to Hel in Niflheim; you know how that would end. Or, she could cast his spirit out, to try and find some passage back to your world, and beyond, to the realm of the Catholic God. If Karl's spirit is strong enough to make that journey, I can't say, but I'd guess that none have succeeded before."

"God doesn't abandon his followers," Rafe said.

"Since when has Karl been a devout follower of any faith?" Eric asked. "He wasn't like you, the Seer, and I; has he changed so much since he married Eloise?"

Rafe scowled, and Eloise cried harder.

"Poor Eloise," Seren said, taking her in a tight embrace. "Once, Rafe must endure, while I with Radsvid. Now Eloise must endure."

Eloise looked up at Seren, her face streaked with tears, and then she pushed her away and collapsed onto the grass, weeping while her closest friends watched. Eric frowned and wished that he could comfort her, but all of the armies of the einherjar can't fight a woman's tears.

Chapter 12

Baroness Elaina

ELOISE

Eloise awoke to the light of an early dawn. She'd passed out upon the grass, and slowly opened eyes redder than an angry sun, her expression forlorn and hopeless. She lay wrapped in several cloaks, none of which she recognized, Eric's strong arms holding her. A dim memory flitted through her mind; she'd once helped carry Eric's severed right arm, rotting and gangrenous, from Eorl Sir Guldwin's lands to the Gates of Valhalla; *Eloise wished that she hadn't come here again, not even for her mother!*

Rafe lay snoring beside her, wrapped in cloaks with Seren, who was holding him in her sleep, protectively, even after all of these years. Old as they were, someday they'd reunite in Heaven, and then their bliss would last forever. Eloise's eyes teared again; she and Karl would never know eternal intimacy. Someday Roselyn would come for Karl, and then Eloise would be doomed to grow old … and face eternity alone.

"Good morning, princess," Eric whispered.

Eloise struggled to sit up, felt too weak to try, and settled back into Eric's arms.

"No one has called me that since …," Eloise started, but she couldn't finish the sentence.

"Days in Valhalla never change," Eric said. "The weather changes. Some days we fight on glaciers, on other days in swamps so thick that armies must swim through pools of snakes and lizards, but the outcome is always the same."

"If Karl didn't die with a sword …," Eloise said.

"He wouldn't be here if he didn't want to be," Eric said.

"He … he slept with her … last night …?" Eloise asked.

"Women were always Karl's greatest weakness," Eric said. "This wasn't unknown to you."

"He married me," Eloise said.

"Until death do you part," Eric said. "You knew that, also."

Eloise bowed her head.

"Once you argued religion with me," Eric said softly. "Arguments don't change a person's faith; each man must feel ultimate truths within their heart, or for them, there are no truths. You can't make another change their beliefs; men have no control over that. Karl's a practical man; he's seen too many gods to ever believe that only one faith is true. You married a man who loves another; you must accept this, or you'll lose what you have today."

"Karl doesn't have to love Roselyn," Eloise said.

"Men don't choose whom they love, either," Eric said. "You know the solution; if you kill Karl in his sleep, then Reginleif won't be able to claim him."

"That would also leave me alone," Eloise said.

"You were never a good liar," Eric shook his head. "You have Karl in this life, and you want him in the next, yet you fear for him to die; *what are you hiding?"*

Eloise glanced at Rafe and Seren, still asleep.

"Do you … promise not to tell …?" Eloise whispered.

"I'd sworn to never tell you about your mother, and by command of my queens, I did," Eric replied softly. "I'll hold all that you tell me in the strictest confidence, but I can't deny my feudal duty."

Eloise lowered her voice to a barest murmur and spoke right into Eric's ear.

"I've become a Druid priestess," Eloise said. "I'd hoped that, if I could become strong and powerful, like Reginleif, then I could turn Karl's attention from her. But I can't; I thought that I'd be as powerful as the Seer, but I'm not."

"As a student, the Seer's powers were intimidating even to his teachers," Eric said. "You have qualities that Athelwynne will never know, such as the need to love, but few mortals attain the Seer's prowess."

"I won't surrender my husband," Eloise said.

"You decreed that separation," Eric said. "Upon death, your spirit shall fly to the Lady of the Druids. If Karl should reject Reginleif, willingly or no, then he'll fall back upon Rafe's faith, and fly to the Gates of Heaven; Karl will never be a Druid."

Eloise melted into quiet sobs, and Eric held her; *she was her own worst foe.* It was the worst truth of all: Karl's spirit would never enter the bosom of the Lady, or see the Blessed Lands of the Elysian Fields. Even if Eloise could hold Karl in this life, she'd insured that she'd lose him in the next.

"Eloise, you must return to England," Eric said. "Don't seek your mother."

"I've known curses worse than any Norse wizard could cast," Eloise said.

"Your meeting won't go as you expect," Eric warned her.

"If she lives, I must seek her," Eloise said.

"Eloise, your mother … isn't the same woman that you knew," Eric warned. "You've more in common than you know, but in other ways …"

"What other ways …?" Eloise asked.

"Just remember, your father died a long time ago," Eric said.

Eloise stared, but Eric said no more, and she didn't have the courage to ask …

Dawn rose slowly in Valhalla. Eric's strong arms were the only comfort that he could give her, and he held her as tightly as her mother used to. Eloise wondered about her mother … and Eric's warning; she'd been very young when her mother had been taken away; *no: she'd chosen to go.* What would she be like? What could they say to each other? According to Eric, she'd left with Eric and Svenson Two-Sword to spare Eloise from the curse of a wizard named Skafti, but was that any excuse? *How could any woman justify abandoning her only daughter?*

Eloise thought about her daughter, little Roselyn, and her sons, Eric and Athelwynne; *did Eric even know that they'd named their first son after him?* Eloise doubted it, but she didn't want to disturb his warm hug with distractions; for the first time in years, Eloise had another adult in whom she could confide, someone who could argue evenly with her, and whose advice she trusted. Eric was too wise to bandy arguments that he couldn't win; Eric just held her tightly and let her argue with herself; it was the best gift that he could've given her. No matter what happened, or where she went, in this life or the next, Eric would always love her; *Eloise took comfort in that.*

"It's nearly dawn," Eric said softly. "Soon I must hie to the fields with the einherjar, and Karl and Reginleif shall come for you; you'd best decide how you wish to greet them."

"I'll always love you, Eric," Eloise said, and Eric squeezed her tightly.

"I hope that you find the happiness in your afterlife that you've given me," Eric said.

"Just do me one favor," Eloise whispered. "Don't fight me."

Four Valkyrie walked amid the thick crowd of einherjar marching out to a grim day's fighting; the einherjar bowed and parted around them. Reginleif, Skeggjöld, Skögul, and Róta approached, and behind them came Karl, his arms outstretched, each hand holding the reins of two winged horses. Eric looked apprehensive as he rose and bowed, but as Rafe and Seren slowly stood, Eloise jumped up and performed a perfect curtsey.

"It's time," Skeggjöld said.

Eloise turned to Eric.

"Farewell again, my dearest Eric," Eloise said, and to everyone's amazement, Eloise seized Eric's shoulders and pulled him in to an ardent kiss, wrapped her arms around the back of his neck and pressed her lips against his with a soft moan of pleasure so sensual that all conversation failed until she was done. Eric resisted at first, but apparently he understood; Eric returned her kiss with equal passion. When they separated, Eric gave no one time to comment; he went straight to Rafe and embraced him, and then he also kissed Seren, although it was a brotherly kiss, nothing like he'd shared with Eloise. When Eric went at last to his brother, Karl was still standing slackjawed, staring at Eloise as if totally confounded, uncertain what he should do.

Eric, who never missed a nuance, ignored Karl's shock and hugged him tightly, whispered something in his ear that Eloise couldn't hear, and then slapped him on the back. Finally Eric stepped back and bowed to his queens.

"Mount up!" Róta said.

Reginleif, seeming unperturbed by Eloise and Eric's kiss, mounted her saddle, and then reached out to Karl, who mounted behind her. Eloise mounted behind Skeggjöld, and Skögul took Seren, leaving Rafe for Róta.

"Bjornson!" Skögul called, smiling wickedly.

"Yes, my queen?" Eric asked.

"You seem to be a good kisser," Skögul said. "After the feast tonight, report to me."

"Yes, my queen," Eric bowed with a grin.

All of the companions laughed, and the Valkyrie shook their reins.

"We named our first son after you!" Eloise shouted to Eric as Skeggjöld spurred, and her mighty horse leapt into the air. Eric raised his hand and waved at her, beaming his brightest smile, and then the steeds of the Valkyrie rose high into the sky and soared away from Valhalla.

Bifrost was an incredible sight; six mighty towers, three on each side, flanked its colorful entryway. The tallest two towers rose in the center, each decorated with metallic rainbows in gold, silver, copper, iron, steel, and bronze. Yet these towers were built for war, for

Ragnarrock, and their formidable appearance was as lethal as they were beautiful. Their designs were similar to the protective palisades atop the walls and towers of Castle Bristlen, only infinitely better designed, and ornate, artistically built atop a wall of massive stone blocks stacked sixty feet high, with many winding stairs leading to different heights. Hundreds of warriors with twenty foot spears stood upon its curved battlements, in matching black armor with a rainbow half cloak; the guards of Heimdal, Watchman of the Norse Gods, who'll arise to wind his mighty horn, Gjallarhorn, when Loki breaks his bonds, and arises in madness, to lead all of the forces of evil in the great and final war. Behind these impenetrable walls rose a great palace, a formidable castle, but so majestically designed that no eye could be displeased, and upon its tallest tower, in a great golden archway, hung Gjallarhorn, the great horn itself, Heimdal's instrument, which had never once been blown. Flanked by four massive guards, it hung by great chains from a golden archway, larger than a carthorse and its burden. The mouth of the horn was so wide that one of their winged mounts could easily fly into it, and Eloise both wondered what it would sound like … and prayed that she'd never hear it.

However, the towers, castle, and legendary horn paled before the sight that shone forth. From the wide gap between the two innermost towers, inside that giant gateway, which no doors could span, the massive rainbow Bifrost stretched in glowing bands of colors so bright that no earthly rainbow could match it, as if every hue were born right there, and each shined clean and pure with a radiance that Eloise loved and longed to enter. Only her first sight of Yggdrasil or the Well of Hergelmir had stunned Eloise as much as Bifrost, and even though she'd seen it once before, her memory paled upon seeing it again.

Many of Heimdal's guards saluted the Valkyrie as they flew past, and the shield-sisters swooped low between their towers and sailed the winds out over the fabled Rainbow Bridge. Then, as they had before, the Valkyrie descended into the colorful bands, flying inside the rainbow. Their steeds leaned forward, and all fell into a terrifying dive. Seren screamed, as she had the last time, but Eloise heard Rafe's howl of delight; no greater thrill existed for a horse-trainer than to ride with the Valkyrie through the radiant bands of Bifrost, the bridge from the realms of the Norse Gods to Midgard. Eloise clutched tightly to Skeggjöld's armor; she trembled, but no greater protection existed than to ride behind the leader of the Valkyrie.

The sheer magnitude of the colors obscured Eloise's sight; she spied the others flying close around her, wings stretched to their utmost as they plummeted through the heart of the rainbow, yet their images were only shadows in the brilliance of brightly shifting reds, yellows, blues, greens, golds, purples, ambers; a paradise of light.

Wind stung her eyes, whipped back her hair, and whistled in her ears. Thousands of feet they plunged through shining, blinding radiance, a freefall of terror and thrill.

Slowly the Valkyrie pulled upon their bridles, and clear blue sky replaced the striving bands of colors. After the endless, terrifying drop, they swooped out of the rainbow. Eloise glanced behind her; the shining remains of Bifrost receded back into the sky until it was lost in the highest clouds. Eloise was amused to see Seren clinging tightly to Skögul's back, her eyes squeezed shut, grimacing. The dive of the Valkyrie wasn't for the fainthearted; Seren had many gifts, but riding horses wasn't one of them.

Below them lay a great shining bay, very wide, and many times longer than it was wide. Surrounding it were countless buildings, and Norse dragonships and knarrs sailed freely upon it. The Valkyrie dove low over the water, past several ships, but not one sailor seemed to see them, as if they flew invisible to mortal eyes. Longwise they glided across the bay, and then they rose over lands and buildings, which slowly gave way to thick forests that passed beneath them in a beautiful carpet of green. Many lakes dotted the landscape, yet the Valkyrie ignored most of them.

"There!" Róta shouted. "There's the tower we seek!"

Eloise peeked over Skeggjöld's armored shoulders; upon a tiny island in a small blue lake stood a single gray stone tower.

Eloise's throat tightened; she'd prayed for and feared this moment. Only the thrill of Bifrost and the dive of the Valkyrie could've distracted her.

Was her mother really inside that tower?

They landed upon the grassy island, Seren still gasping frightened breaths as Rafe helped her to dismount and hugged her. Eloise allowed Skeggjöld to help her dismount, and then they spied the entrance to the tower; an open doorway, and on each side of the stair stood two young girls before tables whose white linen tablecloths were blowing in the breeze. The young girls bowed deeply to them, and then each lifted two silver goblets from the table and held them out to be received. Reginleif, Skeggjöld, Skögul, and Róta stepped forward, took the proffered goblets, and drank without hesitation.

"Welcome, Choosers of the Slain," came a haunting voice from the doorway.

"Mother . . . !" Eloise cried.

Out of the doorway came a woman of statuesque build, not muscular like the Valkyrie, but tall, strong, and mature. She had hair the color of the sun, matching Eloise's bright gold locks, although some silver hairs showed, and she wore a gown of deep burgundy, onto which was sewn tiny mirrored buttons that reflected every light. She stood atop the stairs and curtsied as deeply as Eloise could, but no one could see her face; a white lace cloth, thinly woven, hid her features.

Eloise started to rush forward, but her mother held up both hands, palms outwards.

"Daughter, stop!" Baroness Elaina du Harmonn said so commandingly that even the Valkyrie paused.

"Mother . . . ?" Eloise asked.

"Daughter, if you take one more step forward, then you risk eternal unhappiness," Elaina said. "The curse of Skafti the Wizard shall fall upon you if ever you see my face. Turn, I beg you; my servants shall lead you to a boat; upon the shore stands transport, and a royal barge awaits you in Olso Bay, to return you to England. I would not be the cause of unhappiness to the one I love most in this world; I beg you: *go . . . before you're cursed.*"

"I've borne a curse greater than any cast by a mortal wizard," Eloise said. "I will see my mother again."

Baroness Elaina shook her head, then reached up and removed the white veil covering her face. Baroness Elaina bore the beautiful face of her daughter, but she was no young girl. Elaina had the same smooth skin, glowing cheeks, and cute upturned nose of her daughter, but her beauty displayed dignity and confidence, and her blue eyes possessed a wisdom of years far beyond the reach of any young woman, as if the cold eyes of the immortal half-goddess Hel had suddenly turned bright as midsummer and infinitely warmer.

Eloise rushed heedlessly forward and fell into her mother's arms, sobbing as if she were still a small child. Elaina held her tightly.

"I'm so proud of you," Elaina whispered.

"I love you, mama," Eloise said.

"I love you, and I've missed you every minute since I had to go away," Elaina said.

"Why?" Eloise demanded. *"Why did you go away?"*

"We'll have long years to answer that question, and I'll tell you everything," Elaina promised. "For now, we have guests who can wait no longer."

"How .... *how do you know that?"* Eloise asked, and suddenly she stopped. "Wait ... *you know ... who they are ...?"*

"I'd know the Valkyrie anywhere," Elaina said. "Hail to the Champions of Valhalla: Queens Skeggjöld, Róta, Skögul, and Reginleif."

"We thank you for your greeting, mother of Eloise," Skeggjöld said. "Do you know why we're here?"

"You seek the riddle to a mystic rune," Elaina said. "Show me this rune, and I'll tell you all I can."

Róta lifted a leather wineskin.

"I have it here," Róta said. "This is from Mist; Herfjötur captured her vapors that I might reveal it properly."

Róta pulled the cork from the wineskin and squeezed it firmly. However, instead of wine, a white fog flowed from the mouth of the wineskin and formed a small cloud before them. Within the misty cloud shone the exact symbol of the eye as it had appeared in the Well of Urd. Seeing it, Baroness Elaina stepped forward, looked puzzled, and then glanced at the Valkyrie warily.

"What is it?" Skeggjöld asked.

Baroness Elaina swallowed hard, then drew in a deep breath, as if preparing herself for something unpleasant.

"I've seen this symbol before," Baroness Elaina said. "I've never studied it deeply, for it isn't a symbol of the Norse, nor of the Catholics, nor Druids, nor of any faith still preached on Earth. This is a symbol of ancient origin, from lands far away, such that I know almost nothing about it, of a faith that failed so long ago that few remain who know anything about their true beliefs. This is the symbol of their most-revered eye, as was scribed in early Jewish texts, brought out of an ancient land called Egypt when Moses led his people from slavery into the Holy Lands. Of this symbol, I know nothing but its name; it is called … the Eye of Osiris."

"The Eye of Osiris …," Skeggjöld repeated. "Who's Osiris?"

"Osiris was an Egyptian god," Elaina said.

"Was …?" Skeggjöld asked.

"Yes," Elaina said. "Osiris is … *dead.*"

All stared at each other, confused.

"A dead god," Skögul whispered. "This is a fell omen."

"Osiris was the king of the gods of Egypt," Róta said.

"You know of him?" Skeggjöld asked Róta.

"Only a little," Róta said. "He was the king of a great pantheon of gods, much like Odin … that's all that I know."

"What happened to the Egyptian gods?" Skögul asked.

"Winter," Reginleif said, and all eyes turned to her. "The Lady of the Druids said that Winter comes for all faiths, and that few gods survive their Winter."

"Why would the Norns show us a symbol of a dead god?" Róta asked.

"Does that mean that the Seer is dead?" Skögul asked.

"We've accomplished what we came for," Skeggjöld said. "We've found the meaning of each clue. Now we must report to Odin; perhaps the God of Wisdom shall know more about this Osiris, and understand the clues as to where we can find the Seer. You have the thanks of the Valkyrie, mother of Eloise."

"It's my honor to receive you," Baroness Elaina bowed to the Valkyrie.

"Before we go, I have a question," Róta said. "You knew of our coming, and what we sought: *how …?*"

"Sixteen years ago, when I was forced to abandon my daughter to save her; I came to Norway heartbroken and without purpose," Baroness Elaina said. "There was only one way in which I could keep watch over my daughter; Skafti the Wizard was a wise teacher, and I became his pupil: I'm a Seeress."

Everyone startled, even the Valkyrie.

"A … *Seeress …?"* Eloise gasped.

"A Norse Seeress," Elaina said to Eloise. "Since you and your companions defeated my master and caused his death, I'm the wisdom and council of the kings of Norway. Yet my royal post is ended; whatever the curse of Skafti, I and my Eloise will face it together. I long to see my barony again."

"Can you ferry them home?" Skeggjöld asked, and she raised a hand to silence Reginleif's objection. "We must return to Odin at once."

"I've already seen us, in a vision, sailing together upon two great ships, one a mighty dragon … and one red and gold," Elaina said. "My visions always come true."

"Then we'll leave them in your care," Skeggjöld said. "Mortal concerns can't delay our report to Odin."

"Come, Reginleif," Skögul said sarcastically. "*Say good-bye to your lover … again.*"

Everyone glared at Skögul, but she only sniggered.

"No need," Róta said. "Speak one word, Reginleif, shield-sister, and I'll slay your beloved … and you can bring him back with us."

Eloise looked terrified. Reginleif looked at her, and then she turned to Karl.

"My waiting endures … and my patience wains," Reginleif warned.

"Our daughter is named Roselyn," Karl said slowly. "Our sons are Eric and Athelwynne. They're still too young to know of their namesakes, but I'd like to be there, to tell them, and to help them grow, before I leave them forever."

"Every day alive is a risk that you won't die with a sword," Reginleif said.

"Karl always carries a sword," Rafe said. "And even though it's blasphemy, an abomination before the eyes of the One True God, I've sworn to aid Karl in his quest to die poised for the Valkyrie, even if I must put his sword in his hand and murder him in his sleep."

Reginleif hesitated, and then she nodded her respect and gratitude to Rafe.

"Come, shield-sisters," Skeggjöld said. "Let's fly."

Good-byes were quick, hurried by Skeggjöld, since Skögul seemed to have more taunts to deliver, and even Róta seemed anxious to avoid infuriating Reginleif any further. Reginleif kissed Karl long and deeply, then placed his hand into Eloise's palm.

"Until I come for him …," Reginleif said to Eloise.

Eloise glared at the Valkyrie that she'd once loved like a sister.

"Farewell, She Who Was Once Roselyn," Eloise said.

Chapter 13

The Ban of Odin

REGINLEIF

Göll stood before the throne of Odin and recited the words of the Norn witches:

"Come to see the sisters three,
Prowl the tasty Valkyrie!"

"They failed to find the one they seek,
In waters black and tunnels deep,
Unto three sisters bring their fears,
To die upon Verdandi's shears."

"Bitches of Odin, women slaves,
Fetching those whom Skuld saves,
From those doomed to Loki's power,
Whence Heimdal calls the final hour."

"Blind they sought Urðarbrunnr,
Their funerals in the black water,

With eyes unseeing what they see,
Pathetic, puny Valkyrie!"

"Lost, lost, his battle won,
In distant lands rides no sun,
Forgotten, disremembered, never to return,
His fate one must die to learn."

"Death, demise, murders foul,
Between lovers darkness prowls,
Across rivers, cold sands,
Blind he walks in hopeless lands."

"Colder than cold, 'ere Odin hung,
A land ancient when Yggdrasil young,
Imprisoned where a second crack dwells,
The terror of frozen Mistyhel."

"Eye of a God dead in the sand,
Willingly slain by his own hand."

"Speak not of Gods forever lost,
These Valkyrie must pay the cost."

"In darkness forever, eternal strife,
Only a life can buy a life."

"The time comes for endless grief,
The mortal lover of Reginleif,
The cold eye of immortal strife,
Speaks the mother of his wife."

Odin bowed his head.
"Mistyhel … and Osiris …," Odin growled.

"We know not what it means," Skeggjöld said. "Is there a connection between the deadly doorway and the eye of a dead god?"

Odin brooded long before speaking, such that even the other Norse Gods glanced at each other, their expressions troubled.

"The Seer is lost," Odin declared. "It's a pity; much wisdom have I and the Druid Lady shared, and each are greater for having spoken for so long."

"Let us keep looking, my liege," Prudr said. "I'll enter Mistyhel …"

"No!" Odin interrupted her. "No Valkyrie shall enter that accursed place."

"Master, forgive me, but the Seer was my friend …," Reginleif said.

"I have spoken," Odin said. "The legends say that none who have ever entered Mistyhel lived to emerge … but the legends lie. I've walked into that infernal pit, and I crawled out barely alive; no Valkyrie can withstand the horror within those icy, swirling mists."

"But what of Osiris?" Skeggjöld asked.

"Only death … and endless death," Odin said. "Osiris was a powerful god, who ruled a magnificent, sun-drenched kingdom when Yggdrasil was but a seed. That symbol is also called the Eye of Ra, and the Eye of Horus, who was the son of Osiris, but it is really the Udjat Eye, the Eye of Atum … which Atum …" Odin frowned and rubbed his own leather eye-patch. "… which Atum tore from his body and sent to seek his lost children, Tefnut and Shu."

Gods and Valkyrie staggered, exchanging confused glances as their ears absorbed this unexpected similarity between divine pantheons. Only Loki and Róta kept their visages calm, intent upon Odin.

"But Osiris is dead, passed into oblivion eons ago, and all who seek him are lost," Odin said. "The Seer was the wisest mortal that I've ever known, but if he sought the Dead God then he has died of foolishness."

Reginleif bit her lip; *she couldn't believe that the Seer was dead.* He was nearly a match for Loki, and had proven it on the day that Roselyn had become a Valkyrie.

Róta spoke long to Odin, asking for details of Osiris, but Reginleif barely heard her; the idea of abandoning the search while the Seer still lived seemed abominable. *How could Odin declare the Seer dead when no one knew for sure?* The Seer had opened Yggdrasil to the wisdom of the Elysian Fields, allowing the Norse Gods to communicate with a whole other universe, ruled by one Great Lady. Reginleif stood stunned, feeling strangely hollow, as if the Hall of Odin had suddenly become unreal.

"My Lord," Reginleif interrupted Odin's conversation with Róta. "Forgive me; if I obey your commands, may I continue to search for the Seer?"

"The Seer is lost!" Odin repeated himself, an irate snarl to his tone. "You've other duties to attend to. Obey your liege!"

Reginleif hesitated, then bowed, and without another word, and without being dismissed, she turned and walked out of Odin's hall. She kept her eyes fixed on the marble floor before her, even as she strode outside and mounted her winged steed. Instantly she spurred, driving her horse into the air with no clear idea of where she was going.

She flew, steering her horse toward the clouds, watching the ground shrink beneath her. The strong wind forced tears from her eyes, but she refused to wipe them away; *Valkyrie don't cry for those lost.* She gritted her teeth and tried to restrain her fury; she was a shield-sister, sworn to Odin for all eternity, and yet this order tore her heart apart. The Seer had once been her lover, but she'd never truly loved him, and yet he'd become her friend, an important part of her life, one of her companions who, along with Eric, was all that reminded her of the mortal life she'd once had. She'd never felt fully-accepted by the other Valkyrie; without the Seer, Reginleif felt totally alone.

Hel . . .! How could she tell Hel that her first and only lover was forsaken and assumed dead?

Suddenly a great cloud appeared before her, shaped like . . . *the face of Athelwynne!* Reginleif reined in, forcing her mount to hover high in the sky, and stared at the apparition; *what did it mean?* It was definitely the Seer, his familiar features outlined in the clouds. *Was he sending her a message?*

The face in the clouds grew more distinct, but offered no meaning. Her mount grew irritated, straining to hover in midair, and suddenly a distant voice reached her ears.

"Reginleif . . .!"

A woman's voice reached her, not coming from the cloud shaped like the Seer's head. Reginleif glanced behind; Mist was flying towards her.

Reginleif's heart sank. She hadn't found the Seer, or gotten a signal from him; Mist had created his image to delay her. Mist rode up beside her, pointed to the ground, and swooped into a sudden dive. Reginleif sighed; of all the Valkyrie, Mist watched her progress and judged every action that she made. Mist was the quietest Valkyrie; she spoke only when she needed to, and even then, she chose her words carefully, as if unwilling to waste a single utterance, using brevity as a shield to guard her thoughts. Mist was the Valkyrie least like Skögul, and no love was lost between them.

With a heavy sigh, Reginleif dove after Mist and followed her to the ground. Mist landed in the shade of some tall, fragrant maple trees beside one of the beautiful rivers that snaked across Asgard. By the time that Reginleif had landed, Mist was already dismounted, sitting inside her ethereal veil of white vapors upon a gray rock by the shore, sending little puffs of steam to dance upon the flowing water.

"Valkyrie don't disobey the will of Odin," Mist said as Reginleif sat beside her.

"I know," Reginleif said, "but … Athelwynne …!"

"He was your lover …?" Mist asked.

"Once, but only once," Reginleif said. "Now he's just a friend … a close friend."

"I didn't make you a Valkyrie," Mist said. "I only risked my honor to suggest it. You owe Odin for all that you are."

"I'd never disgrace you who recommended me," Reginleif said.

"I'd be forced to seek revenge if you did," Mist warned. "Where were you flying to?"

"I … don't know," Reginleif admitted.

"What is a god?" Mist asked suddenly. "A god is one who's free to do their will with impunity. Mortals can forego their duties to their fellows, but they may be killed for it. The einherjar, and we Valkyrie, owe our immortality to Odin, who can take it away. Valkyrie may be Queens of Valhalla, but only because we serve; every mortal has a duty; your duty is to Odin."

"I know," Reginleif said. "But Odin wishes for the Seer to be found, and although he's forsaken him, he still needs the Seer to talk to the Lady."

"Odin has forbidden us to enter Mistyhel," Mist said. "He didn't command you to stop looking for the Seer."

Reginleif's eyes opened wide.

"He … didn't …?"

"You must learn to heed the words of Odin scrupulously," Mist said. "He said that you have *'other duties* to attend to', and he's correct, but when you aren't on duty, may you not do as you wish?"

"But … if Osiris is dead, then the only clue that we have left is Mistyhel," Reginleif said.

"You can't enter Mistyhel," Mist said.

"Then, I can look everywhere … except in the one place where the Seer probably is," Reginleif said.

"Odin alone has survived Mistyhel … barely; what chance would you have, youngest of the Valkyrie?" Mist asked.

Mist sent two lines of white steam out over the water; each coalesced into the figure of a woman in armor. One figure wore the suit of mortal parade armor that Roselyn had stolen from her father, and the other wore the shining chain and plate mail of Reginleif the Valkyrie. Then the images shifted; both women stood unchanged, but their armor and clothes fell away, revealing two images of her naked. Yet Reginleif didn't need armor to tell which was who; the way that the figures stood, and the expressions on their faces; she could clearly identify which image was Roselyn the mortal … and which was Reginleif the Valkyrie.

Mist released her lines of steam, and both images swirled and floated downstream, blown by the wind into shapeless puffs.

"I was a sorceress in my mortal life," Mist said softly. "The day after Odin made me a Valkyrie, I thought that I was a changed woman. A decade later, I thought I was a completely different person. Only now, when I've been a Valkyrie for centuries, do I realize how wrong I was; I'm the same woman I always was, only grown. Grow, Reginleif. Grow to accept your new strengths … but don't forget your weaknesses; if you ever leave Yggdrasil, then they'll return. Grow to be a Valkyrie who accepts her strengths … and limitations … and her duty."

Reginleif stared at the flowing waters and sighed.

"I'll always honor you," Reginleif said.

Mist rose without another word; when she'd said what she wanted to, she considered the conversation ended. Without being summoned, her winged horse came trotting towards her, and Mist mounted in a sudden leap so that it didn't slow it down, and the horse suddenly broke into a gallop, spread its wings, and leapt into the air. Reginleif watched her go; Mist was trying to help her, to make her transition from being a mortal to becoming a Valkyrie easier. She should thank her … but she couldn't. A lump rose in her throat that made breathing difficult every time that she thought about the Seer.

Days passed, each minute an eon, and dragged into weeks lasting eternities. Reginleif joined Hrist, Hildr, and Prudr, and they fetched many new einherjars, and she joined Göll, Herfjötur, Hlökk, and Geirahöd on the battlefields of Valhalla, one day fighting in an arid brown desert, another day upon countless dragonships sailing across an endless stormy sea, fighting the weather as hard as they fought each other, and fighting on a dark, sunless day inside a vast, reeking graveyard. Reginleif fought without joy or care, and died many times by sheer stupidity, not ducking for cover when she should, or not reacting quickly enough when they were attacked. Skögul's insults became especially barbed, but Geirahöd rose to her defense, and tried to offer what comfort she could. Reginleif asked Skeggjöld for permission to return to Niflhiem, to inform Hel of Odin's decision, but she was refused: Skeggjöld insisted that she remain with her shield-sisters.

Reginleif shared her evenings conversing with Eric, but he could offer no hope, and his advice was an echo of Mist's.

"Were you not a Valkyrie, then I'd advise you otherwise," Eric admitted. "We answer to the same liege, our Alfather, and I can't advise you against his will."

"What would Eric Bjornson do?" Reginleif asked.

"An einherjar must obey Odin," Eric said. "Yet, if any other commanded me, my father, Svenson, or even Olard, I'd do as I've always done: brave the deeds that earn renown … and to Hel with what others think!"

Reginleif dwelled upon Eric's speech for days, while fighting, riding to Midgard, or feasting in Elvidner, and during every cold, solitary night. She hated all of the advice that she'd been given, but suddenly, in the middle of the night, Reginleif sat bolt upright. *Not all of her companions were removed from her hopes:* Eric was sworn to Odin and had to remain in Valhalla, and Karl, Rafe, Eloise, and Seren were still on Midgard, and she dared not bring them here again, and the Seer was missing, but she still had two companions who would help her.

Under the bright stars, which shined upon her polished armor, Roselyn flew high into the dark sky. She didn't travel far, but rode to a place that she knew was forbidden: Alfhiem. The treetops of the mighty forest looked black and featureless in the starlight, but she swooped low over them, straining to see any light through their thick branches. No light shined; as far as

Reginleif could see, the forest of Alfhiem looked empty, devoid even of animals.

On her third pass over the forest, a small, brown light glimmered to her left; Reginleif banked to meet it. As she neared it, she saw a single tiny fairy, almost just a glowing point, fluttering on tiny brown wings not far above the highest leaves. This fairy wasn't like those that she'd known; it could curl up in the palm of the fairies that she'd come seeking. Reginleif slowed, and finally halted, forcing her horse to flap hard to hover in place, and the fairy flew up close, almost touching her nose. She was a dark-skinned fairy, her skin a deep russet, and she had walnut brown hair, but she seemed to sparkle in the starlight, and she smiled with an innocence that Reginleif had lost long ago.

Slowly the fairy smiled, lifted her closed hand … and hurled some red powder into Reginleif's eyes.

Reginleif screamed as her eyes burned like Muspell. She was instantly blinded, so badly that she toppled, clinging to her reins to keep from falling, and her mount neighed in protest. Then pain erupted from all over, and hanging one-handed from her mount, Reginleif opened her searing eyes: through watery tears that burned like acid, she saw a thousand flying fairies arise from the treetops, many with long, needle-fine spears, and all of them dove upon her. Her horse screamed and flipped, and needles stabbed into her wrists, the backs of her hands, and her fingers. She lost her grip on the reins; Reginleif fell from her winged horse, slapped many leaves, and grasping blindly for any handhold, she plowed into stiff branches and plummeted to the dark forest floor.

Reginleif landed hard; only the padding inside her armor saved her from being killed. Her eyes were still burning, and she wondered if she could sit up, when she heard the buzzing of a host of tiny wings brushing against leaves, descending through the trees. Warrior reflexes took over: Reginleif leapt to her feet, ignoring her blindness and the complaints of her battered and bruised body. She drew her sword, which she slashed through the thickest cloud of fairies as it swarmed upon her. Yet she might as well have been the Wolfqueen slashing hellish claws at the Seer's imaginary lights; the swift-flying fairies darted around her blade with the lithe ease of elvish coordination, which Reginleif hadn't seen in so long that she'd forgotten; fairies had saved Rafe and Seren from the fangs of the Wolfqueen in ruined Grusshire. No matter how fast Reginleif slashed at them, the fairies flew faster.

However, Reginleif was a Valkyrie; when the first needle-spears stabbed her, Reginleif spun suddenly, then dove and rolled; she was much bigger than the fairies, and if they rolled underneath her, then they'd be crushed. She leapt to her feet and ran blindly; she could plow through thick leaves and bushes that the fairies would have to fly around. Yet she could barely see; she ran into several tree trunks, and stumbled into bushes too thick even for her, whose countless branches snagged on every chink in her armor. Time and again the fairies caught up with her, and she was forced to roll upon the ground, then strike out blindly in a new direction.

Suddenly a thin cord dropped over her head: a noose. It tightened upon her gorget, so it couldn't cut into the flesh of her throat, but it took her a moment to break the strong cord, and by then, another had been looped over her free hand. As she pulled to break that, two more encircled her sword, and a third fell again over her head and caught under her nose. As she stepped, fairies dove to loop nooses upon her feet, and before she knew it, dozens of cords entwined her. Reginleif was bound and lifted, hanging inches off the ground inside the dark forest, barely able to see her attackers as anything but flashing sparkles in the night.

Reginleif shifted her grip on her sword, determined to sever all of the cords with one mighty swipe of her sharp Valkyrie blade, when the beautiful russet fairy again appeared directly in front of her nose, only this time she was laughing playfully, and she flung another powder at Reginleif, this one white and softly glowing. Suddenly Reginleif's sight, hearing, and thoughts dimmed.

The sarcastic laughter of a thousand tiny voices awoke her. The first thing that Reginleif saw were glittering trails of fairies flying before her, and then she spied her sword, stabbed into the ground, but the world was upside-down, and a strange disorientation swirled her with vertigo. Her eyes were no longer burning, and she blinked rapidly, trying to restore some order to insanity, when her prison was revealed; she was hanging upside-down, strung immobile by a hundred tiny fairy-cords, bound in midair beneath the trees.

The few patches of the night's sky above her feet were brightening; dawn was rising, but Reginleif had no idea how many days had passed. She tried to focus her thoughts, and then to breathe deeply, to gather her strength before she struggled her way to freedom, out of the thin cords binding her.

Slowly she regained her strength, and her thoughts became clearer; *she'd have to move quickly*. The dark, russet fairy was flying tiny circles before her, waving at the crowd of laughing fairies, and receiving much applause.

Reginleif gritted her teeth; *these fairies would pay for mocking the Valkyrie!*

Their tiny cords were strong, but if she pulled with all of her might, she had no doubt that she could break free, but she had to do so before they cast anymore of their cursed magic powders upon her. Reginleif took a deep breath and tensed, aching to reach her sword and attack.

A trace of Roselyn remained; Reginleif glanced down to see where she'd fall to, and all thoughts of breaking free suddenly left her mind; beneath Reginleif yawned a deep pit, filled with darkness; she could see no bottom to it.

Seeing her startle, the fairies laughed even louder. She was trapped; she dared not risk what might be hiding inside that pit, assuming that it had a bottom, and didn't tunnel all the way to the roots of Yggdrasil. She surveyed her situation, and tried to inventory her resources, but her blood was rushing to her head, and she was angry, and a little concerned that there might be no escape. If the fairies cut their cords all at once, then she'd quickly learn what was hidden in the dark depths of their pit, and she might be dead before she found out.

Dawn rose to a humiliating scene, and finally shone enough that Reginleif could spy sharp metal points in the depths, aimed upwards at her; if she fell, then she'd be impaled by dozens of speartips, and their points looked be thirty feet below the forest floor; if she broke free, she'd only live long enough to fall to her death. There were no trees or branches close enough for her to grab or hook her boots upon; only the thin cords, that suddenly looked far too feeble, held her suspended over doom.

Many fairies flitted past her eyes, making twisted faces at her, or just sneering. Some fairies were a mystery, too small for her to make out their features, as if they were just points of light only seen by glittering trails. Others looked as big as Glororil and Silvana, and a few were even larger, but none looked metallic. Every shade in Bifrost flew before her, and many fairies were strange mixtures of miniature human shapes, but had the textures of sticks, leaves, and stone.

Yet Reginleif could bear hanging upside-down, helpless, no longer.

"Hey!" Reginleif shouted. "Powder-bitch! Come down here!"

The fairies stopped laughing, countless smiles vanished, and bright eyes narrowed. The russet fairy frowned, and she swooped down to hover before Reginleif's eyes.

"What do you want?" Reginleif demanded. "I'm a Valkyrie; *dare you defy the will of Odin?*"

"Odin's will means nothing to fairies!" the russet fairy laughed, her voice surprisingly deep and sensual, not high and squeaky as Reginleif had expected.

"Why are you doing this?" Reginleif demanded. "I came here peacefully …!"

"So do all advance scouts … before their army arrives," the russet fairy said. "The borders of Alfhiem are sealed; none enter without our leave."

"How does one get leave, if they can't enter to ask?" Reginleif enquired sarcastically.

The russet fairy laughed, and opened her mouth to reply, when Reginleif struck: Reginleif shoved her head forward, snapped her teeth shut, and captured the tiny russet fairy inside her mouth. The tiny fairy screamed, and wings flapped against Reginleif's gums.

"Release me!" Reginleif shouted to the other horrified fairies between her clenched teeth. "*Release me … or I swallow her!*"

A thousand voices cried in outrage, and many took to wing. Reginleif was surrounded, and a hundred needle-like spears aimed at her.

"Free me, or kill us both!" Reginleif hissed between her teeth.

It was the strangest sensation of her life; Reginleif could hear the screams of the dark russet fairy from inside her mouth, feel tiny feet pressed against the roof of her mouth … fluttering wings brushing against her tongue … and tiny fists pounding upon the insides of her teeth, but she kept her teeth clenched and glared at the fairies.

"Cut the cords!" one male fairy shouted. "*She'll open her mouth when she screams!*"

"Kill her!" Many fairies agreed. "*Kill the Valkyrie!*"

Suddenly, a brilliant explosion of sunlight blasted.

Chapter 14

Beautiful Life

SILVANA

The first warm rays of a loving sun beamed through the thick forest ceiling of Alfhiem and illuminated a single huge flower, a radiant red rose, its single bud closed for the night. Slowly the rising sun awakened it, and the bud spread its soft, scarlet petals, returning beauty for love, radiance for warmth, as both the sunlight and the rose welcomed each other in perfect bliss, the harmony of Nature. Inside the large red rose, one small figure extricated her limbs from the arms of another, and she sat up with her eyes closed, luxuriating in the sun's first warming touch, a delighted smile widening her lips. She yawned, stretched her arms, and flexed her wings; *today was going to be another wonderful day!*

Silvana opened her eyes to the eternal promise of the dawn. All around her shined bright colors, especially countless shades of green: the vibrant greens of young birch leaves, the deeper, melancholy greens of fir trees, and the joyous greens of holly leaves, proudly displaying bright red berries that shone in the sunlight. Other colors glowed, the sturdy browns and wrinkled grays of tree trunks, the stalkless purple saxifrage, the darker red cowberry, and the proud mottled-white bark of a stand of dogwoods in the distance. Even the happy dirt of the forest floor was a mosaic of subtle colors, fallen leaves and freed pine needles, often similar, but always shifting with the carefree wind. Decorous, glistening morning dew graced everything with a magical sparkle, rounded beads of life-giving water nourishing everything that lived and grew. Above all, peeking through the living leaves, rose a friendly sky of morning blue growing slowly brighter, streaked with yellow beams of sunlight. Silvana delighted to every sight, and paused, as she did each morning, to marvel at the magnificent wonder and beauty of Alfhiem.

Colored lights floated in the air amid the leaves and between the trees. Some glows floated individually, while others spiraled in pairs or small clusters, some slow, while others zipped past at a merry pace, as if making visual melodies in the air. Silvana smiled at them, and she waved, and a few fairies waved back. Slowly she became aware of singing; a soft, distant voice wafted through the morning, an early song to greet the dawn, to awaken those still asleep with gentle harmonies and a welcoming sweetness. An event worthy of great celebration: *a new dawn had come to Alfhiem.*

Silvana glanced at her sleeping companion, and a shadow of a frown darkened her paradise. While Silvana's skin was pure metallic silver, every inch of her resembling the polished metal from the mines, Glororil was completely metallic gold, reflecting the gleam of the dawn as if it were bright noon. Silvana loved sleeping with Glororil; she was always too cold, a reflection of her lunar tendencies, while Glororil was always too hot, like his solar essence, and the two of them blended together perfectly, and they clung to each other every night. Like the moon, Silvana also rose first, but Glororil, unlike his sky-bound cousin, liked to sleep in.

Silvana breathed in deeply, then opened her mouth and began her morning song. Silvana sang no words, but maintained a single note, soft as a lover's whisper, and slowly increased her volume until she joined with the distant, unknown singers. She changed her note, rising like the sun, a gentle trill like a bird's happy cry, and with a voice like tinkling glass bells, she spread her arms wide as if to embrace all of Nature. Then she began a melody that came from the eternal joy within her, spreading it out for all in the forest to share.

Glororil groaned and rolled over, clutched a red rose petal, and pulled it down to cover his head. Silvana's song stuttered with giggles, and a nearby leaf overturned as three young fairies lifted their heads to look at her. One blew her a kiss, which Silvana returned, and then all three young fairies laughed as Silvana lifted the stray petal. Glororil snarled, then tried to cover his eyes with his arms. Still singing, Silvana ran a single fingertip along his chin, down his chest, across his stomach, and lower, and then she leaned over and kissed him. As they kissed, the three young fairies took up her song without dropping a note, and Glororil awoke, and the first sight that he saw was Silvana smiling at him.

Glororil grinned, then lifted his arm and pulled Silvana down on top of him. Silver and golden lights enveloped them, and then everything was music. The large red rose sensed their desire and closed its petals around them.

Their afterglow shining, the lovers sat up as the rose re-opened; something new was happening. More fairies than usual were dashing about, including several armored watchers with spears, who normally guarded their borders. The music had ceased on a strangely broken note, as if disturbed by something unpleasant, which was unheard of in Alfhiem.

"What is it?" Silvana called to a green-clad guard flying past, but he sped by in a flash of emerald sparkles.

"Invaders!" shouted a small indigo fairy, flitting slowly behind him.

"Invaders …?" Glororil gasped. "Dark elves …?"

"Valkyrie!" the indigo fairy shouted as it vanished into the bushes, following its emerald cousin.

Silvana and Glororil exchanged a shocked glance, and then they burst from the rose so fast that several red petals dislodged and floated to happily color the ground.

"Reginleif …!" Silvana shouted as Glororil exploded with the brilliance of the sun, blinding every fairy diving upon their companion, who was hanging upside down over the Pit of Judgement.

"Silvana …!" Reginleif shouted, and to her disbelief, a beautiful dark russet fairy flew out of her companion's mouth, looking both frightened and angry.

As Glororil's brilliance faded, Silvana flew circles around Reginleif, so fast that her companion seemed to vanish inside a cocoon of sparkling silver light. When she finally stopped, Glororil joined her, and they hovered between Reginleif and thirty score fairy watchers, each wielding a needle-sharp spear.

"Stop!" Glororil commanded. *"This is our …!"*

His words ended; *he didn't like humans.*

"… *Friend!*" Silvana insisted, finishing his sentence. "This is Reginleif, who Titania ordered us to protect on her journey from Midgard!"

"She's a Valkyrie spy!" one of the guards growled, and many fairies buzzed their wings in agreement.

"Odin's maids are forbidden to enter Alfhiem!" another fairy shouted.

"I came to see my friends!" Reginleif shouted.

A hush fell over everyone, and then laughter erupted in a great wave. Every fairy was overcome with giggles, and several drooped in midair, laughing too hard to properly fly.

"Get her down … *safely!*" Silvana ordered.

As one, all of the fairies, even the tiniest, rose and swarmed to cover Reginleif. Lines were loosened and cast aside, and Reginleif was lifted, as by a cloud of butterflies, righted, and set gently upon her feet. Then the fairies flew circles around her, a miniature tornado of color and laughing voices, and finally they spread apart, landing on every nearby branch and hanging from every leaf and stem, and each turned to watch and listen.

Reginleif didn't look amused; she frowned deeply, and snatched her fallen sword from the dirt and clenched it tightly.

"Peace, Reginleif!" Silvana shouted, and she winged to hover before her face. "Speak no words here; we need to talk in private."

Reginleif glared at her; the angry glare of a Valkyrie. Her intensity struck Silvana like the hatred of Loki; Silvana screamed and tried to shield herself with her arms, but it was like trying to hold back a rainstorm; it washed over her like the crest of an ocean wave, drenching her with bitter resentment, overwhelming delicate peace with cruel vehemence, her loving openness with selfish hate.

Silvana fell back in agony, only barely aware that any hope still existed in the world, and without that promise of renewal … *she was nothing.*

"Stop it!" Glororil's angry voice rose from the consuming madness. "*Stop … or I'll blind you!*"

The intense pain vanished, but the residual remained, and Silvana was crying; *her own companion had done this to her!* Yet, when she pried open her eyes, Reginleif was holding her in one hand, standing flatfooted, her sword dropped, with her other hand completely covering the whole top half of her face.

"I'm sorry!" Reginleif said. "I forgot!"

"You could've killed her!" Glororil shouted.

"Please …," Silvana wept. "I'm … not injured. I'll …"

"Glororil's right," Reginleif said, and she took her hand from her eyes and held it out for him to settle in. She looked gently upon them, like she was Roselyn again. "It was unforgivable. It's just … well, that's why I need your help. I … I don't know who I am anymore."

"Hurting us won't help you," Glororil said. "You're not even a human now; you're a Valkyrie, sworn to Odin, the God of Violence."

"Odin is Alfather," Reginleif corrected.

"He's the Master of Battles, is he not?" Glororil asked.

Reginleif shook her head.

"I didn't come to argue philosophy," Reginleif said. "I came for council; Athelwynne is missing."

"Missing …?" Glororil asked.

"Talk … *privately!*" Silvana insisted, wiping her tears away.

Glororil held Silvana, comforting her tenderly, which Silvana greatly appreciated; his love was more healing than any amount of rest. She still felt weak, but any contact with Reginleif weakened her more, so Glororil held Silvana upon the ground, rubbed her silvery back, kissed her, and whispered sweet phrases into her ear; Silvana felt strengthened by his love. She wished that he'd speak aloud rather than whisper; Silvana suspected that Reginleif needed to hear loving words more than she did.

Deeply regretting the pain that she'd caused, Reginleif sat against a tree like a soldier, roughly, without the poise or demureness that Roselyn had; *she was a true warrior now.* Silvana felt sorry for Reginleif, and regretted her transformation, even though it had saved her life; *becoming a Valkyrie had distanced them even more.*

The other fairies were gone; they sat beside the Pit of Judgement, which had yawned there since before either Silvana or Glororil could remember. In the distance, they heard many fairies singing, but it was a sad song, almost a lament. Doubtless many fairies were unhappy about having a Valkyrie penetrate their forest.

"What happened … to Athelwynne?" Silvana asked when she could.

Reginleif spared no details describing to Silvana and Glororil what had happened, and effused on how dejected she'd felt since Odin had commanded her not to search Mistyhel, and how she couldn't even seek out Hel to tell her of Odin's commands … and about the ominous chants of the Norns.

"We know nothing of Mistyhel, but we don't fear it," Glororil said.

"Odin barely escaped Mistyhel," Reginleif warned.

Silvana and Glororil exchanged glances.

"She doesn't understand," Silvana said.

"We can't . . . !" Glororil insisted. *"She's a Valkyrie . . . !"*

"She's afraid," Silvana said.

At this, Reginleif sat up suddenly.

"Valkyrie don't fear!" Reginleif argued.

"Only fairies don't fear," Glororil said.

"I'm rested enough," Silvana said. "Come; we must show her."

Glororil hesitated, but Silvana held out her hand and brushed her tiny silver fingers against his lips.

"You must help me … help her," Silvana said.

Reluctantly, Glororil nodded.

"It's the only way," he admitted.

With Glororil's healing caresses, Silvana soon felt ready to fly again, which was itself strengthening. At Silvana's request, Reginleif followed them as they slowly flew ahead of her. They traveled long through the forest, which was difficult, as there were no paths that Reginleif could use, and they had to walk in wide circles around thickets through which the fairies could easily fly, but through which Reginleif would have to hack her way; Glororil had made her scabbard her sword and promise not to draw it again.

"No Valkyrie has ever seen what lies ahead," Glororil said. "You must approach with great reverence, and at its gate, you must leave all your armor and weapons behind. We approach a sacred place."

"Don't fear any fairies, their presence, or their eyes," Silvana said. "You walk to the Holy Fountain of Fairie; we'll protect you … but you must walk willingly."

As they proceeded, they passed more and more fairies, and many joined in the procession. A new song began, but it was so low, so soft and delicate that Silvana doubted if Reginleif heard it. Even the flapping of their fairy wings became a cadence for their song, which Silvana especially liked, for subtlety was prized in Alfhiem, but Reginleif was a Valkyrie; subtlety was not her strongest asset.

As they penetrated deeper into Alfhiem, always walking uphill, more fairies like Silvana and Glororil emerged. Silvana could see Reginleif's startlement; many of the older fairies took on the deeper hues of Nature: fish scales and fins, feathers of birds, and even the contours of rocks, flowers, and trees, of which some fairies actually grew tiny leaves to cover their skin. Some looked even more fantastic, like floating drops of water or flames without substance, hovering before them.

As they neared their destination, the song of the fairies became stronger, higher; *Reginleif had to hear their music by now.* As they neared the Holy Growing Palace, their song grew as loud as thunder, and then silence suddenly fell.

The Living Gate of the Fairies was made of every type of vegetable and fruit ever grown, blossoming into a single huge archway, which sprouted flowers of every imaginable shape and hue, so numerous that their edible treasures were almost buried behind the beautiful bounty of bright petals. Beyond, through the archway, lay a whole other realm, or just a small thicket; it seemed to shift before their eyes with a magic familiar to every fairy, but unknown to outsiders. Silvana knew that Reginleif was used to Yggdrasil, how some places, like Niflhiem and Valhalla, seemed too big for even Yggdrasil to contain it, but that was part of the Nature of the Great Tree, and the entire land of the Norse gods; little did the realms of Yggdrasil make sense to those who paint maps upon parchment with ink. To Silvana, it wasn't a matter of understanding, but of accepting, and if Reginleif couldn't comprehend that, then she could go no further. The Living Gate of the Fairies glowed with the promise of eternal spring, such that it shined so brightly that even mortals couldn't deny its essence, although it was a radiance of emotion more than light.

"Here you must stop," Silvana said to Reginleif. "All beyond this doorway is blessed; no Valkyrie can enter. To pass through this archway, you must accept it fully, wholly, and not be afraid. Here is the Heart of Alfhiem; everything within is pure, as you must be, if you would enter."

Reginleif glanced all about her, at the hundreds of fairies that had followed them and now danced about the living archway. Then she looked at Silvana and sighed; she nodded her head so slightly that most Valkyrie wouldn't even have noticed.

Without a word, Reginleif began to unarmor, undoing belts and tiny latches, and setting everything gently down upon the forest floor. Her sword lay upon the very bottom of her pile, and once her armor was off, Reginleif hesitated, but Glororil gave her an exasperated look, and Reginleif reluctantly continued, shedding her garments until she stood without them.

"Enter," Silvana said.

As Reginleif stepped through the archway, suddenly she gasped, covering herself with her arms, as if trying to hide her nudity, but slowly, almost imperceptibly at first, she seemed to change. She looked astounded, as if surprised by sensations unseen. Her tense muscles softened, her rigid stance smoothed, and where once nervousness had reigned supreme, now a calm such as even Roselyn had never known swept over her.

Silvana smiled, and then flew sharply into the warmth of the Living Gate of the Fairies, and the feeling that every person whom she'd ever loved was suddenly hugging her washed over everyone like a wave of welcome, of belonging, of pure shared delight. Silvana watched Reginleif's stunned expression, which flitted from joy to disbelief to orgasmic ecstasy, as if eternally cycling, too strong to be united.

Flying beside her, Silvana feared that the essence of True Fairy might be too much for Reginleif, that her companion would turn and flee back to the world of the familiar, where violence and strength dominated, but Reginleif stayed, although it couldn't be plainer that she was dazzled by the intensity of powerful feelings she'd never experienced.

"Come," Silvana said to Reginleif. "You must enter the Mere of Mab."

Reginleif turned to stare in wonderment at Silvana; where her glare had once carried pain and hate, Reginleif now effused amazement and pleasure beyond mortal understanding. Silvana was certain that she still didn't understand, like a child looking at the universe, marveling at the complexity of it, but comprehending so little that every sight glowed like an enchanting mystery. Reginleif followed Silvana, but her eyes kept darting about; colors in the Heart of Fairy were pure and clean, so that even the dull seemed to shine, and the bright blazed. The forest looked the same, but these trees were taller, gentler, reaching upwards, seemingly weightless, and perfectly smooth, as if their barks bore the surfaces of brown mirrors, without a shadow or broken branch anywhere.

Hands fell from her body; *no shame existed here, no concealment, no envy, and no regret.* This land, and everything in it, not only accepted Reginleif as she was, but disdained any change within her; this land was eternal beauty itself, and she was part of it. Behind her, fairies streamed inside by the thousands, and the whole world swarmed with sparkles of every color imaginable. Life itself seemed born anew.

Reginleif followed Silvana without hesitation, and they seemed to travel far, although Silvana knew that it could be only a few paces for Reginleif, or it could be miles; distance was a personal aspect here, not a count of steps. Finally Reginleif, or Roselyn, as she now seemed to be, came to a halt before a beautiful grotto, like a stone bowl opened out of a hillside. From the top of the small cliff came a waterfall of blue light, shining and glowing as if the sun's radiance had turned to azure droplets and showered down into a wide pool surrounded by flowers larger than shields: *the Holy Fountain of Fairie.*

Reginleif stepped forward without waiting for an invitation; Silvana smiled. Beauty, external and internal, had flowed into her, and wonder and delight held a Valkyrie in its grasp. The fairies burst into song, a triumphant, celebratory praise of all things, and Reginleif stepped down into the bowl, walked across the luxuriant grass, and stepped barefoot into the Fairy Mere of Mab.

Reginleif's reaction was strong, instantaneous, and every fairy shared her sensations. Her hands softly brushed her thighs, then rose up, lightly gracing across all that she was, reaching her shoulders, her neck, her face, and then diving into the thick mass of her wondrous hair. Every sensation of fairy pleasure and enchantment filled her, and as the warmth of the pool washed over her, every fairy felt the blue Water of Light. They were one; Silvana, Glororil, the oldest fairies, the youngest fairies, the huge blossoms, the smooth trees, the water of light, the love that they shared … and Reginleif. Delight alone existed; *all that every living thing had, or felt, or was … shared by all.*

"Bathe," Silvana said, and everyone, even Reginleif, said it with her.

Reginleif stepped deeper into the water, and its soothing essence soaked into all of them, a foaming wetness sopping even those upon dry land. The water felt perfect, coating Reginleif with affection. The pool sloped downward, and then Reginleif was engulfed; fallen deep within the Fairy Mere of Mab. Effervescent bubbles swirled around her like loving fingers, each touch a caress, as if all the universe were holding her in its adoring arms. Reginleif opened her mouth, but she didn't cough or sputter. The Water of Light beamed throughout her, and she felt transformed, a revelation of what she always could've been … but didn't know how to achieve. Reginleif became one with the light.

"Enough," said everyone. "We must return before you're overwhelmed."

The desire to remain in the water overflowed, but the desire to go was equally strong. Reginleif shined like a human lantern; she yearned to spread her light. Without question or concern, only overwhelming love for Silvana and, to her utter astonishment, for Glororil, and all of the other fairies, Reginleif rose out of the effervescent water and floated upon a cloud of contentment all the way back. A silvery light encased her, held her like a child to its mother's bosom, a comfort beyond belief; Reginleif swayed back and forth, content to stay that way forever.

As she flew out of the Living Gate of Fairy, Silvana instantly recalled the sensations of the world outside of perfection, her own uniqueness, and the singularity of all things. All was a lessening from the perfect glow of the Holy Fountain of Fairie, a diminishment even inside

Alfhiem. Yet Reginleif seemed unaware of the change, smiling widely and contentedly.

"Reginleif," Silvana said softly. "We love you."

"I love you!" Reginleif shouted.

"And you know that we'd never hurt you …," Silvana added.

Reginleif looked up at them, as if wondering why they even needed to say such a thing.

"Don't be alarmed," Glororil said.

"Alarmed …?" Reginleif laughed, as if he'd suggested the impossible.

"Reginleif, flap your wings," Silvana said.

With a bright smile, Reginleif complied, flapping her fluttering wings. Then, slowly, a look of confusion clouded her smile; *Reginleif … had … wings ….?!?*

Reginleif looked up … and her eyes seemed to refocus. Reginleif wasn't sitting on a silvery cloud; she was kneeling in Silvana's palm. She was looking up at tiny Silvana and Glororil, both so small that Roselyn had once carried them like living dolls in her hands, and now their heads loomed bigger than Reginleif's whole body. She was no bigger than Glororil's nose …!

"Love," Silvana said softly.

Reginleif's expression ranged between panic and a new awareness, as if torn between irrefutable logic and undeniable emotion.

"Peace," Glororil said. "Beauty."

Reginleif lifted her tiny hands and looked at them; they looked the same, but … smoother, younger, as if she were a child again. Yet her fingernails looked longer than before … and they were colored: bright, shiny, and dark purple, almost a deep shade of blue, but with a clearly purple hue: her fingernails looked like the petals of violets. She reached to pluck a lock of her long, chestnut hair, and lifted it to drape before her eyes; streaks of violet filled her hair. Slowly, almost reluctantly she looked behind her, and Reginleif saw large butterfly wings protruding from her back; an explosion of colorful streaks extended from her shoulder blades, of all colors, finally fading to a thick band of dark violet that ran around the edge of her wide, thin wings.

"Are you … afraid?" Silvana asked.

Reginleif looked startled by the question, then puzzled, and she glanced around uncertainly. She was tiny. She was a fairy. She was so small that, if she'd seen herself, she'd only be a small spot of light, a tiny violet glow. She'd once been huge and powerful, but strangely, she didn't miss her size or strength; she was with Silvana and Glororil, whom she trusted implicitly, even with her life. She loved them, as they loved her, and she couldn't fear what she trusted.

"She understands," Glororil said.

Suddenly another fairy, just as tiny as she was, flitted down and landed beside her, crowding Silvana's hand; it was the dark-skinned fairy, the russet fairy with brown hair, the one who'd thrown dusts into her eyes, and whom Reginleif had trapped in her mouth and threated to swallow. She seemed threatening no longer. Without waiting for an invitation, she hugged Reginleif.

"She's apologizing," Silvana said, and with that revelation, Reginleif hugged her back.

"Look up here," Glororil said to both of them, and he pointed his huge, metallic-golden finger at a white flower that grew amid the leaves above them. "Imagine what a little brown would do to that blossom."

With a sweet laugh, the russet fairy leapt into the air, zoomed to the white flower, and laid back against its softness. Then she began to spin in midair, as if her tiny bellybutton was her only fixed point, and slowly she faded, and became indistinct, a russet glow that lit the white flower with a whole new color. A light brown, like a caramel radiance, shone forth as part of the flower, imbuing it with a whole new beauty.

"We are Nature," Silvana said. "We're birth, growth, color, and texture."

"We're fairy," Glororil said. "We make the world beautiful."

Reginleif glanced from their huge faces back to the flower; now the smiling face of the russet fairy could be seen amid the brown glow over the white petals. She shined as pure light, and yet real and alive.

"Beauty," Silvana said to Reginleif. "Come; be part of the beauty."

Reginleif nodded vigorously, and then warily flexed her wings, one at a time, watching them uncertainly.

"All fairies are one," Glororil said. "You don't need to learn to fly; feel for how it's done."

For a moment, Reginleif looked skeptical, and then her wings began to flap evenly. Delight washed over all as Reginleif started to rise, and then Silvana removed her silvery hands; Reginleif floated like a butterfly, and a burst of laughter, as soft as a song, erupted from her as she watched her wings move by themselves with practiced ease; *she was flying.* With a glance upwards, Reginleif flew up to the white flower with the russet glow, and hovered before it.

"Love it," Silvana instructed. "Shine your love upon it."

Reginleif extended her tiny hands; slowly the tips of the white flower became violet, with the newly-added brown streaks streaming toward her essence, and where their colors met, the brown and violet merged beautifully on each petal … as if the flower were a magnificent work of art.

"This is only a part of fairy," Glororil said. "Come; there's more that you must learn."

Silvana and Glororil rose upon their translucent dragonfly wings, sparkling of silver and gold, and headed in another direction. Reginleif flew after them, enchanted by her newfound power to fly, and suddenly she felt a hand grasp hers; the beautiful, brown-haired russet fairy had returned, and she pulled upon Reginleif, and then spun her in the air, rolling over and over in a spiral of two lights perfectly matching.

Silvana and Glororil led them to a monstrous waterfall. At her previous size, Reginleif would have stepped across this tiny rivulet and puddle without even noticing it, perhaps even crushed it with her boots, unware of the devastation that she caused. Now it looked like a wide pool of wonder: the shining waters poured over the tall ridge. Gleaming sunlight filtered through it, refracting mesmeric rainbow colors off each bubble. The constantly-washed pebbles looked like polished gems the size of boulders, and the frail grasses that grew around the water were covered with a fine mist, nourishing and revitalizing them as they swayed in the breeze, as if even the nearby plants were intimately contented.

Playing in the water were many fairies, some even smaller than Reginleif. Some fairies darted into the huge waterfall, which splashed upon them in a strangely rhythmic way.

"What … what are they doing?" Reginleif asked.

"Listen," Silvana instructed her.

Reginleif cocked an ear, and Silvana smiled as her companion's expression changed. The tiny fairies were playing the waterfall like a musical instrument, identifying the sounds of each drop as it struck the water and rocks below, and by their depths or density, controlling the notes of the falling water, making a melody so soft and gentle that most humans never noticed it. Reginleif began softly clapping in time to the music, and several fairies joined her, adding a new beat to the melody.

"That's wonderful!" Glororil smiled, and he rose on his buzzing wings, gracefully and dramatically bowed to Silvana, and then he zipped away. A second later he returned, dancing in time with Reginleif's clapping, and then he spun in midair.

Silvana joined him in the air, and together they danced, with unbelievable grace, flitting apart as if torn asunder by terrible trials, and then rejoining with ultimate relief and gladness, as if only by being together could they ever feel happy again. Their every movement was timed to the beat that the smaller fairies clapped and the melody of the waterfall, and Reginleif's eyes alighted as she watched. As a Valkyrie, she'd never have noticed this dance, barely perceiving their movements, and dismissed them as simple flashes of light upon the surface of the moving water.

Long Silvana and Glororil danced, and each minute seemed to strengthen them both, as if their exertions, when creating wondrous beauty, sustained them more than food or sleep. Slowly they ended their dance, not with a great flourish, but descending into a gentle dive, and they landed embraced and kissing, not disturbing the music of the rising water, which the tiny fairies continued to play.

Glororil motioned that they had to go. Silvana reached down, and Reginleif lightly leapt into her hand. Then Reginleif turned to wave good-bye to all of the other fairies, and most of them, those not being splashed by a deluge of water, waved back, and the tiny dark russet fairy winked at her and blew her a kiss. Reginleif laughed, overwhelmed with delight, and then Silvana and Glororil carried her far away. Reginleif peered ahead, as if eager to see what new, amazing thing they were taking her to see.

To her astonishment, they landed not on the ground or on a plant, but upon a huge mountain of shining metal. Silvana set her down, and she walked upon the metal, stepping upon the huge, intricate designs etched into its surface. Then Reginleif turned and looked up at them both.

"Is … is this my breastplate?" Reginleif asked.

"Yes," Silvana said.

"I wear this?" Reginleif seemed doubtful. "But … these symbols: I don't remember seeing them …"

"Now you look with fairy eyes," Glororil said. "Notice what you've always, and never, seen before."

Reginleif stared around her; she was standing upon her armor, which was piled beside a tall, beautiful tree; she was smaller than the smallest ant that she'd ever seen.

"Now you must choose," Silvana said. "Will you stay a fairy … or become a Valkyrie again?"

"Fairy!" Reginleif shouted without hesitation, and her smile beamed.

"Think, before you choose," Glororil warned. "Make no important decision hastily; you're happier as a fairy, but you're not just a fairy; you're Rosie, a mortal child, born rich and carefree, unburdened with chores required to feed and house you, a state which few human children maintain for long. You are little Roselyn, a young girl, who suffered heartless indignities, her dreams crushed by her father … for his profit. You're Countess Roselyn, a woman who fought with a hand axe, and shot a young boy with a bow, who sailed away from England, became a warrior, and who braved many of the worst dangers of Yggdrasil. You're Reginleif, a Valkyrie, whom fallen mortals need to ferry them to Valhalla. You can deliver justice or mercy with the blade of your sword, and without your justice, many may suffer who don't deserve it, and many evils may thrive without you to withstand them. As a fairy, you can make great beauty, but you must abandon all other duties."

"Those whom you love will suffer," Silvana said. "Hel, in Niflhiem, knows not about Odin's decree, and Athelwynne the Seer is still missing, and without you, he may never be found. And there's Karl; *what will become of your dearest love, if you can't swoop to claim him as he dies?"*

Reginleif stared up at them, and her violet wings drooped.

"We can't choose this for you," Glororil said.

"Now you must put doubt aside," Silvana said. "You've chosen a new life many times; in the bedroom where first you saw Karl and Eric, as you faced the Wolflord in his cave, in the crumbling farmhouse where you first slept with Karl, in the Silver Swan where you found Karl making love to Eloise, in Castle Bristlen when you slept with the Seer, in the dragonship as you sailed the North Sea, when you chose to betray Hel and steal Eric, when you accepted Odin's offer to become a Valkyrie, and as you stormed out of Válaskjálf, chased by Mist. With each change of your life, you accepted the new and spurned the old; change always comes with a price. Now you must decide: will you set aside all worldly duties and accept the life of a fairy, without regret for all you've abandoned, or will you return to Valhalla, and by your sword put behind you the regrets that led you here?"

"We've given you a perspective that few ever know," Glororil said. "Whatever you chose, we'll support you, but you must decide who you really are."

"And we'll always love you, whatever you decide," Silvana said.

Reginleif looked about her, then closed her eyes and took in a deep breath.

"Is this real?" Reginleif asked. "Am I really a fairy … or is this just … enchantment?"

"Each of us chooses the world that we see," Glororil said. "Enchantment … or curse … is what we make of our lives."

"You must decide," Silvana said.

Reginleif sighed heavily, and then shrugged deeply, as if filled with deep regret. Finally, she straightened up and stiffened her tiny shoulders.

"Troll dung!" Reginleif cursed. "I understand. Change me back."

Silvana looked down at her companion and smiled; *Reginleif had learned.*

"Not yet," Glororil said with a wry grin. "As a fairy, you're not a Valkyrie; you can go anywhere, and no one will ever know."

"Where would I go?" Reginleif asked.

"Where else?" Silvana smiled knowingly.

Chapter 15

Route of Revelation

KARL

As Karl watched Reginleif and her sister Valkyries fly their magical steeds into the clouds towards Bifrost, leaving them behind, he felt relieved that she hadn't killed him … and also disappointed. Trapped in Norway, their only possible transport home was by ship; England lay seven hundred miles away, mostly over the stormy North Sea. If he survived the journey, then all his political troubles would still be there, waiting for him.

Elaina walked to the edge of her island, called to one of the many small boats on her lake, and a nearby fisherman stood in his boat, bowed deeply to her, and promised to relay her message immediately. To Karl's surprise, before leaving, the fisherman asked Elaina about the weather. Without hesitation, she informed him that no storm clouds were approaching, and he had at least a week before the next heavy rain; plenty of time to repair his leaky roof. Smiling and thanking her profusely, the fisherman sat back down and rowed off toward the outer shore.

Unsure what to do, Karl glanced at all the forested hills he could see across the wide lake. Spring came late in the Norselands. Bitterly Karl recalled the only time that he'd ventured this far north, sailing upon the North Sea, steered by Eric's ghost, only to find themselves trapped amid mountains of floating ice. Fortunately, Elaina's small island wasn't too chill; the snows had melted, and the sprouting greenery encircling her island shined with the fresh greens of new buds, which England had enjoyed a month earlier.

Entering the stone keep, Elaina's small tower seemed unusually warm. Inside her door, she led the way up three small steps to a round central hall with four thick pillars and no inner walls. A small fire burned in each of the four fireplaces set evenly around the outside walls. Ornate, colorful tapestries hung from the ceiling, covering every wall except where the fireplaces lay. Against one wall sat a raised dais, upon which rested a dark throne, yet the raised floor of the dais was covered with drums, harps, lutes, and other musical instruments. No other furniture existed, as if the whole purpose of the main hall was to provide empty space.

Elaina led them up a wooden stairs, built against one long, curved wall, to the second floor. Again, the whole second level was mostly open, with four matching fireplaces, but six long tables with benches stood in its center. Cooks and their helpers were busy in a large kitchen, which was divided from the dining area only by a series of narrow tables set tightly between the thick pillars. Wooden walls separated only one section of the kitchen into a closed room, and Karl spied kitchen servants carrying baskets of vegetables out of it.

The abundance of empty space seemed impractical.

"It's so wonderful to hold you again!" Elaina said to Eloise, pulling her into another tight hug. "I've been able to see you whenever I wanted, but … this is …!"

Words failed, and Eloise received another kiss upon her forehead.

Eloise seemed too stunned to speak, staring at her mother as if she were a beautiful illusion at risk of vanishing.

"Illaria …?" Elaina called to the kitchen workers.

"Supper ready in half an hour," a plump, elderly woman replied, pausing as she lifted a sharp sax over the onions she was mincing. "As soon as the turnips are softened, we'll put on the fish."

"Wine for our guests …?" Elaina called.

"Erica set it out, and Troy and Grim went to pick flowers," Illaria said.

Elaina led them to the tables, upon which was set a large bowl of water with a hefty chunk of ice floating amid three bottles of wine. Rafe helped Seren to sit at the table, and Elaina, Eloise, and Karl joined them.

"Astrid!" Elaina called, and a young girl no older than Edith came bouncing down the stairs from the level above, paused as soon as her head was cleared, and leaned over the rail. "Astrid, pack my clothes …!"

"No!" Astrid's bright young face suddenly contorted with a frown.

"Do it now … and we'll talk later," Elaina said.

Looking as if her dreams were crushed, Astird stomped back up the stairs. Everyone glanced at Elaina curiously.

"She doesn't want me to leave," Elaina said. "Most don't. We've had a wondrous life here …"

"When do we go?" Rafe asked.

"Shortly after dawn," Elaina said. "I knew that you'd come today, but not at which hour, so I had to plan accordingly."

"Leave home forever?" Seren asked.

"Castle Bristlen is my home," Elaina said. "This was the tower of Skafti, whom you slew eight years ago. Of course, it was grim and frightful then, but we … scrubbed all that we couldn't replace. I only saved his scrolls; the rest of his tools we burned or threw into the lake."

"I must see …," Eloise began.

"They're packed and coming with us," Elaina told Eloise.

"Won't miss Norway?" Seren asked.

"I'll miss my friends," Elaina said. "Well, they're really my servants, but I don't think of them that way."

"Who pays for all this?" Karl asked.

"King Ólafr Haraldsson," Elaina said.

"Why?" Karl asked.

"I promised to make him a saint," Elaina smiled.

"Only God can make someone a saint!" Rafe scowled.

"Most certainly," Elaina smiled at Rafe. "God will make King Ólafr a saint… but there's no harm in letting him think that I have a hand in it."

"How …?" Rafe began.

"We've more pressing concerns than King Ólafr," Karl interrupted.

"Actually, we don't," Elaina said. "King Ólafr is providing ships to carry us to England, and he's waiting been waiting a long time to meet you … tomorrow … in Oslo."

Elaina and Eloise spontaneously hugged again.

Dinner was magnificent, and every servant sat crowded around them, as if they were all one family. No one bowed or showed Elaina elaborate gestures of respect, as if she were simply the head of the household, not a baroness or a powerful sorceress. Elaina told Eloise several stories about Eric and Svenson Two-Sword that made everyone laugh, and she was delighted by their news that the two of them were best friends in Valhalla.

"Skafti saved me from both Eric and Svenson," Elaina said. "Eric wooed me, and Svenson offered to marry me, but Skafti warned me that Eloise was sure to hear about it, if I became a queen, and that she'd come seeking me."

"I would have ...!" Eloise insisted.

"Actually, Svenson was already married ... and looking for a way to escape his first wife," Elaina said. "Much to his dislike, I practically forced my company upon Skafti, as only he could tell me what was happening to Eloise. Against his will, I followed him to this island, and slowly I ... learned."

"Can you transport us back to England without sailing?" Karl asked.

"Only gods have gifts like that," Elaina said.

"Only God ...," Rafe said, and no one bothered to refute him.

After dinner, of which little food remained, they left the dishes upon the tables and returned to the main level, fetching several benches, which Karl and Rafe insisted on helping to carry. Several vases of fresh flowers now sat upon the dais, and one old man went to each of the fireplaces and added more wood. Karl thought that the hall was already too warm. He was starting to sweat, when Elaina picked up a harp and sat upon her throne. A bench was set upon each side of her, but only Karl, Eloise, Rafe, and Seren sat upon them. Eight others, mostly the older servants, sat upon the edge of her dais and picked up a musical instrument. The others removed all their shawls and scarves, and then stood still … as if waiting.

Elaina strummed a spritely jingle, and within seconds all of the other musicians began playing to match her tune. Each was a masterful musician, and they laughed as they played, stealing familiar glances back and forth. The trumpet played soft, as Karl had never heard one played before, and the pipers whistled shrill notes equal to it. The drums beat a steady rhythm, and the other harps sprung to life under talented fingers. Apparently these musicians played together often, and Elaina's tower sang out with beautiful melodies.

More amazing, with the first note, all of the other servants began to sway, back and forth, in time with the music. Most closed their eyes, as if concentrating on nothing but the flow of the tune, and slowly they began to step in time. Within a minute, each was dancing, fluttering about, circling the pillars, and cavorting with a freedom and innocence as if none were watching, waving their arms and kicking the air with barely-controlled motions, flitting with complete abandon.

Karl sat stunned, wondering if this was what these people did every night. Each danced with grace, even those of excessive girth or age. The men danced with no less skill than the women, and the few children leapt and spun endlessly, as if they could float like clouds.

Of the companions, only Seren laughed and clapped her hands. Rafe looked astounded, Eloise confused, and Karl didn't know what to think. These musicians and dancers seemed … exuberant, not exhausted as most in Castle Bristlen did after a hard day's work. They played and danced … fearlessly, as if in defiance of the world he knew.

Karl glanced about, noticing something else … not one weapon was visible. No spears rested beside the door, whose brace lay on the floor beside it, as if unused. Other than the cooking utensils, the only weapons Karl had seen here were his and Rafe's swords. No axes hung over the fireplaces, no blades of any kind graced the walls … and no one seemed to be a guard. Even in Demril, no one was this careless about safety, not even the priests in the church.

Yet nothing dulled the delight of the musicians or the dancers. Their smiles beamed, their bright, wide eyes showing no trace of weariness, and each moved as if they'd just risen from their beds.

Over an hour this lasted, until the other musicians slowly silenced their instruments and Elaina alone played. The dancing took a serious change, the movements grew slower and more precise, such that hands seemed to slice through the air rather than wave, and toes stabbed rather than kicked. The slow dancing, balanced beyond belief, and the music of Elaina's harp, rose to a crescendo of artistry, and as Elaina plucked her last notes, the dancers flowed into stances so still and rigid that each could have been turned to stone.

An eruption of applause broke out. Musicians praised the dancers, and the dancers applauded the musicians. Seren rose to her feet, applauding all, and Karl, Rafe, and Eloise joined her. All seemed delighted, and Elaina almost glowed.

"My friends, that was wonderful," Elaina said. "You all know how heavy my heart will be tomorrow, but tonight is a celebration of all the joy we've shared these many years. Tomorrow night, this shall be Úlfhildr's tower, and all shall be as our time together has been, except that I must return, with my daughter, to the land of my birth. I'll miss each of you, but I'll walk proudly, knowing that I'll carry a part of each of you in my heart forever … and it's not like we won't be able to look in on each other from time to time …"

A chuckle rose around the hall, but it was halfhearted. Every face seemed sad. One by one, each servant came forward, and Elaina rose and hugged each long and sorrowfully, and Karl didn't once doubt the sincerity of any hug … or the many whispered words and tears.

Many servants introduced themselves. Especially they all wanted to meet Eloise. All were friendly, and soon Eloise was being regaled with stories about her mother … and how much they were all going to miss her.

Finally someone nudged Karl, and he turned to see Rafe nod at the back wall, and Karl slipped backwards out of the conversation, leaving Eloise to listen to more praises of her mother. They found a stone stairs under the wooden one, and descended into the dungeon under Skafti's tower … all eight steps. In the light beaming in from above, they found themselves on a small, low-roofed stone platform looking down at a flooded basement. On the flagstones beside the wall lay several fishing poles.

"Convenient," Karl smiled. "They can fish in winter."

"Crazy," Rafe said. "Look, this is the end, right?"

"I assume so," Karl said. "The Valkyrie have their answers, and they're gone. Roselyn can find the Seer; they don't need us anymore."

"They could've dropped us at home," Rafe said. "We did solve their mystery."

"We're only human," Karl said.

Rafe gave Karl a knowing glance, and both understood.

"Do you trust Vikings to take us home?" Rafe asked.

"What choice do we have?" Karl asked.

"I won't rest easy until I stand upon Christian ground," Rafe said.

"You'll have a lot to do back home," Karl said.

"If I find one monument to the Valkyrie …!" Rafe warned.

"Don't worry; we're done with them … again," Karl promised Rafe. "When we get home, you can consecrate and bless Castle Bristlen. Host a big ceremony to purge all of the presence of pagans. We'll host a feast to celebrate the cleansing, make it a big deal … invite the whole barony …"

"And what about Eloise?" Rafe asked.

"If you can find a way to control her, I welcome it," Karl said.

The dawn arose bright, the sky shining, and they finally emerged from Elaina's tower. Tearful farewells rained upon Elaina, but she formally transferred rulership of the island and tower to Úlfhildr, a stern-faced older woman with long gray hair but youthful eyes, and Úlfhildr instantly took charge; she commanded the servants not to make Elaina's departure sad.

Two small boats stood waiting, each oared by a fisherman, and Eloise, Seren, and Elaina took one, and Karl and Rafe boarded the other, carrying a heavy chest of Elaina's belongings. Úlfhildr led her servants in a high-pitched, solemn lament to mark Elaina's departure, and Elaina, Seren, and Eloise waved to them the whole way across the lake.

Swiftly they were rowed to the far shore and disembarked before a mounted guard. Ten grim Norsemen met them, amid many horses, two of which were rigged to a large, two-wheeled carriage. Each warrior looked like Eric had when they'd first seen him, gruff, rugged, and garbed in furs, steel swords hanging from wide, brass-bossed belts. One Norsemen bowed respectfully to Elaina, and assisted her, Eloise, and practically lifted Seren atop the open conveyance, behind which they loaded the chest. The other warriors looked askance at Elaina, with distrustful glares, and strongly reminded Karl of how the citizens of Madrone averted their eyes and made signs against evil whenever the Seer walked through their streets.

Saddled horses were provided for Karl and Rafe, who mounted with ease, still listening to the chorus of singers on the small island. From the two-wheeled carriage, the women waved back as they rode off, but Karl kept his eyes forward, wondering where they were being escorted … and why.

An hour they rode through a beautiful countryside, thick forests with many streams and small lakes, and wide, hilly farms plowed and being planted. Then they rode through several small towns, none larger than Demril, and finally they entered a huge city adjacent to the Bay of Oslo. Buildings uncounted covered every hill, and crowds filled the streets, moving aside as they rode through. Again Karl noticed that many townsfolk pointed at Elaina as she rode in the open carriage, and numerous gestures to ward off evil were made … including the sign of the cross.

Their escort led them to a tall building of a crude sort, walled with clay, but roofed with cedar, whereas most of their buildings were roofed with sod. They dismounted before a small crowd of Norse warriors, whose glowers radiated contempt, yet they evidenced no hostility. The crowd parted, and Elaina led their way inside.

The hall was all one room, filled with warriors, most resting upon benches or sitting upon thick furs before low tables, with a few standing. A firepit burned in the center, wafting the smoke out of a large hole in the ceiling. On the far side of the firepit sat a half-circle of six tall-backed thrones.

"Elaina!" called a deep voice, and a huge, heavily-bearded man pushed himself up out of the largest throne.

"King Ólafr Haraldsson!" Elaina said loudly, and she gracefully curtseyed.

As they greeted each other, Karl spied more wardings against evil gestured throughout the hall. Despite his girth, the king bowed to her.

"Rex Perpetuus Norvegiae!" Elaina proclaimed.

"Latin names will never thrive in my lands," King Ólafr said.

"Your descendants will forever praise Norway's Eternal King," Elaina said.

"Today the king weeps," King Ólafr said. "Unwillingly I let you depart."

"Úlfhildr will advise you well, and warn you before your armies sail into storms, or when your enemies gather," Elaina said.

"Hard shall it be for any witch to prove worthy to take your place," King Ólafr said. "Elaina, I shall miss you … *dearly*."

"You needed a Norse wife to bear you Norse sons," Elaina said. "As always, I placed your needs before mine." King Ólafr started to object, but Elaina raised a hand. "A king is a fool who places wants above needs."

King Ólafr sighed.

"For your many years of faithful service, I allow you to depart," King Ólafr said. "Your ships are ready, three ships, which sail with the dawn. Tonight, you must dance for me one last time."

Elaina nodded deeply.

"First, I bring to you those I spoke of … whom I myself witnessed fly to my island upon the winged steeds of the Valkyrie."

"My guards witnessed their magical arrival and hurried to tell me yesterday," King Ólafr said. "Never more foolish have I been, to not be there to greet four Valkyrie. Never again will I doubt you, Elaina, hostess of Odin's shield-maids."

"I bid you welcome my guests, especially Karl, whose elevation to einherjar is assured," Elaina promised. "Hear his tale, and the proofs of our gods."

King Ólafr came forward and shook hands with Karl and Rafe, and bowed as politely as his immense girth allowed to Eloise and Seren. Then he called for jeweled horns of mead to be brought forward, which he gifted to each of the companions, and called for his men to heed Karl and his tale of their journey to Yggdrasil.

Karl obliged, and Elaina translated, telling their story from the beginning. To his surprise, Eloise, Seren, and Rafe were seated in the thrones beside King Ólafr, and two thrones were left empty … for him and Elaina. The whole hall sat silent through their early adventures, but applauded long and loudly when they slew the illusion-casting giant, and thus caused the death of Skafti, Svenson Two-Sword's wizard, who had made the prophesy that had torn Eloise's mother from her beloved daughter. Karl waited patiently for the applause to die down, wondering what Skafti had done to make his own people hate him so.

Only once did a Norseman scoff at Karl's story, when Karl explained how Eloise transformed into the Wolfqueen, which saved them from the zombies of Grusshire. Karl couldn't understand King Ólafr's words as he shouted the man down.

Rapt attention was then paid to the rest of their story, and when Karl finished, Elaina translated his last line, and the hall burst into cheers. King Ólafr pounded the arm of his throne with a meaty fist, and then lifted his horn to Karl.

"Never has so great a tale been told in my hall!" King Ólafr said. "I honor the speaker, and those who travelled with him, for Elaina the Far-Seeing has vouched for these strangers, and the truth of their tale, and her words I hold as vouchsafed as my own."

King Ólafr called for meat, and huge platters of cooked mutton and fouls, still steaming, were carried into the hall. A wide table was set before King Ólafr and piled with food before a single morsel was set upon the lower tables in the hall. Without ceremony, King Ólafr reached for a spiced leg of lamb, but Rafe stopped him.

"May we pray before eating?" Rafe asked.

King Ólafr paused, then nodded.

"Strange indeed are days when followers of Christ bring witness to the Gods of Asgard," King Ólafr said. "We are a kingdom of two faiths, and welcome respects to all."

Rafe spoke a long prayer in Latin, during which Karl spied many furtive glances exchange between the warriors of the hall, and even King Ólafr seemed impatient to eat. Yet all waited, and when Rafe concluded, they resumed as if he hadn't said a thing. Rafe looked displeased, but Karl gave Rafe a knowing glance, and Seren took Rafe's arm to further restrain him; no victory could be gained by arguing against pagans in a hall of Norse warriors.

After dinner, which was a crude, slovenly affair, where only meat was consumed and bones were hurled over heads into the fire with many a laugh while barrels of ale were emptied. All ate their fill, and more meats were constantly carried in. Finally, Elaina stood and stepped forward.

Elaina alone circled the firepit, her arms raised, and cheers burst from all the warriors. King Ólafr clapped his hands, twice, three times, and then every Norseman in the hall began clapping in unison with him. Some drew daggers and pounded on the tables with their pommels, matching the rhythm of their king's claps.

To Karl's amazement, Elaina suddenly kicked one foot high above her head without bending her back, with practiced ease, and then she began to dance. Karl had been impressed with the dancing of the servants in Elaina's tower, but none equaled the artistry of Elaina. She pranced and cavorted like a carefree child, as if Eloise were her mother, and yet with skills no youth could match. She spun so fast that her long yellow hair trailed behind her, a blur before the flickering flames, and she leapt around the firepit with a grace that only Titania, Freyja, and the Lady of the Druids had ever evidenced. Only once had Karl witnessed dancing this perfect, in the fairy glade with the Seer's master, and then he'd been fighting for his life. He sat astounded, watching the older woman display a nimbleness and flexibility that he'd never been capable of, not even as a youth.

Every warrior cheered as they clapped, entranced by Elaina's gyrations. Karl sat mesmerized, and when she finished her dance, with a backbend that would have snapped Karl's spine, King Ólafr and every warrior in the hall jumped to their feet and applauded, cheering as loudly as they could.

King Ólafr approached Elaina, bowed deeply, and then stepped forward and hugged her tightly, and she wrapped her arms as far around him as she could reach.

"I will miss you forever," King Ólafr said to Elaina.

"In another world, you would've been a good husband," Elaina said to King Ólafr, and they kissed long, and the warriors cheered louder.

Eloise gaped, shocked.

Two small, sod roofed houses were provided for the night, one for Karl, Eloise, Rafe, and Seren, and a separate house for Elaina. Eloise objected, but Elaina took Eloise into her arms, kissed her cheek, and promised to rejoin her in the morning. With a loving smile, she departed for the night.

The next morning, King Ólafr personally escorted them to the shore of Oslo Bay, where countless ships bobbed, tied to docks. Two held a dozen warriors each, and the other ship held sailors that spoke both English and Norse, who would sail them home. King Ólafr ordered the execution of each warrior and sailor, should anything happen to Elaina upon her voyage to England, and never was any tone so gruff and serious. At last, Elaina and King Ólafr kissed again, a slow, deep, passionate kiss. When they broke, without a word, Elaina turned to the ships and was assisted aboard, followed by Seren, Rafe, Karl, and a wide-eyed, flabbergasted Eloise.

Chapter 16

Into the darkness

GLORORIL

"Reginleif, wake up," Glororil said softly.

Slowly she stirred, shaking her head.

"What happened?" Reginleif asked.

"The russet fairy put you to sleep again," Glororil said. "It's been two days …"

"Two days …?"

"Almost three," Glororil said.

"Why is it so dark … and what's that horrible smell?" Reginleif asked.

'You've smelled it more than we have," Glororil said.

"It's Niflhiem," Silvana said. "We've brought you here against your will, so that Odin can't blame you."

"Yet we dare not enter the Land of Death alone," Glororil said. "I once blinded Hel … and dropped a house on her and her father; Hel might not welcome my presence."

"Niflhiem …?" Reginleif yawned, lifted her head, and looked out; in the misty distance stood the bridge over the river Gjoll and the tall, dismal Gate of Iron Skulls. Then Reginleif looked at her violet fingernails and glanced over her shoulder to see butterfly wings. "I'm still a fairy."

"We couldn't carry you otherwise," Glororil said. "Nor would it be wise to change back now; as a fairy, you can travel secretly."

"Where's Hel?" Reginleif said.

"In her hall, we assume," Silvana said. "Perhaps … you should lead the way …?"

After she fully awoke, Reginleif flew up; she'd been in Glororil's palm, but the dark of Niflhiem was so pervasive that she couldn't tell. They'd been hiding in the shadows near the edge of a stony outcropping, inside in a crevice. Reginleif flew toward the gate, much slower than the other fairies could fly, and Silvana followed her closely. Glororil trailed behind them.

With disgust, Glororil looked out upon Niflheim; *this was the most horrible realm in Yggdrasil.* All that he could see was barren rocks and dirt … and not one trace of life. In his opinion, the only value of death was that new life could sprout from its remains, but in Niflhiem, decay was eternal. *Hel's realm was an abomination;* it should be wiped clean and left fallow, with the hope that it could be reclaimed. Even in Valhalla, where death permeated, rebirth came every evening. In Niflhiem, nothing was ever reborn. Just being near Niflhiem made Glororil feel sick, and its vile stench only made it worse.

They flew over icy Gjoll, its flowing surface covered with a chill blue mist, passed through the eye-holes of a giant skull in the gate, and winged over the barren wastes of its interior. Niflhiem was flat, looking like a jagged rock pile that every giant in Jontunhiem had crushed beneath their feet. The last time that he'd been here, he and Silvana had been safely encased in Titania's crystal talisman, and had been spared the worst of the smell, although the likelihood that they'd end up being digested inside Garm or Nidhogg had terrified them. Glororil had never desired to ever return to this haunted, reeking land, but Titania had ordered them to protect Roselyn and Athelwynne, and while he could've claimed that they were no longer bound by her commands, Silvana still thought of their companions as friends, and whatever was important to Silvana, Glororil would see done.

"*Attack* …!" cried a shrill voice.

A thousand corpses, fully-armored and armed, rose from the empty plain beneath them; they'd been lying down and covered in rocks and dust, an entire army of death sleeping in shallow graves, waiting to ambush invaders. Silvana grabbed Reginleif and flew high as several long blades slashed at them. Glororil put on a burst of speed and easily dodged three arrows shot at him; he whizzed over their heads and caught Silvana's hand, pulled her even higher, and together they flashed over the unexpected army of deadmen, and soared towards Eljudnir. More dead warriors arose, rising armored corpses, to brandish weapons at the fleeing fairies.

In the center of the roof, between the bonfires burning on each of its four towers, a wide hole in the roof of Hel's hall, which served as a chimney, allowed them easy access, and the fairies flew in through it to escape the last few arrows shot at them.

"*You* …!" Hel shouted angrily.

Glororil separated, releasing Silvana's hand and flying off in another direction, determined to keep Hel's attention on him. Hel was a half-goddess; her gaze was so potent that it could easily kill a fairy, if it focused upon them. Glororil gave her no chance; he flew as fast as he could, visible only as a streak of golden sparkles. Yet Hel's gaze was greater than he'd expected: bursts of fire filled the air behind him, consuming his sparkles to ash.

"Reginleif . . . !" Silvana screamed. *"We brought Reginleif . . . !"*

The midair fires chasing Glororil slowed, and then faded to small clouds of black smoke. Hel turned her gaze upon tiny Silvana, who was hovering, holding her hands closed, tightly pressed against her silvery chest.

"Where's Reginleif . . . ?" Hel demanded, withholding her powerful gaze.

"Right here," Silvana said, flying closer. "We turned her into a fairy, but she can undo the magic anytime that she wants."

Hel looked doubtful. Silvana opened her hands, and a minuscule violet light rose from her, floating down before Hel. Hel was sitting upon her throne, wearing only a thick black robe, and a trail of blood led from her skeletal feet, which were still dripping gore, to her golden pool, where she'd apparently been bathing. Glororil frowned; *Hel had to bathe in blood every day to keep her dead legs supple.*

Hel held out her hand, and Reginleif slowly settled into it.

"Reginleif . . . ?" Hel asked.

"Hel!" Reginleif smiled and waved brightly. "I bring news about Athelwynne!"

Hel looked startled.

"She's a fairy, lost in our joy," Silvana said.

Hel frowned, and looked upon Reginleif with suspicion.

Warily Glororil flew closer; he still didn't trust Hel, but Silvana had flown down to the level of Hel's head, and protecting her was his foremost duty. They hovered before Hel, but she kept her gaze upon Reginleif, who told her everything, even about how Silvana and Glororil had made her into a fairy and brought her to Niflhiem.

"… and I didn't even know that I could change myself back," Reginleif finished with a glance back at Silvana.

"Don't do it yet," Glororil said. "As a Valkyrie, you can't enter Mistyhel …"

"No one enters Mistyhel … and comes out," Hel said. "I've tried many times, even chained a hundred of my subjects together and sent them in one at a time … something inside there pulled them all in, and not one ever returned."

"Never …?" Silvana asked.

"I could hear them scream, but not for long," Hel said. "Something interferes with my control over them; the instant that they enter that accursed cave, I can no longer control them … see through their eyes or hear their thoughts. I've tried a dozen times, and lost over a thousand subjects, trying to penetrate the mystery of those cold mists … and never succeeded."

"But Athelwynne may be in there …!" Reginleif argued.

Hel shook her head.

"I miss him terribly," Hel said to Reginleif. "I don't want to miss you, too."

Glororil raised his golden eyebrows; Hel's voice was twisted with grief, and although she was trying to hide it, no fairy could fail to sense it. *He hadn't thought that Hel was capable of love …!*

"We'll go with her," Silvana said.

"And come back out again," Glororil insisted.

"It's suicide," Hel said.

"Fairies don't die," Glororil said.

"Never," Silvana agreed.

"You're not immortal," Hel argued.

"All things are immortal," Silvana said. "Even you, great Hel, were once a child, and if you could travel forward in time, then you'd find yourself there, even if you're consumed by Ragnarrock. Death can't undo existence."

"Time is unimportant to fairies," Glororil said. "We're all a part of the beauty of the universe, and someday we'll pass into another form, but we'll still be beautiful, just in a different way."

"The Seer was our friend, too," Silvana said. "If we can find him, then we will."

"Will you risk your lives for the hope of finding him?" Hel asked.

"Fear has no place in love," Glororil said. "We're not ready to transform yet, but we don't fear the inevitable."

"Believe them," Reginleif said. "I didn't … but I do now."

Hel held them long in her gaze, looking skeptical.

"Very well," Hel said. "I'll take you to the entrance to Mistyhel, but I can't enter; the madness of the Norns would consume me."

"I believe you," Reginleif said. "I met the Norns."

"We have one problem," Glororil said. "We couldn't carry Reginleif's armor or weapon; when she returns to her Valkyrie form, she'll be naked and unarmed."

"I can remedy that," Hel said. "Yet I can't travel to Mistyhel alone; we'll have to wait."

Hel brought out a bowl of golden apples, which kept both humans and the gods young, but to fairies, they were just a delicious treat. Hel cut off a tiny sliver of apple for each of them, but while the violet light of

Reginleif approached hers, Silvana and Glororil sat down upon the table and only stared at theirs.

"Do you not want yours?" Hel asked.

"We're not ready to eat," Glororil said.

"Don't be offended … or think that your hospitality is unwanted," Silvana said quickly. "Before fairies eat, we sit, sometimes for hours, to anticipate the tastes that we hope to enjoy."

"Fairies savor each bite, some so flavorful that we only need one," Glororil said. "Long anticipation makes the food taste better, and prevents us from growing heavy, which would spoil flying."

"Fairy chefs are the best in Yggdrasil," Silvana said. "And, as fairies eat so little, a single meal can feed thousands."

"If you intend to eat, then you must do so soon," Hel said. "My cavalry approaches, and they ride quickly."

Glororil glanced at Silvana, shrugged, and both picked up their tiny sliver of apple, having to use both hands to lift their portions, while Reginleif knelt atop her slice and took bites out of it, as it was many times larger than she was. Glororil took a moment to prepare, tried to clear his thoughts and anticipate what he was about to taste, and then he slowly bit into his apple slice; it was delicious, juicy and tangy. His first bite was delightful, firm and yet delicate, with a sweetness that only Nature could create, and brimming with the essence of life. He relished the incomparable taste as it swept through him, as it had done each time before when he'd tasted a golden apple. Yet the rancid, horrid smell of Niflhiem soured the taste, and in the end, ruined it. He thought about making a rude comment about the smell, but he was being treated as a guest by the Goddess of Death, and didn't think it appropriate to infuriate her again.

A distant rumbling slowly grew louder, and then it became thunderous, and the ground shook. Hel glanced at her wide doors, and slowly they opened of their own accord. Into Hel's hall rode seven terrifying warriors. Silvana screamed, and even Glororil flew backwards, horrified.

Hel's cavalry were her oldest subjects, rotted until almost nothing remained except putrid bits of dried, ragged flesh hanging upon ash-blackened skulls. Their empty eye sockets burned like smoldering red coals, and skeletal hands gripped the black leather reins of horses free of any trace of flesh, animated skeletons of powerful mounts, as dead as everything else in Niflhiem. Yet their raiment bore no trace of their festering appearance; their armor was spotless, magnificent bands of dyed leather with fantastically etched gold and silver buckles, and mail of the finest kind, welded and polished until each link shined. Red fox and ermine trimmed their collars and shoulders, finely brushed, adding a colorful flourish to their ghastly appearance. Each bore a long black lance, and an inverted teardrop shield, each shield bearing a realistic image of the beautiful face of Hel, their mistress and commander.

As one, every lance rose in salute.

"It's time to go," Hel said. "But first, we must gather that which Reginleif will need."

Hel led them all to a tall, thin wardrobe beside her bed, which was buried in dust and cobwebs. She waved a hand and its door opened, and the firelight brightly illuminated what lay inside.

Gleaming as if newly forged, the most elegant and stylish suit of armor ever made shined before them. Tall, topped with a sleek helmet boasting a single ridge of long steel spines reaching from the forehead to the back, the armor was black, but so shiny that the red of the firelight reflected upon it. Under the stylish, upturned shoulder caps protruded a rounded breastplate that few women could fill, and hanging from it was a thin waist of tiny black scales, each shaped like a grinning skull, which extended beyond a wide, ornate belt to form a skirt to mid-thigh. Slender metal arms and legs dangled from its stand, and each looked impervious. The aspect of the whole suit was designed to strike anyone seeing it with both awe and terror.

"Did you think that I'd face Ragnarrock in my red dress?" Hel asked sarcastically.

Beside the armor rested a magnificent sword. Not a sword designed to hang upon a belt; the mirror-finished blade, reflecting the firelight, was four feet long, and its wide golden guards crossed a handle that reached a foot and a half, balanced by a silver pommel shaped like a miniature head of Garm, Hel's giant wolf pet.

"Bring my armor and sword, and some of my thickest clothes," Hel instructed her cavalrymen. "We ride to Mistyhel."

Her riders saluted again, and then dismounted. Hel swept past them, reached another wardrobe, and pulled from it a thick, long coat of sable fur, which she slid on over her robe. Then she led them outside, and Glororil realized why the approach of the cavalry had been so loud; outside of Eljudnir, the wide plain was now covered with a thousand riders, each an identical copy of the seven age-blackened skeletons that had entered Hel's hall, a legion of mounted dead, and one steed greater than any other. This steed was fifteen feet tall and twenty feet long, a monstrous skeleton with short arms and a long boney tail, like a dragon, but Glororil's eyes fixated on its massive skull and giant teeth. This huge, walking assortment of massive bones turned to stare at them with a gleam in its reptilian eye sockets like emerald fire, the hottest twin embers that ever burned, and Glororil noticed a vast black blanket draped upon its back, beneath a huge saddle decorated with slashes of red and gold.

Hel walked fearlessly toward this reptilian skeletal giant. Eight guards stood before it, holding up a gold-carpeted ramp, upon which Hel could ascend to mount it. Glororil cupped tiny Reginleif in his hand and followed Silvana, who stayed right behind Hel, as she carefully stepped up the ramp and mounted her dragonish steed.

"*Mistyhel!*" Hel commanded, and her cavalry burst into a charge.

Hel's cavalry raced faster than any that Glororil could remember, the skeletal horses clearly the equal of the white horses of the Lady, which had carried the companions to Valhalla eight years ago. Hel's dragony mount kept pace, its huge, clawed feet running in steps wider than any horse's, making the ground shake as each monstrous clawed-foot hammered upon the rocky plain, lost amid the thunder of the countless hooves of the vast skeletal cavalry. Glororil and Silvana easily kept pace with them, beating fast their dragonfly wings, but Glororil had to close his fingers over Reginleif, whose violet butterfly wings would be instantly blown backwards by the foul winds whipping past them.

The dead cavalry rode across the rocky plains of Niflhiem, and the permeating stink of the rotting land seemed to grow stronger. Long they galloped, and yet their morbid mounts displayed no evidence of tiring.

The air grew colder as they traveled, and the ground beneath them became frosted. Soon flecks of snow filled the air, and piles of white gathered upon the icy rocks, growing thicker as they progressed, until the cavalry was plowing through deep drifts of frozen tundra. Large snowflakes began impeding Glororil's flight, and he and Silvana were forced to dodge around thick boulders of snow kicked into the air by Hel's steed. The distant lights of the Fires of Niflheim dimmed as they left Hel's hall far behind them, mile after mile, but their path glowed from the fires of the red eyes of the cavalry and their steeds, and the bright emerald glare of Hel's horrific mount.

Suddenly they were enveloped in thick, blinding mists. Only the brightness of the fiends' eyes showed their direction, and Glororil banked toward Silvana, reached out, and touched her hand; as he'd expected, she was shivering, only her exertions, flying so fast, had kept her from collapsing in the frigid waste. Silvana was always too cold, but Glororil, buoyed by his sunny nature, was never bothered by temperature; he let a trifle of his intense heat run along his arm into Silvana, who instantly stopped shivering; until they left these frozen lands, he'd have to stay close to her.

The chill grew worse; soon they entered an area too cold for snow, the ground lay encased in glacier. Their destination wasn't much farther, and Glororil was relieved when the entire cavalry of Hel finally slowed to a skittery stop upon the snow-covered ice. The air was so thick with fog that Glororil heard, more than saw, Hel's eight guards come running up to her with the same gold-carpeted ramp, and braced it against her skeletal dragon so that she could dismount.

As soon as she reached the dark, mist-hidden ground, thick with ice, Hel held out her hand, and upon the snow burst forth a great fire; a bonfire burning pure air. The sudden light was blinding, and the mists drove back, as if abhorrent to the alien heat.

"Behold Mistyhel," Hel said.

The retreated mists revealed a great pit, a black circle fifty feet in diameter, out of which all of the icy mist seemed to be seeping. It lay surrounded by a vast flat escarpment of ice; spewing an airy gush of white fog from deep within.

"What can you tell us about it?" came a tiny voice from inside Glororil's hand.

Glororil released Reginleif, who flew upwards towards Hel.

"Very little," Hel said to Reginleif. "This pit slopes down to single point, a cavernous entrance which is so small that some mortals must squeeze through it, and from there it slopes down, and the cold grows more intense. Snow falls inside it, so I assume that there must be a large cavern or tunnel in there, but beyond that, no subject of mine has ever returned to report; all have vanished without a trace."

"I could make a quick reconnoiter," Glororil offered.

"Reginleif may need you," Hel said to Glororil. "I'll send ten of my guards in first; whatever fate they suffer, perhaps you'll see it before you suffer the same."

"You'll sacrifice your guards …?" Silvana asked.

"For Athelwynne, I'd sacrifice all that I own," Hel said. "And I prize Reginleif no less; if she doesn't return, then expect no welcome, if you escape."

"Don't kill my friends," Reginleif pleaded. "They came to help."

Hel held out her hand, and Reginleif settled upon it.

"Only for the sake of him whom we both love do I allow you to brave this danger," Hel said to Reginleif. "Come back to me, my dearest friend."

"I will," Reginleif promised.

Hel nodded to her guards, ten of whom had dismounted, and were carrying pieces of Hel's black armor and bundles of leather and fur. With a bow, and no visible reluctance, they stepped toward the icy edge and climbed down into Mistyhel single file. Glororil watched them descend, then looked back at Hel.

"Reginleif, Odin commanded you not to enter Mistyhel of your own free will, and I won't endanger you by asking that you to do so now," Hel said. "Let this act of defiance be my message to Odin for his death sentence upon the Seer."

Hel's hand closed upon Reginleif, drew back, and she hurled the tiny violet point of light into the dark, murky depth of Mistyhel. Glororil and Silvana glanced at each other, and then dove after Reginleif into the great vaporous pit.

Glororil's head snapped back as he entered the pit; before he reached its bottom, past where the skeletal minions of Hel were struggling to climb lower without slipping all the way down. A strange sensation passed over him, as if he were underwater, looking up, seeing only a distorted image of Hel, watching them from the edge far above. He had no recollection of ever feeling this sensation before, and it slightly reminded him of the passage through the Fairy Living Gate to the perfect reality beyond … or the 'crack in the world', through which the companions had passed to enter Yggdrasil. Somehow, Glororil knew that they weren't in Niflhiem anymore; they were entirely in Mistyhel. They seemed to have passed into another realm. *Was it possible … that they'd found another 'crack in the world'?*

And, if so, *where did it lead ...?*

"Reginleif, you must change back now," Silvana said. "You can do it: choose."

Reginleif nodded, and then she clenched her fists, extended her arms, flexed her tiny muscles … and suddenly she grew; Reginleif's wings vanished, and her violet coloring faded, and she became tall and strong again; *Reginleif the Valkyrie had returned.*

Yet Reginleif didn't stand tall; she crumpled and fell to her knees, sobbing.

"Reginleif …!" Silvana shouted.

Reginleif lifted her chin, tears streaming down her eyes.

"It's … over," Reginleif wept. "It was so beautiful, so peaceful …!"

"Don't cry," Silvana said. "Rejoice for what you've learned, and …"

"She must dress before she freezes," Glororil said, and he exuded a steady heat toward her. "Guards, hurry down here!"

Save for the hissing mists, Mistyhel was strangely silent, so much that the scraping of the boots of Hel's guards upon the ice sounded loud. Glororil looked deeper, into the thick, hissing mist pouring from the very bottom of the pit, but the noise and white vapors hid everything.

"Light won't help us here," Glororil said. "We need to see what we're facing before it sees us."

Glororil let a small amount of heat exude from his golden skin farther downward; he dared not produce too much warmth, or he'd incinerate everything, but it was enough. The gushing mists thinned. Reginleif huddled close to him, and when the guards carried their burdens down, Reginleif found that they'd brought her a loose-fitting pair of trousers and a blouse, both made of two layers of soft animal skins, thickly quilted, with a thin layer of fur on the inside. Reginleif slipped them on, along with a pair of tall black boots. These garments were made to fit Hel, who was taller than Reginleif, but they fit her well enough, and the extra material, where it bunched up, just added more padding for Hel's armor. It fit as if it'd been built for her. Reginleif seemed to gain strength from armoring, as if recovering from being a fairy, returning to her natural state as a Valkyrie.

A thick black gambeson went next, and then the heavy breastplate and skull-skirt, and finally her greaves and vambraces. Lastly she strapped on the black, spiked helmet. When she stood, resplendent in the armor of the Goddess of Death, Reginleif looked stronger and more resolute than ever. The guards handed her Hel's two-handed sword, and she took it and held it out, testing its weight.

"Beautiful," Reginleif said grimly, holding up the sword. "Whatever took Athelwynne, I hope I get to sheathe this in it."

Glororil and Silvana exchanged a worried look.

"Have no fear, for me or yourselves," Reginleif said. "I know now what true fearlessness is … and I embrace it eagerly."

With a nod, Reginleif directed Hel's skeletal guards lower, and they proceeded without hesitation. Glororil watched them go, like mindless automatons; puppets with no more thoughts than Hel allowed them.

"Slowly!" Glororil whispered. "Spread out! Single file!"

Following the guards, the three companions slipped down the icy slope. Reginleif was far more dexterous than the guards, but no longer as graceful as the fairies. They came to a passage in the very bottom, where the loud mists spewed thickly, which was so narrow that Rafe and Eric would have to squeeze through it; the thin skeletal guards easily passed through.

"Stop!" Reginleif said. "We won't be able to see them, and they make no sound; how will we know when something happens to them?"

"I don't think that they can speak," Silvana said.

"Let me by," Reginleif said, and when she reached the opening, she peered through. "I hear their footfalls; let's go in a little farther."

As they entered the blind darkness, they found themselves in a tiny, mist-streaming tunnel, sloping downward as the icy wind blew against their faces. Reginleif walked like she'd donned her Valkyrie instincts, feeling her way; they traveled a few paces at a time, and then, as their tunnel widened, she sent one guard forward ten paces, to stand and wait until they reached him. Reginleif listened closely between each interval before proceeding, wary of any sound. Leaving behind them the endless *whoosh!* of the mists escaping Mistyhel into Niflhiem, the deeper cavern was as silent as a frozen grave, and just as dark, and the thick mists blasting past blinded them even more. Their eyes were useless, and even Glororil could see nothing. He yearned to shine forth his light, or to allow Silvana to, but they didn't dare; they rode upon the shoulders of Reginleif, who walked with Hel's sword held before her, ready for anything.

They descended until the tunnel opened fully, but it was more a feeling of wind, of wide expansiveness, than any other clue. They couldn't tell how big the cavern was, or if it were just imagination and not really there. Reginleif whispered, and five of the guards went ahead, one at a time, and Reginleif listened carefully; the only sounds were a faint whisper of wind, like a gentle, constant breath, and the crunching footsteps of the morbid guards walking mindlessly over ice into the unknown. Then a sudden gust of wind arose, and a rumble echoed, like of a small avalanche of snow in the mountains, and then an unexpected deep clap, like the slamming of a great door, filled their ears. Reginleif paused, but no more sounds could be heard; the footfalls had vanished.

"Back!" Reginleif hissed. *"Go!"*

They scrambled backwards, climbing inside the tunnel by feel. After a sharp bend, Silvana released a dim glow.

"Let me go," Silvana said, hovering before Reginleif's face.

"No!" Glororil argued. "Let me …!"

"We still have five guards," Reginleif said, "but we've learned nothing from the loss of the others."

"We learned how far we can go before we disappear forever," Glororil said.

"We can't fight blindly," Reginleif said. "Silvana, you must …"

"I'll go!" Glororil insisted.

"You can't," Reginleif said. "Silvana's light lasts longer, and if she gets into trouble, then she'll need you to rescue her."

"If she cries out, then I'll go, whether you say so or not," Glororil said.

"If Silvana screams, don't wait for orders; I'll be right behind you," Reginleif said. "Silvana, anything could be out there. Fly out, illuminate, and be ready to fly back. Scream and we'll come running."

"Flying," Glororil corrected.

Silvana nodded, and seldom had Glororil seen her look more serious. He trusted her implicitly; and they knew how each other felt; Silvana loved to dance, and

Glororil danced mostly to make her happy. Silvana actually liked to wear clothes, but Glororil didn't, and he liked looking at her body so much that Silvana lived naked just to please him. Their love had lasted eons because there was no limit to what they'd do to please each other. While Glororil had no fear for himself, he worried for Silvana; if she were doomed, then whatever fate claimed her, he'd jump to be likewise claimed, that they'd share eternity together … in whatever form it took.

Silvana flew ahead in a sudden burst of sparkling trail, and then her silver-bluish moonglow lit the darkness, but only icy white mists were illuminated, offering no hope of seeing anything but more thick fog, which filled the chilly air before them and gusted from their breaths. The wind picked up again, and the loud rumble returned, and Glororil and Reginleif exchanged a worried glance.

Silvana screamed, and Glororil blasted out of the tunnel in a shower of golden sparks, trailing after her, but he had to veer; something huge blocked his way. Glororil banked, but the fog was so thick that he could see nothing but her glow in the distance, and the loud rumbling was followed by a sensation that the entire universe was moving.

Glororil let go of his reservations, and his solar nature blasted out, as if too intense to be held inside, like a soap bubble ready to pop. Sunlight and heat exploded upon the misty blindness, and the white fog suddenly retreated.

A terrible roar deafened him so painfully that he had to squeeze his hands atop his golden ears. Yet his sunlight succeeded where her moonlight had failed; Glororil spied Silvana's silver streak flashing past it at unbelievable speed, with Reginleif coming out of the tunnel into a great depression, like a wide dinner bowl, into a chamber more vast than he'd expected. The wintry nature of their enemy was revealed, all of their eyes locked on the monstrosity before them.

A huge white dragon rose, greater than any that Glororil had ever imagined: a horror of the ancient world when Yggdrasil was only a seedling. Nidhogg and the underground green sea dragon that guarded the subterranean lake were infants compared to this mammoth terror; its snow-covered head was bigger than Hel's hall, and its frosted jaws wide enough to swallow Garm whole. The white dragon reeled as the light of Glororil shined upon it, and its cavern rumbled as it thrashed, trying to orientate on the unexpected fairy lights. Glororil didn't wait for his short-lived light to die; he flew toward the ceiling as the tremendous head turned to him, roaring in anger. Great white streams burst forth as a geyser from its terrible mouth, mixed with glistening projectiles of icicles that shot towards him like crossbow bolts. Dodging, Glororil's flying skills were tested as he flew to escape the icicles, barely missed by their frozen points, which flew around him like a spray of daggers.

Glororil reached the edge of the mist; if he flew into it, then he'd be blinded by fog. Instead, he dove, flashing past a mouth the size of a small canyon, with teeth thicker than trees. His own light had failed, but by the glow of Silvana's moonlight, he could see that she was safe, flying free around to the back of the dragon. To his horror, Reginleif had reached the edge of the bowl, running as swiftly as she could.

Without hesitation, Reginleif jumped, sword-first, at the monstrous dragon's shoulder, which was the size of a large hill. She struck its hard, moving surface and stabbed Hel's sword deep into it, but the great frost dragon didn't even seem to notice; Reginleif struggled to pull her sword from the frosty-white shoulder, and then the great dragon's head turned, just as her blade wrenched free; Reginleif tumbled off its massive, frosted shoulder, unable to grip anything solid, and plummeted out of sight.

Shining no longer, Glororil dove. Silvana's gentler glow was flashing as she whirled around and around the massive dragon's head, alternating shadows in the cave between her shining moonlight and the deep shadow of the dragon eclipsed. No longer driven back by the heat, the intense fog, spewing from the roaring mouth of the white dragon, filled the empty space, and darkness resumed.

Glororil dove blindly into the mist, but he flew straight into something hard and icy, although if it was a rocky ledge or a giant icy scale of the dragon, he never knew. He had to see, and dangerous as it was, Glororil again exploded with light and even more heat than before, opening himself to more attacks, revealing all the brightness and heat that he dared, all that he could without risking cooking Silvana and Reginleif. Yet he'd already shined once; each effort was draining, and he hadn't fully recovered. Yet he held on; again the mists were expelled, driven back, and he spied a recent swath in the snow, a gash broken through the crusty white, and even as the dragon roared again, he followed the track downwards as his light began to fail, heedless of his own safety. The white dragon's head was turning to face him, but he could move no faster.

Suddenly Silvana was beside him; she grabbed his hand and pulled, and as they veered away, a heavy blast of vapor and thick icicles shot past, nearly engulfing them both. Glororil allowed Silvana to pull him, as he had little strength left. They darted in wide circles, and then flashed back to the trail in the snow, and followed it all the way down the steep slope. Reginleif lay at the bottom; she'd slid all of the way down, and she was covered in snow; around her lay huge icicles stabbed into the thick drifts, but the armor of Hel had protected her; she was covered in broken icicles which had shattered against Hel's godly platemail.

Suddenly Reginleif jumped up, seized both Silvana and Glororil as they hovered above her, and she pulled them down, against her breastplate, and then she ran. The frozen breath weapon of the frost dragon pelted them, but Reginleif sheltered the fairies and ran as the heavy icicles pelted her, slamming hard into her backplate and helmet, and then she dashed into a crevice, which turned out to be a tunnel in the ice. The massive white dragon roared in anger, but its frozen breath couldn't strike them inside this tiny tunnel.

"Are you all right?" Reginleif asked the companions, holding both fairies up and inspecting them, her sword in her other hand.

"Yes," Glororil said wearily. "How did you know … that this tunnel was here?"

"I saw it when I first fell, but then you blinded me with your second burst," Reginleif said.

The frost dragon roared deafeningly, preventing any further conversation. Reginleif dropped the fairies to press her hands over her helmet, squeezing its padding against her ears, and the fairies stoppered their hearing as well. A fierce blast of fog and icicles struck the tunnel entrance, and they were forced to retreat deeper into the icy cliff.

"We'd best see where this tunnel leads," Silvana said when the roar subsided.

"It seems to be a flow," Glororil said. "Something melted the ice here; something recent."

"What could melt anything in this frozen cave … with the dragon right there?" Silvana asked.

"Athelwynne!" Reginleif said. "He must've come this way!"

"That makes sense," Glororil said. "Otherwise the entrance to this tunnel would've been covered by snow long ago."

Lit by Silvana's moonglow, they proceeded up the ice tunnel, which rose slightly as they went, and was nearly perfectly round, the floor so slick that Reginleif had to use her sword as a spiked crutch. Glororil prayed that Reginleif was correct, that the Seer had made this tunnel, but the possibility troubled him; if the Seer had been here, more than two months ago, then why hadn't he reappeared? Perhaps he'd been trapped down here, and run out of strength, without food to sustain himself, and with no hope of sneaking past the massive, hungry frost dragon. Glororil feared that their quest might end when they came across his frozen corpse; *what a sad end that would be!*

Then he remembered what he'd seen.

"Why didn't Hel's sword hurt the frost dragon?" Glororil asked Reginleif.

"It never touched him," Reginleif snarled.

"You stabbed him …!" Glororil insisted.

"I did … to the hilt," Reginleif said. "But I never reached him; his scales are covered by thick sheets of ice; my sword wasn't long enough to cut through."

"He's the size of a mountain," Silvana said. "Did you really think that you could kill him?"

"If I could've reached a vital spot, like his eyes …," Reginleif said.

"More likely the inside of his mouth," Glororil said. "A good thing that our mission isn't to kill that thing; even Odin couldn't defeat that monster, or it would've been slain long ago."

"Where did it come from?" Silvana asked. "It couldn't have crawled through the tiny entrance of Mistyhel."

"I don't think that it did," Glororil said. "I think that Mistyhel is another 'crack in the world', and that we've entered another universe."

"Then Mistyhel isn't the only entrance to this place, which means that there must be another exit," Reginleif said.

"Perhaps the Seer found that exit," Silvana said.

"The upward slope of this tunnel makes me hopeful," Reginleif said. "As the Seer melted the ice, if he'd gone downhill, then the water would've pooled and drowned him; he would've had to tunnel upwards, so that the water flowed behind him and out."

"Then there's an opening somewhere up here," Silvana said, and she flew ahead.

"Wait!" Glororil shouted, and he zoomed after her. "Anything could be out there!"

Yet when Glororil reached the tunnel's exit, he found Silvana hovering, staring out in wonder. Outside their tunnel was another huge cavern, and beyond it, a vast opening, a gigantic cave's mouth, and beyond its mouth lay ... gray sandy dunes ... under a dim, starlit sky ... just outside the frozen cave.

"Look!" Silvana pointed.

From the tiny mouth of their tunnel, leading downwards, a deep rent split the otherwise smooth snow; it fell straight down the steep slope, as if someone had slid on their backside down the tall hill, and at the bottom, where the slide ended, a set of footprints began, plowing through the thick snow, headed across the wide cavern to the giant exit.

"The Seer's alive!" Silvana shouted back to Reginleif, who was having trouble slipping and sliding upon the sloping ice.

"Be quiet, and dim your light," Glororil said. "We don't want to attract that dragon here."

Silvana's moonglow faded and failed, but the dim starlight outside the cave's mouth provided enough glow to see by.

When Reginleif saw the tracks, she sighed her relief.

"He's alive," Reginleif said. "Hurry; follow those tracks."

As Glororil and Silvana flew out, Reginleif pushed out of the slippery, melted tunnel, and slid on the thick snow and ice all the way down, leaving a second trail beside the one made by the Seer. Then she trudged in his frozen tracks, pushing through the snow, which was higher than her knees.

"Can you warm me up again?" Reginleif asked Glororil. "I'm freezing."

"No, let Glororil rest," Silvana insisted. "We may need his sunglow again."

With her Valkyrie strength, Reginleif plowed on, driving through the drifts, with the fairies flying before her. As they neared the great cave's mouth, they saw a hopeful sign; the footprints in the snow had halted before the huge entrance, fell back, and then proceeded through the mouth of the cave, leaving clear tracks in the smooth, starlit sand outside of the cave. The Seer's tracks continued upon the sand, up the first hill, and vanished overtop its edge.

"Perhaps I should fly ahead," Silvana said. "I can fly in an hour what it would take the Seer days to walk."

"The Seer's been gone for months," Glororil said.

"Best that we stay together," Reginleif said.

Suddenly, just as they reached the spot where the Seer's tracks backtracked, a great fire erupted, filling the mouth of the cave like a great wall, a barrier to their progress. The companions quickly retreated. They had to get through the fiery gate; Glororil didn't fear heat as much as they did, but as he flew forward, the flames burst up again, like an invisible door that burst aflame whenever anyone approached it. These flames were solid, like a moving, impenetrable wall; Glororil slammed into them and was knocked backwards.

"We can't get through!" Silvana complained.

"Athelwynne got through," Reginleif said.

"The Seer's a powerful sorcerer, wielding the secrets of Midgard, Yggdrasil, and the Elysian Fields," Glororil said. "Even Odin didn't have all that. The Seer could probably get through those flames, but that doesn't mean that we can."

"We can't lose him now!" Reginleif argued. "Those are his tracks!"

"We've proven that he's alive," Silvana said. "We can do nothing else here."

"There must be some other way to get into that land," Glororil said, and he flew up, to the very top of the cave mouth, as close as he could come without triggering the flames, and peered out; the Seer's tracks continued in a long line, hill after hill, until they vanished in the distance. Then he flew back down and reported.

"Let's go back," Reginleif said.

"Back … past that white dragon …?" Silvana exclaimed.

"It's our only way out," Glororil said. "But look; that flaming door couldn't have just appeared for our sake; this whole cavern is a prison. Someone, or something more powerful than that dragon, must've forced it into here, and created this flaming doorway to trap it inside."

"Then, whatever the Seer finds out there … may be worse than the white dragon," Reginleif said.

"We must return to Hel," Glororil said.

"Assuming that we can sneak past that white dragon," Silvana said. "It knows that we're here, and it hasn't come after us …."

"It's guarding our only exit," Glororil said. "We've no choice …"

"You two can make it back," Reginleif said. "Tell Hel what we found …."

"We're not leaving without you!" Silvana said flatly.

"Hel would kill us," Glororil agreed.

Reginleif frowned, but Glororil was right, and the intense cold wouldn't let them wait to decide; they had to face the white dragon again, and it would be waiting for them.

"Come," Reginleif said. "If we're going back, then let's do it now, before I freeze solid."

Chapter 17

The Fury of Odin

REGINLEIF

Reginleif squeezed out of the mist-gushing crack, and an instant later, Glororil and Silvana zipped past her, as the roars of the furious frost dragon echoed deafeningly across Niflhiem. They'd done it: they'd escaped from Mistyhel, a feat which only Odin had ever accomplished, and brought with them not only the secrets of Mistyhel, but news that the Seer was still alive.

Reginleif paused to stab her sword between her armor and her belt, and then used both of her hands to scale the icy walls of the pit. The thick snowfall obscured her vision, but she could still see the flickering bonfire, burning nothing but air, high above her; *Hel was still here.*

Yet, to her horror, as Reginleif reached the frozen lip of the pit of Mistyhel, standing before the thousand mounted corpses of Hel's cavalry, and the dragonish zombie mount of Hel, stood thirteen women staring at her: Hel, the Goddess of Death … *and every one of the Valkyrie.*

Her shield-sisters had come to Niflhiem … and caught her!

"Treason!" Skeggjöld shouted angrily. *"Traitor!"*

Reginleif climbed to her feet and stood facing them, wearing Hel's armor, looking more like the ruler of Niflhiem than her sisters.

"Athelwynne the Seer lives," Reginleif said. "These fairies and I witnessed this."

"You defied the will of Odin!" Skeggjöld accused.

"I'll stand by his judgement," Reginleif said, "but I'll never regret what I've done."

Skögul scowled, Mist glared hatefully, and Prudr snorted derisively, but her other sisters, mostly Göll and Geirahöd, merely nodded to her. Róta said nothing, but her eyes narrowed.

"Give me a moment to talk to Hel," Reginleif said. "Then I'll accompany you anywhere you wish."

Sitting upon the Throne of Asgard, Odin the Alfather glared his one powerful eye at Reginleif.

"I ordered you not to enter Mistyhel!"

Reginleif stood proudly before Odin, still wearing Hel's armor.

"A loyal servant must always do what they think will most help their master," she said.

"I decide what my Valkyrie do!" Odin shouted.

Odin leaned back upon his massive golden throne, frowning, his thick beard bristling. The ravens on his shoulders looked like they were pecking at his ears, but everyone knew that they were whispering secrets to him. Gungnir, his powerful magic spear, capable of creating a Valkyrie … or killing one, stood leaning against his throne. His fingers drummed his heavy mail coat, and he glared at Reginleif with his sole eye, hiding behind a leather patch the empty socket that he'd ruined to learn about Ragnarrock. A frightening snarl slipped from his lips.

Behind Reginleif stood all of the other Valkyries, who'd escorted her to face the judgement of their master; they would've brought her bound like a calf, if she'd resisted. Their expressions were grim; Reginleif had broken their most-sacred vow, defied her rightful liege, and disobeyed his will. *Even if Odin pardoned her, it was unlikely that her shield-sisters ever would.*

Many of the oldest and most powerful Norse gods and goddesses stood watching the proceedings. Beside the Throne of Odin stood Thor, Loki, Heimdal, Tyr, Frigg, and Freyja; all glared at Reginleif without a trace of a smile. Many other gods stood to the sides, and all glared hatefully at her. Reginleif faced them resolutely; she'd described what she'd found in the pit of Mistyhel, exactly as she'd told it to Hel, while her shield-sisters had waited impatiently.

"If my death will spare my liege the doom of the same Winter that threatens the Lady of the Druids, then I accept it," Reginleif said.

Odin shook his head.

"I said that the Seer was lost," Odin said. "Now that I know he lives; I'm obliged to seek him. You've burdened your liege!"

Reginleif said nothing, and Odin scowled.

"The Seer is a dangerous power, although not an immortal," Odin said. "I alone had survived an encounter with the great Dragon of Winter, but even I couldn't penetrate the Gate of Ra."

Several of the gods turned to look at Odin, wary looks upon their faces.

"Once, long ago, before I ruled Asgard, ancient Midgard was beset by many frost dragons, such that most of its lands were buried under ice," Odin said. "Back then, ancient gods, from realms far older than ours, rose up and slew the frost dragons, and their reduced numbers forced the glaciers to retreat. One distant land, far to the south, was beset by the ultimately formidable Dragon of Winter, the great Ice Dragon, as big as a mountain, and all of the southern gods combined couldn't slay it. So they drove it into a great cavern, and there they sealed it inside forever, and thus banished winter from their southern lands, which ever since have bathed in sunshine."

Odin reached for his great horn and took a long drink before continuing.

"But Winter came for those ancient gods. As we arose, we, the new gods, including the Lady of the Druids, came to rule Midgard … and those ancient gods failed. The divine realms where they once dwelt are now silent, empty, and dead; nothing remains of what was once wise, strong, and glorious. The Seer is lost in the greatest of those realms; there's no escape from their darkness."

Odin glanced at his fellow gods, and they nodded to him. Odin returned his gaze to Reginleif, standing alone before him.

"Reginleif, you've defied your lord and master; you must be punished!" Odin said.

"I accept your will, and ask only that I might name my punishment," Reginleif said.

Angry hisses came from the other gods and goddesses.

"What punishment would you choose?" Odin asked. "Beware, for you may suffer it."

"Condemn me to this land which cannot be escaped," Reginleif said. "Send me to the dead realm where Athelwynne the Seer wanders; if I can't bring him back, then I'll never return."

Loki grinned widely … while the other gods and goddesses had mixed reactions. Some looked askance at the request, as if it were a trick to avoid a real punishment, and others frowned at the impudence of the youngest Valkyrie.

"The Seer has greatly aided my wisdom, and carried mine to his Mistress," Odin said. "The knowledge that we've combined has strengthened both of our realms, but it's incomplete; his continued services would be invaluable. Therefore, here is my decision: Reginleif the Valkyrie is banished from the Realms of Yggdrasil now and forever, unless she should return to us Athelwynne the Seer, to continue his service. But I can't open the Gate of Ra; finding another doorway to the Lost Realm is your burden. My loyal Valkyrie, return this traitor to the land of her birth, and there abandon her forever: Reginleif is a Valkyrie … no more!"

Reginleif stared back at the King of the Norse Gods … and slowly she bowed.

She was going after Athelwynne!

Without another word, she saluted Odin with the sword of Hel, and then she strode from his hall; her boots echoing on the marble floor. Her sisters followed her, after saluting Odin, and their footsteps followed Reginleif out of the golden doors of Válaskjálf.

Reginleif couldn't help but smile.

In the sunlight, Reginleif looked up at the sky; *Athelwynne would do no less for her.* She'd made the right decision; ever since she'd become a Valkyrie doubts had plagued her, but after her brief sojourn as a fairy, she'd put her doubts aside. It didn't matter if she was called Reginleif or Roselyn, Valkyrie or Countess, or even fairy;

she was the person that she was born to be, and she wouldn't let her sisters make her into something that she hated.

What was banishment to her? She was starting to hate Valhalla, the endless repetition, the daily war with no winner; Reginleif wanted to prove herself, to do great deeds: she wanted to find and rescue Athelwynne … but not for Odin. Odin needed the Seer like a warrior needs an extra weapon; nice to have, but not essential. Hel had offered her the strongest friendship that she'd known since becoming a Valkyrie; Reginleif wanted to reward her friend for making her feel welcome when no one else did: *she'd rescue the Seer for Hel.*

Reginleif turned to face her angry sisters.

"I can't achieve Odin's will alone," Reginleif said, eyeing their frowns. "Take me to Castle Bristlen."

Chapter 18

The Quest Begins

ELOISE

"You're a pagan priestess?!?" Karl shouted at Eloise.

"Karl!" Rafe scolded. "Lower your voice!"

"All these years . . . ?!?" Karl bellowed.

"Please, let me . . . !" Eloise began, looking up at her husband, and for the first time she felt slightly afraid of him; *murder smoldered in his eyes.*

Eloise bowed her head. She'd always known that this moment would come, that Karl would eventually have to be told.

Karl opened his mouth to shout again, but Seren, standing beside him with a plate of fruit in her hands, threw a purple-red grape into his open mouth . . . and Karl choked.

"No shout!" Seren said firmly. "Make matters worse."

Karl spat out the grape and glared at all of them, shifting his gaze from Seren to Rafe, and then to Elaina, and finally back to Eloise. The sunlight streamed in through their open baronial bedroom window; outside, the neigh of a horse sounded between the regular rings of a distant blacksmith hammering rhythmic pounding upon metal, but not one voice rose from the courtyard of Castle Bristlen. No one in the room dared to speak, and all looked ashamed.

Eloise glanced around at her bedroom, at all of her familiar furnishings: at her tall, polished wardrobes, which had stood there since before she was born, at her wide windows with their heavy shutters, now thrown open in a vain attempt to mute Karl's justified rage, to keep him from shouting, and at the new, thick gold curtain, behind which was hidden the treasury closet that her companions had once robbed, and, lastly, at her huge, ornate bed, where her hated stepfather had been knocked unconscious by Eric Bjornson, and where she and Karl had slept together for eight years and conceived their three beautiful children.

Was she about to lose everything?

"Did you know about this?" Karl demanded of Rafe.

"I … um, right before Sir Aledard … I caught her talking … to a fairy," Rafe admitted.

"A fairy …!" Karl shouted, but Seren held a grape threateningly, and he subsided.

"I didn't know that it'd gone any further," Rafe darted an accusatory glance at Eloise.

"Me knew," Seren offered, not trying to deny it, and Karl glared at her. "Found out while Aledard siege castle; made Eloise stop."

Karl shared his angry stare amongst all of them.

"I chose this," Eloise said. "Don't blame them; I kept it secret."

"The king wants us dead, and you're handing him our execution notices!" Karl snarled.

"No one but Seren has penetrated my secret … in six years," Eloise said.

"Six ye…!" Karl shouted, but Seren slapped her palm over his mouth, slamming in another grape.

Karl spit out the grape, his cheeks scarlet.

"You …!" Karl started to shout at Seren, and then he walked around Eloise, putting her between him and Seren, but he lowered his voice. *"You're going to get us killed!"*

"We didn't know that Roselyn was coming," Eloise said. "Eorl Sir Guldwin beat her, whipped you and Rafe, and made me crawl at his feet …!"

"You … killed him …?" Karl exclaimed.

"I killed him," Eloise said, trying to sound stronger than she felt. "Don't look at me like that; he deserved to die … and I faced more danger that day than we did in any land of Yggdrasil. I was trying to save our barony …!"

"Saving the barony is *MY* job!" Karl snapped.

"I did what Eric Bjornson would've done," Eloise said. "I took the risk only upon myself … to help everyone."

"You must've known a different Eric than I did," Karl said. "Eric hated … what you're doing …"

"Sorcery," Elaina supplied the word that Karl wouldn't say, and he snapped his glare to her. "Don't hate me, son-in-law; I wasn't here."

"Like mother, like daughter," Karl hissed.

"I'm a Seeress; I don't do sorcery," Elaina said.

"There's a difference …?" Karl scowled.

"Eloise's magic can do things, but it can't divine truth," Elaina said. "I see what no one else can, and learn what others can't, but I can affect things only in the same ways that you do."

"I can't listen to this …," Karl said, shaking his head, and he turned to walk out the door.

"Karl …!" Eloise shouted.

"I'm through!" Karl shouted, and he slapped the sword on his belt. "I'm not going to wait for you to get me killed; I can die in a hundred ways … *with a sword!"*

Karl reached the door and threw it open. He started to exit through it, obviously determined to leave with a dramatic door-slamming that would shake Castle Bristlen to its dungeon, but a sole, unexpected figure blocked his path.

Reginleif stood just outside the doorway, rigid, wearing the most threatening suit of black armor that Eloise had ever seen, sleek, decorated with red and gold edging, a skirt of the faces of tiny skulls, and with a thin ridge of sharp spines topping her helmet.

Everyone startled, and Karl staggered back, his dramatic exit stopped in its tracks.

"Reginleif …!" Rafe exclaimed.

Reginleif stared at them, a deep frown of utmost misery upon her face.

"No," she said dejectedly. "I … am … *Roselyn.* Odin … kicked me out. I'm a Valkyrie … no more."

Stunned expressions met this revelation, and Eloise stood in a mental blankness of spinning voids.

… A Valkyrie no more …?

Seren recovered first, and she hurried forward to hug Roselyn, who buried her face in her aged friend's long gray hair. Rafe followed Seren's example, and soon the three of them stood in a silent embrace. Eloise exchanged a confused glance with Karl, and slowly questions began to force aside the fogs swirling inside her head.

Roselyn could no longer claim Karl after he died …?

Rafe and Seren escorted Roselyn into the bedroom and sat her on a small chair, the very same chair that she'd been sitting in when Eric and Karl had first seen her.

"I defied Odin," Roselyn explained, her voice strained, but she showed no evidence of tears; *she was no longer the sorrowful maiden regularly beaten by her father.* "Against Odin's command, I entered Mistyhel, with Silvana and Glororil, to look for Athelwynne."

Slowly Roselyn described everything that had happened since meeting Elaina in Norway; her fury at Odin's ban, her weeks of frustration, her transformation in Alfhiem, and how Hel had taken her to the entrance to Mistyhel as a fairy, and hurled her into it. She told them about the massive, terrible Dragon of Winter, whose unbreachable scales lay covered in sheets of ice so thick that even Hel's sword couldn't penetrate them. Finally she described the Seer's tracks in the snow, and the great fire-guarded doorway which even Odin couldn't penetrate, but through which the Seer had passed into a land even more ancient than Yggdrasil.

She spoke as if numb, exhausted beyond words. She told them of how she'd emerged from Mistyhel with Silvana and Glororil, without whom she would've died, only to find all of her shield-sisters arrayed against her, and how her sister Valkyrie had practically force-carried her to face Odin's judgement, who banished her forever, unless she could do the impossible: *find another 'crack in the world', enter it, and bring back Athelwynne the Seer.*

"I've no choice," Roselyn said. "I must go … to seek Athelwynne … alone, if I must."

"*No alone!*" Seren insisted, and Roselyn hugged her again.

"We … mustn't be hasty," Rafe said, his deep voice hesitant. "We need to discuss this … all of it … and sleep on it."

"Good advice," Seren agreed.

Roselyn glanced up at Karl … and a brief smile lightened her face.

"You can't allow yourself to be killed … with or without a sword … right now," she said.

Karl glanced at Roselyn, and then at Eloise, and finally he knotted his fists, pressed them against the sides of his head, and with a long, angry, guttural snarl, leaning his head back as far as utter frustration could bend his stiff neck, Karl stomped through the door and out of the room.

"Welcome home," Elaina said to Roselyn.

Eloise bit back a dozen objections as Seren ordered Rafe out and made Roselyn undress. Seren put Roselyn into Eloise's bed, and Elaina pulled the covers up to her chin; Roselyn objected, but Seren wouldn't be gainsaid, and it'd been two days since Roselyn had slept. Eloise held her tongue, and frowned deeply while the only rival for her husband's heart was tucked into her and Karl's bed. Then they departed, leaving Roselyn buried under warm covers, and closed the door behind them. They proceeded down the hall together.

"I can't believe this," Elaina whispered. "A Valkyrie undone; that's never happened before …"

"Must help her," Seren whispered. "What say Eloise?"

Eloise stopped and stared at both of them; *what kind of an answer did they expect?* She needed time to think, not idle prattle; *there had to be something in her spellbooks to deal with this!* Without a word, Eloise turned from Seren and

Elaina and walked away rapidly, straight to her tower, determined to sort this out.

Roselyn . . . her husband's other lover . . . mortal . . . and back again . . .?

That night, Karl had the cooks bring their meal to a private audience room right off the main hall, and he posted Nate and Phil outside their door as guards, so that no one could bother them. He ordered several minstrels to play loudly all through dinner in the Great Hall, so that no one could overhear them.

Eloise felt uncomfortable. She glanced at the others, who looked no less reluctant to speak. Her spellbooks had revealed nothing that could help her; *even if her magics were as powerful as Athelwynne's, she could never hope to overcome Odin!*

Roselyn looked better for having rested, and more human, wearing a borrowed dress instead of Hel's armor, but she also looked softer and sadder; Eloise wished that Seren hadn't lent her a dress with the excuse that she'd sent Hel's armor to be polished by the smith. In armor, Roselyn didn't look so beautiful. Eight years ago, Eloise had been several years younger than Roselyn, and since then, Eloise had grown into a woman and a mother of three; Roselyn looked exactly the same.

"The last thing that we need is to start another pagan quest," Karl said, standing up and facing everyone at the table.

"Hear, hear!" Rafe agreed.

Eloise glanced at her mother, who sat beside her, drinking wine from her goblet. Elaina looked the most casual at the table; she'd always support her daughter, Eloise knew, but she'd never been to Yggdrasil, and never faced the horrors that she and the others had witnessed.

Seren and Rafe looked a little haggard; Eloise had overheard them arguing before the meeting. They were her biggest threats, as they were both impartial and wise; they'd support what was best for everybody … but about her husband, Eloise reserved the right to be possessive.

"I have to find Athelwynne," Roselyn said, her tenor determined and undaunted; *the defiance of a Valkyrie.*

"No, you don't," Rafe contradicted Roselyn, his gruff voice rivaling hers for certainty. "Odin turned you out; Christ would never do that."

"Humans aren't to blame for the whims of gods," Karl added.

"I … I don't know if I could … come back," Roselyn said. "I swore an oath to Odin, and even if I hadn't, I've been a Valkyrie, an immortal Queen of Valhalla; what's left for me here?"

Eloise stiffened at these words; in Valhalla, Roselyn had stolen her husband for a night of passion … and shamed her. In Castle Bristlen, Karl was a married man, and Roselyn would have to stand aside forever. If she didn't, then she and Karl could be excommunicated. Yet … *who would hold Karl's deepest affection?* If Karl chose Roselyn, instead of his wife, then Eloise could not only lose her husband, she could lose her baronial title … and her barony … *she could lose everything to Roselyn!*

"Your father's dead," Karl said to Roselyn. "Your brother's beaten …"

"His army stands, and your only protection is their fear that I'll descend upon them again," Roselyn said. "What do you think that they'll do when they hear that I'm here … and no longer a threat? I know my brother; he'll seek revenge."

"You could … assume a disguise …," Rafe suggested.

"Countess, Valkyrie, and then … what?" Roselyn asked. "Spend my few remaining years afraid to show my face? Hide in shadows, hoping that no one ever sees me? Live in a convent behind sealed doors, wearing a veil so that no one recognizes me?"

"At least you'd live in the eyes of God," Rafe said.

Roselyn's expression changed; her eyes hardened, almost turning red, and a mien of fury such as she never could've revealed before masked her face. Valhalla had wrought countless changes upon her. She barely looked human, more like the avenging goddess that had dropped out of the sky, with her shield-sisters, to destroy an army.

Rafe met her fearful gaze with his own, ready for a confrontation. Their war of faiths seemed about to explode. Eloise didn't want them arguing, but she feared to speak up.

She didn't want her oaths to the Lady to become enmeshed in their argument.

Seren spoke up suddenly, diverting their attention with her soft voice.

"This no help," Seren said. "Odin not problem; Seer lost. Him one of us; we can't abandon."

"The Seer can take care of himself!" Rafe argued.

"Athelwynne sacrificed his life to save yours … to save all of our lives," Roselyn said. "He threw himself into the Well of Mimir …"

"He did that for his pagan Lady, not for us," Rafe said.

"He made that bargain before She arrived," Roselyn said. "He martyred himself to spare the rest of us. His last request was for Her to help us."

Rafe snorted, but he took a deep drink of ale rather than reply.

"What if Glororil need help … or Silvana?" Seren asked.

"Wife …!" Rafe hissed warningly, but Seren ignored his attempt to silence her.

"When Reginleif need help, fairies leave Alfhiem and enter Mistyhel," Seren said. "They take great risk. If Rafe need help, or Karl, would they not come?"

"It's not that simple," Karl said. "Things have changed. We have a barony to manage."

"Barony safe from invaders," Seren said.

"We can't accept another godless quest!" Rafe insisted, and Roselyn rose to her feet, facing him angrily. Palpable glares streaked between them.

"May I speak?" Elaina asked, and when no one objected, Rafe and Roselyn let their retorts go unspoken and returned to their chairs. "I didn't go on your last adventure, but it seems to me that, before you embark upon another, you'd best think about how you'd accomplish it."

"Exactly!" Karl said. "We had a plan before … well, the Seer had a plan, and we only succeeded by following it. What're we supposed to do, sail to Egypt and ask total strangers: 'Excuse me, but can you point us to the nearest 'crack in the world'?"

"We did have a plan, and we ended up going the wrong way," Roselyn reminded him.

"Who says that we won't do that again?" Rafe asked.

"My fear is that we will," Roselyn said. "Don't you see? If we'd gone straight to Valhalla, then Hel wouldn't have ever come there. We would've failed, or we would've been forced to travel all the way to Niflhiem and back, twice as far, with Loki chasing us both ways. When we first arrived, Loki tried to force our secrets from us, and would've killed us, if not for Garm.

Something … or someone …. more than Athelwynne's plan … was guiding us back then, and they may be doing so again."

Eloise startled at this revelation. Everyone stared at Roselyn, trying to digest her arguments.

"Who …?" Seren asked.

"The Norn witches," Roselyn said, grimacing. "I've seen them. I've felt their power, and I watched it repeatedly defeat my sisters, despite their centuries of wisdom. Who sent us to find Elaina? Who told us where the Seer had been sent, knowing that I'd insist on seeking him? They knew that either I'd die in Mistyhel … or that I'd make it back with proof that Athelwynne lived. If they set us on this path, then it's a thread that they're weaving, and I know better than to trust them."

"Another reason why we shouldn't go!" Rafe insisted.

"Perhaps the Norns erred," Elaina said. "Many blessings resulted from your last quest: a new Valkyrie was born, Hel gained eternal friends, Odin gained a great einherjar, The Lady and Odin became close correspondents, the Seer became a great power, and Loki was humiliated; of all of those, only the last is what the Norns could have wanted."

"The Norns probably expected us to die," Karl said. "They probably wanted Loki to learn of the 'crack in the world'."

"Precisely; what other goal could they have had?" Elaina asked.

"None know the desires of the Norns," Roselyn quoted.

"We failed in our quest," Rafe said. "Did you never consider that God was testing us, to see if we'd abandon His path to help a bunch of pagans?"

"Example of Jesus be helping others," Seren said.

"I will not return to Yggdrasil," Rafe said flatly, and he rose to his feet and glared at all of them.

"Sit down, Rafe," Karl said. "We're not going to Yggdrasil, even if we agree to go on this quest."

"We shouldn't even be discussing this!" Rafe bellowed.

"Fine!" Roselyn rose to her feet. "All that I ask is a horse …"

"Two horses," Elaina corrected her. "Surely you don't think that you'll find a 'crack in the world' … with just your sword?"

Roselyn looked surprised, but then she smiled.

"Thank you, Seeress," she said to Elaina.

Eloise stared at her mother; *Eloise was willing to let Roselyn go on this fool's errand, but she didn't want her mother accompanying her!*

"I haven't agreed to let you go," Karl warned.

"I'm still a Valkyrie," Roselyn snarled.

"Odin kicked you out," Karl reminded her.

"I can kill every person in Castle Bristlen … and take all the horses I want," Roselyn said, her glare unbroken.

"Spare Seren!" Seren said, and Eloise couldn't repress a chuckle as Seren and Elaina laughed.

"Husband, you've no right to detain Roselyn," Eloise said. "You're a baron, but she's still a countess, of higher nobility. But you, Mother …," Eloise turned to face Elaina, "… you shouldn't volunteer for this; our last quest almost killed us a hundred times."

"Each time, your friendship saved you," Elaina said to Eloise. "If you abandon that, what will you have left? Roselyn can't find a mystical doorway without a seeress."

"Seer one of us," Seren said. "He come help, if any of us in trouble. If Roselyn go, Seren go …"

"No!" Rafe shouted. "You're my wife! *You're not going!"*

Seren turned a stare upon her husband that only Roselyn's could equal, so intense that Eloise was taken aback. Rafe met his wife's stare undaunted, ready to fight.

"Enough," Karl said. "The last time that you two argued we lost to Ruthedhel and were almost killed by Utgard-Loki. Seren, I'm afraid that Rafe's right; you couldn't walk from here to Demril without needing several days to rest, and you wouldn't dare attempt to climb back up the Cliffs of Othar on foot … even on the smooth trail. We don't know what we're facing. Do you really think that you could march across another universe, as different from this one as Yggdrasil?"

Seren glared at Karl, but she said nothing. Rafe smiled widely.

"Rafe," Karl continued, "you can't come, either."

"What …?!?" Rafe shouted.

"Brother, no man alive can match you in a saddle, but the first thing that we had to toss, after we went through the 'crack in the world', was our saddles," Karl said. "Seren can manage Castle Bristlen, but you need to be here to rule the barony. All our guards obey you, all the villagers respect you, and everyone knows that you speak with the power of my office."

"You need me!" Rafe said.

"Eloise and I need you here … to raise and crown our children, if we don't make it back," Karl said.

"You need me … to protect your souls," Rafe said. "Without a representative of Christ, you never would've survived Yggdrasil."

"The barony can't spare both of us," Karl said to Rafe. "One of us must stay behind."

Rafe looked furious, but he only shook his head and frowned.

"Then I'll find someone to go with you; perhaps Friar Thomas ...," Rafe sighed.

"Anyone that you send with us will be welcomed," Karl said, and he glanced at Roselyn. "Apparently my soul won't be claimed, if I die right now, and I don't want it gobbled up by some Egyptian god."

"Then ..., *we're going ...?*" Eloise asked.

"I can't let that stupid Seer claim to be a better friend than I am," Karl said, but his jaw was clenched, obviously trying not to smile. "Wife, you can stay, if you want ..."

"You're not running off with ... without me," Eloise said firmly. "So you, I, mother, and Roselyn will go ...?"

"Not alone," Karl said. "We're not as young as we used to be; we'll take Nate and Phil with us."

"What about Edith?" Eloise asked.

"I can't imagine explaining to Sarah Tiller why we took her daughter into danger," Karl said. "She'd hang us all by our ears."

Eloise slowly nodded; *at least Karl was taking her, not running off alone with Roselyn!*

"Thank you ... all of you," Roselyn said.

"Don't thank me yet," Karl said. "Eloise, can you mark a man's boots ... so that we can follow his ghost to the Egyptian land of the dead?"

Sadly, Eloise shook her head; *she couldn't perform any spells that complex.*

"Elaina, are you sure that you can find a 'crack in the world'?" Karl asked.

"Such magics are beyond even the wisest seeress," Elaina said. "But I'm willing to try; the closer that we get, the more likely I'll succeed."

"So, we don't have any sure means of finding another 'crack in the world'," Karl said to Roselyn. "We'll go, but we can't search forever; by sail, we can arrive in

Egypt in a few weeks, perhaps by the end of spring, but if we haven't found a clue to the entrance to where the Seer is … by the end of summer … then we're done. That's the price of our help, Roselyn; we can spare you the whole summer to try and find the Seer, but if we can't, then you must promise to give up this quest and return to Castle Bristlen."

"You … are asking me to give up being a Valkyrie … if we can't accomplish our goal in three months?" Roselyn asked.

"In almost four months, actually," Karl said. "We have other responsibilities, too; that's the cost of our help."

"Do you swear you'll do all you can, until the end of summer, to aid me, and not to hinder me?" Roselyn asked.

"I swear it," Karl said. "Do you swear to come back with us if we fail?"

"No," Roselyn said. "However, I won't hinder your departure."

"That's not good enough," Karl said.

Roselyn sighed heavily. "Very well … you have my oath."

Roselyn's gaze turned to Eloise, distrust in her eyes.

"I need a vow from each of you … that you won't hinder my search," Roselyn said.

"I swear it," Elaina said quickly.

All eyes fell on Eloise. She grimaced; she didn't want to go, but she couldn't let her husband traipse off to foreign realms with only Roselyn; *when could Karl ever be trusted alone with an attractive woman?* And they might need her magics; *she couldn't let herself be left behind with Seren and Rafe.*

"I swear it," Eloise said … although her words tasted like bile.

"May God have mercy upon all your souls," Rafe said.

Making arrangements for a long voyage, without making it look like they were making arrangements, was a daunting task, in which Eloise could help only a little. None of Svenson's dragonships remained; they'd all been stolen in the night and sold before the companions had returned from Yggdrasil, carrying wineskins of the Water of Life to the king, with which they'd bought their coronets. The coffers of the barony were mostly empty, so Karl had to sell a large tract of land, and then go with Nate and Phil, and several reliable sailors, to find and buy a large, sturdy ship. They returned only days later; they'd found a nearby Scottish merchant willing to sell them a well-built knarr bought from a Norse trader, which Karl liked because it was a Norse ship, so he knew how to sail it, having helped sail one to the icy waters of the frozen North Sea. Yet all of this had to be done in secret; no army would attack du Harmonn since news had spread of Roselyn's brother's army being defeated by thirteen immortal Valkyrie flying winged horses, but the threat of assassination still loomed, and Nate and Phil constantly hovered over Karl, protecting him from anyone unknown.

Rafe's absence didn't help; shortly after Karl had left with his squires, Rafe had ridden off to find a representative of Christ to journey in his place. Friar Thomas refused to go on this pagan mission, as had Father Duncan, several priests in a neighboring district, and one fat monk who lived alone in Wolven Forest behind Farmer Tiller's lands. Day after day, Rafe rode off, and several nights had not returned, and then he rode to ask his last hope: Deacon Michael James of the Abbey of St. Dunstay, who was two day's ride away.

Eloise and Seren kept the cooks busy, preparing meals for the voyage. They'd leaked the story that the ship would contain an envoy to the Pope, and would be sailing all the way to Rome, Italy, to explain the reports of pagan goddesses raining upon Castle Bristlen.

Although she'd recovered her black armor, Roselyn was forbidden to wear it, and as she'd predicted, she became virtually a prisoner in Castle Bristlen, forced to wear veils whenever she left her room. Eloise tried to assign a guard to watch her, but Roselyn objected, and when Eloise insisted that she needed to be guarded, Roselyn punched her guard unconscious with one blow. Afterwards, no other guard would take the post.

Worse, Roselyn got her hands on a bow, and out of pure boredom, she spent a happy hour upon the battlements of Castle Bristlen, near Eloise's tower, and she put every arrow that she could find into a seagull or migrating duck flying past the white cliffs of Othar, and legends were already rampant about the *'fowl rain'* that showered Demril.

Elaina took to keeping Roselyn company, and tried to seek a vision of their goal, but Egypt was too distant; all that she gained were glimpses of ocean waves, a great river winding past vast coastal cities, strange trees, stone mountains built of giant bricks, with four flat sides and sharp, pointed tops, and what looked like a beach … but it went on as far as her eyes could see.

"A beach …?" Roselyn asked. "Rocky shores and driftwood?"

"No water at all," Elaina said. "Endless miles of dry sand, surrounded by mountains and valleys of rock …"

"A desert," Roselyn said. "A baking wasteland."

"What's a desert?" Elaina asked.

"They don't exist in the northlands," Roselyn said. "It's the worst terrain, the most hated by the einherjar."

"They have deserts in Valhalla?" Elaina asked.

"Valhalla suffers every type of terrain, under every condition of weather," Roselyn said. "Better a blizzard, or a tempest so cold that rain falls like tiny icicles, or hail so heavy that any man without a helmet or shield can be killed by it, than a desert. Only storm-tossed seas at night are said to rival the evil of deserts, where the heat is so intense that many warriors can't bear armor, and fight wearing only billowing sheets to protect their northern skin from blistering under the rays of a relentless sun, whose heat sears flesh anywhere it touches metal."

"How horrible!" Elaina said.

"It is," Roselyn said. "And that's where we must go."

Rafe returned the following evening, shortly after Karl and his squires had arrived with their new boat. To everyone's amazement, he had a stranger riding behind him: a young nun.

"Nate, Phil; assist Sister Aspertine down," Rafe ordered.

Without hesitation, both boys ran forward and helped Sister Aspertine dismount.

"Rafe, what's this …?" Karl asked, looking at her white wimple and deep blue habit.

"I couldn't find anyone willing to go," Rafe growled. "Even Deacon Michael James refused, but he assigned Sister Aspertine …"

"We can't take a nun!" Karl argued.

"You must have a representative of Christ!" Rafe insisted. "That's why I chose Sister Aspertine; she's young and strong; she won't slow you down."

Sister Aspertine was indeed young; she looked to be no older than seventeen, although her stiff wimple and holy robes hid most of her thin shape.

"You promised," Rafe reminded Karl. "You must take her … or me."

Eloise gaped; *another woman? A young, pretty nun? That's the last thing that Karl needed!*

Rafe glared adamantly, and Karl swallowed hard. He'd promised; *like it or not, Sister Aspertine was going …*

Chapter 19

Trapped aboard ship

KARL

Karl glanced up at the moon, which was slowly traversing the cloudy, pre-dawn sky over England. The vanishing of the dimmest stars warned of the approach of an important day, perhaps the last morning that Karl would ever see his beloved children. He'd said his good-byes to all three, and now they were sound asleep; Rafe and Seren would care for them. He lowered his head and steered his horse toward the ledge overlooking the cliff, to the worn path of the winding trail, leading a line of five other riders: Eloise, Elaina, Roselyn, Nate, and Phil.

To keep their journey secret, only Rafe, Seren, and Edith watched their departure from Castle Bristlen in the pre-dawn silence, having sent all the other guards from their usual posts. Rafe and Edith were still frowning about being left behind, and Seren had deluged them in hugs and kisses, insisted on several last good-byes, and promised that she'd pray for them three times every day. Karl had thanked her, but then he'd asserted that they had to be off. Their sailors and Sister Aspertine were awaiting them, and they departed with hands waving good-bye.

Karl was glad to be leaving the politics of Castle Bristlen. Life as a baron wasn't as exciting as he'd imagined when the king had first set his golden coronet upon his head. Headaches and intrigues filled the mind of every royal, and distrust and dishonesty, even the slightest of which was punishable among peasants, was common among the nobility. His father would've beaten him for voicing even one of the lies that he had to maintain every day.

Karl couldn't stand noble arrogance or justify the royal's extravagances. Alone, Eloise had ruled the Barony du Harmonn for their first year; she was far wiser after their venture to Yggdrasil, and she'd kept Karl involved in every political detail. He slowly got the knack of lying, but it still didn't come naturally.

The recent assassination attempt against him, upon the castle wall, still haunted him. He was sick of at least one of his squires waiting outside the privy, and hovering over him day and night, as if he needed their protection. *Hadn't he proven that he could take care of himself, indeed, that he was unbelievably courageous, leading his troops on the riskiest charges?* Seeing him so protected, any watcher might think that he was as weak and helpless as Baron Vandeslidge du Harmonn; *a short vacation away from politics would be a blessed relief… and remove him from the likelihood of another attempted assassination.*

The idea of passing through another 'crack in the world' didn't bother Karl; after seeing what it'd taken to find and open the last one, Karl found it amusing to believe that any mortal could find a second magical portal. The promise that he'd extracted from Roselyn, to return at the end of the summer, made their success even less likely; chances were that they'd only take a long, relaxing sail to warmer climates, to see the lands that he'd only heard about in the tales of traveling minstrels, which made the southlands sound enchanting, and then they could all return to a peaceful winter in Castle Bristlen, free of their duty to the Seer.

However, Karl felt troubled. Eloise and Roselyn were obviously quarreling, even though they hadn't spoken openly against each other. He'd hoped that this mission might distract their rivalry, that they'd set aside their differences to focus on finding the Seer. Eloise had been unhappy that he'd slept with Roselyn in Valhalla, but a million warriors had been watching them, and Karl didn't think it wise to refuse one of their queens under that kind of scrutiny, especially not if he intended to join their ranks someday.

His one night with Roselyn hadn't been perfect, much to their mutual displeasure. He hadn't really wanted to sleep with another woman since he'd married Eloise. Eloise had always been more adventurous and demanding than he, always looking for new methods to pleasure him. After their long separation, Roselyn had seemed cold and distant, more queenly than he remembered. Their love-making had been intense, slow and sensual beyond any frenzied lust, yet it had been strangely silent and perfunctory. Karl loved Roselyn, but he was a married man, pledged to Eloise, and Roselyn had been Reginleif, Odin's Valkyrie, not the mortal woman whom he'd sworn to love forever. Karl's feelings confused him. Both Eloise and Roselyn wanted him to choose them, but if he chose either, then he'd plunge their company into chaos, and make their mission impossible … and his pleasant vacation to Egypt would quickly become Niflhiem on Midgard.

Sloping down, Karl reached the start of the rugged path, the steep cliff-side trail to Demril, and pushed his worries aside and focused on his horsemanship; falling off this high ledge, and bouncing all the way down the stony Cliffs of Othar, wouldn't resolve his problems in any acceptable way.

They reached the poor fishing village of Demril long before daylight, as the Cliffs of Othar kept Demril in shadow until the fully-risen sun's rays peaked over its summit, yet the black sky above them was lightening to blue. From the bottom of the trail, past the long rows of rebuilt houses and shops which lined Demril's only street, he could see their immediate destination, the end of their horse's ride.

Beyond the docks, he spied their starlit knarr bobbing in the harbor, its naked mast swaying. The villagers were doubtlessly still sleeping as they rode past, and they tried to go as quietly as possible to keep their departure secret.

As they reached the dock, the sweet, innocent smile and bright blue eyes of Sister Aspertine greeted them. After spending the night in prayer with the village priest, praying for God's grace upon their voyage, she was standing alone on the dark dock. Beside her stood a young page, whom Rafe had sent to take their horses back to Castle Bristlen.

From their places on the ship, five rough and rugged-looking sailors arose. They'd been sitting on barrels and chests stuffed with provisions and clothes, tightly packed for the journey, and the sailors bowed deeply to their baron and baroness. Karl frowned; it'd taken him a long time to get used to people treating him as nobility, and it still bothered him occasionally. He'd prefer to stuff his coronet in a chest and forget about it for the voyage; *make it a true vacation.*

Hand-picked by Rafe, these sailors were all loyal men, but they had no idea where they were really going. Unlike the sailors, Sister Aspertine had been fully informed of what their mission was, and Rafe had even told her about their adventures in Yggdrasil, and charged her to guard their souls; *Karl wasn't worried about the sailors, but Sister Aspertine was a serious liability.*

With barely a word, they climbed aboard the sturdy knarr and set sail. These sailors knew their business; minutes later they were coasting out of the harbor, crossing the same breakwater that they'd bobbed upon when following Eric's ghost.

Karl's hope of sailing the ship quickly faded; these sailors knew their tasks and attended to everything without hesitation, and Karl's awkward attempts to help them accomplished nothing but getting in their way. Soon he was quietly sitting against a rail, frowning, with Nate and Phil watching him intently, when not staring out to sea, pretending that they weren't guarding him, as Rafe had doubtlessly ordered them to do. Obviously, Elaina had purposefully seated herself between Eloise and Roselyn, and Sister Aspertine sat upon a barrel, her young face aglow, smiling as if she didn't have a care in the world.

They sailed for hours, and around mid-morning, they left sight of land, but by evening they spied the rocky shores of southern England; they were sailing away from the island of his birth. Karl had never been this far south before, and he was disappointed that the clouds had moved in and made the sky gray and dreary; he'd expected to see nothing but the eternal southern sunshine promised by the minstrels. Yet he held his tongue, and, after Sister Aspertine led them in a prayer of blessing, Karl accepted his small quarter of a cooked chicken, which he ate, and then threw its bones overboard.

Karl mused in silence; *at least this quest wasn't starting with a horde of vikings invading England and killing everyone in Castle Bristlen!*

Elaina brought out a small harp that Karl hadn't known that she'd packed, and she began to play. As before, she played masterfully, and her music relaxed everyone; Karl wondered if she'd anticipated the rivalry between Roselyn and her daughter, and brought the harp to distract them; he hoped that she had.

After her first song, Sister Aspertine asked if she knew the Latin hymn 'In Paradisum', and Elaina said that she'd never played it before, but that she'd give it a try. As she started to pluck the harp's many strings, Sister Aspertine started to sing.

"In paradisum deducant Angeli;
in tuo adventu suscipiant te martyres,
et perducant te in civitatem sanctam Jerusalem.
Chorus angelorum te suscipiat,
et cum Lazaro quondam paupere
æternam habeas requiem."

Amid a chorus of music and good spirits, such that even the sailors paused to listen, the evening passed into night. Karl noticed how the sailors always seemed busy, even on the knarr, which was much smaller than the huge dragonship that they'd sailed to the 'crack in the world', but upon which they'd done practically nothing, which had proven to be a great disadvantage when a storm almost sank them.

Before darkness fell, at Eloise's request, the sailors raised a tarp over the fore of the knarr. Tired of sun and wind, Eloise insisted on eating inside, and handed out bread and cold sausages. Roselyn insisted on tapping a small keg, Sister Aspertine said a blessing, and they all dined and drank beer. Nate suggested that they slice up some of the large store of cheese that they'd brought, but Elaina insisted that the cooks had sealed the cheese in wax, and that they'd best leave it untouched until their perishable supplies grew low.

Everything went calmly until night had fully fallen. Three of the sailors were already snoring in the windy aft of the ship, wrapped in wool blankets. Elaina passed out several more blankets, but when Karl ducked to enter the tent, both Eloise and Roselyn lifted an edge of their blanket, offering Karl a place to sleep beside them.

"I think … I'll stay up and … help steer," Karl said, and he pulled the flap closed without entering.

Frowning, Karl scavenged through the sea chests on the deck outside of the awning, and he finally found a short fur cloak, probably packed for Sister Aspertine, as it was too small for anyone else. Karl wrapped up in it; he'd much rather bed the night snuggled against Eloise or Roselyn, but he'd rather spend an uncomfortable night in the cold wind than to be forced to choose between them.

His sleep was troubled; *if he had to, how would he decide?* Eloise was his wife, and he could've asked for no better partner in life, but they'd grown apart in the last six years, when Eloise's unexpected absences had begun, and her insistence on secrecy had interfered with their peaceful nights. He should've expected that she was learning the forbidden arts of the Seer; the Seer had told her that she had an affinity for magic, and Eloise had always been desirous of power, having been born to the aristocracy and determined to rule.

Karl shook his head. Eloise was a woman, and the king would never support her as a leader of men. If the truth of her practicing Druid magic ever became common knowledge, then the populace would turned against them both; they'd be excommunicated, and the king would finally be able to get rid of them, and again sell the barony for his profit.

Eloise's choice to learn Druid magic didn't bother him as much as it had infuriated Rafe. Karl wasn't heavily religious: he was born Catholic, and saw no reason to change, but he'd witnessed the realities of multiple gods … multiple sets of gods … from multiple universes … yet he never worried about it. Since their venture into the roots of Yggdrasil, he'd assumed that Reginleif would come for him, and that he'd spend his afterlife with her. But Reginleif was Roselyn again, no longer a Valkyrie, and she couldn't restore him if he died.

Karl briefly wondered what he truly believed, since he seldom worried about such things. He attended mass each day, and prayed as his mother had taught him to, but he considered himself a friend of the Lady of the Druids, and a subject of Odin the Alfather, and as more than a friend to Hel, the beautiful Norse Goddess of Death, whose tingling kisses still haunted his dreams some nights.

He wondered what Jesus would say if he suddenly appeared at the Gates of St. Peter. Karl doubted if he'd be allowed to choose where he wanted to go; he wondered what afterlife he'd be doomed to, since he wasn't as religious as Rafe, Eric, or the Seer. He always tried to act in a Christian manner, but he assumed that

Jesus wouldn't be pleased with him. *Would St. Peter condemn him to Hell?* That thought troubled him deeply.

Karl's feelings for Roselyn hadn't lessened over the years, but they seemed somehow distant. Reginleif was very different than Roselyn. He couldn't blame her; being an immortal queen, and a champion warrior, for eight years, worshipped by a million subjects, with direct access to several dozen gods; such a transformation would alter anyone.

Karl wasn't the same, either; becoming a baron was more of a change than he'd expected. He was wiser, calmer, and physically older, his body bulked out to that of a grown man. He wondered how Roselyn saw him; once they'd been the same age. She looked almost unchanged; physically, she was only different in her longer hair and the muscular enhancements of her limbs. Otherwise she was still a beautiful girl in her late teens, while he was an adult man in his mid-twenties. Neither thought like a teenager anymore; when he'd first met Roselyn, she'd been an abused countess bartered by her father to bear a bastard grandchild, a pawn to give him control over du Harmonn, and Karl had been a poverty-stricken runaway, forced by hunger to become a castle guard, a position whose trust he'd betrayed at great cost, but which would've killed him, if he hadn't. Now, Sir Karl du Harmonn could rule and manage an entire barony.

Was he still a man whom Roselyn could love?

Dawn comes early at sea; the sun rose agonizingly as Karl tried not to open his red, stinging eyes. Chills shivered him, and his forehead felt bruised, rocking against the hard inside of the wooden hull as the boat swayed, clenching the too-small, too-thin fur cloak tightly about him, even in his sleep. He heard, rather than saw, movement beside him.

"Where … where are we?" Karl asked weakly.

"Headed toward the Bay of Biscay, the north-east coast of Spain," the sailor said. "We've made good speed all night."

"Are … are you the captain?" Karl asked.

The sailor looked taken aback.

"Lord Sir Rafe Giant-Bane said that you were our captain, my baron," the sailor said. "I'm Henry Sinkula."

"A pleasure, Henry …"

"Thank you, Captain Baron Sir Karl du …"

"Just Karl; my head hurts too much for titles."

"Aye, aye, … Captain Karl."

Karl shook his head.

"Each one of you knows more about sailing than I do," Karl said.

"Begging your pardon, Captain Karl," Henry said. "Being a captain isn't about knowing how to sail; it's about commanding … and discipline."

Karl nodded, too tired to argue. He cocked open an eye and saw Henry and two other sailors listening to him; the other two were still sleeping … under far larger blankets than Sister Aspertine's cloak.

"Listen," Karl whispered to them. "We all want this to be a quiet, peaceful voyage. We need to sail to the farthest corner of the Mediterranean Sea, and we'll probably be there most of the summer, and then sail home. Can you manage that?"

"Sail, we can," Henry said with a glance at the other two sailors, who looked apprehensive. "Peaceful, only God can tell; no foreign waters are safe, even in good weather, and all seas are temperamental."

"I don't expect miracles," Karl grinned. "As long as you can get us there and back, I'll ask no more of you."

"Captain, Lord Sir Rafe promised to give our families a silver coin every month until we return," Henry said, "and two silvers each, should we bring you back alive and safe."

Karl's jaw dropped; *where was Rafe going to get the silver? The barony was broke … and Rafe shouldn't be promising wealth that they didn't have!* Yet he'd take that up with Rafe; *these sailors didn't need to know that.*

"So, you see, Captain, your continued health is very important to us … and to Lord Sir Rafe," Henry said.

"I didn't know that," Karl confessed.

"He made each of us swear to lay down our lives for you, Countess Roselyn, Lady Baroness Eloise, and Baroness Elaina," Henry said. "If it comes to a fight …"

"I don't run from battle … or allow others to fight for me!" Karl said flatly.

"That's why we agreed," Henry smiled. "You've taken risks that few nobility dare. Alone, you snuck into Sir Lasky's castle and killed him … while we in your army were sleeping outside. Some call you Karl the Reckless, and others Karl the Brave."

"We're honored to serve you, Captain Baron Sir Karl," another sailor said.

"Here's my paramount order," Karl said. "The next time that I sleep on the deck, make sure that I get a warmer blanket."

They all laughed, and one man reached down and picked up a thick blanket, then handed it to Karl. Karl took it, but he was awake; he stood up to face the chill dawn and wrapped the warm blanket around his shoulders.

"Captain, we can handle the ship at night," Henry said. "You can sleep under the awning …"

"Here's my next order," Karl said, and he again lowered his voice to a whisper. "Never say that again, especially not to my wife, and if I ask if you need me at night, always say 'yes'."

"I understand, Captain," Henry whispered back. "I'm a married man myself."

Sister Aspertine climbed out from underneath the awning first, looking only slightly disheveled, with her fresh, ironed habit now wrinkled, and a few stray locks of hair the color of dried hay sticking out from her wimple. She glanced about them at the wide, white-foamed sea, spied no coast, and looked surprised. Yet she smiled at Karl and bowed slightly to him.

"God bless you this morning, Baron Sir Karl," Sister Aspertine said. "May I ask if you've said your morning prayers yet?"

"Uhhh … no," Karl said.

"Then I'll join you," Sister Aspertine said, looking about at the crowded deck. "Shall we kneel here?"

"Perhaps we should wait … until the others awaken …?" Karl suggested.

"I'll lead them in prayers later," Sister Aspertine said. "One can never pray too much."

"I'd rather pray with them," Karl said.

"As you wish, Your Excellency," Sister Aspertine said, and she bowed again.

"You do realize … that we don't know where we're going?" Karl asked.

"I know that you seek something that doesn't exist," Sister Aspertine smiled. "Deacon Michael James told me that Lord Sir Rafe was a good man, but that he suffered from delusions. You should've heard the wild farce that he told me … about traveling to some pagan world. Nevertheless, I'm to journey with you and see that God's will isn't forgotten, and I'm pleased to do so; I've always wanted to see the Holy Lands, and our destination is close to them."

Karl nodded, and then turned away to stare out to sea. He was accustomed to their story of visiting Yggdrasil being laughed at; he'd once laughed at the mere suggestion that dragons and giants were real. He actually hoped that Sister Aspertine was right, that they weren't going to find another 'crack in the world', but he wondered what Sister Aspertine would do if they did. *Would she enter a 'crack in the world' with them? A nun in a pagan land?* Karl doubted if she would, and if she didn't, then he wouldn't mind leaving her behind; whatever lay beyond this 'crack in the world', it was no place for the innocent.

Sister Aspertine led them all in prayer; even the five sailors knelt and whispered in Latin along with her. Only Roselyn refused to pray, manning the tiller while the others knelt. With amusement, Karl noted that Nate knelt closely on one side of Sister Aspertine and Phil knelt even closer on the other side, and both prayed ardently; *his squires contested on everything.*

Afterwards, they ate a sparse breakfast, and then sat back to look at the sky and waves. It was another overcast day, and Karl was disgusted; he'd been certain that they'd be enjoying endless sunshine by now.

"Were you able to help steer the ship last night?" Roselyn asked him pointedly.

"Uh …, yes," Karl lied. "Did you sleep well?"

Roselyn only glared at him, and Eloise's stare equaled hers.

"I'll bet these sailors know some good songs!" Elaina interrupted them.

Their unwanted conversation delayed, Karl made a mental note to thank Elaina later, when they were alone. They'd seldom been alone; Elaina was a beautiful older woman, much like Seren had been when they'd first met her, although cleaner, less worn by a life of hard labor and laying under men for coins. Elaina was as lithe, blonde with streaks of silver, and as pretty as her daughter. Aboard the Norse dragonship, on their voyage back to England, Karl had decided to avoid being alone with Elaina as much as he could, as Eloise's mother was still attractive, and he had a known weakness for beauty.

The sailors did know some good songs, and one of them, Samuel, had a clear and resonate voice. When he sang, it was as if pure emotions flowed from him, and pulled at you like a tide.

After the singing ended, Elaina spoke up.

"Have any of you sailed to Egypt … and learned about their gods?" Elaina asked the sailors.

"I know nothing of the gods of Egypt, but I've seen their statues in Alexandria, and their likenesses are horrible," Samuel said. "They're giants, or at least, their statues are. They're terrifying monsters of humans and animals fused together, men with the heads of birds and crocodiles, women with the bodies of vultures and hippopotamuses …"

"What are hippopotamuses…?" Nate asked.

"River monsters, like the fattest pig you've ever seen, wider than any horse," Samuel said. "A hippopotamus submerges underwater, then rises and crushes any ship that challenges it, and its jaws open so wide that any sailor trapped within them will be bitten in half."

"Fill our ears with stories of God, not legends of monsters," Sister Aspertine laughed.

"Hippopotamus aren't legends," Samuel said. "Every sailor on the Nile River sees them every day, floating their bloated bodies just beneath the surface, only huge nostrils, watchful eyes, and twitching ears visible above the shining waters. It's the ears that sailors most watch, for when they twitch, wise men flee."

Every day and night they sailed south, sharing songs, and as one quiet evening approached, they spied towering cliffs of dark gray stone.

"Gibraltar, the Pillars of Hercules," Henry said, pointing at the cliffs. "That gap is the portal to the Mediterranean Sea."

Before sunset they neared the cliffs. Many other ships were sailing toward Gibraltar, and they sailed alongside a large vessel filled with heavily-armed black-skinned men, whose captain wore long feathers in his hair.

"Moors," Henry said to his fellow sailors. "Ease the wind out; let them go first."

The other sailors complied, and their ship slowed, while the Moors sped ahead.

"Damn!" one of the sailors cursed. "Look at that!"

"What?" Karl asked.

"Stay down!" Henry hissed. "Don't move, anyone; we may be in trouble."

With an air of nonchalance, Henry looked around the ship in every direction.

"Four ships full of Moorish warriors," Henry announced. "All armed and ready."

"We're surrounded," another sailor said.

Karl lifted his head and looked aft; two large ships of black men were converging on them from behind, one still distant to the side, and the foremost was ahead of them, dropping its sail.

"Can we out-sail them?" Nate asked.

"No," Henry said. "And we can't fight and win; our best bet is to parley."

"I'll do it," Karl said.

"They probably don't speak English," Henry said.

"Their lead ship is slowing, cutting across our path," a sailor said.

"Drop the sail, Captain?" Henry asked. "We're not going anywhere."

Karl nodded, and soon they had to slip aside to let the spar settle upon the deck. Henry raised his hand in greeting, and the captain of the lead ship did likewise. As they slowed, the two ships coming from behind caught up, and the other ship of black warriors converged upon them from the east. Karl counted at least thirty warriors on each ship; a dozen to one … *they were vastly outnumbered.*

After a few attempts at communication, Henry and their captain settled on French, and Karl needed to have everything translated. Elaina, Roselyn, and Eloise spoke French, and the gist of their conversation was that they'd allow the men to strip naked and swim to shore, if they could make it; they wanted everything else, including the women.

"Eloise, is there anything that you can do …?" Karl asked.

"I'm not the Seer," Eloise said. "I brought my tools, but against a hundred … I doubt it."

Suddenly Roselyn stepped forward and addressed their captain in French. After she spoke, all of the black men burst out laughing.

"What'd she say?" Karl asked.

"She challenged their captain to personal combat," Eloise said. "She offered to be his slave and cater to his every desire if he wins, but that all of his people must leave us untouched, if he loses."

After their leader replied, Roselyn spoke again, loudly, so that all could hear. Every black man on all four ships laughed again.

"Did he agree?" Karl asked.

"Yes," Eloise said. "She said that he must give her a moment to dress for battle."

Roselyn vanished under the awning while Karl stared at the many warriors besieging their ship. The black men were all smiling, their white teeth gleaming against their dark lips, and their captain shouted something in French.

"He asks, begging your pardon, if Englishmen always hide behind women's skirts," Henry said.

"Tell him that I don't waste words on fools about to die," Karl said.

With these words translated, the smiles of the warriors and their captain vanished. From inside the awning, the clink of metal warned that Roselyn was hurrying, and when she came out, she was wearing a dress no more: the black armor of Hel, Goddess of Death, covered her, and her hands held Hel's long, naked sword.

The Moors gasped and gaped, disbelieving, and Sister Aspertine made the sign of the cross.

"Tell them that this is a warrior-goddess," Karl said. "Offer to let them go, if they will flee without fighting."

Eloise addressed the black captain; Karl could understand only three names amid her French: 'Valkyrie',

'Reginleif', and 'Odin'. Yet their captain looked unimpressed; he raised a short, ornately-carved spear in one hand, and unscabbarded a long, curved sword with the other.

"Roselyn," Karl said. "Do your worst."

With a cry, Roselyn ran across their deck and jumped, bounded off their front rail, and leapt nine feet through the air, to land upon a shocked crew of black warriors, many of whom tried to scramble out of her way; she ignored them as she might disregard rats scurrying past her armored boots. The captain thrust his spear at her, but her first sword-swing severed its sharp metal tip, sending it splashing into the sea, and their captain drew back only its useless wooden haft. Roselyn's next blow caught his sword and knocked it aside, and her third swing came straight down upon his head … and his blood sprayed upon every man on their ship.

Roselyn didn't stop; she laid about with her sword, hacking into heads with a rapidity at which most farmers couldn't thresh wheat. The black warriors screamed, and many raised weapons, but every flex of Roselyn's Valkyrie muscles turned the blade of her slashing sword before her opponents could gather the sense to attack en masse. Arms and heads flew overboard with such a flurry of death that a wave of blood seemed to splash up and engulf the whole fore of their ship.

When the last *splosh!* of blood rained down upon their ship, the sea, and the shocked warriors, Roselyn alone stood amid the red-coated shapes of a dozen slaughtered corpses, her sword raised, poised to attack, facing the two dozen warriors that had crowded back against the rear of their ship. Screams came from everywhere else: from the wounded, from the other ships, from Elaina, from the five sailors, and especially from

Sister Aspertine, who stood horrified. Only on the late captain's ship was there not a sound; twenty-four warriors stared disbelieving, with wide, white eyes bulging from blood-splattered faces, frozen, holding many spears and curved swords pointed at Roselyn, who stood her ground amid their fallen comrades, ready to conclude her assault.

Eloise shouted to the black men facing Roselyn, but they ignored her. One tall, muscular black man rose and cast his spear at Roselyn, very hard and at close quarters; Roselyn struck the spear so that it glanced straight up, flew far above their mast-top, and when it finally fell, she slapped it twice more with the flat of her sword; her first slap poised it, and her second slap sent it flying back to stab through the chest of the warrior who'd cast it.

The remaining Moors cried out and jumped overboard, even the wounded, into the sea. The other three ships' captains were shouting; their warriors raised their sails and steered away as fast as they could; not even one arrow flew at Roselyn. In only two minutes, twenty-three men were bobbing in the water, swimming away, while their fellows were sailing in three different directions. Only then did Roselyn, drenched in blood, relax her stance. She grabbed a rope from among the dead bodies and cast it to Henry, who caught it and pulled their ships together.

"Someone's going to have to clean my armor," Roselyn said as she climbed back aboard the knarr and unbuckled her spined helmet.

"Nate and Phil will do it," Karl answered, and both boys nodded.

"Sister Aspertine, you can help me bathe," Roselyn said, and she handed Phil her helmet and pushed underneath the awning.

Sister Aspertine stood aghast, her mouth open, too stunned to move.

"I'll do it," Elaina said, and she glanced at the corked barrels. "I'll need clean water."

She vanished inside the awning. Karl snapped his fingers, and Phil set down the bloody helmet and snatched up an empty bucket while Nate hurried to uncork a water barrel.

Chapter 20

The Theft

PHIL

The next morning, Phil picked up an entire severed human arm, noticed the wide armband upon its black skin, and grimaced as he pulled it off. The armband was made of some kind of bone, intricately carved, and big enough to encircle a muscular man's bicep; *what kind of monster had bones that big?* Seeing no rings on the fingers, he dropped the gruesome limb overboard, then bent low and dipped the armband into the salty sea water, rubbing it with his other hand to scrub off the blood. It was grisly work, but Karl had ordered them to do it, and he and his brother were sworn to obey.

He glanced across at his younger brother, who was stripping a sword-belt from another corpse, with his skinny, bare back exposed; Phil wondered if he, like Roselyn, could kick his brother hard enough to send him flying ten feet over the rail. Of course, he could never ask Roselyn … she was a countess and a Valkyrie, and he wasn't good with words, especially when many ears were listening.

Phil and Nate had stripped to their waists to search the bloody bodies ... right in front of Sister Aspertine, who'd *'eeped'* and turned away, so that she couldn't watch. Teasing her was fun; being married to God, neither of them could seriously consider Sister Aspertine as available, but she was young, cute, and guileless, and her attentions, however unwilling, were another trophy that they could compete over.

Phil smiled; he was older, with large, chiseled muscles, and he never failed to deride his younger brother for being smaller and weaker. Phil was determined to keep wooing Sister Aspertine; it would prove another contest in which Nate couldn't hope to beat him.

Watching Roselyn fight had impressed him. He hadn't been surprised when she'd decimated the Moors; he'd watched her and her shield-sisters defeat an entire army before Castle Bristlen; he only wished that he could fight like a Valkyrie.

Phil picked up a beautiful, blood-drenched helmet, blackened-steel, etched with fine traces of gold in an ornate pattern that looked like some savage beast, but which only shined into prominence when the sunlight hit it just right.

"Wow!" Nate said. "I claim that!"

"I found it!" Phil argued.

"I claimed it!"

Ten seconds later, Nate splashed overboard, after a brief but very brutal struggle, during which Karl shouted at both of them. By the time that Nate surfaced, sputtering and cursing, Phil had already buckled the prized helmet onto his head, and Karl was yelling angrily. Obeying Karl's orders, Phil pulled Nate back onboard the

Moor's ship, and to settle the argument, Karl allowed Phil to keep the helmet, but decreed that Nate could have his pick of everything else, and that Phil could claim nothing more until Nate had claimed everything that he wanted. Nate tried to avenge his pride by claiming everything, but Karl reminded them that everything either boy was wearing belonged to him … just like they did … and that he'd be sure to tell their father if they fought again.

Over an hour later, the Moor's ship floated away, stripped of everything, including two large purses of foreign coins, many weapons, and seven unusual suits of armor, strangely decorated, and many chests of fresh food, which their rowers had sat upon, a large box of odd jewelry, and two barrels of a potent drink that they couldn't identify, yet which Karl, Roselyn, and their five sailors gladly shared.

Phil stood, wearing only his ornate helmet above his waist. Nate was wearing a coat of the best mail, which had a pattern of twisting serpents made of brass-dipped rings woven amid the blackened steel, which matched Phil's helmet, and silver-etched vambraces so strong that they nearly matched Hel's armor, and a wide black belt with real gold on its lion-head buckle, which had gleaming red stones for eyes. He also wore new boots, and carried a long, wickedly-curved pole axe, a beautiful matching sword and dagger, and both coin purses, now empty; Karl let him keep everything except the coins. Phil sorted through the rest, but he disdained it all; his brother had taken the best body armor, but he'd won the prized helmet, and he didn't want anything that wasn't better than what his brother had.

A second ship would only slow them down, and nothing of value was left on it, so they pushed it off and set sail. Its fore was still drenched in blood and starting to attract flies as the morning air warmed, so they quickly put as much distance as they could between them and the empty ship of the Moors. Perhaps the Moors' other ships were still watching, from a safe distance, and would reclaim their vessel. Phil didn't care; the majesty of the stone pillars of Gibraltar loomed impressively overhead, not as tall as the familiar cliffs of Othar, and yet ominous, bolder and more majestic.

They sailed through the gap in the mighty pillars, and now that they had more food and drink than they needed, they rode in grand style, indulging in gluttony. The day passed in slothful delight and relaxation, save for the tedious chore of cleaning Hel's armor, which Nate and Phil attended to without bickering. Karl had threatened them both with horrible punishments if they started fighting again, and neither relished the idea of wearing Eloise's dresses for the rest of the voyage.

Everyone relaxed, although at one point, a fishing vessel sailed up beside them, spied the huge pile of weapons and armor stacked aft, and asked if they were the ship carrying the Goddess of War. Elaina scolded them, and told them that they were fools to believe in such rumors, and Karl ordered their prizes to be shifted to the fore, under the awning, where they wouldn't be seen.

One person didn't relax: Sister Aspertine hadn't smiled since the fight against the Moors had begun. She stared at Roselyn as if afraid to ask if she was the devil in a woman's semblance.

Phil knew every detail about Karl, Eloise, and Roselyn's adventures in Yggdrasil, and he knew Karl well enough to know when he was lying; Karl always swallowed hard, and then spoke with a dry mouth, whenever he had to deceive. Yet few believed their story of a universe centered around a giant tree, and Karl and Rafe often publicly denied it; better that their story became a legend, an unbelieved rumor that people told around fireplaces while getting drunk; that way the clergy, who hated the story, couldn't use it against Karl.

Sister Aspertine spoke very little, and Phil wondered if he could use her silence as a means to penetrate her confidences, to get closer to her, if only to annoy Nate, who, despite all proofs to the contrary, boasted that he was the ultimate desire of all women.

Phil continued to scrub and polish Hel's armor; he had no doubt that this armor belonged to the legendary Goddess of Death, as Lady Seren had described her so completely. The armor was steel, but it was the smoothest and strongest that he'd ever seen, and each plate seemed too heavy for its size and thickness, as if it were denser than mortal-forged armor. The black color wasn't just oil that had been poured onto it while the metal was still glowing from the forge; it shone black like obsidian, as if made of an entirely new metal. It also bore faint flutes, slightly-raised ridges that ran along the length of each plate, and its girdle of tiny black scales, each shaped like a small grinning skull, was beyond the skill of just any blacksmith; each scale was so identical that Phil couldn't tell them apart. The artisan who'd made this suit was a master at metalsmithing.

Phil had grabbed and was cleaning Roselyn's helmet, the like of which neither of them had ever seen, with its single ridge of long, steel, needle-sharp spines reaching from the forehead to the back; no one could wear it and not look threatening. It made the helmet that he'd stolen look amateurish. Yet Nate had foolishly grabbed the ornate breastplate, and then blushed to realize that he could've worn either breast-cup as a metal cap.

"Are you sure that you know what you're doing with those things?" Phil teased as Nate scrubbed the blood from Hel's domed breast-plates.

"I've played with these before," Nate replied smugly, polishing both breast-cups extra-vigorously.

Roselyn casually leaned over and whispered to them.

"If you boys are talking about my armor, then I may just take all of your teeth for a necklace."

They finished cleaning Hel's armor in silence.

When Roselyn was satisfied that Hel's armor was properly cleaned, dried, and oiled, she took it under the awning and changed back into it. While Phil washed his hands overboard, Nate went and sat on a sea chest beside Sister Aspertine, whose lips were pressed together tightly. She was glaring at the closed flap of the awning, listening to Roselyn armor. Wary, Phil stepped quietly up behind him.

"You don't like women wearing armor?" Nate asked softly.

Sister Aspertine startled to find that she was being addressed, but she returned her gaze to the awning.

"No one with a soul fights like that … especially not a woman!" Sister Aspertine said in a furtive whisper.

"I can't do it," Nate shrugged, sounding as if he were equally disturbed by Roselyn's sword-skills, which Phil knew was a lie. Phil hated his brother's penchant for dishonesty, but secretly envied Nate's ability to talk to total strangers … and to tell stories that commanded the attention of a whole crowd.

"You … have you known these people long?" Sister Aspertine asked him.

"Since Phil and I were children," Nate said. "Long before Karl became baron, and when Roselyn was only a countess."

Sister Aspertine shot him a reproachful glare.

"You … believe in their … that story?" Sister Aspertine asked. "That … *she* … is a Valkyrie …?"

"I believe that … if one word of it's true, then never has God worked in more mysterious ways," Nate said. "But Sir Karl's my knight; I'm honor-bound to …"

"Your first duty is to God!" Sister Aspertine whispered angrily.

"Of that, I've no doubt," Nate said.

Sister Aspertine took a deep breath, then let it out slowly, as if fighting to restrain herself. She nodded to Nate and whispered something to him conspiratorially, too softly for Phil to overhear.

Nate returned her nod, and then pretended to yawn and look out over the sea, examining the tall pillars of stone now far behind them, rapidly dwindling in the distance. Phil turned his face from theirs so they wouldn't see him scowl; *Nate was having private, secret talks with Sister Aspertine!*

What was he planning …?

Did his little brother really hope to seduce a nun …?

Even Nate wouldn't do that …!

Phil stole a few glances at Sister Aspertine while she was watching the closed awning, waiting for Roselyn to emerge. He didn't understand nuns. Sister Aspertine was young, pretty, and had smooth skin; it was a waste for any woman to spend her life in virgin innocence. Yet, like it or not, she was a nun; any playful flirtations with her could never become anything more … for him or Nate.

Phil and Nate had been listening to Karl's stories of Yggdrasil since they were children. Both believed that many gods existed, but Phil acknowledged that God was his god. Nate believed in nothing, having long ago rationalized that, even if every god and goddess ever worshipped actually existed, it didn't matter; the Divine Ones wasted few cares on human suffering.

Nate walked over to stand by the awning, pretending to be looking out at the sea, and then he closed his eyes, bowed his head, made the sign of the cross, and folded his hands, quietly, subtly, and knowing that Sister Aspertine was certain to be watching.

Phil hated how phony his brother could be. He could expose him, but how can you prove that someone isn't praying? He was likely to lose a war of words, and if he tossed his brother overboard again, despite how badly Nate deserved it, Karl was sure to be angry, and his duty wasn't to infuriate his knight.

This contest wasn't over! Phil thought determinedly while Nate continued pretending to pray. *Nate would lose again!*

Almost a week later, after making excellent time, with a brisk, warm wind filling their sails, they came in view of a magnificent coastal city.

"Italia!" one of the sailors said, and the other sailors smiled.

"Italy?" Karl asked. "Perhaps we should stop."

"We have to find the Seer by the end of summer," Roselyn reminded him with unconcealed contempt.

"We'll sail faster if we lighten our load," Karl said. "We don't need extra armor, it's taking up deck-space, and selling it will give us more coins for food, so that we don't have to go back early for lack of funds."

"I can get coins anywhere," Roselyn said.

"We're not thieves," Karl said.

"We stole from the Moors …!" Roselyn argued.

"We took only what they abandoned; we didn't steal it," Karl said. "They approached us as thieves; we helped them to see the error of their ways."

"My husband's right," Eloise said. "Karl and I are representatives of the English crown; we can't be accused of common thievery."

"They weren't Catholics," Sister Aspertine said, as if that settled the matter. "Still, their pagan souls might be worthy of a prayer. Perhaps we should donate their armor to a church …?"

"We may need the extra coinage, begging your pardon, my knight," Nate spoke up. "However, if we don't use it, then we could give it to Lord Sir Rafe; he'll spend it on God's will back in du Harmonn."

"An excellent idea," Karl said, clearly decided upon this course.

Nate glanced at Sister Aspertine; she met his eyes, then nodded so slightly that only he and Phil saw it. A brief smile played upon her lips. Then Nate turned away from her, so that she couldn't see his face … and grinned smugly at Phil.

They sailed into a huge, noisy port. After paying a slight moorage fee to the dock master, Karl rented a handcart, and had Nate and Phil pull it, with the help of two of their sailors, Henry and Samuel, who got out of the boat to assist. Karl ordered their remaining three sailors, Dennel, Thorkel, and Rishard, to guard their ship.

They piled everything that they didn't need into the handcart, including all of the extra armor, which made the cart so heavy that, even with Karl helping, they found it hard to drag uphill. Roselyn finally had to help them. Despite that she was wearing a large hooded cloak to hide her armor, her Valkyrie strength pulled the armor-filled handcart uphill, although even she seemed to labor from the effort.

A huge marketplace wasn't far from the docks, and their arrival sparked unwarranted interest. The merchants pressing them, trying to sell them every commodity in Italy, quickly grew alarming, and soon seemed overwhelming. Men and women alike seemed affronted to see Roselyn wearing a suit of black armor under her cloak, but as Sister Aspertine walked with them, most crossed themselves and said nothing.

Phil could understand a little Italian, but the merchants spoke with such speed and heavy accents that he quickly gave up all hope of understanding. Elaina, Eloise, and Roselyn all spoke Italian, and the women walked from merchant to merchant, displaying their cart, and slowing selling all the extra armor and weapons that they had.

By late afternoon, only a few items were left unsold, and little of it was worth much. Karl was smiling, a new bag over his shoulder heavy with coins.

"Let's go back," Karl said.

The merchants loudly objected to their departure, shouting what Phil assumed were bargain prices for everything that they had.

On the walk back, the two sailors alone were able to manage the nearly-empty cart, and Nate stepped up to walk beside Sister Aspertine too quickly for Phil to intercede; instead, he squeezed himself between Elaina and Roselyn.

"That's a handsome church!" Nate pointed to a tall, ornamental cross atop a steeple.

"Indeed," Sister Aspertine said. "It's been too long since any of us have received communion …"

"We don't have time," Karl said.

"There's always time for attending mass," Sister Aspertine said.

"We promised Roselyn …," Karl began, and Sister Aspertine stopped so suddenly that everyone halted, if only to avoid running into her.

"Lord Sir Rafe and Deacon Michael James entrusted me with the keeping of your souls!" Sister Aspertine insisted.

"We are not all …!" Eloise began, but Karl cut her off.

"We are all devoted Catholics!" Karl said emphatically, so loudly that several passersby paused to look at them suspiciously.

"Perhaps … we should … pray," Nate said, looking around at the many strangers eyeing them.

"We don't want to draw attention …," Elaina whispered.

"I will not go into …!" Roselyn started.

"You'd best wait outside," Eloise said to Roselyn. "Some might not find armor appropriate … on a woman … in a church."

"Just a quick prayer," Karl said. "We can't stay for long."

Covered by her cloak, Roselyn suggested that she could guard the handcart alone, but Karl argued that trouble was less likely to approach the cart if three, rather than one, stood around it. They left Roselyn with Henry and Samuel, and entered the church to find that mass had just started. Phil managed to sit beside Sister Aspertine; Nate tried to push him aside, but Phil had wedged into the pew first and blocked him with his thicker body. Nate couldn't start a physical confrontation in a church, but he glared daggers at his older brother. Phil removed his Moorish helmet, and watched smiling as Nate suffered, trying to remain perfectly still, as his fancy armor loudly clinked in the quiet church.

Karl looked impatient as the mass dragged on, and when the last prayer ended, he was the first to rise. He did leave a respectable donation with the priest, although it was only half of what he usually tithed; nobody here knew him, and he wasn't wearing his coronet, so the demands to keep up royal appearances didn't seem required. Yet Sister Aspertine insisted on thanking the priest, and introducing herself, and everyone had to wait while they conversed on the doings of the church and what abbey had raised her.

When they finally emerged, they found Roselyn and the sailors impatiently waiting. Within twenty minutes, they returned to the harbor.

Yet, as they approached the streets near the docks, a great pandemonium greeted them, and distant screams echoed across the city. When they finally reached the wooden planks, grim-faced men crowded its boards, making pulling their cart through the crowd difficult.

"*Our boat …!*" Henry cried, looking over the heads before them. "*Baron Sir Karl, our boat's gone …!*"

Abandoning the cart, they rushed forward. Henry pushed through first, and he found a dying sailor, soaking wet and coated with blood, laying upon the wooden boards of an empty dock.

"*Rish!*" Henry shouted. "*Rishard, what happened …?*"

"They didn't have a prayer," one of the men standing nearby said in broken English.

"What happened?" Karl demanded as Henry kneeled to comfort Rishard.

"They struck only ten minutes ago," the stranger said to Karl. "Seven men came walking up the dock, carrying those crates." He pointed to a pile of empty wooden boxes. "Without warning, they dropped the crates and jumped aboard your ship with knives flashing; your men didn't stand a chance. This one …," he pointed at Rishard, "was the first one stabbed, and half of them were setting sail before the other two were fully dead. He's got seven holes in him, but he managed to jump overboard as they pushed off … unlike his murdered companions, God save their souls. Their boat … your boat, begging your pardon … floated away from the dock in seconds, and sailed out of the harbor less than two minutes later. There was nothing that the rest of us could do; it happened too fast."

"Where's Dennel and Thorkel?" Samuel demanded.

"They didn't dump them overboard," the man on the dock said. "At least, not close enough for us to see."

Elaina knelt beside Rishard, examining him.

"He's not dead," she said. "But he's dying. Eloise, can you help?"

Eloise looked wary, but she stepped forward.

"No!" Karl hissed. *"We can't draw any more attention …!"*

"The only thing we can do for him is pray," Sister Aspertine said firmly, and she folded her hands and bowed her head.

Eloise glared at Sister Aspertine, who tried to ignore her.

"Stand back," Eloise ordered them all.

The crowd looked confused, but Henry and Elaina instantly moved aside. Eloise untied a silk pouch upon her belt and drew out a perfectly round white stone; the Seer's moonstone.

"Eloise …!" Karl said warningly.

Eloise knelt beside the dying sailor and held the moonstone aloft; its polished white brilliance shone in the sunlight. Then she lowered it and placed it upon Rishard's bloody chest.

"What is she …?" Sister Aspertine demanded, but Phil shushed her.

"Knife," Eloise said, and she held out her hand expectantly.

Phil drew a small dagger and placed it into her hand. Eloise held up the knife in both hands, bowed before it, and then, with the tip of the knife, she traced the line of Rishard's deepest wound, across his stomach. Then she turned its blade toward her dress, and without hesitation, she pulled out the fabric of her dress and stabbed through the cloth, then pulled at both rough edges of the hole until a wide rip opened over her midsection. Her pale stomach bared, Eloise kissed her fingertip, then touched the knife-wound upon Rishard's stomach, and slid her finger lightly along it. Then she pushed her finger deep into the wound; Rishard cried out, but Henry and Elaina grabbed and held him still.

Eloise lifted her blood-dripping finger, and taking a deep breath, she painted the line of Rishard's wound upon her own stomach. Instantly she cried out, and doubled over, shaking and trembling, as if she'd been stabbed.

The whole crowd stepped back, and many made the sign of the cross.

"Dear sweet Jesus …!" Sister Aspertine exclaimed.

Eloise recovered slowly, tears flooding from her eyes, looking as if she were going to retch. Slowly she reached down and examined another wound, this one on Rishard's side. She traced the line of his cut with the tip of the knife.

"I don't have the strength," Eloise whispered, and she held up the knife to Phil. "Cut my dress … along the side."

Phil glanced worriedly at Karl, who looked furious, but Karl nodded, and Phil took the knife and opened a hole in the side of Eloise's dress. Eloise closed her eyes tightly, as if gathering strength, and then kissed her bloody fingertip, traced the line of the second wound, dove her finger in as deep as it would go, and then drew the same mark upon her skin, between her own ribs, with his blood.

Eloise's scream rang out, deafening, and more signs of the cross were made, but no one moved to stop her. Sister Aspertine tried to step forward, but Nate grabbed her by one thin arm; everyone except the nun seemed to know better than to interfere with magic; the stories that he and Nate had learned as a child explained that magic mustn't be interrupted, and the strangers on the dock seemed too horrified to speak.

Eloise writhed and fell onto her side, sobbing, but her mother held her firmly, and slowly pulled her back up. With one hand, her mother reached down and wiped her palm over the first wound on Rishard; his stomach was still bloody, but the wound looked half-healed.

"It's working," Elaina said to her daughter. "You must go on."

"Those two wounds aren't mortal," an Italian sailor whispered, pointing to cuts upon Rishard's arms, "… but there's one on his back …"

Karl helped Phil turn Rishard over; he had a wide cut beside one of his shoulder blades. Eloise took the blade, and traced the cut with its tip, despite her shaking hand, and then held up the knife. Without asking, Phil cut a hole in Eloise's dress, exposing her back, and Eloise repeated her motions, this time screaming, falling over, and thrashing so hard that Phil, Henry, and Karl had to hold her still to keep her from further hurting herself.

Eloise collapsed limply, wavering on the edge of consciousness, unable to walk. She could heal no more; they bound up Rishard's remaining wounds as best they could; several sailors gladly donated their shirts, tearing them into strips for bandages. At Karl's insistence, they recovered the handcart, and bundled Rishard and the unconscious Eloise into it, and pulled them away as quickly as they could.

"Be warned, each of you!" Elaina said to the crowd before they departed, laying a hand upon Roselyn and drawing open her cloak to reveal the black armor of Hel and the long, bright sword resting in her belt. "What you've seen today, and the rumors you've heard of a ship full of Moors, will seem trivial to any who dares speak of this. Beware the curse of the Valkyrie: *no man can withstand them!"*

Roselyn glared at the crowd of sailors, and then reached out and took from the hands of one old sailor a metal hook which was imbedded into the wood of a thick, strong pole. It took her several seconds, but finally there was a loud *'crack!'*, and Roselyn dropped both halves of the broken pole onto the dock.

As they pushed out of the crowd and walked away from the dock, no one followed, and not a sound was uttered behind them. Phil wasn't surprised to see Sister Aspertine staggering, looking horrified, walking beside Nate, who was helping her walk … and grinning stupidly.

Frowning, Phil shook his head; *some things were more important than rivalry.*

Chapter 21

The City of Italia

NATE

"This party is cursed!" Sister Aspertine shouted angrily. *"We travel with a demon and a witch!"*

Nate bit back his smile and struggled not to shake his head. They were crowded into a single, smoke-stinking room in the back of a seedy tavern, trying to save the coins that they had. Most of their wealth, including the foreign coins from the purses that they'd found upon the Moor's ship, had been aboard their now-stolen ship, along with their coronets, spare clothes, all of their food and gear, and most of Eloise's magical tools. The sale of their captured armor, added to the few coins from Castle Bristlen that they'd carried to the marketplace, would feed them aplenty, but were insufficient to buy a new, ocean-worthy ship.

Their cramped room looked like it'd formerly been a low-class brothel; three aged rope-beds filled the room, each with a stained straw mattress and a single worn blanket, with thin wooden walls whose boards were pockmarked with knotholes, half of which seemed to have fallen out. Some of the knotholes were plugged with oily rags, but enough remained to send lonely beams of light streaming into their windowless room. Lacking enough room for everyone to stand, Elaina, Eloise, and Sister Aspertine sat upon one bed, and Roselyn, Phil, and Henry sat upon the other. Karl, Nate, and Samuel stood leaning against the wall, all staring at Sister Aspertine. Upon the third bed was Rishard, who was still alive, but moaning in his sleep.

"You knew what we were before you came," Karl said to Sister Aspertine.

"How could I be expected to believe …?" Sister Aspertine demanded.

"Exactly," Eloise said weakly, still tired from her spellcasting. "Like everyone here, you chose to believe; don't blame us if you chose wrong."

"Blasphemy!" Sister Aspertine cried. *"How dare you, witch …?"*

"Sister, Rishard can't continue; he has to be taken home," Karl said. "Perhaps you should remain behind and escort him … when he can travel … and see to his needs."

Sister Aspertine glared at all of them; her bright blue-eyed gaze could've seared them alive, and her frown couldn't have been deeper.

"That … ridiculous story that Lord Sir Rafe told me … *was it true?"* Sister Aspertine asked.

"Do you know any mortal women who can do what I can?" Roselyn asked.

"If anything that Lord Sir Rafe said was true, then you're sworn to a pagan devil, and your soul's already forfeit," Sister Aspertine said to Roselyn.

"Then my soul is equally lost," Eloise said. "As is the soul of the Seer, whom we seek to rescue. None of us invited you or welcome your presence; perhaps it's best if you leave now … to perform your duty."

Sister Aspertine scanned their faces and alighted on Nate.

"What of you?" she asked. "Are you sworn to Holy God … or …?"

Nate glanced at Karl.

"Lord Sir Rafe himself baptized me right before I was squired, and I've attended mass at least once a week since then," Nate said.

Sister Aspertine turned from him to Phil.

"And … you?" she asked.

Phil frowned and swallowed hard.

"I was … also baptized … by Lord Sir Rafe," Phil said softly. 'But I … can't deny what I've seen."

"What've you seen?" Sister Aspertine asked.

Phil glanced at Roselyn … and pulled at the collar of his tunic, as if to give his throat room for words.

"I've seen the Valkyrie ride the skies … on winged horses … and defeat an entire army," Phil said.

Nate grinned; he'd seen the same, but he was too clever to admit it, unlike his stupid older brother. Their mother had taught him and Phil about Jesus, but their father had always insisted that they attend the monthly summer moon-dances, which were always exciting, and more fun than a Catholic mass. Nate had never been drawn to church as his older brother had; religion was just a bunch of people arguing philosophy, not the revelry and excitement of watching beautiful women dance with moon-lanterns. When he'd turned fourteen, Karl had taken him and Phil as squires, mostly because of the deep friendship between Castle Bristlen and their dad. Since then, Nate had learned to accept all three religions, and he never worried about religious rivalries; if he was forced to choose, he'd side with Odin; the Norse faith, fighting and drinking in Valhalla, sounded more fun than floating clouds or fancy gardens.

Fun seemed to be the only reason for following any faith. After all, the companions had risked their lives to bring the Lady of the Druids to Yggdrasil, and what reward did She give them? Horses! Their adventures had given Odin a new einherjar, and instead of rewarding them, he'd taken Roselyn for himself. They'd given Hel the first taste of friendship that she'd ever known, and what did she give them? Hel had chased and tried to kill them. Some Catholics suffered miserable lives, and starved to death, while praying for relief; *gods and goddesses don't help people.*

"Did anyone else witness …?" Sister Aspertine asked.

"We all saw it," Eloise said. "If you hadn't been hiding in a convent …!"

"The Lord's work is not *'hiding',*" Sister Aspertine snapped.

"Enough," Karl said. "Sister Aspertine, we'll give you enough coins to escort Rishard back to England."

"No," Sister Aspertine said. "I made a promise to Lord Sir Rafe, a true man of God, and I won't break that oath for the wills of pagans. Obviously my presence here is all that saves you from Heaven's wrath …"

"I don't fear Heaven's wrath," Roselyn said.

"Blasphemy!" Sister Aspertine shouted.

"Rishard's wounds will take months to heal," Elaina said. "If we take him, either he'll slow us down … or we'll have to abandon him somewhere worse than Italy."

"What about a local hospital?" Nate suggested. "We could pay for his care … and pick him up on the way home …?"

"Pay with what …?" Henry asked, and then he froze, as if afraid to have spoken so boldly. Karl frowned at him.

"Henry, speak up anytime you want," Karl said. "Squire, you're right, of course. I'd hoped to use this as an excuse to send our young companion home, although Rafe would be furious with me. Sister Aspertine, let me be blunt: the further that we go on this mission, the less you'll like it. You'd be wise to leave now, with honor, to care for this man …"

"Only now do I see why Lord Sir Rafe insisted that I come," Sister Aspertine said. "The further that you go on this mission, the greater jeopardy your souls will be in; I'll do my duty and turn you from your heathen ways."

Roselyn and Elaina both opened their mouths to object, but Karl silenced them with a gesture.

"The women will take the beds, save for the one that Rishard is using. The men shall sleep on the floor," Karl said. "Nate and Phil, tomorrow we'll have to sell our armor, and then we'll leave Rishard at a hospital and try to find a boat that we can afford."

After prayers, Phil took off his helmet and stretched out on the floor by Rishard's bed. Nate laid down in a corner, wearing his armor, draped his thin cloak over him, and leaned his head against a wall. The laughing customers in the tavern, whose drunken voices often rose in anger, floated through the thin walls; Nate wished that he could join them. Those drunkards had few troubles that drinks couldn't wash away, and their befuddled arguments could be settled by fights.

All problems were like that. He sometimes felt that he should be in charge of their company, since he was the only one who made quick decisions. Phil's constant competition against him made no sense. Nate was younger and smaller, and maybe a bit weaker, but Phil was an idiot who couldn't figure out how to coil a rope in a circle. When the need for intelligence arose, Sister Aspertine would see which brother was truly superior, and then all of Phil's attempts to usurp her attentions would be lost.

Rishard was left in the caring company of a convent of white-habited nuns, who ran a charity hospital, and were grateful to accept Karl's coins to care for Rishard until the end of summer. Karl ended up paying more than their usual charge, since Sister Aspertine had refused to deceive other nuns, and introduced Baron Sir Karl and Baroness Eloise by their regal titles. She ignored Roselyn, whose title as a countess seemed to be negated by her status as a 'Valkyrie trying to regain the favor of a pagan deity'. Holding only their weapons and their purse of coins, having sold everything except Hel's armor and their swords, they emerged from the well-tended hospital onto a narrow lane in which few strangers were traveling.

"We should go back to the docks," Roselyn insisted. "Just tell me which ship you want …"

"No killing!" Karl insisted. "Also, no thieving, not if we can help it."

"It's a sign from God," Sister Aspertine said. "He wouldn't have taken your ship if He wanted you to go on this mission."

"I, too, was raised Catholic," Elaina said. "The hand of God could also be seen in our determination to continue; most of the saints overcame hardships."

"Your betrayal of God's faith is the greatest sin," Sister Aspertine said to Elaina.

"Don't tell us what God demands," Eloise said, rising in defense of her mother. "Of all the deities worshipped in this company, He's the only one that no one has ever seen."

"Enough!" Karl shouted as Sister Aspertine started to object. "No point going to the docks; we don't have enough to buy a boat big enough to carry all of us. But we're still a baron, a baroness, and a countess of England; let's see if that gets us anywhere. I had Eloise ask the sisters; the local ruler is Prince Fernando; we'll go see him … and ask if he can help."

They headed toward the busier streets, and there the women asked where Prince Fernando lived, and everyone pointed them to a great white palace upon a hill, distant, but easily seen from most of the city.

Most of the day was spent walking up the crowded main streets, and Roselyn complained that it was too hot to wear a hooded cloak over her armor.

"If you weren't wearing armor, then you wouldn't need the cloak," Eloise said.

"The armor of Hel isn't to be cast aside," Roselyn said.

"Hell …?" Sister Aspertine asked, but no one answered her.

"Just stay in the middle, where you're least seen," Karl said. "Squires, Henry, Samuel: close ranks around her."

Eloise gave Roselyn a nasty glare, then wrapped her arm around Karl's waist, walking close beside him.

Nate smiled; Eloise was his knight's wife and his baroness, and Roselyn was his first love; Karl was right to keep both women on a string. Nate wished that he had two beautiful women competing over him. Yet Nate kept his mouth shut; he was too smart to interfere in the obvious rivalry between Baroness Eloise and Roselyn the Valkyrie, but he felt certain that the success or failure of their quest in Egypt would hinge upon which woman got the sole right to claim Karl.

Personally, Nate had always felt that Karl should stay with Eloise as long as she was young and beautiful; when she grew too old, then Roselyn the Valkyrie would still be young. Yet Roselyn was no longer a Valkyrie; *which should Karl choose now?*

Nate wondered what the name of this city was, but he didn't ask Sister Aspertine; better to save their talks for private conversations. Italy was certainly a beautiful place, although as hot as summers in England ever got, with sunny cobblestone roads and tall, elegant buildings, and it was full of flowers growing in hanging pots … and people smiling. Its busy marketplaces were thriving, and Karl bought them all some hard, brown breads and red wine.

As they walked through the crowd, Nate smiled at many of the pretty girls, all of whom blushed and smiled back at him coyly. The dresses that they wore looked different from those he saw in du Harmonn, fancier, many with traces of delicate lace, and of all colors, as if every woman wore a party gown, and their dark eyes and hair effused an exotic look that Nate found strangely attractive. Meanwhile, the men of Italy seemed fascinated by pale Eloise, Elaina, Roselyn, and even pretty young Sister Aspertine, to whom they all bowed respectfully, but they looked askance at the men, who clutched their weapons as they walked.

Several city guards watched them pass by with narrowed eyes, and some seemed to be following them.

Nate spied two guards waving signals to others, and one whispered into the ears of a small boy, who then ran quickly ahead, right past them. As they walked up a long, straight, narrow road, the white palace of Prince Fernando clearly visible not far ahead, Nate wasn't surprised to find their path blocked by a line of guards, and another half-dozen suddenly filled into the lane in their wake.

"Danger!" Roselyn whispered, and all of them stopped.

Elderly mothers shucking peas in the street paled as both paths of the strange, armored foreigners were blocked. Playing children were snatched up, and the city guards ignored the anxious peasants who hurriedly fled between their armored ranks. All nearby shutters and door slammed shut, and unseen braces scraped, barricading all escapes. Karl motioned the companions to silence, staring at the guards. All who carried weapons reached for their grips.

"No one draw," Karl said. "Eloise, ask what they want."

Eloise spoke in Italian so slowly and deliberately that Nate could almost follow their conversation, and several city guards chuckled as she conversed with one tall man, who was obviously their leader.

"They want our swords and our money," Eloise told Karl. "He says we look like assassins …"

"Is every man in Italy a thief?" Karl sighed.

"I can …," Roselyn began.

"You can't kill them all instantaneously," Karl said to Roselyn. "We have four swords; Eloise, Elaina, and Sister Aspertine must be defended."

Suddenly Sister Aspertine spoke to the leader of the guards, and he bowed politely to her.

"She asked if the women could be allowed to stand aside while they dispute," Elaina interpreted. "Their leader agreed."

Roselyn and Elaina glared at Sister Aspertine; Nate knew that she shouldn't have spoken without permission, but Karl angrily nodded.

"Henry, Samuel, you don't have swords; stand by the women, and be prepared to defend them," Karl said.

"I can do this alone," Roselyn said.

"We fight as a company," Karl said. "You take out those in front; we'll guard your back."`

As the others moved aside, Roselyn pulled off her hooded cloak and threw it to Samuel. Three swords slid from various scabbards, and Roselyn drew the long sword of Hel from her belt and raised it high. The city guards all smiled; *there were over a dozen of them …*

Roselyn stepped clear of the men, and suddenly she jumped almost six feet straight up in the air, fully armored, performed a flip, slashed her blade on both sides of her, and landed on her feet with ease. The city guards lost their smiles; Roselyn raised her sword threateningly and glared at their leader; *everyone knew who her first target would be.* The city guards held their swords and spears grimly, realizing that they were facing more than they'd expected.

"Whenever you wish," Roselyn said to Karl.

"Slay only those you must," Karl said. "We can't expect favor if we kill all of Prince Fernando's guards."

"ODIN!" Roselyn cried.

The battle began. She'd done enough acrobatics to frighten her foes; Roselyn stepped forward almost cautiously, her poise perfect, her blade held ready. Their captain and two guards stepped backwards, but three guards tried to rush her, two swinging for her blade, one stabbing with a spear. Roselyn jumped back to let their swords swish through empty air, and then sliced the spearhead off its haft, and before any of the guards could react, Roselyn spun forward and dropped to one knee … and slashed Hel's heavy blade with all of her might, a wide, sweeping swing that sliced through armor and knee-joints. Three half-legless guards fell screaming, blood shooting from their knee-stumps.

Those behind them charged as a wall, and Roselyn rose and swung; the blade of Hel sliced through the sword of the guard closest to her, and Hel's black armor deflected three spearpoints as she rapidly spun, and then Roselyn jumped forward, too close for their longer weapons to threaten; three more fell dead or wounded, and the remainder ran backwards, too daunted to fight.

"No!" Phil cried, and he charged forward.

Roselyn spun to find a city guard, whose skin and armor had been slashed, but not too deeply, had jumped to his feet, wielding in one hand the speartip whose haft Roselyn had severed. The attacking guard hesitated as Phil's sword pointed at him, his speartip inches from Roselyn's back. Then the blade of Roselyn rested against his throat, and Nate's swordtip touched his back.

"Don't kill him!" Karl shouted. "Drop that speartip! Roselyn, let him go."

The guard's weapon clattered to the cobblestones, and Roselyn drew back her sword, leaving his neck unbloodied save for the drippings from Hel's razor-sharp edge.

"We're going to see Prince Fernando," Karl said to their shocked leader.

"Forgive me, but we're sworn to protect …!" their leader said.

"We're not here to harm anyone … who lets us pass in peace … or your Prince Fernando, to whom I shall report your attempted thievery," Karl said.

"Uh … Thank you, Master," the leader bowed, as if afraid to argue. "If I may humbly ask … as I'm a watch captain … forgive me …, but … what business have you with Prince Fernando?"

"Three of our company were attacked, at the docks, by a different set of thieves," Karl snarled. "Two were killed, and our boat was stolen, while we were in church. We require a loan so that we don't have to become robbers … *like you!*"

"Begging your pardon, my lord, but you need no credit, if you desire money …," the leader said.

"What do you mean?" Karl asked.

"There's a gladiator hall in the city," the leader said, glancing nervously at Roselyn. "A good wagerer could triple their money with each fight, if they bet wisely … and you have a warrior who can't be beat!"

"No," Karl said.

"Why not?" Roselyn demanded. "Better to earn: *warriors don't beg.*"

Karl almost smiled, and Nate understood; *when Karl told his story, those were Eric's exact words on the first day that they'd met.*

"It's late in the day," the leader said. "Allow me to escort you to my home; it's not big, but we have a warm fireplace and food for all of you … and if you'll allow me to place a few side-bets, then I'll cover the entry fees."

After a long walk to his house, the home of Captain Markus Gavino was indeed small, but warm and homey. His wife, Gia, objected, but at Captain Markus' insistence, Gia hurried out to the marketplace to purchase more bread, meat, and especially strong ale; the latter at Roselyn's insistence. Captain Markus had several children, including a three year old boy who hid under the table at first, but slowly came out, and eventually amused himself by climbing over all of them. Nate and Phil were given the task of cleaning Roselyn's sword and armor again, and her suggestion that they clean her breastplate silently was met with strict obedience. Captain Markus gladly provided the boys with rags for cleaning, and when Gia, their eldest son, and their daughter returned with provisions, a delicious meal was quickly prepared.

Afterwards, they sat before the fireplace and enjoyed their evening as best they could.

Nate noticed that Roselyn kept eyeing the children, especially the three year old, but when he tried to climb upon her, Roselyn picked him up and passed him to another. Yet she surrendered him reluctantly, if she were trying to keep up an appearance, but really wanted to play with the child. After each release of the boy, Roselyn quickly drank from her mug of ale. At first, Nate had thought that Roselyn was going to hurt the child, but then he recalled her playing with his little sister back when Edith was only two; Countess Roselyn had loved children, but her life as a Valkyrie, dying in Valhalla, couldn't be good for bearing offspring. Nate suspected that other people's children reminded Roselyn of the sons and daughters that she'd never have ... and of the three children that Eloise had already given to Karl.

Nate indulged in the unwavering attention that Sister Aspertine lavished upon him, especially after he asked her to say grace before they ate, and again before they slept. Nate obliged her by praying long and loudly, and Sister Aspertine smiled every time that she saw him fold his hands and bow his head.

Since he'd first seen Sister Aspertine's bright blue eyes and pert figure, Nate had known that he needed to win her favor away from his stupid brother, whose height and physique brainless women seemed to admire. Pretending to be religious was easy … for him, but Phil couldn't conceive or execute a convincing pretense. Phil never once volunteered to pray aloud, and when forced to by their mother, Phil's prayers were always short; Nate suspected that he couldn't recall a long scriptural passage, despite having heard them at every mass since they were children. Nate didn't believe in the power of prayer, but praying when someone was watching, when he'd get credit for it, was eminently rewarding …!

Chapter 22

The Basement Coliseum

ROSELYN

Roselyn awoke instantly as the thin arm touched her ribs; in the dying glow of the fireplace, Roselyn startled to realize whose arm it was: *Eloise.* Eloise had sat beside Karl to eat, and when they stretched out to sleep, she'd claimed the spot on the other side of Karl. Under the blankets that Captain Markus had provided, they'd fallen asleep, Karl sandwiched between them. At first, Roselyn was infuriated; Eloise was her rival, and for Eloise to rest her forearm upon Roselyn's ribs was going too far … but Eloise was sound asleep, unknowing, cuddled up against Karl by habit, while Roselyn was cuddled against his other side by sheer force of will; Roselyn was unaccustomed to sharing a bed with anyone. Yet, to her mirth, Karl lay squeezed, even in his sleep, with both of his arms pressed at his sides, pinned as if bound by Herfjötur. Unable to escape, Karl looked worried even as he snored; Roselyn grinned at his predicament: *trapped even in sleep!*

The touch of Eloise's arm hadn't bothered Roselyn until she'd become a Valkyrie. Roselyn had given up worrying about the differences that she'd had with her former self; in the Blessed Pool of the Fairies, Silvana and Glororil had taught her the importance of not worrying about change; anybody would be changed if they'd lived eight years as a Valkyrie, and doubtless she'd change further still.

The most useless struggle of all was to fight against change.

Roselyn felt angry with herself; *Karl belonged to her,* but she couldn't blame Eloise for wanting to keep him. She'd defend Eloise with her life, if she had to; as a Valkyrie, Roselyn would disgrace herself if an enemy killed any companion of hers.

If a Valkyrie truly wanted one of her companions dead, then it was her duty to kill them.

A worse trouble bothered her; *her failing Valkyrie skills.* Sitting beside that river in Asgard, Mist had said that her strength would leave her if she returned to Midgard. Roselyn was so accustomed to being strong, to never feeling tired, that she barely recalled weakness, but on the road, before she'd slain or wounded half of Captain Markus' men, Roselyn had jumped six feet into the air; in Valhalla, Roselyn had once jumped eight feet, and Skögul had drilled her until she could barely stand, to insure that she could do feats that few others could; her training under the tutelage of Skögul had been the most intense experience of her life, and the most painful, often ending in dying. Skögul would've scorned her recent puny jump.

Also, she'd almost lost; Phil had saved her from being stabbed in the back. Phil hadn't needed to attack; his shout alone had given her sufficient warning, but the fact that she'd needed his warning felt troubling. Kicked out of Valhalla, where she'd constantly drunk the Water of Life, eaten the golden apples of immortality, and trained every day against the toughest einherjar, Roselyn was losing her edge. She knew what she had to do … it was just harder to do it.

Was she truly becoming Countess Roselyn again …?

Worst of all, a strange weight seemed to be dragging at her, as if heavy chains shackled her limbs. She felt each movement of her body more intensely than she could remember, as if each stretch and flex strained her, or as if all of her energy had been siphoned away. She even felt tired, as if she hadn't gotten enough sleep, and then she recognized the nearly-forgotten sensation: *weariness.* For the first time in eight years, Roselyn felt exhausted, despite having just awoken, and sleeping on the hard floor of Captain Markus' house had felt … *uncomfortable.*

Today, Roselyn had to fight for her life before a crowd of beer-sodden revelers betting upon her prowess against professional gladiators; despite any weariness, *Valkyrie don't lose.* If she didn't win today, even if she survived, she could never face her shield-sisters again.

If she didn't win, then never again would she be a Valkyrie.

Almost reluctantly, Roselyn rolled away from Karl and rose with absolute silence; *some Valkyrie skills were still hers!* Everyone else still slept; she glanced at Hel's armor, but if she put it on, then its noise would awaken everyone. She began carefully stretching each joint, slowly but fully, even her fingers and toes, flexing each muscle, and making sure that she was at her fighting prime. She was no longer in Valhalla; *death on Midgard was death forever.*

The squalid, reeking tavern displayed no sign over its door, nor customers at its tables, but Captain Markus gave the barman a copper coin for each of them, and he opened a false wall and let them pass through a too-narrow hall, which led to a dark, smelly stairs. They descended the creaky steps, listening to a loud murmur, until they pushed past a thick wooden door. A burly gatekeeper stood there … and eyed them suspiciously, especially Sister Aspertine. Inside the room was a round, wide pit, around which were three levels where spectators could stand, and look overtop each other, to see down into the pit. Six tall torches surrounded the pit, which was eight feet deep and fifteen feet in diameter.

Everything reeked of rotting blood.

Each small, swarthy knot of people stood gathered around a big, heavily-armored warrior. No other women could be seen, but one man on the top-most row stood before a stand of kegs, from which he was pouring foamy beers. Despite the six torches, the room looked dark; every filthy wall was caked in soot.

Markus led them to a small table, behind which sat a bald fat man.

"Aren't you a city guard?" the fat man asked contemptuously.

"Not today," Captain Markus said.

"Not if you win," the fat man said. "What if you lose?"

"I have my own gladiator," Captain Markus said. "I'm not here to lose."

Many laughed at this, and all eyes turned to look at Karl. Captain Markus dropped a silver coin upon the table, and the fat man scooped it up, then looked at Karl.

"Be warned, stranger; once you enter that pit, expect no mercy," the fat man said.

"On the contrary," Karl said. "Our best will spare any warrior that admits defeat and begs for mercy … and everyone who pays their bets."

Everyone but the fat man laughed.

"Who's your champion?" the fat man asked.

In answer to his question, a four-foot gleaming blade rose out of Roselyn's cloak and reached out to touch the fat man's throat. Everyone looked surprised, but Roselyn's face was hidden by her hood.

"I'll bet fifty, or a hundred against anyone who gives me odds," Captain Markus announced to the crowd.

"Why should we give you odds?" the fat man said, trying to peer inside Roselyn's hood. "Let's see your champion."

Slowly, as if desiring to heighten the anticipation, Roselyn reached out her gauntleted hand and unfastened her cloak clasp. She waited until every man in the room had paused to look at the new champion before she jerked off her hooded cloak, revealing herself, without removing her blade from the fat man's throat.

A moment's silence was followed by loud laughter and competing shouts of ever-increasing odds. The armored warriors all stood up to look at her, and one shouted:

"After she's dead, can we keep her body?"

Many laughed, but Roselyn turned to face the warrior who'd shouted, a tall, hairy, muscled brute in thick mail.

"I'll kill you for those words," Roselyn said.

"I'm Galwarth, killer of thirty men," the brute replied, and he strapped on a simple helmet, a metal cap with a short nasal, and lifted an iron flail with three metal balls on short chains attached to a long metal bar, with a nasty spike protruding from the other end. With a laugh, he jumped into the pit, and then motioned for Roselyn to join him.

"Five-to-one on Galwarth!" a man with many rings shouted.

"I bet for the woman; are there no better odds?" Captain Markus challenged, but no one else spoke.

"I, too, have coins to wager," Karl said.

"I'll match all of your bet!" the man with the many rings said.

"We're strangers," Karl said. "How do we know that you'll pay … if you lose?"

"Any who can't pay their debts must themselves enter the pit," the fat man said.

"At your odds, I'll bet all that I have," Karl said, and he held up and shook his purse of coins.

A moment later, Roselyn jumped down into the pit amid shouts of glee and sadistic laughter. Galwarth leered at her; if she lost, then he'd do more than kill her.

Roselyn knew why he'd chosen the flail; he had no fear of her. His confidence that he could beat her into submission, and then rape her for the pleasure of the crowd, would be his undoing. She silently flexed her muscles and tightened her grip upon Hel's sword. More than ever, she had to obey the lessons of her shield-sisters: *the Fighting Secrets of the Valkyrie.*

Roselyn suspected that he'd want to toy with her first, but neither of them had a shield, so that assumption was foolish; she could test it, but she couldn't rely upon it. If the chance to kill came, then she had to take it. She extended her arms and carefully inched forward; soon her blade was in reach of his flail, even if she wasn't. If he fell for her bait, then she'd know his skill level.

As Roselyn expected, his flail swung; an amateurish attack, unworthy of an einherjar. He was clearly an experienced warrior, but stupid enough to underestimate an unknown opponent. Roselyn pulled back her sword at the last moment; only the lightest *'ting!'* sounded as his spiked iron balls nipped the edge of her blade. Yet it told Roselyn everything that she needed to know: the speed at which he swung, the angle of his most basic attack, how he counterbalanced to avoid being pulled off his feet by the momentum of his swing, the arc of his thickly-muscled arm, which could be told by the steady sweep of his elbow, how he held his other arm back, to keep it out of her range, the wideness of his stance, and how he stepped off the inches between them, whether or not he leaned forward as he attacked, which showed his confidence of winning, and, most important, his eyes, which never left her face, and which showed an overconfidence that Roselyn found childish. He was dreaming about satisfying his lusts in the middle of a fight; *in Valhalla, this fool would never live past noon.*

Roselyn knew how to kill this man, but if she showed her full skills, then no man would bet against her.

If he wanted to play, then she'd play …!

Roselyn stepped forward and let him swing again (the exact same swing; a fool's attack). She held out her sword and let his chains wrap around it. She allowed herself to be pulled in close, and she turned and slammed her back against his chest; as long as she kept his weapon tied up, then he couldn't hurt her; he held no other weapon. She had to reign in her disgust as he wrapped one arm tightly around her, and he seized her and tried to kiss her cheek.

Roselyn shoved him back against the wall, carefully not using her full strength, and then she pushed away from him; had he been holding onto her arm, her belt, or something which could give him control over her movements, something against which he could grapple, then Roselyn wouldn't have acted so cocky, but Galwarth had cupped his wide hand over her right breast-cup … to many roars of laughter from the crowd; *he'd pay for that!*

Roselyn slashed wildly, careful not to even come close to hitting him, and she purposefully stumbled away, backing up against the far wall. Galwarth laughed loudly, and howls of merciless mirth echoed from above; *she was putting on a grand show.* Her opponent had sized her up as just a petty plaything, yet Roselyn knew to be careful; even the worst fighter could get lucky, and if an enemy gets lucky at the wrong instant, then it could be your last.

However, *skills increase and luck fails.* Galwarth kept looking up at the crowd, encouraging their shouts of adulation and their jeers against her. Roselyn would never take her eyes off any opponent until his head was free of his shoulders.

"Throw down your sword, my pretty!" Galwarth teased. "Let me sheathe my best weapon in you … and maybe I'll let you live. No? Imagine what I'll do once you're so beaten that you can't stand! Better surrender now … while you can!"

Roselyn was too focused to shake her head; talking during a fight was a waste of breath. Taunting your opponent was asking for them to fight at their best, and to risk certain death or the chance of a double-kill, acceptable in Valhalla, was intolerable in this filthy Italian death-pit.

Roselyn couldn't resist; she paused … and loudly blew Galwarth a kiss.

The crowd exploded with laughter.

Amused, Galwarth threw several sloppy blows, two of which approached close enough that Roselyn had to block them with her sword, and he kept pressing her, trying to keep her pinned against a wall. Then he attacked her head-on, a bold challenge, swinging overhead to crush her helmet.

Roselyn caught his swing; again his chains encircled her blade, and he jerked up his arm, lifting her off her feet, trying to pull her sword from her grasp. Again she spun, and slammed her back-plate against his chest, but this time Roselyn hammered back her head, and the sharp steel spines of the Goddess of Death, which covered the ridge of her helmet, stabbed into his face. As he cried out, Roselyn spun away, and smiled as she saw four blood-spurting holes in his face, one on his chin, and three on his cheek, leading upwards at an angle; he must've ducked his head to the side as they collided; she'd just missed his left eye. His free hand wiped his cheek, and then he glanced at his blood on his hand; his smile vanished … and the laughter from above altered to gasps of sheer incredulity.

No more games: Roselyn had scarred and disgraced him; he'd come at her fully now. She held out her sword, knowing that he'd again strike at it, and as his chains wrapped around her blade for the third time, he rushed forward. Roselyn raised her pommel and pulled it back, which lowered her point, and then she shoved her swordpoint forward, striking him just below his heart, piercing his armor just beneath the joint where his lowest ribs met his breastbone. Roselyn stabbed him through, deeply and cleanly, sliding his wrapped chained-spiked-balls all the way to her hilts.

Yells of dismay filled the air, but the expression on Galwarth's face told Roselyn that he'd fight no more. He wasn't dead; as his clinking flail fell from his hand, Roselyn pushed him away, and he collapsed onto the dried-blood floor, choking and gasping. To her amusement, Galwarth rolled onto his hands and knees and tried to crawl away like a wounded infant.

Now it was Roselyn's turn to play for the crowd.

Most men's armor was notoriously lacking in protection for the seat of a man's pants, and watching him crawl away, Roselyn spied the perfect scabbard for her sword.

In Valhalla, such an attack was considered an unforgivable disgrace, and many soldiers awoke every dawn to go out and face the same opponent, day after day, century after century, always the same challenge, the same fight, to avenge this ultimate insult. No pause in this vendetta would ever come, save for Ragnarrock itself, and it was said that those feuds would continue even after the Great Final Battle of the Gods … if anyone survived to keep fighting. But here, in this grimy pit, this attack would only become the best gossip in Italy, a story which would last forever and bring this filthy basement into an eternal prominence which it would never otherwise have. Roselyn lowered her blade … and stabbed at his retreating anus, hard and deep, in a gesture so quick and sure that it could be no accident.

Galwarth screamed his last scream.

Deafening cheers fell upon Roselyn as small grappling hooks were thrown down and Galwarth's corpse was snagged and lifted out of the pit; Roselyn ignored the cheers, looking up to see who her next challenger would be. Instead, she saw Karl and Captain Markus accepting handfuls of coins from a frowning man with many rings, and Henry and Samuel were holding Sister Aspertine's unconscious body; the young nun looked to have fainted. Eloise was watching her approvingly, although only the slightest smile upturned her lips. Elaina was cheering her as loudly as any man, including Nate and Phil.

A giant of a man stepped to the brink of the pit; this man had been born a warrior, and looked fiercer than many einherjar. He had long blonde hair, tied back in a braid, and a short beard. He was thick; any belt around his waist could encircle her girth three times. His arms resembled the biceps of Prudr, and his sleek studded armor was as black as the fur of Sleipnir, Odin's horse. He looked like he preferred grappling to any weapon, but he lifted up a heavy knobbled steel bar, a mace which could crush any bones that it struck. Roselyn doubted if even the armor of Hel could protect her from repeated hammerings of that weapon.

Without hesitation, he jumped into the pit. His eyes never left hers, and as he crashed to the blood-soaked floor without effort, he held up a hand in warning.

"Gladiators wait until all bets are made," he said slowly.

Roselyn nodded; she was only here to make enough money to buy a boat … and stay alive.

"Who are you?" she asked.

"The greater question is: who are you?" he asked. "Or should it be: what are you? Are you really a woman under there? Or are you a man who wears a woman's armor … so that he's underestimated?"

"I've a woman's heart, a woman's breasts, and a woman's ire," Roselyn said.

"I'm Halgard of Sweden," he said. "It'll be no pleasure to kill you; you resemble our legends of the Valkyrie."

Roselyn startled, then she rose to her full height and lowered her sword.

"You're Norse?" she asked.

"From Oslo," Halgard said proudly, almost defiantly.

"Speak more respectfully of Odin's shield-maids, if you would bow before your queens in Valhalla," Roselyn said.

"No mere woman could kill Galwarth," Halgard said. "If I thought that you were a Valkyrie ..."

"Then you'd fight your best, to prove worthy of Odin's call, the summons of the Choosers of the Slain," Roselyn said. "No man worthy of being an einherjar would do less."

"Are you a Valkyrie?" Halgard asked.

"If you can kill me, does it matter?" Roselyn asked. She smiled wickedly at him, and he returned her smile with a grin just as evil.

"All bets are made!" shouted the fat man. "Kill the whoring bitch!"

Roselyn frowned ... and momentarily glanced upwards.

"He bet on Galwarth," Halgard explained.

"He'll pay later," Roselyn said.

"No, he won't," Halgard said.

Halgard cautiously raised his mace. Slowly, by fractions of an inch, they approached each other. Halgard was good; his movements were slow and subtle, not showing any sign of what he was capable of when fighting in earnest. Unlike Galwarth, Halgard's free hand was heavily armored: a thick casing of stitched leather crossed with spiked bars covered his right hand, almost a weapon more than a gauntlet. He carried his mace in his left hand; Roselyn noted this carefully, as left-handers fought differently; most fighters were right-handed, so they were used to fighting their own kind; lefties took advantage of their unusualness, and were able to throw and block blows that were difficult for right-handers, but they had their own weaknesses: lefties were best at blocking attacks on both their right and left sides, where they were usually attacked; their weakness was in their middle. A lefty's best attack was swinging wide, around at their opponent's back, as they could reach targets that most fighters couldn't; Roselyn had to be sure to twist fully, if he tried that tactic, and to attack his exposed arm, which had to be dangerously extended to reach those back-targets.

Halgard stepped forward and swung fast and hard, directly at her center. Roselyn blocked with her sword and jumped backwards, but Halgard rushed forward, and before Roselyn could react, he was upon her. His mace clanged against her blade again, clearly just to keep her from bringing it to bear, and he reached to grab her with his spiked gauntlet. Faster than any human, Roselyn twisted and spun, rolled underneath his arm, and she slashed as she rolled, and deeply-scored his armor before she regained her feet, but she'd inflicted no real wound. Instantly he turned and chased her; Roselyn swung several blows, forcing him to block, but he kept pressing her. Finally, with a flurry of blows, she drove him back … enough to catch a much-needed breath.

Roselyn drew back to lean against the filthy wall behind her, her sword held between them. She felt winded; he was good, and he swung his heavy mace as easily as she could slice with Hel's sword; if she'd had a lighter blade, then she could swing faster. He obviously wanted to grapple, to force this fight into a contest of his best ability; Reginleif could've matched his strength, but Roselyn didn't have a prayer.

Their weapons tight in their hands, he inched toward her, mace raised; she couldn't let him close. With a feint to drive him back, Roselyn turned and ran, and as she reached the far wall, she jumped onto it, running so fast that centrifugal force supported her; she ran around the circle with incredible speed, and as Halgard gaped at her, she slashed at his head.

Halgard ducked her swing, which would've decapitated him, and suddenly his gauntleted fist hammered into her; she turned her head at the last instant, so the spikes only scratched and grooved Hel's helm, but he fouled her momentum; she started to fall, and then his mace smashed her to the ground. Roselyn was instantly up, her sword raised high, but suddenly his huge arms surrounded her, and her long sword wasn't as good at close range. Pressed face to face, he squeezed with a crushing strength that forced the air from her lungs; if she didn't escape soon, then she never would.

Strength against strength they struggled, but without the replenishment of the Water of Life, the strength of Reginleif failed Roselyn; *she couldn't defeat him.*

Her blade needed range to swing, but he was wearing no helmet. With all of her remaining will, Roselyn lifted Hel's weapon over him and smashed the ornate, Garm-shaped silver pommel of her sword onto the top of his head; *once, twice, three times.* He fell back, stunned, staggering, and Roselyn slashed hard and suddenly: Halgard's severed head flipped twice before it thudded to the ground beside his collapsed body.

"V... Valkyrie ...!" Roselyn coughed, hoping that one of her sisters would hear ... and claim this worthy foe.

Roselyn was gasping so hard that she could barely hear the shouts above her, and she couldn't tell if they were cheering or cursing. A wineskin was hanging upon a hook; Roselyn staggered to it, yanked it free, and drank the weak, tart wine that filled it, and then spat most of it out. As hooks lowered, and a servant descended the ladder to claim Halgard's head and the fallen weapons, she examined herself; the spiked gauntlet hadn't hurt her, but it'd come close; she'd almost been badly scarred, and Hel's armor bore several dents. She struggled to focus, to clear her mind, and to hear Mist's voice in her head as it drilled the rules of combat into her.

The Fighting Secrets of the Valkyrie were all that she had.

Her third challenge was over before she learned his name; he was clearly no equal of Halgard or Galwarth; she deeply sliced his sword-arm with her first swing, and he was dead before her third struck. Then Roselyn called for a break; she needed a rest.

"Roselyn, do you want to stop?" Karl asked her, kneeling down and leaning over the pit.

"Do … do we have … enough?" Roselyn asked.

"We've a lot, but you're more important," Karl said. "We can go whenever you want to; we can't afford to lose you."

"Valkyrie … don't lose," Roselyn said.

"We don't take risks unless we have to," Karl said. "You look exhausted. What would Eric do?"

Roselyn looked up and gave Karl a feeble smile.

"I'll stop when we have enough," Roselyn said.

"Don't take chances," Elaina knelt beside Karl and said to Roselyn. "When we get to Egypt, we'll need you."

Roselyn nodded, then leaned against the wall, waiting for her next opponent.

Her fourth challenger was tall and thin, and didn't look heavily-muscled, but he bore a tall shield that reached from his shoulders past his knees, and he had a well-notched sword. Roselyn suspected that he was an experienced fighter, but new to gladiatorial games, as one of its first rewards was a better weapon. They traded blows for almost four minutes, which was a long fight, but he hid like a turtle behind his shield, and hid his sword's initial swings behind it until it was almost too late. He was fast; twice Roselyn was only saved by Hel's stout armor, which suffered several more dents. Yet, as he was about to rush in, Roselyn, unable to penetrate his defense, blocked his swing, and then kicked his shield just enough to press it against his body; with his shield pinned against him by her foot, she stabbed before he could raise it to shield his eyes. He jerked back his head at the last instant; her swordtip stabbed into his forehead, just over one eye. He didn't die, but bled profusely. Blinded by his own blood, he freely accepted his defeat, and had to be helped out of the pit and carried to a healer.

A young man, too young to have been fighting long, entered next, and he grinned at Roselyn; in each hand, he held a short, light blade, and strapped across his back was a large shield, and he wore mail and a simple iron cap; Roselyn wondered if he'd ever fought in a gladiatorial pit before. He seemed confident: either he was a fool … or a real threat.

As they met, his resounding attacks rang from her blade, and she was forced backwards, but he was all attack; Roselyn dodged aside and gained a few feet of distance, and then waited for him to lose patience. When he came at her again, Roselyn smashed her sword hard at both of his weapons, knocking them aside, and then slashed across his gut, which didn't cut through his mail but knocked the wind from him, and then she stabbed … at the same time that he did.

Roselyn felt the resistance in her blade as it entered his chest, but then she felt the familiar pain; *she'd been stabbed.* Her blade was rammed through his chest, probably piercing one of his lungs, but he'd found a newly-opened gap in Hel's armor, and his sword was lodged in her gut, between two of the black steel skulls. He tried to swing his other sword to finish her off, but he was too hurt, and as Roselyn pushed him away, they both fell to the blood-wet ground.

"Don't enter the pit!" the fat man's voice shouted. "Nothing's finished until one fighter's dead!"

Roselyn crawled away; she was out of range of the young man, and he was staring at her, barely able to move. She gritted her teeth and fought to control the pain; *she hated dying, and Odin's Rainbow wouldn't save her here.*

"What if they both die?" Eloise's voice asked.

"If both die in the pit, then all bets forfeit to the house," the fat man answered her. "If one of them can climb out, even if they die later, then bets must be paid."

Roselyn and the young man both glanced at the small wooden ladder: *their mutual path to survival …*

"What if they both climb out?" Elaina asked.

"One must win, or we push them both back into the pit," the fat man said.

The young man started to crawl toward the ladder. Roselyn flushed; she was bleeding badly, but she wouldn't be defeated. She pressed her back against the wall, and inverted her sword, used it as a crutch, and levered herself up. Pain shot through her, but she'd known pain greater than any man alive. Roselyn pushed away from the wall, staggered four steps, lifted her inverted blade, and as she had with Mist, she fell upon the retreating young man with all of her armored weight. Hel's sword pierced his wooden shield and mail; with a pathetic cry, he collapsed and died.

However, Roselyn hadn't won yet; *now it was her turn to crawl.*

Leaving behind Hel's heavy sword, she inched overtop the boy's still corpse toward the ladder. Shouts and jeers rained upon her from above; many wanted her to die … to avoid having to pay Karl, but other voices encouraged her. Slowly she crawled to the ladder, seized the first rung, and tried to pull herself up … but she fell back, gasping.

The first three stanzas of her training chant flashed through her mind:

The more tired you are, the harder you fight.

Pain evokes anger, anger summons strength, and strength overpowers all.

No excuse justifies losing.

Roselyn focused, tried again, and pulled herself up, rung by rung, until she was almost standing, leaning against the ladder, clinging to it to keep from falling back down. If she fell, then she'd never make it out.

Karl appeared above her.

"Damn the bet; Roselyn, I'm coming …," he said.

"Master!" Phil shouted. "Wait! Give her a chance!"

Roselyn looked up; Nate and Phil both looked pale white, shocked so deeply that the blood had fled their faces … and they weren't even bleeding. Despite her wound, Roselyn grinned, and she tried to pull herself up, but she couldn't. Men were shouting. Her head was spinning. Her world was going black.

"Roselyn …," Eloise's steady voice floated down to her. "Roselyn, climb the ladder. Please."

Eloise, Roselyn thought dimly, *her former best friend … who'd stolen her lover …!*

Pain stabbed, and dizziness swelled, but Roselyn lifted her foot and stepped up onto the lowest rung.

Chapter 23

Prince Fernando

SISTER ASPERTINE

"Dear Lord and Heavenly Father, look down upon this poor wounded soul, and in Your infinite mercy, spare her, if it be Your will, for although she's turned aside from her true faith and worshipped false idols, still she's one of my charges. I must do all that I can to restore Your light to her soul before her body returns to dust and she is damned to Hellfire for all eternity; for this, I pray to You. Amen."

Sister Aspertine doubted if Roselyn would survive, but her holy duty was to pray for all who were dying. If her faith allowed it, then Sister Aspertine might've wished that Roselyn would die, as she was obviously a pagan demoness whose soul was already damned, but Sister Aspertine couldn't pray for death upon anyone.

Grim faces stared at Eloise, in the center of their room, in a far more reputable inn than their previous hovel. Eloise was kneeling before Roselyn, who lay pale and unconscious, her wound still bleeding despite the pressure that Elaina was applying to it. Nate and Phil were each holding a candle, and Henry and Samuel had just returned from the market, where they'd bought and slaughtered a lamb. They'd carried back the carcass, which they were cutting up and cooking over the fire, along with a bucket of its blood, which Eloise had used to draw a four-fingers-wide circle around the bed. Then she and Elaina knelt inside it, on opposite sides of Roselyn. Yet despite Eloise's ardent prayers, and her repetitions of the motions and chants that had saved Rishard on the docks, Eloise never screamed, and no healing came.

"Eloise, what's wrong?" Karl finally asked.

Eloise bowed her head, sounding exhausted and exasperated.

"It's not working," Eloise said. "I've cast the spell five times: nothing."

"Will she live?" Karl asked.

"Not without healing," Elaina said. "She may last a few days … because she's so strong …"

"You must save her!" Karl said.

"I'm trying …!" Eloise said.

"Let's rest," Elaina suggested. "Gather your strength, and then we'll try again."

Eloise picked up Roselyn's sword, which Nate had recovered, and set it on the floor, its tip just touching the blood-painted circle, and she exited over its point.

"If only my altar hadn't been stolen …," Eloise said wearily, and she stumbled to a different bed.

Elaina replaced the thick bandage back upon Roselyn's wound, set the Seer's moonstone aside, and then climbed over the bed and exited the circle at the same spot, where Hel's sword touched the bloody ring. Sister Aspertine glared at her; these pagan rituals were heresy, and should never be practiced. Doubtless anyone healed by them would be cursed in the eyes of God. Yet these people had been poisoned, not just by heathen beliefs, but by familiarity with … unnatural forces … in forbidden lands.

Sister Aspertine couldn't believe that God had allowed their mythical journey, if, in fact, it wasn't just a satanic delusion, but neither could she doubt the reality of these strangers: she'd never seen any man or woman who could fight like Roselyn, and having watched Eloise heal Rishard, no doubt existed that Eloise was a witch and a harbinger of evil.

But … *didn't Jesus heal people?*

How could healing be bad?

When Sister Aspertine had started this voyage, she'd been naive, light-hearted, thinking that all she needed to do was to enjoy the ride and remind Baron Karl and Baroness Eloise to say their prayers. Now she didn't know what to think; she'd never seen a man killed before, and since their ambush by the Moors, every day had been horrible. Nothing in her upbringing, an orphan raised in a convent, had prepared her for this; *what was she supposed to do?* She'd promised Lord Sir Rafe that she'd stay with Karl, Eloise, and Roselyn no matter what, and never leave them, but Rafe's delusion, however impossible it sounded, now tormented her. As bad as Rafe's journey to visit lands beyond God's world sounded, this journey to Egypt seemed even worse.

They sat in silence for an hour, and then Elaina roused Eloise.

"Daughter, we need to try again," she said.

Eloise rose wearily from the bed, the gap in her ruined dress, exposing her stomach, now wider than ever, red from the five lines of Roselyn's blood that she'd drawn upon herself, but which had somehow failed to heal. She started to approach the circle, but Elaina stopped her.

"Baron, if we're to do all we can, then we must use every method to infuse purity into the healing chant," Elaina said. "To do this, we must unclothe; you men must leave while we work."

Karl nodded, still frowning, and gestured for all of the men to follow him, but Sister Aspertine stayed; she'd noticed the slight look of surprise upon Eloise's face; *something was amiss.*

After all of the men left, Elaina braced the door firmly behind them.

"Why …?" Eloise asked.

"Because we need to talk," Elaina said, and with a glance at Sister Aspertine, she stepped close and held Eloise at arm's length. *"Daughter, can you honestly say that you want to heal Roselyn?"*

Eloise lowered her chin.

"She's my friend," Eloise mumbled.

"She also loves Karl," Elaina said.

Eloise looked away.

"I love you," Elaina said to Eloise. "You've always been the most important thing in my life. When Skafti predicted that you'd suffer eternal unhappiness, I gave up my greatest love to spare you. For sixteen years I lived apart from my only daughter, and I don't regret that, although I fear that our reunion will cause Skafti's prediction to come true. Now you're faced with another curse: Roselyn will die if you can't save her."

"The Lady saves, not I," Eloise said.

"The Druid Lady would save Roselyn; She did it once, when She saved all of you. Roselyn is beloved by the Seer, her chief servant. It's you who must be saved. Until you're saved, healing won't come."

Eloise glanced at Roselyn; she was barely breathing.

"I can't surrender Karl," Eloise whispered.

"This isn't about Karl," Elaina said. "This is about two proud rivals; jealousy is holding you back."

"Let her die," Sister Aspertine interjected suddenly. "All healing comes from God, and the best that you could do is reject pagan deities, stop practicing forbidden rituals, and kneel down and pray. By her own admission, she's been cast out of the Norse faith, and she never worshipped the Druid witch. Leave her to God's mercy."

Eloise started to object, but Elaina stopped her with a gesture.

"You would condemn Roselyn to eternal Hellfire?" Elaina asked Sister Aspertine.

"Only Almighty God is eternal," Sister Aspertine said. "Even to Heaven and Hell, there shall come an end. God's judgement shall be fair."

"Like God was fair when he drowned the whole world?" Eloise demanded. "Like God was fair when he took my father's life?"

"Never question the will of God!" Sister Aspertine said.

"That's the ultimate blasphemy," Eloise said. "I've seen gods … and nearly been killed by them …"

"Those weren't gods!"

"And every one of them echoed your words: *never question My will*," Eloise said.

"Your thoughts sin," Sister Aspertine said.

"Appeasement of any god is a sin to another," Eloise said.

"There's only one God!" Sister Aspertine argued.

"Who healed Rishard?" Eloise demanded.

"Rishard would've been better off dying a Christian than living healed by wickedness," Sister Aspertine said. *"As will Roselyn …!"*

"I'll save Roselyn!" Eloise shouted.

"Then do it," Elaina said to Eloise. "Let go of your jealousy: *heal Roselyn!*"

Eloise glared at her mother, and then at Sister Aspertine, her face a mask of determination. Angrily, she stepped over the tip of the sword, into the circle, and then she kicked the sword aside before her mother could follow.

Eloise snatched up the moonstone, knelt beside Roselyn, yanked the bandage off her bloody stomach, and threw it onto the floor. Roselyn moaned in her sleep, but Eloise grimaced, snarled, and spread her arms wide.

"Blessed Mother, my Lady,
Let now my eyes see,
All I am that I can be,
For I am all eternity,
All the universe bring to me,
Blessed Mother, my Lady."

Eloise bowed her head and began her ritual again. Her prayers were ardent, her voice pleading, and when the time came, she grabbed the edges of the cut in her ragged dress and ripped it so wide that no repair was possible. Roselyn writhed as Eloise stabbed her finger deep into Roselyn's wound, and when Eloise drew Roselyn's wound upon her own stomach with Roselyn's blood, Eloise screamed so loudly that Sister Aspertine started forward, determined to help, but Elaina seized and held her back.

Sister Aspertine prayed ardently to God to spare Eloise's suffering, but Eloise fell over, and a pint of her own blood flowed from her drawn-wound: Eloise was truly suffering from Roselyn's sword-cut. She writhed and cried out, and Karl's shouts came from the other side of her door, and fists hammered against it, but the door was braced, and Sister Aspertine's frail muscles were no match for Elaina's strength.

God Almighty, help her!

Sister Aspertine's prayers went unanswered. For long minutes Eloise thrashed about upon the floor, and then she stilled and moved no more.

Softly, Roselyn groaned in her sleep.

An hour later, Elaina removed the brace and Sister Aspertine walked out of their rented room, pale and shaken, to find Karl and the others. By shouting at them through the door, Elaina had ordered them to go away, and then she and Sister Aspertine had sat for most of the hour, holding hands, wondering if both Eloise and Roselyn would die. Pressed side-by-side in the same bed, both girls had awoken almost simultaneously, and although they moved so slowly that neither appeared to have healed; when they saw each other, Eloise and Roselyn silently intertwined fingers.

The men sat in the common room of the inn, drinking from tall wooden mugs, and all rose and cheered when Sister Aspertine stepped close and nodded. At first, she couldn't speak; the words stuck in her throat, and then she reluctantly reported the healing of a pagan demoness by a heathen witch, which was a godless tragedy. Karl sent Nate and Phil to the tavernmaster to ask for rags and buckets, to clean the floor, while Karl led both sailors back to their room.

Once they were all out of sight, Sister Aspertine fell onto her knees and sobbed, heedless of the many strangers in the common room.

Dear God, save me! Show me Your light!
Prove to me that these evils and witchcraft
shan't lead me into blasphemy and disrepute!

Spare me, or take my soul now, before I am corrupted by Lucifer himself! God, show me Your way, Your plan, and don't deny me entrance to Heaven as a witness to heresy! Please … I beg you!

"Are you the suora that fainted during the gladiatorial game where the woman fought?"

Sister Aspertine stopped praying and lifted her head; a dark-skinned boy no older than thirteen stood before her.

"Who … are you?" Sister Aspertine asked.

"I'm a royal page of Prince Fernando," the boy said. "He invites you to the palace. He desires to meet this woman who fights like a demon."

Sister Aspertine scowled.

"Any woman who fights like a demon should be locked in a convent to pray for her soul," Sister Aspertine said.

"Yes, suora; that's what the cardinal said," the boy replied.

"Cardinal …?" Sister Aspertine asked. "There's a cardinal at the palace?"

"Oh, yes; he specifically said that."

Sister Aspertine thought carefully. She'd always wanted to meet a cardinal. Surely such a high-placed man of God would advise her well.

"Could the Prince help us buy a ship?" Sister Aspertine asked.

"The Prince owns many ships," the boy said.

"Tell the Prince that we'll come as soon as we may," Sister Aspertine said.

"Thank you, suora," the boy said, and he bowed and ran off.

Nate and Phil were still scrubbing lamb's blood from the floor, hiding the evidence of their blasphemy. Henry and Samuel were cooking thick slices of lamb over the fire, and Elaina and Karl were already eating. Roselyn and Eloise were both unconscious, still resting side-by-side, looking as if each had barely escaped the Angel of Death. Sister Aspertine raised her head, stepped inside, and closed the door behind her.

"I've found someone willing to sell us a boat," Sister Aspertine announced.

"Really …?" Karl asked.

"Prince Fernando," Sister Aspertine said. "He sent a page, who invited us all to the palace … as soon as possible."

"The palace …?" Elaina asked, but no one answered her.

"Where's this page?" Karl asked.

"He went back to report that we were coming," Sister Aspertine said.

Karl frowned, but Sister Aspertine stood silently, making no sign that she registered his displeasure. She'd accepted a royal invitation without consulting him, but she smiled sweetly and assumed an appearance of devoted subservience.

What could he do … chastise a nun?

"Master, if I may …?" Henry said. "We have enough money for a ship that can take us to Egypt, but not a great ship, and after we buy it, we'll have no money all summer."

"Thank you, Henry," Karl said. "Very well; we'll go as soon as Eloise and Roselyn can walk."

However, despite some healing sleep, neither Eloise nor Roselyn could walk far … or up hills. The next day, Karl sent Nate and Phil to hire a wagon, and their ride was long and uneventful. Sister Aspertine rode in the back, eager to meet the cardinal, and trying to hide her smile. Almost two hours later, they arrived at the doors to the palace, where guards and servants came out to meet them. They were greeted like royalty, and then escorted inside with a fanfare of trumpets and deep bows.

Prince Fernando's palace was enormous. Sister Aspertine appreciated its Italian-style architecture, with massive, thick walls, sturdy piers, well-crafted groin vaults, tall towers, and highly-decorative arcading, including many beautiful statues of angels, which relieved Sister Aspertine; *this was the kind of palace where a cardinal should live.* Each building had a clearly-defined symmetry, with rows of lancet arches; tall, narrow, and steeply pointed. Smooth granite blocks rose to vast heights, offsetting woodwork of polished acorn and lemonwood, and every corner bore gilt, swirling edgings. Flags of white and dark green boasted a heraldic device of a gold cross entwined by a red wyvern, and all of the guards at the gate wore these colors, with matching, high-crested helms.

Eloise walked hidden inside their biggest cloak, which she kept tightly closed, as her only dress was ripped to shreds, and even though she'd washed the blood of Rishard and Roselyn off her skin, her dress made her look like she'd been fighting in the gladiatorial pit. Yet her hood was thrown back, her sun-yellow hair falling about her shoulders, and despite her weakness, she walked like a baroness. Roselyn wore Hel's armor, and walked shakily with Nate on one arm and Phil on the other, both with Karl's orders not to let Roselyn fall. Henry and Samuel offered to wait outside, but Karl insisted that the company stay together at all times; *no one entered or left unless they all did.*

Outside huge doors they stood, halted by servants, until a musical performance ended, and then the doors were suddenly flung wide, and the companions were escorted inside amid a flourish of high-pitched flutes. A tall guard announced Karl and Eloise's formal titles and names in a rich baritone, echoing to the ends of the wide, formal hall.

Prince Fernando's appearance surprised them all; thin and barely sixteen, he sat upon his throne with a scantily-clad woman on each side, one bearing a plate of baked sweets, while the other held his golden wine-cup, which looked like a church's chalice. He returned Karl and Eloise's elaborate bows with a cursory nod, and then he scanned them all and focused upon Roselyn.

"You must be the warrior-wench!" he said with a laugh, in English, although with a heavy Italian accent.

Despite her weakness, Roselyn snarled and rose to her full height.

"This is Countess Roselyn," Eloise interrupted what would've surely been his beheading. "She's newly-arrived from … from the Norselands, where women fight as well as men."

Prince Fernando laughed sarcastically; Karl laid a restraining hand upon Roselyn.

"Prince Fernando, we regret to announce that we were robbed in your city," Karl said. "When we returned to the harbor …"

"Your ship was stolen … and two of your men killed," Prince Fernando said. "My guards say that a witch brought one of your men back to life."

"He was only wounded," Karl said. "He lies in a local hospital, and must lie a'bed for months, so he wasn't healed."

"Countess Roselyn," Prince Fernando ignored Karl. "You have a pretty face. Is your true shape as impressive as the armor that hides it? I charge beautiful women a heavy toll for entering my city …"

Hel's sword slid from her belt, and she held it pointed at the prince, but she grunted from the exertion.

"Prince Fernando, take care with your words," Eloise said, stepping between them. "We came here as guests; if you don't desire our company, then we'll gladly leave."

"You'll stay as long as I *desire*," Prince Fernando said contemptuously. "This is *my* city, and I do as I please with all within it."

"*You …!*" Karl began, but Sister Aspertine stepped in front of him and cut him off.

"Is the cardinal here?" Sister Aspertine asked.

As if for the first time, Prince Fernando looked at Sister Aspertine, and a wicked smirk twisted his smile.

"Cardinal Isbano does dwell here, and he'll be delighted to meet you," Prince Fernando said.

"Thank you, Your Excellency," Sister Aspertine bowed politely. "I have important matters of the church to report to him. I'd be greatly honored if you'd allow my companions to join your court while I speak privately with the cardinal."

"By all means; guards, escort this nun to Cardinal Isbano," Prince Fernando said.

A soft hiss of whispers broke out among the court, but Sister Aspertine ignored them and followed the guard, leaving her companions behind. The guard escorted her down two long hallways, and then up three flights of spiral steps to a landing surrounded by a brightly polished rail. Gold curtains hung upon every wall, and ornate tapestries depicted holy scenes, and she was escorted to a tall pair of arched doors. After waiting to be announced, Sister Aspertine entered an office as ornate as a king's chapel. Standing before a large rowan desk was a white-haired man with bright caramel eyes wearing long red robes embroidered with many crosses.

"Cardinal Isbano," Sister Aspertine bowed to him.

"Greetings, in our Lord's name, dear sister of faith," Cardinal Isbano said in an eager voice. "Come in and feel welcome."

With a nod from the cardinal, the guard left, leaving them alone.

"Forgive my intrusion …"

"By what grace of God do you call this an intrusion?" Cardinal Isbano interrupted her. "This is a wondrous meeting. Tell me, child, what's your name?"

"Sister Aspertine, from the Abbey of St. Dunstay, in England," she said. "Your holiness, I'm desperate for advice, for I've seen and learned many things that have troubled my heart … and made me fear for my soul."

"Peace, daughter of Christ," Cardinal Isbano said. "Tell me everything."

Sister Aspertine spoke long, as if at confession, and revealed every heresy and act of witchcraft that she'd seen. Cardinal Isbano's eyes widened, and his expression ranged from doubt to amusement with such rapidity that Sister Aspertine feared that he'd think her mad. Once started, she couldn't stop. She spewed every thought and experience that she remembered, from the day that she'd been summoned to meet Lord Sir Rafe to the magical healing of Roselyn.

Throughout her tale, Cardinal Isbano remained silent, but his eyes roved over her, as if looking for some sign of deceit. She couldn't blame him. When she finally finished, he stared at her until she could bear it no more.

"You question my sanity, as do I," Sister Aspertine said. "I swear: these things my senses witnessed …"

"Rest your fears," Cardinal Isbano said. "Poor child! Forced to associate with devils and their spawn; even Heaven must forgive you, as your thoughts have remained pure. Your thoughts have remained pure, haven't they?"

"Never have I doubted my faith," Sister Aspertine said.

"The Lord blesses your constancy," Cardinal Isbano said. "He's already blessed you, has He not? Forgive an old man, but never have I seen such freshness of youth, such smooth, perfect skin. God has given you many virtues, has He not?"

Sister Aspertine was taken aback; *this had nothing to do with her pagan companions!*

"Your grace, what should I do?" Sister Aspertine asked. "Some of my companions seem to be honorable Christians, but others …!"

"You must end your companionship with them," Cardinal Isbano said. "Their diabolical influence upon you is already evident."

"But I made a promise to Lord Sir Rafe …!"

"I absolve you of that promise, but you must repent, and perform penance for the rest of your life."

"I will, bless you!"

"And you must stay here, where you'll be safe from heretics and antichrists."

"Stay here …?" Sister Aspertine asked. "Not return to England …?"

"The Church of England is strong, but the return journey would corrupt the soul of even the most devout," Cardinal Isbano said. "I won't feel secure in your

Heavenly reward unless I know that you're protected, and I can see the salvation in your pretty eyes."

At Cardinal Isbano's insistence, Sister Aspertine fell silent while he poured her a drink and handed her the tall, narrow silver goblet. When he raised his, they both drank, but Sister Aspertine choked and coughed as the fiery liquid burned her throat.

"I – I'm sorry … I thought it was wine …," Sister Aspertine said, her cheeks flushed with embarrassment.

"It's Holy Whiskey," Cardinal Isbano said. "You must drink it."

"Holy Whiskey …?" Sister Aspertine asked. "I've never heard of …"

"It's new!" Cardinal Isbano explained. "The pope drinks it with every meal now; I'm surprised that you haven't heard of it."

"I really don't …," Sister Aspertine began.

"Have you refused your habit already?" Cardinal Isbano demanded, his voice suddenly deep. "Has Lucifer seduced you …?"

"No!"

"Sister Aspertine, you've been infected with heresy," Cardinal Isbano said. "Cleansing you of the devil, without resorting to burning at the stake, will be hard and difficult. You must submit your will to mine, submit yourself to my care, and embrace every treatment I ordain without regret or complaint. Can you do this?"

"Yes, your grace," Sister Aspertine said.

"Swear to me," Cardinal Isbano commanded her. "Vow upon your faith in God that you'll obey without the slightest qualm or refusal."

"I will, your grace," Sister Aspertine promised.

Cardinal Isbano smiled widely.

"I hear your vow and accept it, in the name of our blessed Lord," Cardinal Isbano said. "Kneel before me and accept my blessing … and accept your place in my care."

Sister Aspertine dropped to her knees and lowered her head; she wasn't happy about this turn of events, but he was a cardinal, a Father of the Church, and her duty was to obey. She regretted abandoning her charges, even though they were ungodly, but she had to put her faith in Cardinal Isbano and trust that he knew best. *The Lord works in mysterious ways;* surely He'd led her to a place where she could be cured.

"Remove your wimple," Cardinal Isbano said softly.

At first, Sister Aspertine was certain that she had misheard, but then his brows lowered, and she obediently lifted her hands to the pin underneath, and then her head was uncovered. Her long, pale hair fell unbound about her shoulders; *she felt ashamed.*

"Throw it upon the floor," Cardinal Isbano instructed.

Sister Aspertine bit back a gasp; she didn't dare show reluctance so soon after her vow: *she had to trust the cardinal!* Her hand trembling, Sister Aspertine dropped her precious headgear, and let it fall onto the rug.

"Very good," Cardinal Isbano said. "Receive now the blessing of your master."

Cardinal Isbano placed his hands upon her shoulders, leaned over, and kissed the top of her head. Sister Aspertine prayed to feel the holiness of God enter her and purge her of all unworthy thoughts, but every muscle in her body tensed with misgivings. Cardinal Isbano kissed her long, so long that she felt uncomfortable, and his hands squeezed and flexed upon her thin shoulders with an unnerving intimacy. Unquiet screamed in her ear, but she had to resist it, to be strong and obedient.

Finally Cardinal Isbano rose, and he looked very concerned.

"You need to be baptized again," Cardinal Isbano said. "You must wash off the sins of satanic associations. Rise, Sister Aspertine. Come with me."

Sister Aspertine glanced at her fallen wimple, and reluctantly followed, leaving it behind. She chided herself for her doubts; he was a cardinal, and she'd taken vows of subservience.

To her surprise, he led her into, not a chapel, but into an ornate bathing room. Before them stretched a square pool of steamy water, easily big enough for six grown adults.

"Your condition is unworthy of a nun's habit," Cardinal Isbano said. "Remove it, and prepare to be born again."

Impossible fears stabbed Sister Aspertine; *what was he saying?* No man had ever seen her unclothed, and few women; *this was unheard of!* Cardinal Isbano was a confirmed man of God, a church elder, saintly; she'd always dreamed of meeting a cardinal, and imagined the joy of his spiritual presence. Yet an unexpected panic seized her. She glanced at his face; a frightening, hungry look shined in his eyes, which blazed with the fierceness of a forest predator.

Obey, Sister Aspertine said to herself. *Obey, and God will protect you.*

As her fingers lifted to the long row of buttons down her back, tears started to leak from her eyes. *It was the cardinal's right to give her orders, but never had she felt so wrong.*

"Yes," Cardinal Isbano whispered. "God has sent you to me, to return what you've lost … the peace of His will. Blessed are you, for the needs of those who lead His church are great, and you'll relieve the deepest stresses of his most-worthy servant. A new life begins for you today; a new life for both of us!"

Cardinal Isbano leered as Sister Aspertine plucked each button free. Sobs burst from her before she undid the last button, and then she turned away, facing the raised pool, unable to look at him anymore. In one more minute, she'd be facing a life that she couldn't comprehend. Man of God or not, no woman could mistake the desires burning in his eyes. His *'new life'* arose like a Luciferic shadow, engulfing her.

She couldn't do this!

She was a bride of God, an ordained nun, a …!

Grasping hands reached through her long hair, touched her blessed habit, and pulled it apart, exposing her bare, naked flesh. Sister Aspertine bit back a scream, and then she looked down to see a large, thick, brass water vessel beside the cardinal's bath, empty, but giving her an unholy, unthinkable hope of escape …

At the tall, arched doors, Sister Aspertine paused and calmed herself, straightened the wimple restored to her head, and then she opened the arched doors and walked across the narrow balcony to the stairs. She'd left nothing behind her but a drink that she'd never finish, an unconscious cardinal, and a deeply-dented water vessel.

Guards jerked their heads to stare as she walked past, but she ignored them; few men would block the passage of a nun in a hurry. She descended to the main floor and followed the long hallways back to the main chamber, hearing loud and raucous laughter coming from the court.

Inside Prince Fernando's throne room, Sister Aspertine found Roselyn holding Hel's sword in one hand, clutching her stomach with her other. Karl and both of his squires had drawn their blades, and more than a dozen guards stood before them, protecting Prince Fernando with swords and spears. Even Eloise and Elaina had carving knives in their hands, and Henry stood beside Karl, shoulder-to-shoulder, his fists clenched, and Samuel was holding a small bench like a club. One guard was already lying upon the floor, blood pooling under him. While the court laughed, Prince Fernando pointed at the companions.

"Kill the men!" Prince Fernando shouted. "*Kill the men … and all but the woman warrior will be yours … until I tire of her!*"

The court laughed louder.

Sister Aspertine entered the room without flinching, without even acknowledging that they were there, let alone about to begin a bloody fight. Protected only by her staunch demeanor and the sacred garments of the church, Sister Aspertine crossed to the center of the room, walking between the surprised guards, and stopped before the dead guard. The fallen guard had a large dagger upon his belt; Sister Aspertine bent and drew the dagger, and then she turned and walked right past the guards to stand defiantly before Prince Fernando.

"Order your guards back, and let us go in peace," Sister Aspertine said to Prince Fernando, and she pointed the guard's dagger at him.

Prince Fernando laughed sarcastically.

"Nuns don't murder," Prince Fernando sneered.

"No, we have foolish, petty monarchs excommunicated," Sister Aspertine said. "*Excommunication;* you'll lose your palace, your whores, your luxuries, your city, and perhaps your head … *for murdering a nun.*"

Prince Fernando's smile inverted.

"You will not touch any of my people, you or your guards," Sister Aspertine warned. "Once word spreads … and your immorality is revealed, then you'll lose royal favor … lose everything that you have … lose everything that you … *desire …!*"

Prince Fernando glanced at his guards.

"Kill this bitch!" he shouted.

His guards looked askance; not one came forward.

"Your men know that, if one of them kills a nun, then you'll have to kill them … to save yourself from prison … or the hangman," Sister Aspertine said. "I and my friends are leaving. Don't follow. Stay here. Indulge in your … licentiousness … and pray that you never see me again."

Sister Aspertine turned her knife to point at the guards, and they stepped back, clearing her way. She motioned to Karl and the others; without speaking, they started backing toward the huge doors through which they'd entered. Sister Aspertine followed them slowly, never lowering her knife.

"May God Himself judge you … for what you are … and have done," Sister Aspertine said, glancing at Prince Fernando, his guards, and his entire court, and then she backed out of the palace.

Chapter 24

Storms at Sea

ELAINA

Elaina closed her eyes, raised her arms, and danced. Her companions sat silently watching her, but she tried to ignore them; she'd always danced in Skafti's tower in Norway, and she felt stiff and sore from having done so little dancing lately. She wished that she had music; in her tower, her beloved servants were all musicians, and their melodies filled her tower and spilled out onto the shores of her island. Many fishermen loved to catch salmon in her lake just to hear their music and watch her ladies dance upon their shore.

As she danced, Elaina listened intensely.

All the world is music, if you know how to hear it, and Elaina had spent the last sixteen years learning to listen. Skafti had taught her how to listen, but he'd scowled at dancing, and refused to submit himself to the music of reality.

Foremost, her ears were filled with the breaths of her companions, and the subtle creaks of the crude rope beds and wooden chairs beneath her watchers as they shifted uncomfortably, and the groaning of the aged boards beneath her quick-stepping bare feet. Behind those sounds, the soft clicks and gentle thumps of the building, their third inn in three nights, echoed almost inaudibly. Even fainter, distant voices, and the clip-clops of hard hooves upon dirt roads, wafted in from the street through the thin walls.

These sounds were traps. Elaina focused … to go deeper.

Overtop the buildings, tree limbs flexed in the warm breeze, which drug across the land like the long train of a wedding veil as a giant bride walked across the sky. Leaves danced in the wind, their flutters applauding in time with the gusts that loved them, and refreshed its scent by flitting against their soft greenery. Long grasses rubbed against each other lovingly, adding an endless *'swish'* to the backdrop of the harsher notes of small waves crashing against the docks, waters tinkling in streams, the deep barks of dogs playing and romping all around the city, the cries of restless babies, and the high-pitched chirps of small birds singing their joy of living.

Everything was a note, a song, a cadence; Elaina listened and danced.

The slow, steady motion of the sun, and the faster flight of the less-reliable moon, bore no sounds, but as conductors in an orchestra, they led the motions of all things. Eternal stars twinkled ten thousand glittering spotlights, and on nights of the greatest magic, Elaina had stared amazed above her northern tower as the sky itself danced, illuminated by swaying sheets of translucent colors. She'd joined their beams of countless hues, sharing in their dance, and becoming one with their cosmic magnificence.

When her dancing reached its fevered pitch, when her arms stretched to their limit and her feet alone guided her, she fell away and became nothing but her dance: *only then could she truly hear.*

The Music of the Universe was beautiful beyond the euphony of any instrument or dream of composer. Soft, light, eternal, cycling; trilling notes echoed from her soul, eager to be set free, and the sounds of love and concinnity, of patience and harmony, of infinity and eternity, burst forth in a crescendo of melodies played only upon heartstrings, never the same, but endless and abundant.

The boundless richness sang to her, and she submitted to it utterly, uncaring, baring her feelings and yearning to sense more. Elaina swayed, pirouetted, and let the music transport her as waters in a strong current might flow her where it wills, unrefusing, heedless, trusting wherever it led. She jumped, leaped, and gently touched down, bent, flexed, and flung herself about in thrall to the irresistible will of the dance.

Elaina performed no magic. Unlike her daughter, she knew no spells, no incantations; desire for control would only deafen her to the oneness she sought, the culmination of all things that she longed for, the climax of perfection when her dance united with the music of the Oversoul at the zenith of all things. Then she'd hear the truest song, of which she'd become its longest note, and the universe would hear her as clearly as she wanted to hear it. Then would the echoes of her needs be responded to, like the tight skin of a drum reverberating to each tap, as she and the music of all became one, and their rhythms returned what she needed.

Time became irrelevant, reality unimportant. Elaina gave herself utterly to the freedom of movement, the music which filled her, and which she returned full-willing; the dream-like haze of a dancer dancing with eternity.

Slowly certainty wafted upon her: a red ship, golden sails, and everything that they needed. She could hear it; waves against its hull, creaks of swaying ropes, and tiny squeaks from a lost and hungry mouse in its hold. A seagull upon its topmost spar squawked three times low, then three times high, and then a pair of beating wings married with the wind to lift it away. These strange sensations filled her; *she knew where she had to go.*

The Music of the Universe had responded to the harmony within her, and the subtle sounds of infinity faded into the coarser, less-harmonious sounds of reality, and Elaina was spinning, dancing in their room … in the inn … with her mesmerized companions watching her.

"Well …?" Karl asked as she stopped.

Elaina paused to steady the rhythmic gasps which heaved her chest.

"I … found our ship," Elaina said. "Red, with golden sails; I know where it is."

After they awoke the next day, Eloise tended Roselyn again, and then they left, purchasing no breakfast because they needed to save their coins to buy the promised ship. They hurried to a remote section of the harbor which they'd never been. Many ships bobbed there, but none of quality; any red ship with golden sails would be easy to spot amid these floating wrecks. Yet no worthy vessel bobbed visible, and when Sister Aspertine asked which berth held a ship matching Elaina's description, the sailors replied that no such ship had ever berthed there, and that none had ever seen such a ship in these waters.

Karl scowled, but he said nothing, although his glower displayed his doubts. Nate and Phil looked disappointed. Samuel and Henry both tried to stand apart and say nothing, although their discomfort couldn't have been more obvious. Sister Aspertine alone smiled; Elaina suspected that she was pleased that her scrying dance hadn't worked.

But it must have worked! The universe couldn't be wrong!

Elaina cast about, walking farther out on each dock, looking for even a trace of faded red paint or worn gold sails … only to find nothing.

Long she searched, and her companions seemed to grow increasingly irritated. Karl asked if they were in the wrong section of town, but Elaina ignored him.

It had to be here!

Nate opened his mouth to speak, but three low squawks of a seagull drowned out his words. He made to speak again, but Elaina stopped Nate with a gesture, looking up: upon the topmost spar of an old, age-blackened ship sat a spotted gray seagull, looking directly at Elaina. She hesitated, and then she stepped toward it. Seeming alarmed by her approach, the seagull squawked three more times, but these cries were high-pitched, alarmed, as if to frighten or warn away strangers, and then the seagull spread its large wings, leapt into the air, and flew away. Elaina watched it go, listening to the familiar flapping of its wings, mixed with the lapping of the water against the hull of the age-blackened boat, as the seagull flew out of sight.

Elaina stepped closer to the ship; it wasn't painted black; it was filthy, darkened by rotting seaweed and brine. Its mast wobbled in the wind, shaking tattered ropes that looked ready to break. Elaina held her breath and listened; softly, from somewhere inside the aged wreck came the squeak of a mouse.

"This is our ship," Elaina said.

"What …?" Karl asked. "You said that it was red with golden sails!"

Elaina met his argument with a steadfast silence.

"This thing isn't going to make it out of the harbor," Karl argued. "Look at it; it can barely float! A strong wind will blow it to splinters!"

Elaina turned her cold eyes upon Karl.

"We must sail on this ship," Elaina said flatly. "You trust a Druid priestess. You trust a Valkyrie. Trust me."

The argument that followed lasted half an hour, and many raised voices protested Elaina's choice, but she wouldn't be gainsaid. Both Henry and Samuel declared that the ship was waterlogged and leaking, and unlikely to survive to Egypt even if it sailed empty, and that no one had washed or tarred it for years.

Eloise supported her mother, although she looked askance at the vessel, whose stink wafted vile, and her words bore no conviction. No one seemed happy, but Karl finally turned to see Roselyn resting against a large barrel, still barely recovered from her wound.

"Roselyn, are you well?" Karl asked.

Roselyn shook her head.

"Just get aboard," Roselyn said.

"Are you jesting?" Karl asked. "Board that … floating coffin? If we try to sail to Egypt …!"

"Have you heard the prophesies of Odin?" Roselyn asked. "Have you been tortured by the Well of Urd, or met the three foul giantesses, the Norns, and cringed as they laughed at you? I've seen illusions to pale the deceptions of Utgard-Loki, and magical trickeries of dark elves. I've bathed in the Immortal Pool of the Fairies; if you disbelieve, then you'll thwart our plan.

"I have to find Athelwynne; if Elaina says that's our boat, then I trust her."

Roselyn almost fell as she pushed away from the barrel, and Nate and Phil rushed to help her. Slowly she limped toward the ruin of a ship, and with much help, she climbed aboard. Karl seemed furious, but he asked who owned the boat, and when one old sailor came forward, asking a fortune for his boat, Karl gave him half of what he asked, which was still twice what the boat was worth, and showed him the point of his sword; the seller walked away smiling, and they all climbed aboard.

Their dirty, ragged sail raised, Henry took the tiller and sailed them toward the open sea. They sailed very low in the water, and Samuel, Nate, and Phil had to begin bailing almost at once. They had only one bucket; Samuel used it, while Nate and Phil tore an old rag in half and dipped it into the bilge, and then wrung it out over the side.

As they floated away, on the dock behind them, every sailor laughed.

Many sailors upon passing ships also laughed, and no one could blame them. The companions had to bail constantly, and it was good that they didn't have any belongings: the ship was small, cramped, and barely bore their weight.

They had no awning; that night, they slept in the open, everyone cuddled under the only three cloaks that they had, and every few hours one of their ropes would break, and they'd have to repair it. One fisherman, from whom they bought their only food, gave them a spare bit of rope out of pure charity; Henry and Samuel saved the new rope until it was needed, and coiled the worn, old remnants of rope that had come with the ship to help retie the rest of their old ropes when they broke. Without Henry and Samuel, their ship would've fallen apart and dunked them into the Mediterranean Sea, but even their expertise finally failed; they couldn't make new wood out of old. The fish that they'd bought was raw, but they had no choice; they ate it or starved.

Roselyn insisted on helping bail, but Karl refused her.

"Roselyn, you're our strength," Karl said. "We need you to heal … more than we need you bailing."

"The strength of the Valkyrie is leaving me," Roselyn said. "I … I don't know how long I'll …"

She choked, as if she couldn't say the words, and Elaina felt sorry for her; as a Valkyrie, Roselyn had scorned weakness, and soon weakness would be all she had.

"I have faith in you," Karl said. "We'll need a good fighter, if we ever find the door to the land where the Seer is."

"If you guys would learn to fight properly …!" Roselyn scowled.

"Learn …?" Nate asked. "Do you mean … you could teach us to fight like you?"

"I can't divulge the Fighting Secrets of the Valkyrie," Roselyn said. "But I know some tricks, and training techniques, like Eric never dreamed of … until he reached Valhalla."

"Can you teach us?" Karl asked.

"Somewhat," Roselyn said. "But the best training is in Valhalla, where if you fail, you die."

"I hope that you're not going to be that extreme," Karl said.

"I won't," Roselyn said. "You must."

Phil went first, since there was no room for more than one to practice at a time. Roselyn stood in front of Phil and ordered him to climb onto the very front of their rickety boat, balance there, and then to jump over her head without touching her, and to land balanced on the starboard rail, some six feet away. Phil said that he couldn't do it; *Roselyn kneed him in the groin.*

To Nate's horror, he went next, and seeing his brother's punishment, Nate actually tried … and he almost crashed down on top of Roselyn. However, before he hit the deck, Roselyn's knee had struck the same target, and he was writhing before he landed on the boards.

"How are we supposed to do this?" Karl demanded.

"Fearlessly," Roselyn said. "If you're afraid of failing, getting hurt, or falling overboard, or thinking about anything else, then you won't make it. Each of you can do this; in Valhalla, they make you jump over a ravine filled with spears. If you fail, then they march you out the next morning and make you try again. They keep doing this until you learn to not be afraid."

"What's to be afraid of in Valhalla?" Karl asked. "You can't die."

"When you've felt the agony of death a hundred times, then you won't ask that question," Roselyn said. "I've died several times in just the last month. Eventually you lose your fear of death, and when that happens, you lose your fear of everything. You become totally free … and able to do things that you'd thought impossible. You don't risk; you just do. To fight well, you must lose mortal fear."

Everyone exchanged a wary glance.

"Your turn, lover," Roselyn smiled at Karl.

Karl jumped high, but at a sharper angle, not directly over Roselyn, and he hit the rail with one foot, slipped, and fell overboard. Henry and Samuel were hard-pressed to stop their fragile ship and go back for Karl without breaking a rope, tearing their ragged sail in the strong wind, or snapping their aged mast. When they finally reached him, Roselyn helped pull Karl aboard, and then she slammed her elbow into his stomach and dropped him to his knees.

"You're learning," Roselyn said, and she looked at the sailors. "Next …?"

Henry and Samuel paled.

"We're bailing," Samuel said.

"If you succeed, then you'll be able to keep bailing," Roselyn smiled.

Over the next four days, Elaina slept too little. Sleeping on the smaller ship was cramped and damp, the boards were dank and smelly, and bailing was required day and night. Their Norse trading ship, that had been stolen, was far more comfortable, smelled better, and the rocking of the sea had made sleeping pleasant.

Elaina was glad that she wasn't a man, although she and Eloise had to bail while Roselyn gave lessons … until the men recovered. When they weren't bailing or sleeping, Roselyn had every man exercising until they almost passed out, and then she inflicted some impossible task upon them, and punished them every time that they failed. Karl ordered her to stop, and he awoke an hour later with a ringing headache and a lump on his brow.

"Do you think that all of the einherjar agree to this?" Roselyn demanded. "Most argue, and beg us to stop, but we can't; this is the training that every warrior needs."

Sister Aspertine alone objected, calling the training *'barbaric'*, but Roselyn ignored her. Eloise kept herself busy; convinced that her mother had to be right, she cast spell after spell to transform their wreck of a ship into a beautiful red vessel with golden sails; none worked.

Under the burning blaze of the sun, day after hot, sweaty day, their ship seemed to leak a bit more, to creak and snap a lot more, and several boards actually broke free and had to be quickly repaired. Elaina felt ashamed.

She'd never known the universe to lie to her.

Next, Roselyn had the men lift each other, one at a time, over their heads, and then set them down gently. Nate simply wasn't strong enough, and suffered tremendously. Although wounded, Roselyn was deft at inflicting pain with very little effort, and twice demonstrated that she could do everything that she was asking them to do; the exertions cost her, but she was healing faster with Eloise's daily treatments, although she still clutched at the thin scar across her stomach. No contention showed between them; Roselyn helped Eloise whenever she could, and they slept with Karl sandwiched between them.

Fortunately for Karl, everyone was too tired to not sleep.

Elaina tried to dance again, to unravel the mystery of their woe-begotten boat, but the sway of the tiny ship interfered, and her mind couldn't focus; she'd doubted her ability … and doubted the universe. Yet there was nothing else that she could do but try. Ashamed, she offered to help bail more, but after a few days, she regretted her offer; bailing was hard, uncomfortable, and she was always sweating and exhausted before she was relieved.

By the sixth day, every companion had bail constantly, even at night.

A sudden storm swept over them one night; with no warning, they couldn't reach land in time, and before the men were fully awake, their only sail had been blown to shreds. They tried to row, but the waves splashed over their rails, and the black sky offered no clue as to which direction promised land. Their boat wasn't built like a flexible dragonship; the waves beat at it mercilessly, and it began to leak in earnest; all constantly bailed just to keep from sinking. When the rain came, it dropped like a waterfall, and all had to bail faster.

Karl insisted that this storm was nothing compared to what they'd faced on the North Sea, when the Seer had summoned Eric's ghost to save them, but his words eased no fears. Sister Aspertine couldn't swim, but she proved that she could scream every time that a bolt of lightning crashed over their heads and thunder reverberated in their bones.

Their ruined vessel couldn't survive. Slowly, inevitably, it sank, despite everything that they could do. Fortunately, the storm broke first, and the dark clouds divided, revealing a bright blue dawn rising over the Mediterranean Sea.

However, as the sunlight illuminated them, Henry and Samuel were waist-deep in sea water, trying to hold several broken boards in place, while the rest of them bailed, and yet their boat sank to where their port rail dipped underwater.

"Ahoy …!" cried a voice, and the companions turned to see a great ship sailing at them, filled with wicked-looking men holding bared weapons: *pirates.* The swarthy sea-thieves were laughing at them, brandishing their weapons threateningly, and crowded to their fore, eager to hear their captain taunt the companions, whose boat was surely about to go under.

"Nice women you have there!" shouted the pirate captain. "Surrender them … and we might save you!"

The pirates laughed louder.

Every one of the companions smiled: *the pirate ship was red … with golden sails.*

"Ladies, stay here … and keep bailing," Roselyn said, and she lifted Hel's sword. "No time to armor: men, draw your weapons … or fight without them."

Fifteen minutes later, every pirate was dead. The men had fought like Valkyries; the pirates had never seen the like, and the last combatants quailed beneath the deadly swords of the companions, who jumped about the red ship like avenging angels heedless of death, and attacked the pirates from all sides. Roselyn attacked foremost, screamed the loudest, and often drew the attention of the pirates away from the others, letting them attack the unaware backs of the pirates, stabbing and slashing with blows that landed unblocked. Roselyn actually fought very little, and in the end, she crumpled as the last pirate died, clutching her stomach, yet she smiled and never lost consciousness.

Hel's armor was quickly transported off the horrible wreck before it sank entirely, and they had nothing else to save.

Henry suffered a sword stabbed through his left arm; Eloise insisted on healing him despite her pains. The Lady answered her prayers quickly, and afterwards both Henry and Eloise felt much better.

While Henry was being tended, Samuel took command, delighted to be sailing a strong, sturdy ship again. Within minutes of pulling the last woman aboard, out of the sea, their old, ruined ship slipped completely underwater, and Samuel turned their bright golden sails and steered them toward Egypt.

The configuration of their new ship was strange to all but Henry; it was Arabic, possibly a royal pleasure craft from Persia, intricately decorated with carved dragons, stylized curls, and held together with thick rivets of bronze.

As before, Nate and Phil were tasked to strip the dead pirates of anything valuable, and then to dump their bodies overboard. Elaina wasted no time praising the men; they'd all fought like Valkyries to commandeer their elegant new ship. Of course, all of the men, and Roselyn, were covered in blood; every fisherman who sailed too close made the sign of the cross and hurried to steer clear.

When the squires were done, they had another pile of stolen armor and weapons, although nothing as fine as the haul from the Moors that they'd sold before their first boat had been stolen. Those needing new armor and weapons chose freely from the pile, and Henry found a strangely-curved sword. Henry lifted it and slashed it through the air.

"I like this," he said.

"It's an Egyptian blade, which they call a khopesh," Samuel said. "The curve cuts deep on unarmored flesh."

Henry smiled and slashed it through the air again.

Sister Aspertine discovered several trunks full of food and stolen clothes; before the sun lowered to the horizon, everyone was washed clean with soap, even their hair, dressed in bright, dry clothes, eating their fill, and drinking the pirate's grog.

Dressed in a white chemise and a bright red outer dress from the pirates' plunder, Elaina smiled, delighted.

Their new ship looked exactly as it had when she'd seen it during her dancing-dream. Now they had the sturdy, sea-worthy ship that she'd predicted, plenty of food and drink, new clothes and armor, and they were on their way to Egypt to find an entrance to the lands of the Forgotten Gods.

The universe hadn't lied to her.

Chapter 25

Sailing to Egypt

KARL

Karl awoke squeezed between Eloise and Roselyn; once he'd dreamed that both women would be content to share him, and that the three of them could grace the same bed every night. Some of the whores in The Bent Hook, Demril's only tavern, did exactly that, although they charged a lot for it. But Eloise was a baroness, and Roselyn was a countess-turned-Valkyrie; Karl suspected that suggesting it would be the fastest way to get himself tossed overboard.

Karl struggled to extricate himself without waking either woman … and failed entirely, but managed to crawl out from between them as they fought to claim his spot without opening their eyes. Samuel was holding the tiller; the morning sky was bright enough to see by, although the sun had yet to peek over the horizon. Yet it was already hot, too hot for a spring morning; for the first time, Karl realized that they'd truly entered the lands where it never snowed.

To most of the people in England, these lands were as much a legend as Yggdrasil.

The sea was choppy because of the strong wind, and their sail billowed, their powerful, well-built ship pounding a steady course through the chop. They could go no faster without storm-winds on their tail.

Samuel nodded respectfully to Karl, who felt chagrined. Their baronial regalia had been stolen with their ship, but these sailors didn't care; Rafe had well-selected them for this journey. Karl nodded back, then sat down and yawned, watching the many fishing boats sailing out to cast their morning nets.

"We should be there in a few more days, your excellency," Samuel said.

"Just call me Karl; we're a long way from du Harmonn."

"Sir, that wouldn't be proper …"

"Out here, our titles may cause us more problems than they remedy," Karl said.

"Your excellency, you wear the white belt and gold chain of a knight," Samuel said. "Half of you speak like royalty. If we don't show respect, then others will assume that you're a fraud who stole your regalia, that you have no right to wear them, and that we're all thieves."

Karl pondered this as the sun rose into the sky. Samuel was probably correct. *Should he hide his badges of office, the highest honors that he'd ever been given, and try to pass himself off as a peasant?* Karl shook his head; he could easily pass for a peasant, but Elaina, Eloise, and Roselyn couldn't, and since few peasants could act like the nobility and not cause trouble, it'd only make matters worse. Yet Karl was tired of pretending to be noble; he was a farmer's son who'd gotten lucky, and he'd proven that he'd rather go seeking a second 'crack in the world' than face another royal audience.

Politics, intrigue, lies; Karl yearned for a simpler life, with one woman whom he could love forever, an honest, straightforward duty to perform, and a noble cause worth striving for. He glanced back at Eloise and Roselyn, now sleeping comfortingly together, side-by-side; their animosity had been delayed by Eloise's saving Roselyn's life, but both were almost healed now; *their peace was tentative.* Roselyn had started wearing parts of Hel's armor again, adding more as she found that she could bear the weight. Since Eloise had healed Henry's arm, she'd been growing stronger, too.

When both reached full-strength, would their animosity resume?

When everyone had awoken, Sister Aspertine led them in morning prayers, infuriated that none of the other women would join her. She seemed unusually upset these days, and Karl couldn't fathom what was bothering her now. After their prayers, Sister Aspertine offered to lead the women in special prayers for their souls, if they'd join her; none would.

"You're disgraces to our sex," Sister Aspertine scolded them, her youthful voice filled with undisguised vehemence.

"I'm a servant of The Lady," Eloise said to Sister Aspertine. "My prayers would only be a pretense, and that would be blasphemy …"

"Prayers to God will be your only hope when you realize too late that your *'Lady'* is a witch and a siren!" Sister Aspertine shouted.

Eloise's eyes flared and her brows furrowed, but she withheld her temper.

"If I thought that your words were of any importance, then I'd be angry, and you wouldn't enjoy that," Eloise said calmly. "I summoned Death and killed Eorl Sir Guldwin from my tower …!"

"Then you're a murderess and should repent on your knees, if even that can save you!" Sister Aspertine said.

"My powers are insignificant beside the wonders of the Seer," Eloise said with a wicked grin. "He is Her greatest servant; if we do find him, then I suggest that you keep your opinions of the Lady silent."

"I'll never be silent while God's words are on my tongue," Sister Aspertine said, and then she turned to face Roselyn. "And you, demoness? By your own admission, your false gods have cast you out; will you not return to God?"

"Norse gods don't listen to prayers," Roselyn said. "Norse gods watch deeds … and reward those that they deem worthy."

"Many Norse pray, especially the women," Elaina contradicted Roselyn. "I've watched them do it. But, if any god's ever answered a prayer, I've yet to witness it."

"You're the greatest blasphemer of all!" Sister Aspertine said to Elaina. "These two have been on a … path of delusions … which caused their doubts to turn them from the One True God. You weren't deceived by divine intervention; you abandoned God."

"I haven't abandoned God," Elaina said.

"You don't pray …!" Sister Aspertine argued.

Elaina shook her head.

"I don't worship …," Elaina began.

"Blasphemy!" Sister Aspertine snapped.

"Prayer is a pale substitute for communicating with the universe … or any of its gods," Elaina said. "Listening … dancing … and singing in harmony with the Infinite All is far more intimate, almost a joining with the gods, rather than simply praying to them."

"Heresy!" Sister Aspertine shouted.

"You've seen proof …"

"Lies …!"

"You watched Eloise heal …"

"Witchcraft!"

"We stand on the boat that I predicted …"

"Coincidence!"

"You've seen Roselyn fight …"

"Sacrilege!"

"Enough!" Karl shouted. "You're giving me a headache!"

"God is punishing you!" Sister Aspertine turned her fury upon Karl. "You're a baron, appointed by the church; your duty is to uphold His church, not cavort with witches and demons!"

"Leave him alone!" Elaina shouted. "You're not the only devout follower here, you innocent, sanctimonious …!"

"Whore of Babylon!" Sister Aspertine shouted. "*Tramp! Slut!*"

"Bitch …!"

Suddenly both women lunged at each other, screaming incoherently, slapping, scratching, and clawing; Nate and Phil moved almost by instinct; Phil seized Elaina, and Nate pulled Sister Aspertine back, and both moved with such Valkyrie-taught speed that neither woman hurt the other.

Roselyn laughed as both kept screaming.

"Master, there's a method for settling fights aboard ship," Henry shouted to Karl over the screeches of the women.

"Then do it!" Karl shouted.

Henry and Samuel glanced at each other, nodded simultaneously, and then both walked over to the ruckus. Without hesitation, Henry grabbed Elaina, and Samuel grabbed Sister Aspertine, and in one fluid motion, they lifted them up into their arms … and tossed them overboard on opposite sides of the ship.

Both women screamed … and then splashed loudly.

"Mother …!" Eloise shrieked.

Roselyn laughed hysterically while Eloise ran aft; neither woman was in sight.

"They can't swim …!" Eloise shouted.

"Boys, go get them," Karl said, and with smiles on their faces, Nate and Phil dashed aft, jumped off the rail, and dove overboard.

By the time that Henry and Samuel had turned their ship around, Nate and Phil were each treading water, a frantic, wet, angry woman clinging tightly to each of them. As they pulled them aboard, looking like drowned cats, but with eyes like Hel in her most-murderous rage, Karl asked both if they'd care to resume their religious argument.

Neither answered.

Karl wished that all their problems could be solved so easily.

Shortly afterwards, having changed into gaudy sailor's clothes, since they had no more dry dresses, Elaina and Sister Aspertine sat on opposite sides of the ship, saying nothing. Meanwhile, after some hard breads and a little wine, Roselyn began her trainings again; the men were getting better, but still not accomplishing everything that she asked, since she always asked a little bit more than they were ready to give. She made each of them select a small dagger from those collected from the pirates, and hide it inside their clothes. After each had done this, she challenged them to see who could draw their hidden dagger fastest. She won, of course, and made the slowest hide their dagger better, and they continued practicing drawing their hidden daggers for an hour … and Roselyn won each time.

Roselyn turned out to be a great teacher; she showed them things that they never would've guessed.

"In every fight to the death, there's one decisive blow," Roselyn said. "It could be a stab, or a slash, or a wrestling move that breaks or crushes your opponent; either way, the sooner that you do that killing attack, the sooner your opponent will fall."

"How do we know which attack will work?" Nate asked.

"All kill-worthy attacks work," Roselyn smiled. "However, for each of you, the best killing blows are the ones that previously succeeded. Every man moves differently, and each warrior wields their blade the way that they think; if you were able to kill a man with one blow, then chances are that the same blow will kill another. Each time that you kill, remember the pose that you were in when you dealt that blow, and practice that pose until you can do it at will. Imagine that you're posing for a sculptor at the instant that you killed your last opponent; that's the pose that you need to practice most."

"But all opponents move differently, and defend themselves differently," Karl said.

"Don't worry now about how enemies defend," Roselyn said. "Einherjar seldom defend; their goal is to attack in such a way as to make their opponents defend. Only the person who's attacking can kill."

"But a good defense can tire out an opponent," Henry said. "It takes more energy to attack than to defend."

"That's why you strive to kill as fast as possible," Roselyn said. "That's why you practice killing blows, so that those attacks can, if possible, be the first and only blow you throw; so that you can kill each enemy with as little effort as possible. But don't confuse using little effort with holding back; to fight well, you need to put every ounce of strength that you have into each attack; in the long run, you'll kill more enemies."

"So … when do you rest?" Phil asked.

"When the battle's won … or you're dead," Roselyn said.

"We don't drink the Water of Life," Karl said. "All mortals tire."

"You must practice resting as hard as you practice fighting," Roselyn said, and she turned to Nate and Phil. "You boys are the worst at resting; when you're done practicing, no matter how tired you are, you waste breath bragging or demeaning each other; fools like you never rest. When you're done fighting, stop moving, stop talking, and learn to recover in seconds what might otherwise take minutes. Learn to get an hour's rest in a few breaths; then, while your enemies are licking the wounds you gave them, or amassing to attack you again, then you can gain all the rest you need in a few precious moments … because without that rest, you'll tire and die. And you can only do this if you've practiced recovering quickly. How you breathe helps; before you rest correctly, you must know how to breathe."

Roselyn showed them several different ways to breathe properly, in through the nose, out through the mouth, as long and as deeply as they could, and to hold each inhale several seconds, and then to expel every ounce of breath before taking another. The first breathing method was for fighting, and preparing to fight;

it psyches warriors up, brings tension to their muscles and awareness to their mind. The second breathing method was for slowing breath when gasping, and bringing down body temperature as quickly as possible; quick inhales with lips pursed, normal exhales with mouths wide. This method was only to be used when breathing normally couldn't be achieved. She instructed them to always breathe with the lower half of their lungs, not the upper halves; the lower halves are bigger, and can expand against the stomach without being confined by ribs. Her last method was rapid breathing, which no warrior should ever do for long, lest the brain become fogged, but this gains a sudden revitalization, only to be used immediately before first attacks, so that they could step into range suddenly and strike once without having to draw a second breath.

A few hot, sweaty days later, Roselyn saw Phil pour water over his head after practice, and called them all together.

"Never pour water upon your head if you're too hot," Roselyn said. "Cooling down the head before the body costs awareness and reaction time; it may be an hour before you can think properly again. Pour cold water upon your feet first, even over your boots; you'll cool off quickly and safely. Then put a wet towel around your neck. If you have time, then rest and pour small palmfuls of water upon your face, one at a time, and wait until the cooling evens out before you begin another. Always use clean water to wash the sweat from your face so that the sweat-salt doesn't sting your eyes. Save pouring a bucket of water over your head until you're ready to fight again: this'll let you return to battle cool … and stay cool longer. However, water is weight, and if you carry an extra five pounds of water into combat, soaked into your hair and gambeson, then you'll move slower, jump shorter, and tire quicker."

Samuel showed Roselyn a killing blow that he'd used on one of the pirates; bending low to the side and stabbing upwards.

"A good attack position," Roselyn said, but then she reached out with one finger and pushed against him while he demonstrated; Samuel fell backwards.

"What was wrong with his pose?" Roselyn asked.

"Balance," they all said.

As Samuel stood up, Roselyn had him assume the same pose, but she turned one ankle so that his feet weren't pointed in the same direction, widened his stance, and leaned him forward more. Then she had him stretch as far as he could in that position, and go even lower.

"If your opponent has a shield, then every inch matters," Roselyn said. "How low can you go, and still attack with enough force to kill?"

Samuel tried to go lower and not fall over, but toppled onto the rocking deck.

Suddenly Roselyn whipped out a large dagger, ducked and dipped, and assumed the same position that Samuel was doing, only deeper, her hair piled upon the deckboards, one shoulder almost resting on the planks, and she stabbed her blade upwards with undeniable force. She held her position long seconds as the ship tilted, but she grunted and looked pained, and placed a hand on her stomach as soon as she stood back up.

"You're getting stronger," Karl said. "A week ago, you couldn't have done that."

"The … the strength of the Valkyrie has left me," Roselyn said, and she cursed profanely.

"You've wisdom and experience, more than any man alive," Karl said. "We're all better fighters."

"You'll need to be," Roselyn said. "Even Hel's sword feels heavy now."

All of the men demonstrated a killing pose, and Roselyn corrected each position, stretching their stances to gain every inch, and showed the sailors how to twist their hips to deliver more-powerful attacks, how to walk by sliding their feet, rather than stepping high, and how to lean properly. By then, Eloise and Elaina had their midday meal ready, and they all held their tongues while Sister Aspertine blessed the food and the company, *'despite its heathen elements'*, and then they ate sparingly.

After eating, Roselyn had Phil stand before her, and each held a single sword, gripped by both hands, facing the other.

"Watch how my sword doesn't move," Roselyn said.

Suddenly Roselyn took a wide step to the left; Phil rotated his sword to defend against her new position, but her swordhand hadn't traveled with her; Roselyn stabbed lightly forward and lightly touched Phil's chest with ease.

"Control," Roselyn said. "Control your opponent, control the fight. He moved sideways because I did; *I controlled him.* This's how you kill an opponent with one blow; make him think that you're throwing something different. He blocks where your sword isn't, defending, not attacking, and you're free to kill."

"That sounds great," Henry said, "but surely an experienced fighter wouldn't be fooled twice."

"That's why you kill with your first blow," Roselyn said. "Many einherjar practice long sequences of tricks … because they fight immortals. Your enemies aren't reborn; they don't know all the tricks."

"Tricks …?" Nate asked.

"Distraction is the only trick that I'll teach you today," Roselyn said, and she set down her blade and picked up a short piece of rope.

"Eric showed me how to distract," Karl said. "He … smiled."

"Gather around and I'll show you another way," Roselyn said.

The men inched closer, and Roselyn closed her eyes, placed her left hand upon her right metal breast-cup, squeezed … and softly sighed. All of the men's eyes stared at her hand, caressing her metal breast, even Karl. Then Roselyn slashed her short rope hard, in one wide swing, like a sword; her rope struck each of their throats before they could move.

"Five of you … decapitated," Roselyn said, holding up the rope. "Distraction controls your opponent's eyes."

"Eric made me look at his face," Karl said.

"Eric could do the same now with a fraction of that obviousness," Roselyn said, and she suddenly glanced strongly over the starboard rail. All of the men turned their heads to see what she was looking at, and her rope slashed across all of their throats a second time.

That evening, the men collapsed, exhausted, and even Roselyn seemed weary. They drank some wine and nibbled on some dry white cheese as the stars came out, but no one talked. Roselyn suggested that they all start wearing the pirate's armor, even while they sleep, to strengthen them. The men groaned.

Karl stretched out on the deck, still breathing hard. Roselyn lay on one side of him, and Eloise laid her bedroll on the other side of him, but as he tried to find a comfortable position to sleep in his armor, Eloise suddenly cried out.

"You hit me with your links!" Eloise complained.

After her third injury, Eloise furiously threw back her blanket and stormed across the deck to stand in the fore and look out at the night.

Karl glanced at Roselyn, who was staring at him with a stony expression.

"I'd better go talk to her," Karl said.

"Why?" Roselyn demanded, and Karl knew what she meant.

"She's my wife," Karl said.

"Only until death," Roselyn said.

"Yes," Karl agreed, fearing to say anything else. "Until death."

Roselyn made no sign of acceptance, but Karl rose and went after Eloise. The rivalry that he'd feared most had returned; he hoped that he could quell it. He walked up beside Eloise, still wearing her gaudy sailor's outfit, but she didn't turn to face him.

"Why aren't you sleeping?" Eloise demanded. "You're tired; sleep."

"I want you beside me," Karl said.

"But not me alone," Eloise scowled.

"Wife, we can't afford this," Karl said. "Your training on the fairy isle; was that without difficulties? I'm in training, and wearing armor …"

"I can't sleep against mail and vambraces," Eloise said.

"Then, go sleep," Karl said. "I'll sleep over here … alone."

Eloise turned around and stared into his eyes.

"I'm your wife … and the mother of your children!" Eloise whispered. "I will not be … *supplanted …!*"

"No one's supplanting you …," Karl said.

"This can't go on," Eloise said. "You need to choose …"

"Rafe and Seren almost broke our company apart when they argued," Karl reminded her. "We're at the start of this quest; we can't quarrel …"

"Kiss me," Eloise said.

"What?" Karl asked.

"I'm your wife," Eloise repeated. "I deserve a kiss."

Karl frowned, and then leaned over, and suddenly Eloise threw her arms around his neck and kissed him hard and long. Karl startled; they hadn't kissed like that since before Eloise had started becoming so secretive, hiding her training in the Seer's arts, and Karl had forgotten how good a kisser she was.

When finished, Eloise slid back and grinned wickedly, and then she walked back to her blanket. Karl watched her go, appreciating the sway of her hips, which was even more mesmerizing now than in her youth, but then he caught sight of a pair of steely Valkyrie eyes staring at him from the darkness, and he paled and turned away.

Eloise was doing it again, manipulating him … and infuriating Roselyn!

Eventually they'd wait no longer; *what would he do then?*

Karl prayed that he'd die before that day came.

"There it is!" Henry said as they breakfasted on some hard bread under the already baking, unrelenting sun. "Egypt!"

The landscape was definitely drier, and many miles of bare coast showed in the distance, but there was also much greenery near the shore.

"We'll be reaching the mouth of the Nile soon," Samuel said.

"Where's the sand?" Elaina asked.

"Not far away," Henry promised them. "From the river, you'll see all the sand you want … in the distance, not next to the water."

"Where's the Nile River?" Nate asked.

"Oh, we're still a long ways away," Henry said. "Past the city of Alexandria; that's where we'll find the mouth of the river. But it won't be easy sailing; the Nile River flows north, and we'll see how this ship manages when we hit the Nile current; we'll go much slower as we sail upstream."

All the companions gazed at the hot, unfamiliar coast, which was covered with strange trees, bare of branches, but which rose to a tremendous height, and then burst outwards with long, fern-like leaves. Karl grimaced, wiping the sweat from his brow.

They'd reached Egypt, their first destination, and now their quest could begin in earnest.

For the next step in their journey, all that they needed was to find a 'crack in the world' … which no one knew of … could be hidden anywhere… and might not even exist.

Karl shook his head; the easy part was over … now they faced their real challenge.

End of Book 1 of

The EGYPTIANS! Trilogy

ABOUT THE AUTHOR

Born in Tripler Army Medical Center, Honolulu, Hawaii, Jay Palmer works as a technical writer in the software industry in Seattle, Washington. Jay enjoys parties, reading everything in sight, woodworking, obscure board games, and riding his Kawasaki Vulcan. Jay is a knight in the SCA, frequently attends writer conferences, SciFi Conventions, and he and Karen are both avid ballroom dancers. But most of all, Jay enjoys writing.

JayPalmerBooks.com